the Cheetah Girls

the Cheetah Girls

Off the Hook!

Volumes 13–16

Deborah Gregory

JUMP AT THE SUN

HYPERION PAPERBACKS FOR CHILDREN
NEW YORK

Printed in the United States of America

First compiled edition, 2005

3 5 7 9 10 8 6 4

This book is set in 12-point Palatino.

ISBN: 0-7868-5654-8

Library of Congress Catalog Card Number on file.

Visit www.cheetahrama.com

Acknowledgments

A Hyperion shout-out to talented editor Jaïra Placide and my favorite marketing Big Daddy, Angus Killick, who "loves to shop." Primo thanks to Beth Miller and Gary Marsh at Disney Channel, as well as Whitney Houston, Debra Martin Chase, and Alison Taylor for their dedication in bringing the Cheetah Girls to the big screen, where they belong. Also, Andy McNicol and Eric Zohn at the William Morris Agency for their integrity. There is not enough thanks in the world I can give to my spiritual mentor, Anath Garber, the one person who was committed to healing my childhood wounds when there was no one else I could turn to. And, most important, this is for all the cheetah girls around the globe: thank you for all the letters, e-mails, cheetah drawings, and photos you've sent in your cheetah-licious outfits. Keep running wild and showing your spots. Growl power *forever*!

Contents

❀ ❀ ❀ ❀ ❀ ❀ ❀ ❀ ❀ ❀ ❀ ❀ ❀ ❀ ❀ ❀

The Cheetah Girls Credo

To earn my spots and rightful place in the world, I solemnly swear to honor and uphold the Cheetah Girls oath:

- Cheetah Girls don't litter, they glitter. I will help my family, friends, and other Cheetah Girls whenever they need my love, support, or a *really* big hug.

- All Cheetah Girls are created equal, but we are not alike. We come in different sizes, shapes, and colors, and hail from different cultures. I will not judge others by the color of their spots, but by their character.

- A true Cheetah Girl doesn't spend more time

doing her hair than her homework. Hair extensions may be career extensions, but talent and skills will pay my bills.

🐾 True Cheetah Girls *can* achieve without a weave—or a wiggle, jiggle, or a giggle. I promise to rely (mostly) on my brains, heart, and courage to reach my cheetah-licious potential!

🐾 A brave Cheetah Girl isn't afraid to admit when she's scared. I promise to get on my knees and summon the growl power of the Cheetah Girls who came before me—including my mom, grandmoms, and the Supremes—and ask them to help me be strong.

🐾 All Cheetah Girls make mistakes. I promise to admit when I'm wrong and will work to make it right. I'll also say I'm sorry, even when I don't want to.

🐾 Grown-ups are not always right, but they are bigger, older, and louder. I will treat my teachers, parents, and people of authority with respect—and expect them to do the same!

🐾 True Cheetah Girls don't run with wolves or hang with hyenas. True Cheetahs pick much better friends. I will not try to get other people's approval by acting like a copycat.

🐾 To become the Cheetah Girl that only *I* can be, I promise not to follow anyone else's dreams but my own. No matter how much I quiver, shake, shiver, and quake!

🐾 Cheetah Girls were born for adventure. I promise to learn a language other than my own and travel around the world to meet my fellow Cheetah Girls.

Oops, Doggy Dog!

For Kristina Paris in NYC,
Show your spots, *mamacita*!

Chapter 1

I'm sitting in the green waiting room at Lincoln Hospital, but I'm not sick or hurt. I'm here with Chuchie and her mom, 'cuz it's time for Miss Cuchifrita to have the cast taken off her foot. I say a prayer: "Pleez, God, let Miss Cuchifrita's sprained ankle be healed, so the Cheetah Girls can be revealed—as the singing stars of the future, that is!"

The Cheetah Girls are me, Galleria "Bubbles" Garibaldi; Chanel "Chuchie" Simmons (my best friend in the whole world); Dorinda "Do' Re Mi" Rogers; and those fabulous Walker twins from Houston, Aquanette and Anginette.

Believe me, we Cheetahs are hungry! We've been waiting forever to take advantage of our biggest break yet—the chance to go into the recording studio with Mouse Almighty, the world-famous record producer, and make a demo tape for Def Duck Records! Once the A&R peeps at Def Duck listen to it, they'll decide if they're gonna give us a record deal. And with Mouse in the house, we like our chances.

We were all set to rock a month ago, when Chuchie sprained her ankle. That set the whole process back, and we're *still* waiting. This Thursday's supposed to be the big day, but who knows? Between now and then, anything could happen, especially with Chuchie involved, you know what I'm sayin'?

Even if Dr. Reuben says Chuchie can hang up her crutches, we still have to go straight over to my house so my mom can check her out. Mom doubles as the Cheetah Girls' official manager (or "head cheetah in charge," as she likes to refer to herself). She knew Chuchie was getting her cast off today, so she went ahead and made the appointment for us with Mouse Almighty. But if Mom doesn't think Chanel can stand on her ankle for hours in the studio, she'll cancel, and we'll be right back on that old treadmill to nowhere.

When I'm nervous, like I am now, I can't sit still. And the part of me that just won't stop—no matter what—is my mouth. Without even thinking, I start pulling on my bubble gum like it's a yo-yo.

"Stop it, Galleria," Chanel's mom hisses under

her breath. She thinks I'm a bad bubble-gum influence on Chuchie, and she's even complained about it to my mom.

"Sorry, Auntie Juanita," I say, throwing out the gum (even though it's my last piece and I'm not done with it).

I know Chanel is nervous, too, because she starts tapping one of her crutches on the floor. "What if I walk funny without the crutches?" she says.

"We're going to Mouse's studio to record songs, not put on a show," I point out. "So what does it matter if you get a little wobbly or something?"

"*Madrina's* not gonna let us go," Chuchie sighs, referring to my mom.

"You'll be lucky if *I* let you go," Auntie Juanita butts in, smoothing her ponytail.

Then she turns to me. "Dottie didn't already make an actual appointment with that producer—without asking *me*, did she?"

Oops. I bite my lip, looking for a way out. This is no time to ruffle Auntie Juanita's feathers. Luckily, just then the receptionist calls out Chanel's name. Chuchie hops up on her crutches, and we follow her into an examination room.

No sooner are we in there than Juanita starts in again. "Well? Did she?"

I hate giving her a reason to fight with my

mother. Those two are always at each other. But it looks like I have no choice. "Yes, she did, but that's her job. She's our manager." I wince as I wait for the boomerang to come back at me.

"We'll see about that." Auntie Juanita plops her purse down on the chair and whips out her cell phone.

"I'm sorry, but you can't use cell phones in the hospital," the nurse informs her, then points to an empty corner. "And could you please put your stuff over there." Auntie Juanita huffs a couple times, but complies.

Meanwhile, I help Chanel sit up on the gurney, and set her crutches against the wall.

"Can we burn them after?" she asks, giggling.

"Not so fast," Auntie Juanita snaps, crossing her arms impatiently. "You may be walking out of here *with* them. *Está bien?*"

Chanel and I keep our beaks closed. We sit in silence for another ten minutes, and I'm beginning to feel like we're playing a game of hospital musical chairs, because we're *still* waiting to see Chanel's doctor, only in a different room.

Finally, the door swings open. "How are you, Chanel?" Dr. Reuben asks, breezing in and taking a pen from her lab coat pocket.

"*Estoy bien!* I'm okay," Chanel says, perking up.

Dr. Reuben scribbles on Chanel's chart, then bends over to remove the soft cast. "Have you been keeping your weight off your ankle?"

"Yes."

"Good, good, it looks fine. Let's weigh you, then get your blood pressure."

When Chanel steps on the scale, she almost loses her balance. "I can't believe I gained two pounds!" she shrieks.

I give her a look, like, *Just chill.*

Dr. Reuben ignores Chanel's protests. "Weight or no weight, you're to do absolutely no exercising for three weeks."

"Oh . . . okay." Chanel looks defeated. After Dr. Reuben bids us good-bye and leaves, she says, "I'm never gonna eat again."

"What do you expect after lying up in bed for two weeks?" Auntie Juanita asks her.

I can't *believe* she's being so unsympathetic. If Auntie Juanita gained an ounce, she wouldn't eat even a sunflower seed until she lost it back. Trust me, I know her. She spends all day exercising in the studio she built in her loft—belly dancing, salsa, yoga, whatever.

I'm tempted to run into the hallway and ask Dr. Reuben if it's okay for Chanel to perform. I mean, she said, "no exercising," but what about just standing up for hours and singing? Now, if my mom was here, *she* would have asked Dr. Reuben. I guess that's why she's our manager and Auntie Juanita isn't. Mom knows how to handle our business—and other people's, too!

Chanel gets down from the gurney and makes her first careful steps without crutches.

"Wow," I say, encouraging her. "I feel like I'm watching the first woman astronaut walking on the moon!"

"Galleria, you're so dramatic," Auntie Juanita says.

She should talk! You'd think she'd be pleased that Chanel is finally walking without crutches, but I can tell she can't wait to call my mom and ruffle her feathers about our big studio session.

Auntie Juanita and my mom were both models back in their day, but my mom was more successful, and I think it bothers Auntie Juanita even now. And all this drama over our singing group really takes the cake, okay? It seems like they're always fighting over Cheetah Girls stuff. Auntie Juanita doesn't want us to "rise for the prize," but my mom does, because she knows how important it is to me and Chanel to be in a singing group. That's all we've ever really wanted to do!

"Can we go eat?" I ask, listening to my stomach

grumble. "I know I'll get my grub on when I get home, but I need a pit stop first."

"Okay," Juanita says, "but I'm not eating."

As we walk up to the door of Dunkin' Donuts, Chanel lets out a yelp, which makes me think there's something wrong with her ankle again.

"No way, José!" Chanel blurts out. "I'm not eating here—I'm too fat!"

"Awright, just wait while I get a Dunkaccino and jelly doughnut to go," I say, relieved it's not her ankle after all. "You can watch me eat it." When I'm hungry, my stomach cannot be denied.

"Oh, okay," Chanel chuckles, giving in without even a fight, "I'll get a Vanilla Bean Coolatta—just to keep you company."

"I knew you couldn't resist," I tease her. That's Chuchie for you. Her willpower is like rubber—it bends whenever you push it, then comes right back. You know she'll be complaining later about how fat she is, and saying: "Galleria, why'd you let me order that Coolatta? So much sugar!"

Chanel and I slurp and munch our gooey concoctions happily while Auntie Juanita sips a Diet Coke, then makes the call on her cell phone. "Dottie, did you make an appointment with that producer for the girls?" she says, breathing fire. "Chanel is barely off her crutches, and I don't want her running herself ragged, like she did before the accident. . . . 'But' nothing. I know Galleria is trying to get everybody all worked up about this singing group, but—let me finish, Dottie."

Get everybody worked up about this singing group? Jeez, Louise, Auntie Juanita is like a dog with a bone, she just won't leave us alone! I'm so tired of her acting like the Cheetah Girls are just some after-school soda-pop group, sitting around drinking milk shakes and giggling. I can't wait till we prove to her—and everybody else in this world— that the Cheetah Girls are down for the twirl. Then they'll *have* to take us seriously, even if we are a bunch of teenagers.

"Well, I'll think about it," Auntie Juanita says, still huffing. "'Cuz I'm not sure she's up for it, that's why. Okay, fine, fine." Auntie Juanita snaps the phone shut. "Galleria, you and Chanel go on. I have to go jogging." Then she says something to Chanel in Spanish before leaving.

"What did she say, Chuchie?" I ask, curious.

"That I'd better not say anything to your mom, and I'd better be home by nine o'clock." Chanel breaks into a big grin. "Hey, forget about her—I'm off my crutches, *mija*!!"

We do our Cheetah Girls handshake, then give each other a fierce hug.

Chapter 2

"You don't think she talked *Madrina* out of letting us go to the studio with Mouse Almighty, do you?" Chanel asks, coming right back down to earth.

"You never know. But we'll find out soon enough, when we get to my house." I'm feeling so nervous about Auntie Juanita jinxing our date with destiny that I clutch Chuchie's arm and steer us to Singh's deli for some fresh bubble gum. Gotta have it, even though I've only got five duckets in my cheetah wallet.

"Gimme too, *mamacita*," Chuchie whines, grabbing her own pack of Biggies Bubbles, then ripping off the foil wrappers one by one until she's stuck a whole pack in her mouth.

"'Gimme too?' What are you, on *Sesame Street*?" I giggle, paying for hers because Chuchie has even fewer duckets than I do. Auntie Juanita has had her on a starvation budget ever since Chuchie, alias the shopaholic, borrowed her credit card and maxed it out.

Chewing away like a pair of chomp-happy cows, Chanel and I are strolling arm in arm down the hallway to my apartment when I hear a door being unlocked behind us. "It's Mrs. Brubaker," I whisper, shushing Chuchie.

Mrs. Brubaker is my "Wicked Witch of the West" next-door neighbor. Her hair is dyed such a bright red, she looks like a rooster. My mom calls her "a snob without a job."

I get ready to put on my polite face and say hello to Mrs. Brubaker. I wouldn't care if she never spoke to me if it wasn't for her little bichon frise, Buffy, who is the cutest dog in the world—besides my Toto, of course. Buffy is—get this—*paper trained*, because Mrs. Brubaker doesn't take her outside to do her business. "Buffy could pick up diseases!" she always says.

I wonder what Mrs. Brubaker wants. It looks like she opened her door when she heard the elevator coming. She must be expecting someone.

"Galleria!"

"Oh, hi, Mrs. Brubaker." I realize suddenly that Mrs. Brubaker has been waiting for *me*.

"Ooo, can I play with Buffy?" Chuchie asks excitedly. She is so shameless, she'll do anything just to pet a fluffy pooch!

"Well, that's exactly what I need to talk to your mother about," Mrs. Brubaker says to me. "I've rung the bell, but she doesn't answer, even though the doorman told me she's home."

Why, all of a sudden, do I feel like *I* did something wrong? "Oh? What do you need to talk to her about?"

"Never mind, just tell your mother I need to see her *immediately*."

"Can't I see Buffy for just a second?" Chuchie pleads, oblivious to the fact that Mrs. Brubaker is radiating supa attitude.

"No, you may not!" Mrs. Brubaker backs up and slams her door right in Chuchie's face.

"She's definitely got a bee in her stupid bonnet," I hiss, loud enough for Mrs. Brubaker to hear me right through the door. "Buzzzzzzzzzzz."

We go on into my apartment. Mom is there in all her cheetahness, sitting at the dining room table reading *Billboard* magazine and sipping iced tea. Usually she works really late at the store, but I guess that conversation with Auntie Juanita got her uptown faster than Bisquick rising.

"What are you doing home so early?" I ask, like I don't have a Blue's clue.

"You *know* why I'm home," Mom snaps at me. "Juanita sounded like she was going to have a coronary! Chanel, honey, come over here and let me see you walk, so I can decide if you're going to keel over at Mouse Almighty's studio."

"Yes, *Madrina*," Chanel coos, then runs over to my mom with no trace of a limp, and gives her a big, happy kiss.

"Well, you seem to be moving fast enough to record a hit record, don't you?" Mom says, giving Chanel a good look-over.

"Thank gooseness!" I say, relieved. No way, José, did I want Mom to cancel that appointment! "Oh, by the way, Mom, Mrs. Brubaker says she rang the bell but nobody answered."

"I know. I looked through the peephole, saw that prune-dried face, and tiptoed right back into the kitchen. I'm in no mood for any of Esther's drama today. I mean, how can you talk to someone who hasn't changed her hairstyle in twenty years?"

It's true that Mrs. Brubaker is always bothering us about something. Either we didn't put the recycling bags in the right place, or didn't tie them tight enough. Or we left too many newspapers and magazines in the incinerator room. Or Toto is barking too loud. Or we played our music too loud on a weeknight. And if she's not bothering *us*, she's bothering someone *else* in the building with one of her pet peeves. I guess Mom's right—who cares what Mrs. Brubaker wants?

"What I want to know is, what are you girls going to wear to Mouse Almighty's studio on Thursday?" Mom peers at us over the top of her cat-eye-shaped cheetah eyeglasses. "It'd be nice if you came up with something new, but true to your look."

"I don't know what we're wearing," I say, "'cuz we sure don't have new-but-true duckets."

"Wake up and smell the vinyl, darling. You want Mouse to think you're the next-best thing since the Spice-Rack Girls?" Mom says with a twinkle in her eye. I can tell she's got something sneaky up her sleeve. I just hope it results in some duckets in my pockets! "I could be convinced to give you a few duckets for a head-turning accessory that will bring your cheetah-ness to a glorious new level," she says. "But *in exchange . . .*"

Now I see that there is a point to this joint. "In exchange for *what*?"

"For that ticky-tacky, cow-curdling *bubble gum*—which I want banned to never-never land for at least one week! You two girls are too fierce and fabulous to sound like firecrackers wherever you walk. You probably scare half the neighborhood with that noise!"

"Mom!" I shriek, wondering where Daddy is when I need him to defend me. Of course, I *know* where he is. He's at the factory he runs in Brooklyn, where all the clothes are manufactured for Mom's Soho boutique, Toto in New York.

"'Mom' nothing! If I even see a gum *wrapper* on the sidewalk near you, the deal's off!"

Instantly, Chanel spits her big wad of gum into a tissue. "Done deal-i-o!" she says.

"Chuchie, that is disgusting," I moan.

Mom stares at me harder.

"But how am I gonna live up to my nickname?" I ask in despair.

"I don't know, but it's gonna be awful hard recording a demo and chewing gum at the same time!" Mom says, not budging.

"Oh, come on. I mean, have you ever heard of a 'Bubbles' without any gum? That's like a Backstreet without a 'Boy.' Or a Destiny without a 'Child.' Or a Britney without a 'Spear.'"

Mom is looking at me like I'm from Mars.

"Okay!" I grab another tissue and spit mine into it. "Done deal-i-o."

"So we have a deal?"

"In *principle* . . ."

"Then empty out your pockets and gimme your emergency stash," Mom commands.

"I don't have any more, Mom!"

Chuchie grabs my backpack, with all my packs of bubble gum in it, and runs for the door. "I'm gonna dump these in the incinerator, *Madrina*!" she yells, giggling.

Just when I thought Chuchie couldn't go any lower for a chance to "shop in the name of love!" The first chance I get, I'm gonna hang her like a piñata, then whack her to see if any candy comes out. "I can't believe this. Gum-jacked in my own living room! Is there nowhere safe in the world for an innocent child?"

"I'm sure that's not how *Eddie Lizard* thinks of you—which is all the time, judging by his phone calls," Mom huffs back at me.

"Has Eddie called me?" I ask excitedly, instantly forgetting about anything else.

"No. Why do you ask?"

"Oh . . . no reason . . ." I say. See, Eddie Lizard is this really cute boy I met at our Saturday vocal class, at Drinka Champagne's Conservatory. I just *love* his eyes. I've never seen eyelashes so long. So when he asked me for my number, I gave it to him.

For the first week, he was calling me every other minute. But it's been two whole days now since I heard from him! Hmm . . . maybe he called me at home instead of on my cell phone, even though I told him not to. Yeah, that's it, I'll bet he called, and Mom picked up and scared him off!

I can tell she doesn't like him. She thinks Eddie Lizard is gonna drag me into a snake pit or something. She's upset because he's the first boy I've ever liked. But I'm fourteen! She should get over it, okay?

I can hear Chanel talking to someone out in the hallway. It doesn't take long to figure out who it is, either—*Mrs. Brubaker*. Bigmouthed Chuchie is spilling the refried beans! "Yes, she's home. She was busy before!" Chuchie is really gonna get it later. She heard my mom say she didn't want to be bothered with "Esther the pester."

Chuchie comes back inside and says, all chirpy, "*Madrina*, Mrs. Brubaker really wants to talk to you."

"Fine, Chanel, tell her to come in," Mom says, rolling her eyes.

"Look, Bubbles, Buffy is here!" Chanel says, moving out of the way so that Buffy can come waddling into our apartment.

Jeez, Louise—Chuchie isn't the only one who's

put on weight! Buffy looks like she's had more than her share of Bow Wow treats lately. She is definitely extra plump-alicious.

I wonder why Mrs. Brubaker brought her over here. She knows Toto is gonna pounce on Buffy like always. Sure enough, Toto comes barging out of the kitchen like an arrow shot from Cupid's bow.

"No, no, no! Get him away from her!" Mrs. Brubaker cries hysterically.

I grab Toto and hold him while he squirms for dear life. "Stop it!" I hiss at him under my breath.

Mrs. Brubaker calms down, then takes out a doggie wipe and cleans Buffy's paws! She is definitely a major-domo clean freak.

"Hi, Esther, what can I do for you?" Mom asks, without even inviting Mrs. Brubaker to sit down.

"You know, Dorothea, we've been neighbors for quite some time, and this is very difficult for me," Mrs. Brubaker starts in. "I've asked you very nicely to keep Toto away from my Buffy. I know you and Galleria think that may seem unkind, but now look at what he's done!"

"What exactly are you getting at?" Mom asks, puzzled.

"I took Buffy for her checkup, because I was worried about her weight—and the doctor

21

informs me that she is *pregnant*, and about to deliver any day!"

"And what does that have to do with Toto?" Mom snipes impatiently. "I mean, if he came anywhere near your dog, you'd skin him alive!"

"Well, obviously, Toto has . . . um . . . *had his way* with Buffy. So I think you should pay for all her medical expenses."

We look at her like she's crazy. "You know, I've heard a lot of scams in my time, but this one really takes a bite out of crime!" Mom snarls. "If you want to sue for paternity payments, perhaps you should go sniffing around someone else!"

"Dorothea, I do not allow Buffy out of the apartment, so I know it's impossible for any other dog to be the father," Mrs. Brubaker says, choking back tears. "He has always managed to sneak around her somehow. I don't know how he does it."

"Well, I guess we're gonna have to have a paternity test, aren't we?" Mom shoots back. "And maybe we should call in Sergeant Snausage, the pet detective," Mom says, referring to the TV cartoon character.

"That's enough, Dorothea! You people are impossible!"

"*You people?*" Mom says, her voice getting scarily sarcastic.

Thank gooseness Daddy comes in right then, just in time to save Mrs. Brubaker from getting whacked over the head with one of Mom's cheetah purses.

"Daddy!" I yell, running to the door and throwing my arms around him.

"Come stai, cara?" Daddy greets me in Italian, his native language.

"Molto bene, ma senti! La signora ha detto che—" I start to say, trying to clue him in to Mrs. Brubaker's wack accusations.

"Hello, Esther." Daddy interrupts me.

Mrs. Brubaker's angry face has contorted into what looks like a wrinkled prune. "Your dog has impregnated Buffy. Your wife insists that isn't possible, but I *know* that somehow, Toto has gotten to her. I don't understand why you never had him fixed anyway."

"I don't understand why *you* didn't get *Buffy* fixed, if you're so worried about male suitors!" Mom hisses, then looks at Dad like she wants him to handle this situation.

Instead, Daddy breaks into a big embarrassed grin, and starts wringing his hands like he's nervous.

"I don't see what's so funny," Mrs. Brubaker says.

"Well, I guess I should have said something

earlier," Dad says. "Ah, Esther, do you remember the day they were putting the new furniture in your apartment?"

Mom sees what he's getting at. "Franco! How could you let Toto get at Buffy!" she blurts out angrily.

"They were playing in the hallway," Daddy says innocently. "I felt so bad for Toto. He never gets to see Buffy, and I thought it wouldn't hurt. *Va bene?*"

Mom gives Daddy that look that used to scare me when I was little. She is really mad at him.

"Well, I expect you'll be paying for all Buffy's medical expenses," Mrs. Brubaker says triumphantly.

"What about the puppies?" I blurt out.

"We'll discuss that another time. I must be getting home," Mrs. Brubaker says hastily, then leaves in a huff.

I want to yell for her to wait, but I know better. Mom is really mad at Dad. He's gone off to the kitchen, trying to disappear, but I know that won't work for long. They are going to have a big fight later, when they're in their bedroom alone and the door is closed.

"Can I have one of the puppies, *Madrina*?" Chuchie asks shamelessly, sounding like a puppy dog herself.

Oops, Doggy Dog!

"Wake up and smell the latte, darling," Mom says, annoyed. "You know Juanita isn't gonna let you get a dog. We'll be lucky if *we* get one from that woman." She punches a number into the phone. "What a day. I'd better let Juanita know you're going to the studio, whether she likes it or not. *And* that I'm going to be a *grandmother*!"

Chapter 3

The next morning I wake up with a serious case of "lockjaw." I guess it's from chewing so much bubble gum yesterday—*and* wearing braces for a thousand years (okay, five). I'm supposed to get them taken off real soon, and my teeth are dying to get out from "behind bars."

"Momsy-poo!" I scream, like I'm in pain. When I was little, I used to do this to see how fast she'd come running to my rescue. Now I do it just to annoy her.

Mom ignores me, so I hop off the bed and march into her room. She's sitting at her mirror, putting on one of her many wigs.

"If I have to give up chewing gum," I start in, "then can I least get my braces taken off before the studio session?"

"I told you, Dr. Gold is booked solid. You can't

26

get an appointment with him until the next drought," Mom says, being dramatic. "Galleria, you've lived this long with braces, a few more weeks won't kill you. Be happy that I'm giving you money to buy something new for your studio session."

Mom is right. I accept her twenty-dollar bribe without a fight. "You said we should get a new look . . . like what?" I ask, fishing for advice.

"Add some wigs to your act. It worked for Tina Turner and the Ikettes, it'll work for the Cheetah Girls."

Mom's gotta be kidding. Tina Turner and the Ikettes were really famous in the '60s and '70s, but what would the Cheetah Girls look like shaking a tail feather? Well, it *is* her twenty dollars, so I could think about it, I guess. Whatever makes her clever.

"Mom, could you talk to Mrs. Brubaker and make sure we get the puppies?" I ask hesitantly.

"Oh, don't you worry, I'm going right over there before I leave for work." Mom turns away from her mirror and gives me her full attention. "And you do mean *puppy*—not puppies—because we are not running a bichon bed-and-breakfast here!"

"Okay," I say, giving in. "One puppy, pleez."

As soon as I'm out of the house, I make a beeline to Singh's deli to buy some forbidden bubble gum.

"Mr. Singh, where's the gum?" I ask, eyeing the empty racks.

"Your mother was already here," Mr. Singh says, chuckling.

I feel my face burning as I realize that I've been outfoxed by my own mother—*again*! What'd she do, sneak out last night after fighting with Auntie Juanita? *That's right, she took Toto for a walk!*

Busted by Mom behind my back!

"Awright, Mr. Singh. I'll see you later." I storm down First Avenue toward the subway station so I can catch the train to school. As I pass Ricky's Urban Groove, this new cheetah-licious drugstore that opened last month, it occurs to me that I could sneak inside and see if they have any Biggies bubble gum. But before I can take a step, I notice a display of pink, blue, and purple bob wigs in the window. Suddenly, Mom's advice comes back to me—"Add some wigs to your act"—and a light-bulb goes off in my brain.

Holy, cannoli! The Cheetah Girls are gonna show up at Mouse's studio decked in pink wigs! Humming all the way to the subway, I forget about the bubble gum—until I get to school and see everyone clamoring around Chanel, because she's finally walking without crutches.

"*Mija*, are you gonna take ballet classes

again?" asks Daisy Duarte from our homeroom.

"Yes. No. I mean, I'm just gonna do the warm-ups, but not anything else," Chanel responds sheepishly.

"I heard your singing group broke up. Is that true?" LaRonda chimes in.

"Who told you that?" I ask, butting in. I wonder how LaRonda could say something so wack! I mean, we thought she was chill with us.

"A lot of people at school are saying that," LaRonda explains, embarrassed. "I don't remember where I heard it."

I know she's telling a fib-eroni. I wrack my brains trying to figure out who's trying to squash our limelight by spreading such a nasty rumor. I mean, the list of sneaky-deaky culprits could go on till the break of dawn.

"We haven't done anything lately, but that doesn't mean we're not still together," Dorinda pipes up in our defense. Where'd she come from? I didn't even see her in the crowd—probably 'cuz she's so tiny.

"We're going into the studio tomorrow with Mouse Almighty, the famous producer," I chime in.

"Really?" LaRonda says, like she doesn't believe me.

"Why do you say it like that?" Now I'm getting defensive, even though I liked LaRonda. Until now.

"Last time I asked you, you said you hadn't heard from the record company or anybody," she explains.

"Yeah, well, here's a blow-by-blow, so don't act like you know!"

"Awright, Galleria, calm down. So y'all gonna go in the studio and do your songs?"

Dorinda throws me a quick glance, like, "Here we go with round number two."

"No, LaRonda, we're not gonna do *our* songs," I say, feeling suddenly embarrassed and insecure about this whole studio thing. "We don't know yet what songs Mouse wants us to sing. It's, um, just a demo tape."

"Yeah, but at least it's something," LaRonda says, trying to reassure us now.

"Yeah, or a whole lot of nothing," I quip back.

Dorinda nods her head in agreement. I notice that she has dark circles under her eyes, and I wonder what drama is going down at her house this time. See, Do' Re Mi lives uptown on 116th Street, with her foster parents, Mr. and Mrs. Bosco. Last month they took in another foster child—their tenth or eleventh. So things are even more hectic than usual at Do's house these days.

"I'll see you in a minute in homeroom," Daisy Duarte says to Chuchie, and trails off down the hall. The rest of the pack of peeps huddled by our lockers slowly scatters.

"I can't believe LaRonda said that," Dorinda says.

"Yeah, whatever makes her clever," I say. "But I'll bet you I know who started the rumor. It was probably The Red Snapper." The Red Snapper, alias Derek Ulysses Hambone, has a gold tooth, *and* a crush on me. We also call him "Mr. DUH" because of his initials. And because he's pretty dense.

"It could be the Mackerel, too," adds Chuchie, referring to Derek's main man Mackerel Johnson, who has pointy front teeth and a crush on Chanel.

"I heard that," Dorinda says, nodding in agreement. "But it could be anyone. There's always somebody stirring up flackeroni in this school."

"Listen up, chicklets, I got an idea that will definitely show off our spots at Mouse's studio," I say excitedly. "Ricky's has these shocking-pink wigs in the window. Let's snatch us some, and wear them with our pink leopard tops for our studio debut!"

Chuchie jumps up and down, panting like a puppy, but Dorinda doesn't look sold.

"Are you okay, Do' Re Mi?" I ask, concerned. "You don't like it?"

"No, it's cool, but, um . . . I really don't have any money right now, 'cuz the Youth Entrepreneurship Program is closing until next semester."

"Oh, I didn't know that," I say, feeling guilty. See, Dorinda works three days a week after school at the T-shirt stand in the lobby of the YMCA on 135th Street. That's how she gets money for all the little extras Chuchie and I take for granted. Even Aqua and Angie get an allowance, and their dad pays for them to go to the beauty parlor once a month to get their nails and hair done.

"Maybe we should wait till we see Aqua and Angie after school?" Dorinda suggests sheepishly. "You know, see what they think?"

"Awright," I say, not wanting to make Dorinda feel bad. "But you know, my mom gave me enough money to buy something for both of us."

Dorinda doesn't say anything, and I wonder if I've stuck my foot even further into my mouth. I decide to change the subject, pronto.

"Toto's pregnant," I blurt out, then correct myself. "I mean, Toto got *Buffy* pregnant."

"Word?" Dorinda chuckles, taking in this hot dog news.

"And my mom said I can keep one of the puppies!" I say excitedly, then instantly feel bad. What was I thinking without blinking? What if Dorinda wanted one? I mean, she probably doesn't even have a *stuffed* pet, let alone a real one.

"I'll see y'all after school," Do' says, hiking her cheetah backpack on her shoulders and scooting down the hall. Now I *know* she feels bad, 'cuz she left on the supa-quick tip.

Cuchifrita Ballerina obviously doesn't care. All she wants to know is how she can get her paws on a puppy. "Bubbles, you haven't said anything—I mean *nada*, *nada*—about *me* getting one!"

"Oh, stuff the fluff," I snap at her. But she continues whining all the way to homeroom class. That's where I spot our number one suspect— Derek Ulysses Hambone. Derek majors in Design, same as Dorinda, but from the looks of his Johnny Be Down get-ups, I think "talent" is just a word he knows how to spell. Maybe Derek dresses like all the other kids—like a hyena following the pack.

Cheetah Girls are not about being copycats. Oh, snapples, that would make a good line in the Cheetah Girls Credo, I realize, and whip out my KittyKat notebook to scribble it down. This furry, spotted notebook is strictly for my songs, thoughts, and ideas—nothing to do with school. I carry it with me wherever I go, and however I flow.

"True Cheetah Girls don't run with wolves or hang with hyenas. . . ."

Chuchie gives me a nudge, and cuts her eyes over to Derek. Mr. Hambone is huddled with his crew. I can see that he's talking about us, because he is cutting *his* eyes over in *our* direction.

"*Mija,* you were right," Chuchie whispers. "It was Derek *bocheenchando* gossiping about us."

"Whatever makes him clever," I mutter under my breath, tapping my pencil on the desk impatiently. Mr. Drezform, our homeroom teacher, hasn't arrived yet, and the natives are getting restless. *God, I wish I had some Biggies Bubbles!*

To get my mind off chewing bubble gum, I start daydreaming about Eddie Lizard again. Maybe I should call him after school. After all, there could be a very good reason he hasn't called me. Maybe he's sick, or hurt, and couldn't reach me. Or maybe his father threw out my phone number by accident. Or maybe they're both out of town on an emergency. There could be lots of good reasons he didn't call! Yeah, sure, lots of reasons . . .

What did I ever see in the Red Snapper? I guess I liked the attention. But now that I've met Eddie Lizard, Derek can flap his stupid snapper someplace else!

* * *

After homeroom, Chuchie and I decide it's better to hightail it out of the classroom than to stick around for a flack attack with Derek and his crew. But I should have known Derek would try to reel me in. He always does.

"Hey, Cheetah Girl," he riffs, fumbling with the deep-sea pockets on his baggy-to-the-max jeans with the logo JOHNNY BE DOWN scribbled on the pockets. I look over and smile, and that's when I notice something new around his neck: Derek is sporting a gold nameplate with his initials—D.U.H.—in big script letters.

"You like it?" Derek asks, catching me eyeing the merchandise.

"It's so loud I almost can't hear you," I snap back, smirking.

"Check out my new moon watch," Derek says. Oblivious to my snap, he flashes his wrist at me. "It's from Apollo 13—qualified by NASA for space missions."

"Well, I guess you're ready for takeoff any day now, huh?" I say, squinting my eyes.

"Yeah, looks that way," Derek says, flashing his gold teeth. "Oh, remember that fashion show I modeled in—Mad Millennium?"

"Yeah. How could I forget those designs by 'up and coming' students at Fashion Institute of

Technology?" How could I also forget that after the fashion show Derek had the nerve to kiss me on the cheek and *ask me out on a date*? "Someone needs to call the fashion police and have you thrown in fashion detention," I snap.

"Arrest me, yourself, Cheetah Girl," Derek says, crossing his hands and thrusting them in front of me.

"Never mind, we've got bigger fish to fry. Like getting ready for our studio session," I hiss at Derek, who is really getting on my nerves.

"Oh? Last I heard, the Cheetah Girls had run off looking for some hyenas to play with," Derek says, confirming my suspicions. So he *is* the one flapping his lips about us around school.

Grabbing Chuchie's arm, I give Derek one last morsel of remorse. "Yeah, well, it looks like we found them!" And then we're out of there, before he even figures out what I said.

"Mr. DUH" may have loose lips, but Little Ms. Fierce got the last word this time!

Chapter 4

*C*huchie, Dorinda, and I hop on the #1 train uptown to meet Aqua and Angie at their school—LaGuardia Performing Arts Annex, on 68th and Amsterdam. This way, we can catch the crosstown bus together to go to Ricky's Urban Groove and check out their digable wig collection. I think Aqua and Angie will start "thinking pink," after they see how ferocious we look in the wigs.

We keep our eyes peeled for the twins' matching press-'n'-curl bobs to surface in the rowdy crowd pouring out of their overcrowded school. "There they are." Dorinda points to the twins, who are wearing denim jackets and jeans.

"Hey, y'all!" Aquanette exclaims.

"Wow, you go to school with all these peeps?" Dorinda says, squinting her almond-shaped eyes and looking up at Aqua and Angie. Dorinda is the shortest of our crew. She's not even five feet tall.

"Well, we don't all sit in the same classroom, if that's what you mean, Miss Dorinda," Angie explains. "Ooh, look, 'member that girl we told you about?"

"Which one?" I ask.

"JuJu Beans Gonzalez."

"Oh, right, the next Mo' Money Monique," Dorinda remembers.

"Yeah—and she wants to be a diva 'fore she can even spell it." Angie shakes her head.

"Well, she sure looked like she saw a ghost when she heard we were going into the studio with Mouse Almighty," Aquanette says triumphantly.

Angie hoists her book bag. "Where we going now?"

"Well, I told you that we should go into the studio and rock it to the doggy bone with a new look," I begin.

"That sounds good," they say in unison, nodding their heads. I always wonder how they do that. I guess it comes with being twins.

"Wait till you see what I have in mind," I say.

"Well, I sure hope this ain't a wild-goose chase, 'cuz we have lots of homework to do, plus clean the whole house," Angie says seriously.

"What's up with that?" I ask. "The *whole house*?"

"You don't understand, Galleria," Aqua says, coming to her twin's defense. "Daddy is on our tail all the time now that he's his old self again."

Mr. Walker's ex-girlfriend, High Priestess Abala Shaballa Hexagone, put a love spell on him, to steal his love for life. Luckily, the twins came home early and peeped the witchcraft situation. They called me and Chanel, and we got Eddie Lizard to call in his father, the famous Doktor Lizard, who is a bona fide hoodoo practitioner. He uncrossed the spell. And that's the whole hexarama.

Now that their father is unhexed, it seems things are back to normal in the Walker household. See, their father is kinda strict, like a military officer. He has very specific tasks for the twins, and a new schedule every day.

As we're getting on the 68th Street crosstown bus, Aqua brings up a sore subject. "How is Eddie Lizard?" she asks. I can hear a twinge of jealousy in her voice.

"I wouldn't know," I sigh, plunking my MetroCard into the slot on the fare box. "He hasn't called me all week, and I'm not chasing after him like a little lost cub." (I'm thinking about doing just that, actually, but I'm sure not gonna tell Aqua!)

"Well, he didn't seem like he was worth the bother, anyway," Aqua says.

"Oh, yes he is," I hiss, defending him. "You're just green with Gucci envy!"

All five of us get quiet as clams. We're standing on a crowded bus, and we don't want everybody to know our business, so we pretend our beef jerky is squashed.

"Guess who's gonna be a daddy?" Chuchie tells the twins, getting excited. After we finish telling them all about our escapade with Mrs. Brubaker and Buffy, Angie asks, "You sure he's the daddy?"

A lady with a baby carriage looks up at Angie and smiles. I get embarrassed, because I know she thinks one of us is pregnant. But that's not going to happen to me until after I'm famous and live in a castle. For true!

"Why, yes, Miz Anginette, Mr. Toto is going to be a proud daddy indeed," I say, imitating the Southern accent the twins brought north from Houston.

"What's gonna happen to the puppies?" Angie asks excitedly.

"Well, that's what my mom is gonna find out," I say.

We fall silent again, and suddenly, this tune pops into my head out of nowhere. I start whistling it, and the other Cheetah Girls pick it up, nodding and smiling. Everybody looks at us as we start humming it together in perfect harmony. It's amazing how easy it is for the five of us to get in that groove together.

After we let the melody die down, we get real quiet for a minute. It's almost as if we're all thinking the same thing—and three of us are not even twins!

"I wonder what kind of songs Mr. Mouse Almighty is gonna have us recording," Angie says, a concerned look in her eye.

I know what she's worrying about. The twins are very religious, and they're particular about what kind of songs we sing. They definitely don't wanna do anything too "bootylicious," if you know what I'm saying.

"Yeah, what if he picks songs for us that are really wack?" Chanel asks.

"Don't worry," I assure my crew. "Mouse Almighty knows what he's doing. He's produced joints for Kahlua Alexander, Karma's Children, Sista Fudge, and In the Dark."

But to tell you the truth, I'm worried, too. Mouse is definitely the real deal as a producer, but how do we know he'll really get our global groove? See, we Cheetah Girls have our own special vibe—and I'm not just saying that because I'm the main songwriter and leader of the group. Truth is, we don't look, sound, or act like any other singers. We have our own way of singing and harmonizing. Mom says that's what sells records, and if it's true, then we should sell them by the bushels, 'cuz we have "growl power" to the max!

I know I shouldn't ask Mouse Almighty if we can record *my* songs—but why not? I know our groove better than he does. It's a question that's been on my mind for weeks, but I keep it to myself. I don't wanna make Chuchie jealous.

See, she wants to write songs for us, too. Trouble is, she doesn't really know how. I let her help me with this one song, and she's been pushing ever since to write some more. I don't want to make her feel bad, but Miss Cuchifrita has a lot to learn in the songwriting department.

"Well," I tell my crew, "if we don't like the songs he picks, we have to say something, okay?"

"I heard that," Dorinda says, nodding in agreement.

"Even if it means not recording a demo, that's what we'll do—'cuz we're not going out like that," I decide right there on the spot. Nobody argues with me, though Chanel looks like she wants to.

Angie gasps when she sees all the stuff in Ricky's window. "Wow—how come we ain't got a store like this in our neighborhood?" The twins live on 96th and Riverside. It's definitely a lot quieter up there, with tree-lined streets and chirpy birds.

"Just hold your breath. I'll bet you the 'Urban Groove' is coming your way any day," I exclaim, walking into Ricky's like I'm stepping inside my very own groove factory.

Aqua and Angie zone right in on the hair-care section. They love spritzes and sprays even more than Chanel does. "So far so good," I whisper into Chuchie's ear as the twins scamper around, oohing and aahing at everything. "Now let's see if the twins are down for the 'do.'"

I can't believe Mom even gave me the money to buy a wig. I guess she's just as happy about us getting into Mouse's studio as we are. While the twins are oogling over racks of fairy dust glitter in little pots, I ask to try on one of the wigs.

"You have to put on a wig cap before trying one on," the salesgirl informs me.

"Oh. I don't happen to have one in my backpack," I tease her, hoping she'll let me slide.

"Well, you can buy one for ten dollars."

"Ten duckets?" I respond in disbelief. "They should be ten dollars for a *dozen*."

Now the rest of my crew is on drama alert, so I turn to them and say, "Listen up, chicklets, we gotta make a mad dash to my house for a Minute Rice moment."

"What for?" Aqua asks.

"To borrow five of my mom's stocking caps."

"What do we need stocking caps for?" Angie asks. The twins are always a little slow on the uptake, but I'm used to it by now.

"So we can try on wigs."

"We're not wearing *those* wigs, are we?" Angie asks, gasping in disbelief.

"Yes, ma'am, we are! We're gonna at least try them on, to see if they show off our spots." I walk out the door so we can move this caravan along to my house, and all the time, I'm talking to my crew over my shoulder.

"Remember when we saw the Ike and Tina Turner videos, and the three Ikettes were swinging and flinging their hair like windmills? That added a lot to their act, you know what I'm saying?" I know Mom would agree with me. See, once a month we have Seventies Appreciation Night. We watch videos of all the old-school performers, so we can study their acts and learn musical history. It's part of our Cheetah Girls "boot camp" training.

Angie and Aqua nod their heads in agreement and keep quiet. See, the twins are definitely the best singers in our group—that's why they got into

LaGuardia Performing Arts Annex. On the other hand, they know that Chuchie, Dorinda, and I have mad flava in the style department. That's why *we* go to Fashion Industries High.

Still, I can see they're not happy, and I know it's gonna be a hard job getting them up to speed with the program. "I thought those wigs in the window were just for decoration and stuff," Angie finally says. "We're gonna look funny in them. I mean, people already make fun of our Cheetah Girls costumes as it is."

"Peeps who aren't down with our flavor aren't the fans we savor," I hiss, which shuts Angie up for the moment.

Getting off the elevator and walking down the hallway to my apartment, I'm tempted to knock on Mrs. Brubaker's apartment. "This is where Buffy lives," I whisper, then peep through the peephole, which makes my crew giggle.

"Who's there?" Mrs. Brubaker yells through the door.

"Oh, snapples!" I shriek, then hurry up and get my door keys out of my cheetah backpack—but not before Mrs. Brubaker flings her apartment door open. She gives my crew the once-over, then barks, "What were you doing outside my door?"

"We weren't doing anything, Mrs. Brubaker," I say politely.

"How's Buffy?" Chuchie cuts in, batting those big brown eyes like she's so innocent, when she knows *exactly* what she's doing. She is so shameless!

"She's just fine," Mrs. Brubaker snaps back.

"When is she going to, um, have the babies?" Chanel asks.

"They're not babies, they're puppies. And why do you want to know?" Mrs. Brubaker must think she's a pet detective!

Chanel blushes, then stammers, "I—I just want to know."

"Well, Buffy's delivery date is none of your business."

"Did you, um, speak to my mother?" I ask. I'm trying to be polite, but I'm getting tired of her hooty-snooty behavior toward me and my crew. She doesn't have to treat us like we're a bunch of kids.

"No, I haven't spoken to your mother. Two can play the same game, you know."

I give her a blank look, because I don't follow her drift. What is she talking about?

"It'll be best if *all* of you just leave Buffy alone. What I do with her litter is my own business. Tell your mother *that*," Mrs. Brubaker says, then closes her door on us.

"I can't believe she dissed me like that," I mumble, shoving the key in my own apartment door. I decide to call my mom and tell her about this latest Buffy drama. Dialing the number of her store, I suddenly realize what Mrs. Brubaker meant by "two can play the same game." Mom doesn't open the door when Mrs. Brubaker rings our doorbell, so Mrs. Brubaker must have done the same thing to Mom this morning!

"Yes, I'm sure," I tell Mom. "She said, 'What I do with Buffy's litter is my business, so fly away,'" I explain on the phone. "I swear that's what she said. Chanel, Dorinda, Aqua, and Angie are right here—they heard her, Mom!"

Chanel grabs the phone from me. "*Madrina*, she said to forget about the puppies and leave her alone. She wouldn't even tell me when Buffy was going to deliver the babies! Like I'm gonna kidnap them from the hospital or something."

I'm going through major withdrawal. I have to get a wad of Biggies in my mouth or I'm gonna burst like a bubble! "Gimme the phone, Chuchie," I say, getting impatient. "Mom, what are we gonna do?" I ask.

"Sue," Mom says calmly.

"Sue?"

"Yes, we'll take this matter to family court. Let a judge decide if we're unfit parents."

"But they're *puppies*," I remind her. Mom may be our manager, and she may read *Billboard* magazine every week, but that doesn't make her the legal eagle of 67th Street.

"Darling, you can sue someone for putting a run in your stockings if you want to. This is New York," she says. "We'll go to family court first thing in the morning, and file a complaint. That's the least we can do."

"Okay," I say, sighing deeply. Inside, I feel like we stand a better chance of winning the $5 million jackpot in the lottery than getting Buffy's babies. I don't care what Mrs. Brubaker says, they *are* babies—*my* babies.

"Mom says we're gonna sue for custody of Buffy's litter," I tell my crew as I rifle through Mom's drawers, looking for extra stocking caps.

"Wow," Dorinda says, impressed.

"Look at all your mom's wigs!" Angie exclaims, peering in at the doorway of Mom's bedroom.

When we've found enough stocking caps, we walk back to Ricky's. "Maybe we'll get to keep *all* the puppies!" Chuchie says as we turn the corner.

"Chuchie, get it out of your piñata head that

you're getting a puppy!" I snap. "I'll be lucky if *I* even get one," I quickly add, noticing the hurt look on Chuchie's face. "Awright, let's get Operation Big Cheese in full effect," I say, changing the subject, and hand stocking caps to the rest of my crew.

With the caps on, we look like aliens. "Beam me up, Scottie!" I chuckle, staring into the mirrors behind the cosmetic counter. I ask the salesgirl, "Can I have one of the pink wigs, please?" I figure maybe if I try a wig on first, everyone else will go with the flow.

"Wow!" Chuchie says. "You look good enough to eat, *mija*!"

"Okay, chicklets, are you ready to think pink yet?" I ask the twins, then stare at my reflection. "Wow, I kinda dig it."

"*Mija*, I like it!" Chuchie says excitedly.

"Galleria, that may look good on *you*—*and* Chanel and Dorinda—but what about me and Angie?" Aqua objects. "We're a lot darker than y'all—and we got big ole heads!"

"Don't be radikkio," I tell her. "Two of the Ikettes wore blond wigs, and they were just your complexion. Remember we watched a video of them on the *Dick Clark Show*, shaking a tail feather?"

"Yeah, well, why do we have to look like we have tail feathers on our heads?" Aqua huffs, rolling her eyes. I *hate* when she does that.

"Just try it, Aqua," Angie says, coaxing her sister. "Gimme one, I'll try it."

The salesgirl gives us four more pink wigs, and I help Dorinda put hers on.

"*Mira*," Chuchie says, motioning for us to huddle together and look in the big mirror. I can see that she's now totally into our transformation. I knew I could count on my ace señorita to get into the groove! "Wow, we really look like a singing group now," she says.

"Either that or cotton candy," Aqua retorts, still unsold. "I don't think this is such a good idea."

"Oh, Mommy, look!" exclaims this little freckled girl, running toward us and pointing at our wigs. "They look so cool! Can I get one?"

"Okay, you can try one on," the mother says, beaming.

See? I want to say to Aqua, *Get with the program.*

"Come on, let's look around," I say, grabbing Chuchie's arm. If Aqua wants to rain on our parade, she can do it all by herself. I walk around the store, looking at other stuff, and *all* the customers comment on our wigs.

"Are you girls in a show or something?" asks

this older lady who is wearing a pink sweater set, pink pumps, pink lipstick. Guess we can tell what her favorite color is!

"Well, not exactly," I explain. "We're in a singing group—the Cheetah Girls."

"Is that right? Well, you're gonna knock 'em dead." She puts on her bifocals to read the label on the bottle of Pepto-Bismol she has in her hand.

Aqua walks up in back of us, staring over my shoulder at the bottle of Pepto-Bismol, then blurts out, "That's what we look like in those wigs—a bottle of Pepto-Bismol, ready to get shaken, stirred, and thrown out of the studio!"

I refuse to give in to Aqua's protestations. It's funny how much more dramatic the twins are than when we first met them. In their case, a little knowledge is a dangerous thing!

"Look, I got the blue one," the little girl says, running over to us.

"Blue is you!" I say, smiling warmly even though I'm so mad at Aqua I could scream.

"It's my favorite color," the girl says, grinning from ear to ear. "I'm gonna wear this to school!"

"No you're not, dear," her mother warns her. "It's just for fun."

"Yeah, blue is our favorite color, too," Aqua says wistfully.

Oh, now I get it. She thinks we should be wearing *blue* wigs instead of pink ones. No way, José. I'm definitely not feeling blue.

"Ooh, look, *mija*, pink false eyelashes!" Chuchie says, grabbing them off a rack.

"Now, that's going too far," I moan.

"Well, if you ask me, *this* is going too far!" Aqua says grumpily.

"Okay, fine!" I snatch the wig off my head. "We'll go bald, how's that?"

"You don't have to get so dramatic, Galleria," Aqua says, sucking her teeth and rolling her eyes again.

"Maybe that's why Eddie Lizard likes *me* instead of *you*!" I blurt out suddenly. Chanel looks at me, shocked. *Tooooo bad.* I'm tired of pretending like I don't know what bee Aqua has in her bonnet. The reason why she thinks Eddie Lizard "isn't worth the bother" is because he likes *me*, not her!

"I don't like Eddie Lizard, so why should I care if he likes you?" Aqua counters. "The way you were sticking to him like a frozen Popsicle, he didn't stand a chance anyway. No wonder he hasn't called you!"

Now I've had enough of Aqua's fluff. I hand the wig back to the salesgirl and thank her. Behind me, I hear Dorinda trying to reason with Angie. "You sure we can't do this, Aqua? I think they look dope on us."

"No, thank you, ma'am," Aqua says, determined not to give in. "I'd rather show up at the studio wearing hair rollers. That's the only thinking pink I'm doing with *my* big head!"

I'm almost out the door when I hear Chuchie yell, "Galleria, wait for us!"

I stand outside, fuming, while they return their pink wigs to the counter.

"We can still wear pink cheetah tops," Chuchie offers, giving me a hug.

"Yeah, that's a good idea," Aqua says sheepishly.

"Thank gooseness you like *something*," I snap. Then I get down to business, so I can just bounce, and get away from Aqua and her attitude problems. "I guess we'll see you at the studio at four o'clock tomorrow." I kiss Chuchie and Dorinda good-bye, then march around the corner to my house.

Now, I wonder how Aqua knew Eddie Lizard hasn't called me?

Chapter 5

Before I reach my building, my Miss Wiggy cell phone rings. *Oh, please, let this be Eddie Lizard!* I answer it with bated breath, but try to sound on the chill tip.

"Wazzup?"

I'm soooo disappointed when I hear Mom's drowsy-sounding voice on the other end of the line.

"Hi, darling." She sounds like she's on her deathbed.

"What's wrong, Mom?" I ask, trying to forget about my drama for a second.

"I feel like the Grim Reaper is raking me over some cobblestone coffins," she says in a low voice.

"Mom, that doesn't make any sense."

"Well, read between the lines. I'm coming home,

and please don't play any loud music, hum, or even scribble in that notebook of yours. And have some gingersnap tea ready, with a dollop of fairy snap."

"Right, Mom," I say, finally catching her drift. She's just acting punchy because she has too much work to do. "Okay, I'll see you in a few minutes."

Why won't Eddie call me? I wonder, running quickly past Mrs. Brubaker's apartment door like a scaredy-cat. Now that we're taking this puppy matter to court, I've lost my gumption for giving her a piece of my mind. I hurry inside my apartment, flop down on my cheetah bedspread, let out a deep sigh, and stare at my Miss Wiggy telephone, willing it to ring. I reach over and pick up the receiver, then slam it down. No way, José am I calling Eddie Lizard! Bending over to take off my suede cheetah boots, I notice a big wad of white gum stuck to the left heel.

"How disgusting!" I yelp to Toto, who is resting on his front paws and looking up at me. Suddenly, I feel guilty for all the times I stuck *my* used-up wads of Biggies on the bottoms of desks in school, underneath chairs in Micky Dee's, or railings in subway stations.

"What kind of ticky-tacky gum is this?" I examine the evidence like an autopsy expert. "This gunk looks like it's gonna need a blowtorch to get off my heel." Rifling through my nightstand, I find my favorite Swiss Army knife, sit down at the dining room table, and start scraping the gum off. Then I hear Mom's keys in the door, and I have to laugh. She's gonna love this.

"Hello, darling, is my tea ready? Galleria, what are you doing? Ah, I see your bubble gum charades have finally backfired on you."

"It's not mine!" I protest lamely.

"That's even better—maybe now you'll see how disgusting a habit it really is." Mom plops down at the table and starts to look through the mail. "And I hope you're telling the truth, or the cheetah fairy is gonna strike you with her wand."

"Yes, I am! A deal is a deal."

Mom looks closely at me, because she finally realizes that something is wrong. "And I'm proud of you keeping your side of a bargain. At the end of the day, the only thing you have left is your word. If that's no good, nothin' else is."

"Well, it doesn't matter anyway, because I'm not gonna need the money you gave me—thanks to Aqua, Miss Country Hick on a Stick."

"Oh. So you've had a little drama this afternoon?" Mom walks to the kitchen and picks up the teapot.

"Oh, I'll make it for you," I say, dropping the boot on the floor. "I told you I would."

"Good," Mom says, rubbing her temples. "I need to sit and rest. What a day at the shop!"

"Busy?"

"You know what it's like this time of year." She massages her brow some more, then says, "So tell all, darling. What happened?"

"Aqua hated the wig idea," I moan, getting out the tea bags.

"If I had a penny for every woman who hated wigs, but secretly envied how fabulous *mine* looks, I'd be richer than the Supremes," Mom says, smirking. (The Supremes were the biggest girl group in the sixties, and we've watched a lot of their videos.)

"I thought the Supremes ended up broke," I say, puzzled.

"Whatever, darling, I can't think straight right now. Anyway, my whole point is that wigs—not diamonds—are a girl's best friend, and don't ever forget it."

Best friends. Suddenly I feel sad, because of this beef jerky with Aqua.

"I hope you still plan on going to the studio," Mom says suspiciously.

"*Of course.* I just feel like Aqua's trying to stop

our flow." I don't mention that Aqua is all crushed and mushed over Eddie Lizard. I don't even want to mention his name right now. "She's always giving me a hard time about improving our 'cheetahness,'" I explain, leaving out the specifics.

"Well, have you ever heard the word 'compromise'?" Mom asks. "If she wouldn't go for the wigs, why didn't you girls put your stubborn heads together and try something else?"

"Why should I—I mean *we*?" I stammer, but I don't want to back down. "The wigs are the jointski."

"Well, if you hadn't been so busy trying to get your way, you might have noticed something else in Ricky's that would make your group 'growl,'" Mom says, sipping her tea slowly.

"Whatever," I mumble under my breath. "Mom, could you go talk to Mrs. Brubaker before you lie down?" I ask, trying to ignore the fact that Mom just dissed me hard.

"Hmm. All right," Mom says, getting up slowly. "Come on, then. We might as well do this together."

Mom rings Mrs. Brubaker's doorbell several times, but no one answers it. There's still time to run.

"I guess two can play at the same game," I

whisper to my mom, and explain to her what Mrs. Brubaker said earlier.

"Yeah, well, we'll see who wins this round," Mom huffs, ringing the bell fifty more times.

Finally, Mrs. Brubaker yells out from behind the door: "Who's there?"

Mom responds very sweetly. "Esther, darling, can we talk to you a second?"

I almost gag when Mrs. Brubaker flings the door open and invites us in. We haven't been inside her apartment since before Buffy was born and I was still wearing a little cheetah fur coat and matching hand muffler.

"Let me move these," Mrs. Brubaker says, pushing aside three iron sculptures of frogs holding musical instruments. "I just got them, and I'm taking them to my country house this weekend."

"Oh." I stare at the frogs' bulging glass eyes, and the curly iron antennae on top of their heads. *Jeez, Louise, those are some ugly statues!* I also wonder what caused Mrs. Brubaker's change of heart— usually she only talks to us through the crack in the door, like she was guarding Fort Buffy or something.

Walking into the living room on the powder blue pile rug, I suddenly feel bad for thinking such bad things about Mrs. Brubaker. She probably felt sorry for being so mean to me and Chanel and the rest of our crew, and realized that we should squash this situation like neighbors. Yeah, that's probably it.

"Sit down, please," Mrs. Brubaker says.

I maneuver my way around a huge brown leather hippopotamus footstool, but I almost trip. "Oh, I didn't realize there are two," I say, noticing the little hippo footstool hidden behind the bigger one. I haven't been in Mrs. Brubaker's apartment in so long that I forgot how treacherous it is!

"You all right, Galleria?" Mrs. Brubaker asks, like she's more concerned about her hippos than me.

"I'm coo—yes, I'm fine," I say, catching myself. Sometimes I forget to talk on the regular tip when I'm around adults.

Sitting on the blue alligator couch, I look around for Buffy. I wonder if all the animal furnishings frighten her, 'cuz they sure frighten me, if you know what I'm saying. Staring down at the wooden coffee table etched in flying salamanders, I notice a keepsake box covered with photos of bichons.

"That is so cute!" I exclaim, then pick it up to show Mom.

"I had that made for Buffy's fifth birthday," Mrs.

Brubaker says nervously, then sits down across from us on an armchair covered with dancing blue elephants.

"Oh, how did they do that?" Mom asks.

"It's called découpage. First they put Buffy's picture on the wood, then they seal it with special glaze," she says proudly.

"Oh, you mean those pictures are Buffy?" I ask in disbelief. Now I'm jealous. How come we don't have stuff like that with Toto's picture?

"Yes, that's her. A couple in California make them. I'll give you their number. They also do picture frames—costs a pretty penny, too." Mrs. Brubaker jumps up and goes into the kitchen, then returns with something wrapped in brown paper.

"Where's Buffy?" Mom asks, curious.

"She's in the bedroom . . . *resting*," Mrs. Brubaker says, while scribbling down the number on a piece of paper. "Now, I have to show you something. I just got it framed." Ripping off the brown paper wrapping, Mrs. Brubaker holds up an oil painting of a dog that looks like Buffy.

"This is Polka Des Brill Mignons, Buffy's ancestor, in France, around 1944," Mrs. Brubaker says proudly. "At that time, Buffy's breed was referred to as Bichon à Poil Frise—a Belgian lap dog related to the Bolognese, the Tenerife dog, and the toy poodle. Look how black his eyes are—round, and not almond like those of his cousin the poodle—and his delicate dark nose, the tail turned back into such an elegant curve."

Mrs. Brubaker takes a deep breath for a second, and I figure she's finished her bichon history lesson. I should have known better.

"Now perhaps you can see why I was so adamant about Toto not being around Buffy," Mrs. Brubaker says, smiling first at Mom, then at me. "I was trying to protect her pedigreed lineage. I would have arranged for her to breed with the finest pedigree bichon—when the time was right."

"Oh, well, we're terribly sorry about that, Esther," Mom says. "God knows Toto's breed is a mystery to us, since we adopted him from the ASPCA. But he was lost on Park Avenue, if that makes you feel any better."

"Yes, I know it was not intentional," Mrs. Brubaker says, pausing, "but it's all water under the bridge now."

"Good, I'm glad. We will certainly give *our* puppy the finest care, you can rest assured," Mom says, then puts her hand on top of mine. I'm so relieved that I sink back into the couch.

"I didn't say anything about giving you a

puppy, Dorothea," Mrs. Brubaker says, looking surprised.

I shoot straight up in the couch in disbelief. Okay, I get it. It's Nightmare on 67th Street, and Mrs. Brubaker is Freddy Krueger with a bad hairdo!

"Esther, you cannot be serious!" Mom says, the starch rising in her voice like bubbling grits.

"I cannot let you have any puppies from Buffy's litter," Mrs. Brubaker says. "I just explained to you my predicament about her lineage."

"No, what you did was show us a ghastly painting," Mom huffs. "If I'm not mistaken, dogs peed and pooped on the sidewalk even back in France in 1944. Or are you gonna tell me that poor Buffy's great-grands were also paper-trained and held hostage in an apartment that looked like a safari expedition about to stampede Kmart!"

"I think this conversation is over," Mrs. Brubaker says, standing up. "And I hope you'll be so kind as to leave me and Buffy alone. I told your daughter that this afternoon. I thought I made myself perfectly clear."

"Esther, what's clear is that we're taking you to family court and letting a judge decide if we're fit parents for one of Buffy's puppies." Mom adjusts the cheetah bangles on her arm carefully. "Maybe

I'll even run to Kmart and get a bichon painting to bring to court!"

"Oh, don't be ridiculous, Dorothea—you'll simply be wasting your time," Mrs. Brubaker says, obviously shocked by Mom's decision.

"Oh, but you're wrong. I like shopping at Kmart," Mom says indignantly.

"I mean about taking me to court!" Mrs. Brubaker says impatiently.

Mom clutches my hand and we both stand up from the couch as she says, "Well, Esther, I guess it's my time to waste, isn't it, *darling*?"

Chapter 6

Mrs. Brubaker's apartment isn't the only place crying out for a makeover. The whole vibe at Family Court (which is way downtown near Wall Street) is so gray and dingy—the walls, the floor, the security guards in uniforms—that I start feeling self-conscious about my outfit, a bright pink leopard top and brown leopard miniskirt.

"Honey, don't you think that skirt is a little too short to wear to school?" Mom asks me as we're standing in line to go through the metal detector.

"No, I don't think so," I retort. I've decided to wear my cheetah outfit because I have to go straight to school after we file our petition. Then, after school, it's straight on to Mouse Almighty's studio on 52nd Street and Ninth Avenue to record our big demo tape!

"Well, I guess sixteen-inch hemlines is de rigueur with you girls," Mom sighs. She walks through the metal detector, and of course, it goes off.

"Take off your jewelry and empty your pockets, ma'am," the armed security guard says gruffly. "Place everything in the basket." First Mom takes off her bangles, then her Agatha Paris Terrier charm earrings. Then she fiddles with the clutch on her gold Agatha Paris watch with terrier face. Terriers are Mom's favorite dog, but she fell in love with Toto because he clung to her shirt when she took him out of his cage at the ASPCA.

"It's thief-proof, what can I say?" Mom chortles at the guard, who is staring impatiently, waiting for her to finish.

Once we get upstairs, there is an equally long line to see the clerk at the front window. Mom explains our situation to the indifferent clerk, who I can tell would rather be on his lunch break.

"You wanna do *what*?" the clerk asks Mom in disbelief.

"File a petition to gain custody of a dog's litter. Well, one puppy," Mom says, trying to be patient.

The clerk ponders the situation, then says slowly, "Well, it's not exactly parental rights. . . . Wait, let me get this straight—you want someone to give you their *dog*?"

"No, no, we want to gain custody of one of the puppies from her dog's litter, because our dog is the father." Mom is trying hard to maintain her cool, I can tell.

"I think you'd have better luck filing a petition in Small Claims Court," the man says. He just wants to get rid of us, but Mom isn't having it.

"Young man, I'm not suing for money, but for custody of a living, breathing *creature*. That's why I'm filing the petition in *Family* Court and not Small Claims."

"All right, then," the man says, defeated. "Either way, you're gonna have to serve the plaintiff with a summons. Fill out this form, get a cashier's check for twenty-five dollars, then fill out the summons and get both notarized. Then come back. Next in line, please."

"What—where is the notary public around here?" Mom asks quickly, before she's trampled on by the long line of people in back of us breathing down our necks.

"Across the street, at the County Clerk's Office in the stationery store. Next in line, *please*," the clerk repeats gruffly.

"No wonder people never file petitions," Mom huffs. "You're too exhausted from dealing with the red tape and bureacracy to care if you win the case or not!" She goes to a counter and takes a form. We both look it over, trying to figure it out.

"What should we put here?" Mom asks, pointing to the line marked REASON FOR FILING.

I shrug.

"Because I'm tired of her trying to run us over with her hippopotamus footstools and haughty attitude!" Mom snaps, which makes me chuckle.

"No, Mom. I don't think that would get us even one of Buffy's biscuits."

"You're right, darling. I'd better word this in a way that leaves my personal feelings out of the matter. Do you know, the first few years your father and I lived in the building, Mrs. Brubaker never even spoke to me?"

"Yes, Mom," I say, because I've heard the story so many times.

"Okay, let's see. 'Upon discovering that my'— no, no—'*our* dog, Toto Garibaldi, impregnated our neighbor's dog, Buffy . . .' Should I put her pedigree name, or Esther's last name?"

"I think we should put both, like Chuchie does," I say. Chuchie is Dominican and Puerto Rican, and it's the custom in Latin culture for a child to use both their maternal and paternal last names— which in Chuchie's case is Duarte Rodriguez Domingo Simmons.

"Okay, Buffy Mignon Brubaker. 'We kindly'—no—'politely'—Oh, forget it! 'We asked for'—no—'We *requested* custody of one of the puppies from Buffy's litter, and such request was denied.' How's that?"

"Sounds cool," I respond, "but how are we gonna serve Mrs. Brubaker a summons? She's never gonna open the door for us again."

"Oh, that's the easy part. We get Nunzio from the florist shop to deliver flowers to dear old Esther. But inside the card will be a big, fat surprise—the summons!" Mom smiles, proud of herself.

"That sounds good to go," I say. "What kind of flowers are you gonna send?"

"Oh, some nice roses . . . with some nice *thorns* on their stems," Mom chuckles. "Hey, baby—you nervous about going into the studio?"

"Definitely," I admit. "I mean, we don't really know what Mouse Almighty is like, and he's worked with such Big Willie stars. Maybe he thinks we're just a bunch of wannabes."

"Well, I can assure you, a producer like that doesn't waste his time nibbling at stale cheese. He wouldn't even be doing this if he didn't think there was a big fat 'chunk' in it for him."

"You're right," I say, wrapping my arm through

Mom's. She always has her own way of explaining things. I'm glad she's our manager, even though we fight sometimes.

After we go to the Notary Public and get an official seal stamped on our documents, we return to Family Court. Luckily, we have another clerk this time, but he isn't any friendlier. "If you don't show up, you forfeit your decision, and the defendant automatically wins the judgment," grumpy clerk number two explains.

"I wish I could be there to see Mrs. Brubaker's face," I tell Mom as we leave the building.

"I'm sure her eyes are gonna bug out bigger than the ones on those ghastly frog statues!" Mom says.

"I just feel so bad for Buffy," I say wistfully. "I mean, you can tell she really loves Toto."

"Imagine that—and they're not even from the same pedigree class," Mom laughs. "Never underestimate the power of a bona fide charming personality."

"What if Mrs. Brubaker doesn't show up for the court date?" I ask.

"All the better. Then we win by default. You heard the clerk, it works both ways. Don't you worry. The judge will figure out all this nonsense."

"Okay, Mom. I'll see you later," I say, kissing her on the forehead.

"And, please, don't ask Mr. Walker to take you girls anywhere after the studio session," Mom says, pulling down my skirt trying to make it longer. "He's already been informed to bring you straight home."

Dance class is the last period of the day, and it's my favorite, for three important reasons: 1) I get to groove, 2) It's the only class I take with Chuchie and Dorinda, and 3) Our teacher, Ms. Pigeonfeat, has some ultraslick moves of her own. The one thing I don't like is that I always sweat so much, which really messes up my hair, and today we have to race to the locker room to shower and get ready for our big studio session with Mouse Almighty.

"*Ay, Dios mío*, this place is smelling ultrafunky today," Chuchie moans, spritzing her Yves Saint Bernard cologne in the locker room.

"Yeah, it sure could use a few stick-ups," I moan. "Let's hurry up and beat our faces," I command my crew, "because we have to get to Mouse's studio, and I don't want to be late."

"Aqua and Angie will probably be there before we are," Chuchie says.

"Well, they should be. Their school is closer to the studio than ours," I say, without adding another riff on the twins. Right now, I'm definitely not trying to open that can of refried worms.

"Maybe Aqua and Angie will change their minds about the pink wigs," Chuchie says, trying to be nice. "*Tú sabes*, when we do a show."

"Sure thing, chicken wing," I say sarcastically, "but that won't be anytime soon."

Chuchie winces, because she probably thinks I'm blaming her injury for pushing back our Def Duck Records showcase. I guess I *am* blaming her.

"God, I look like a bush baby," I moan, looking in the mirror at my ten-foot fuzzball of a hairdo. "I gotta work some abracadabra today." I bend over, brushing my hair carefully so I can get busy with the blow-dryer, which I had stuffed into my cheetah backpack this morning, along with a few jars of hair gunk and makeup.

After blowtorching my fuzzy locks for twenty minutes, I'm finally ready to beat my face. Then I look over at Chuchie's face, and gasp in disbelief. "Holy cannoli! I didn't know Santa was looking for a new helper!" I've been so busy obsessing about my fuzzy locks that I didn't notice how much makeup she was putting on.

"Where did you get this?" I ask, picking up the bottle of Glamorama foundation.

"It's *Mami*'s," Chuchie says, getting defensive.

"But Auntie Juanita is darker than you."

Chuchie ignores me and flicks her powder brush—now she's depositing too much blush on her cheeks!

"Chuchie, if you put on another coat of makeup, you'll be dressed for winter!" I'm annoyed now, because I'm worried we're gonna be late. Still, we can't show up with Chuchie looking like this! "We're not leaving here until you wash your face and start from scratch."

"What happened? I'm not washing my face!" she protests.

"Yes you are, because we're not going to the circus today. We're going to a recording studio."

Dorinda gives us a look, like, "Here we go again, round number three." By now, she's used to us fighting, so I don't feel bad. Besides, if Dorinda doesn't want to say anything about Chuchie's finger-painting escapades, that's her prerogative, but I'm not gonna zip my lip, not when it comes to Cheetah Girls' business, okay?

After Chuchie wipes her face and puts on some of Dorinda's foundation—they are both the same honey-caramel-cocoa shade—I whip out my hot-pink eye shadow, and hold up the applicator to her face. "Give me your eye," I command.

"I wish I could," Chuchie giggles.

By three-thirty we're on the move, tearing up Eighth Avenue like a bunch of roadrunners, rushing to get to Mouse's studio on 52nd and Ninth.

"Coming through," I mutter to the lollygaggers in front of us. Sometimes the streets of New York are so crowded, you gotta work your moves like a snail. All of a sudden, I feel a hand grab my backside!

I turn and see this scary-looking guy with big teeth. Seeing the cheetah fire in my eyes, he turns and starts making tracks like greased lightning. "You'd *better* run!" I scream loudly after him.

"What happened?" Chuchie asks, scared.

"He grabbed my behind, that's what happened!" I say, choking back tears because I'm so angry. "He's lucky he ran. If I ever see that Big Bad Wolf again, I'm gonna spray him with my Miss Wiggy Mace."

"Are you all right?" asks a lady carrying a briefcase.

I'm too embarrassed to look at her in the face, so I just shake my head.

"What a bozo," Dorinda says, grabbing me by the arm so we can keep walking. I'm so upset, I just wanna run after that guy until I find him, and beat him down hard! With my mouth poking out like a platter, I let my crew lead me on until we get to the lobby of Mouse Almighty's studio.

"You awright, *mamacita*?" Chuchie asks, concerned.

I try to shake off the whole thing and act like I'm okay. "Thank gooseness there is a mirror here," I say. Looking in the mirror intently, I wipe the mascara smear from under my lashes with a tissue. "You still wish you had a nice round butt like mine?" I tease Dorinda, who's always moaning about when she's gonna "develop."

Do' Re Mi gets a sheepish look on her face, then shrugs her tiny shoulders and shivers with disgust. "No, I guess not," she says.

Chapter 7

Chuchie was right. Aqua and Angie are already upstairs at Mouse's studio waiting for us. They're wearing the pink cheetah tops I told them to wear, but with navy pleated skirts and matching tights! If you ask me, they look like twin cheerleaders instead of cheetahs. All they need are some oversized pom-poms to shake, and they'd be good to go. I know Aqua and Angie aren't into fashion like we are, but sometimes I wonder if they dress in the dark, okay? I mean, who wears pink and navy together?

"Wazzup, buttercups?" I say, trying to act like everything is chill between us. But Aqua isn't putting on the same charade. She throws me a look that's far from Southern comfort.

Angie picks up the vibe and starts to shrink against the wall. "Do we look okay?" she asks me.

"Yeah." I turn quickly to the receptionist and open my mouth to introduce myself. "We're—"

"I know who you are!" The receptionist cuts me off, chuckling, then points to the sprawling black leather beanbag couch. "Now that you're all together, have a seat. Mouse is in a meeting. He'll be finished soon."

We all sit on the big leather couch, and now I'm starting to feel nervous. Chuchie looks over at me and grimaces, which means she's got a bad case of the squigglies, too. My heart is beating so loud, I think it's gonna jump out of my chest! I look around at the studio walls. There are tons of posters, certified gold and platinum CDs, and bottles of hot sauce on shelves.

"Wow, somebody likes it hot!" Angie chuckles.

"Oh, yeah, one of the engineers, Son Seven, likes to collect them," the receptionist explains. "He gets them from all different places."

"You mean, like, different countries?" Dorinda asks.

"Yeah, he travels quite a bit." The receptionist grabs a ringing phone and answers it. "Studio."

I don't want to seem like I'm listening to her conversation, so I stare at the framed CDs and posters.

"Look," Chuchie says, motioning to an

autographed picture of the LoveBabiez, the group that opened up for Mariah Carey at the Garden. "I didn't know he worked with them."

I get up to read the inscription. "'Mouse, you're the man. We owe everything to you. One love, your Babiez.'"

Wow! Mouse Almighty worked on their debut album, too! Still, I try not to act too impressed. After all, the Cheetah Girls have got what it takes to be up on this wall, too. "They just need to lose the diapers and baby carriage from their act," I whisper to Chuchie, sitting down on the couch again.

All of a sudden a door opens, and the sound of men's voices fills the hallway. "Wazzup, Cheetah Girrrrls!" Mouse greets us. "Come on back."

I smile at the "man with a plan," and notice how short and wiry he is. We've only met Mouse once before, at the Def Duck Records office, but he was sitting down at the conference table. He's got really long dreadlocks and *really* big white teeth. With him is a guy in jeans, Mecca T-shirt, and base-ball cap. I wonder who he is—probably some Big Willie. "This is my man Seth Seidelman," Mouse says, introducing us to him.

"We're the Cheetah Girls," I tell Seth, my heart pounding in my chest. I can feel Aqua's eyes on the back of my head. I just hope she squashes our beef jerky, at least until we get out of the studio.

"I'm doing a demo for them," Mouse tells Seth. "Maybe they'll be blowing up like your girls." Mouse chuckles, then explains that Seth is the executive producer of the new reality television show, *So You Wanna Be a Star.*

"We love that show!" I exclaim, wishing Chuchie and I had auditioned last year. There were posters plastered up everywhere, casting female talent for the show's resident girl group, Eden's Blush. We didn't, in the end, because we are a girl group for real, not some manufactured hype.

But now it turns out Seth's here looking for songs for Eden's Blush. After the show finishes its season, they're gonna go on tour and cut an album. Hearing about it makes me jealous. What are *we* gonna do, record a wack demo? I mean, with a little help, we could be gettin' down like that.

"Did you put these Cheetah Girls together?" Seth asks Mouse.

"No, this a little something I'm doing for Def Duck, man," Mouse explains.

"Chuchie and I have been friends since we were born," I say, pointing to her. "Then we met Dorinda, Aqua, and Angie."

Aqua and Angie smile at Seth. I can tell they're a little nervous, too.

"Well, you're in good hands now," Seth says, then does the hip-hop handshake with Mouse.

I hope we are, shrieks a voice inside me.

"Come on in," Mouse says, and we all pile into one of the recording rooms. Mouse sits on a swivel stool and gives us the once-over. "Y'all have gotten big."

Seeing the shocked look on Chuchie's face, he chuckles. "No, no, I *like* it! Look at Missy 'Misdemeanor'—girls gotta claim their spot, know what I'm saying?"

Feeling uncomfortable, I start pulling my miniskirt down. I'm starting to think Mom was right. Maybe I should have worn a longer one.

"Awright, I want you girls to listen to the songs I've picked out for you—new licks from some up-and-coming songwriters." Mouse motions for us to sit.

My heart sinks. *Up and coming?* I was kinda hoping that we would get to record songs from a few Big Willie songwriters. I shoulda known better. But if we're doing stuff by unknowns, then why can't we just record *my* songs?

I know I'd better not say anything, so I just chill

and sit down, waiting for the lyrics to flow before I get kaflooied.

"The first song is 'Not a Chance,'" Mouse says, cuing the engineer to roll the music.

I cut a quick glance at Chuchie. "Not a Chance"? I definitely don't like the title. I mean, it doesn't have our kind of flavor—you know, growl-licious and different.

Mouse hands us the sheet music to the song, and we all read the lyrics.

> *I saw you hanging with your friends*
> *From day to dusk to dawn it never ends*
> *But when you wanna come and fetch me*
> *There's never any* please
> *Just an attitude like I should do the dropping*
> *If you think you're gonna play me*
> *That's not how you can slay me*
> *So don't even try to say to me*
> *Not a chance, not a chance*
> *We've had our last dance*
> *And baby I take that stance . . .*

I look around at my crew, and they seem to be digging the song. Everybody is smiling and nodding along. After it's finished, Mouse swivels around on his stool and looks at us, smiling. "You digging that, right?"

"Yeah!" Aqua and Angie say in unison. The rest of us nod our heads, too. Even me. I mean, the song's not bad, considering it isn't mine.

"The songwriter is Mystik Man. I think it's got some nice catchy lyrics, tight musical arrangement, and harmony potential for y'all. As a matter of fact, Seth got one of Mystik's songs for his girls, Eden's Blush, so you know it's just a matter of time before he's gonna blow up."

His girls. I'm definitely glad the Cheetah Girls aren't going out like that.

As if reading my mind, Mouse quickly adds, "I see you girls as these strong, independent Cheetah Girls, coming up strong, doing your thing, not taking no shorts. Am I right?"

We nod our heads as Mouse continues his riff. "See, when I got in the studio with Karma's Children, I thought their vibe was similar to yours—sweet but strong—and they were just about your age when I started working with them."

"Really?" Chuchie asks excitedly.

"Yeah, they were. But Kahlua was a little older, about sixteen, so I decided we could give her a harder sound. You know, she's got an edge, that street-but-sweet-type thing."

"That's true, she comes at you with the lyrics," Dorinda chimes in.

"So you know it's gonna take some time for us to get to know each other, but I want to come right out of the box with some product that the record company can comprehend. You know what I'm saying? 'Cuz the bottom line is about selling records, moving product. When I take this demo to Freddy Fudge, all he wants to hear is the sound of *ka-ching*. You know what I'm saying?"

We all nod like little cheetah cubs.

"Now, I've put a few acts out there, so you've gotta trust me on this."

We nod our heads again, and I'm starting to feel like, *Well, he is the man. Let's just do this whole thing his way.*

"See, I don't want y'all to sound like a bunch of kids. We're gonna go the sophisticated route, so you can go out there, be marketed to the youth market, get a little adult action, too. Is that cool with y'all?"

We nod our heads again. "Yeah, we definitely don't want peeps looking at us like we're a bunch of kids," I say, trying to convince myself that this is the move.

"Now, I know y'all got some songs, but we don't want to come out the box with the gimmick, you know? I wanna record some songs that are gonna get you a record deal. Are y'all down with that?"

We nod our heads yet again. "So it's cool with y'all that we rehearse this one?"

"Yeah," I say, since Mouse is looking directly at me.

"I'ma ask Cindy to order down from Chunky Cheese. Y'all want anything? Some shakes and burgers? 'Cuz we're gonna be here awhile."

"Yeah," Angie says excitedly. I smile weakly at her. She *would* get excited over grub.

After we down our cheeseburgers and shakes, we practice the Mystik Man joint for an hour before Mouse feels that we're ready to lay down some tracks. "This is Son Seven, my master engineer," Mouse says, pointing to the bald man in the control room.

We wave at him, then put on our headphones and get ready to jam. I look over at Chuchie and Dorinda, and I can tell they're totally psyched, just like I am. At least I feel like we're a real girl group now—laying down tracks, taking meetings, performing for peeps, and cutting a demo. *Finally!*

After we finish laying down the tracks for three different versions of "Not a Chance," Mouse comes into the room and flashes a big grin. "You hooked it up!"

"Thank you for the cheeseburgers," Dorinda tells him as we head back out to the reception area.

"Yes, thank you," I chime in, remembering my manners.

We sit in the reception area, waiting for Aqua and Angie's dad to pick us up. Mouse leans over to the receptionist and gets his messages. There's a big stack of them. "Ayiight—that's too bad, he's gonna have to wait."

Now I really feel glad and excited that we're working with such a big-cheese producer. All of sudden, I wanna scream, *"We're in the house with Mouse!"*

Chuchie is staring at all the CDs on the wall. "What's it like working with Kahlua?" she asks Mouse excitedly.

"Oh, she's mad cool," Mouse answers, smiling. "You know, she may look like she's large overnight, but she's been in the game more than a minute."

"So when do we get a record deal?" I say, joking with him because I'm totally amped.

"Hang on to that thought for a minute," Mouse says, chuckling. He pushes his long dreadlocks off his face. "We have to do two, maybe three more songs, then see what happens."

"I heard that," Dorinda chuckles.

"Y'all got that deep vibrato going," Mouse says, pointing to Aqua and Angie. "I'll bet you tear it up in a choir, don't you?"

"Yeah, we've been singing in church choirs since we're six," Aqua says proudly.

"You've got great voices," Mouse says, nodding like he's grooving to a beat. "Brings a lot of harmony to the mix."

I feel a sting on my cheeks, but I just keep smiling. How come he didn't say anything about *our* singing? I don't look at Aqua or Angie, because I feel insecure. I can tell by looking at Chuchie that she feels the same way, because she starts twirling her hair in the front, something she only does when she gets upset.

"Awright, so check this," Mouse says. "I'm gonna holler at your mother, set up another session with you girls, awright?"

"Right," I say, nodding.

"Awright, you girls get home safe. I'm out, gotta go to this club and check out some product from a new songwriter." Mouse rubs his forehead, and I can tell that he is tired. I know it must be really hard being a Big Willie producer, and keeping the hits coming. Or the "product," as he calls it.

Mr. Walker arrives, and Chuchie greets him happily.

"Hi, Daddy," Aqua says, and I can tell by the sound in her voice that she's real tired.

Mr. Walker looks at the CDs and photos on the

wall. I can tell he's impressed, because he just nods his head silently.

"Bye, Cheetah Girls!" the receptionist yells after us as we leave.

I wave good-bye to her even though she's on the phone, and she winks back at me while she talks. "No, there's no studio time tomorrow, he's booked solid."

As we ride in the back of Mr. Walker's Bronco, I start feeling sad again about Eddie Lizard not calling me. I just feel so amped and excited that I want to call him and share every tidbit about our studio session with him. "Should I call Eddie?" I ask Chuchie.

"Not a chance!" Chuchie shoots back, then giggles. Dorinda joins in, too, but the twins just stare at us. I look Aqua straight in the face and smile. She smiles back, but there is a look in her eyes like, *I'm gonna get you later.*

Well, let her simmer in her Southern stew just a little longer. Eddie Lizard likes *me*, not her.

At least, I *think* he does.

But then, why hasn't he called me?

Chapter 8

"**H**ow was your session?" Mom asks as soon as I come through the doorway.

"Fabuloso!" I tell her, sitting across from her at the dining room table. In the kitchen, I can hear Daddy humming and clattering as he rustles up some grub for us. "He wants us to come in two or three more times. He said he's gonna call you to set it up!"

"I know, darling."

"You know?"

"I called the studio after you girls left and spoke to Mouse. He seems to think it went really fabulous."

"He said that? Hot diggity!"

"He also said it's gonna be a couple weeks till he can clear enough time for you girls to have another session."

"A couple weeks? That's so long!"

"Well, it's Christmas season coming up, and you know, Mouse Almighty is a very busy man."

"I know, but jeez . . ."

"Now, now, let's talk about other things," she says, brushing off my blues. "Don't you want to hear the latest on Operation Get a Puppy?"

"Yeah!" I say. "What happened? Give me the blow-by-blow."

Mom laughs. "My little florist delivery plan worked like a charm. I understand Mrs. Brubaker was yelling so loud that Peter Pruitt down the hall stuck his head out of his door and told them both to shut up! Peter says she even tried to stuff the summons into Nunzio's back pocket!"

"Did Mrs. Brubaker tell Mr. Pruitt if she's gonna show up tomorrow in court?" I ask.

"No, she didn't. But you know Esther Brubaker, she's more slippery than a buttered escargot."

"Hi, *cara*, have you eaten?" Daddy asks me, coming out of the kitchen and pecking me on the cheek.

"No—and why is the kitchen sink covered?" I ask, noticing that it's got a drop cloth draped over it.

"A pipe broke in the basement. Everybody is backed up in the whole building, so don't use it, or maybe a rabbit will jump out," Daddy explains, waving his hands. "José is coming to fix it." José is the handyman who fixes everything in the building, even my computer when it broke once.

"*Va bene*," I say.

"I'm surprised you can get anyone to fix anything around here," Mom humphs. "Leave it to the landlord to raise the rent even if the roof fell in."

"Oh, by the way, did Eddie call me?" I ask sheepishly.

"No, thank goodness," Mom says, putting on her cheetah reading glasses and starting to do her paperwork from the store, which is piled up in front of her on the table.

There has gotta be something wrong. Now I wonder if Eddie's even gonna show up to class at Drinka Champagne's Conservatory on Saturday.

The doorbell rings, and I jump up like RoboCop. Maybe it's Eddie Lizard! I'll bet he's already heard through the grapevine about the Cheetah Girls' big studio session. I look at my watch, and see that it's already nine o'clock. If it *is* him, Mom is never gonna let me go out this late on a weeknight. I fling the door open and see José the handyman's face.

"Hi, José," I say, smiling to try and hide my disappointment.

He beams back at me, then waves at Mom and

Dad as he walks into the kitchen with his toolbox. "Very big night next door," he says, smiling at Mom.

"Oh, really?" Mom says, peering over her cheetah reading glasses at him. "What happened? Esther make a rabbit roast?"

José chuckles at Mom's joke, but I can tell he is excited to tell us something.

"What's the deal-i-o, José?" I ask, butting in.

"The little Buffy—she have the babies already!" José says in his thick Spanish accent, proud of his spying skills.

"What?" I gasp in disbelief. "I can't believe Mrs. Brubaker didn't even tell us!"

"Well, darling, if you were expecting an engraved invitation to the baby shower, forget about it," Mom says sharply. "After all, we are suing the woman."

"What'd they look like? How many?" I badger José like I'm a detective on a case.

"They look nice, very little," he says, cupping his hand to show me how tiny they are. "She have them in a little basket. I have to fix her sink, too, but I was looking at them, and she come over, nasty, you know? Waving her hand for me to come to the kitchen."

I can tell that José doesn't like Mrs. Brubaker,

either. Nobody in the building likes her because she's mean to everybody.

"How are we gonna get those puppies?" I ask out loud, my face contorted from worry about my babies.

"Darling, let the judge decide tomorrow. That's what arbitration is for," Mom says. Then she shakes her head. "That sneaky Esther. I'm surprised she didn't sell them off already!"

"Mom!" I moan. "I wanna see them."

"There's nothing we can do about it now," Mom snaps at me. "We simply have to wait until tomorrow."

José fixes the sink while I sit and sulk. *No puppies and no Eddie Lizard.*

"Well, if you keep pouting, I'm not going to give you your present," Mom says, staring at me.

I stop instantly, sitting up straight in my chair. "Why didn't you say so!"

Out of Mom's bag comes a book—*Buffy: From the Garbage Can to the Catwalk, Doggie-Bag Tips from a Furry Fashion Hound.*

"I saw this book in the window of Barnes and Noble, and I thought it was so funny that they both had the same name," Mom says, pointing to the foxy black terrier on the cover. "Her fashion advice is a hoot—she's such a dog!"

"Thanks, Mom," I say, reaching over and kissing her on the cheek. Leafing through the pages, I stop at the picture of Buffy marrying her dream man, Bosse—a three-year-old Hollywood hound—in a fancy "muttrimony" ceremony, in front of a preacher and everything. Suddenly, I feel a pang of sympathy. "Mom, why can't Toto marry the Buffy next door, the love of his life?"

"Darling, not even a shotgun wedding is in the cards for those two," she says, shaking her head sadly. "That is not the kind of bone you want to pick with Mrs. Brubaker. We'll be lucky if she doesn't try to get a restraining order against Toto, so he can't get within a mile of Buffy till his dying day!"

"Oh, that is so unfair!" I sigh, resting my head on my left arm. "Mom, I'm not going to be okay if we don't get at least one puppy out of Buffy's litter."

"Don't you think I know that, Galleria?" Mom asks, looking at me like I'm a basket-case bozo. "I've already called all over town, and gotten a tentative appointment with a top child psychologist for you if we lose."

"I'm not a 'child,'" I say, looking up at Mom, challenging her.

"That includes *troubled teens*," Mom says, correcting herself. "I double-checked."

"Mom, I'm not joking."

"I know, darling. But what will be, will be."

José comes out of the kitchen. "Everything is okay," he announces, holding his toolbox.

"How many in the litter?" I ask him.

"Six."

"Six!" I repeat, feeling warm inside just thinking of those little cuties.

"But as far as you're concerned, *one* is the only number that matters!" Mom says firmly, gazing hard at me.

"I know, I know." I give up and start mindlessly leafing through the pages of the doggie picture book. "One is better than none."

"How was your music today?" Daddy asks, changing the subject.

"I think Mouse Almighty's a good producer," I say. "I just wonder if he really likes us."

"Why do you say that?" Mom asks, curious.

"Because, I mean, why won't he look at the songs I wrote?"

"Darling, when you have a gold record, he'll not only listen to the songs you wrote—he'll spoon-feed you!"

"*Cara,* you're just fourteen years old," Daddy says. "I mean, he is a businessman, no? He knows his business."

"I guess so," I say, not really convinced, but not wanting to talk about it anymore. "I'm going to sleep," I mutter, then rise from the table and kiss Mom and Dad good night.

I close my bedroom door and lie on my mattress in the dark, staring up at the ceiling. I know I should be imagining a golden future for the Cheetah Girls, but I can't help feeling sad. It's not because we're not recording any songs I wrote, either. I can live with that—for now. And I know we rocked it to the doggy bone in the studio, too. But it all went away as soon as I got back home. And I know why.

It's Aqua. When me and my crew aren't together in spirit, nothing else is right. And why aren't we together? Because she's jealous about me and Eddie Lizard, that's why.

It's funny, you know? She's mad because he likes me. But if he likes me so much, then why hasn't he called?

As I walk to the kitchen in the morning, I hear Mom and Dad whispering about me. "What will be, will be!" Dad whispers in a hushed voice. At least someone is concerned about me, which is more than I can say for Eddie Lizard. I didn't sleep the whole night, worrying about him.

95

But I'm not gonna tell *them* that. Instead, I moan about the other thing that's on my mind. "I don't know what I'm gonna do if I don't get my paws on Buffy's litter. I've gotta have a puppy!"

"What would you like for breakfast, darling?" Mom asks, ignoring my whining.

"Some Biggies bubble gum," I snap. "I'm having a massive gum attack."

"That's not gonna solve your problems, Galleria," Mom snaps right back.

"*Cara*, hurry up and eat, so I can drive you downtown to the courthouse," Dad butts in. He places a cereal bowl in front of me.

"You look nice, darling," Mom says. "At least your skirt is long enough today."

Remembering what happened to me on the street on the way to Mouse's studio, I have to admit she was right about not wearing the miniskirt. "Sorry, Mom. You were right," I say, giving her props. After all, she's a great mom and a great manager. And it's not *her* fault Mrs. Brubaker is acting like such a bozo.

If I thought I'd seen the worst of Mrs. Brubaker, I was wrong. After Daddy drops us off at the courthouse, we run into the "defendant" in the lobby. From the look on her face, I decide I'd rather run into the Wicked Witch of the West. We all get into the elevator together, but I can't get the nerve to say anything to her.

Glancing downward, I notice how chipped Mrs. Brubaker's nails are. I mean, they look raggy. Shame on her! I chuckle to myself, even though I don't feel so chuckly, because my stomach has a bad case of the squigglies.

When the elevator door opens, Mrs. Brubaker shoots out like a cannonball.

"Did you see her nails?" Mom snips, as we walk down the corridor to Room 101A. "She doesn't need a manicure. She needs to be declawed!"

I'm really nervous now, so I clutch Mom's hand tightly till we get inside. The courtroom is a lot smaller than I thought it would be—not like the ones you see on television. Sitting down at a long table, I try to avoid Mrs. Brubaker's glare, but Mom doesn't care. She stares right back at her until Mrs. Brubaker looks away.

The judge comes into the room and sits at the head of the table. A court stenographer positions himself in front of a funny-looking little typewriter.

"Good morning, my name is Judge Fowler, and I'll be presiding over this arbitration. I will listen to both sides, then render a decision. You will receive such decision by certified mail the next business day."

I sit there staring at Judge Fowler's hair. It's long, red, and straightened, which makes him look like Simba from *The Lion King*. I look over at Mom, wondering what Judge Fowler means by the next business day? I'd raise my hand and ask, but this isn't school—it's a courtroom—and I don't know the rules of behavior.

"The plaintiff, Mrs. Gari . . . boodi, may proceed first," Judge Fowler says, peering at Mom's name on a piece of paper on his desk.

"That's Mrs. Gari*baldi*," Mom corrects him.

"Pardon me—Mrs. Garibaldi. Please proceed," Judge Fowler says, without cracking a smile. I sink further down into my chair, afraid of what might happen next.

"Our dog Toto, whom we love and adore—I mean, we adopted him from the ASPCA even before my daughter was born—" Mom takes a cheetah handkerchief from her purse and starts sniffling.

I stare down hard at the table, because I can't believe that Mom is putting on such a Broadway show. How shameless!

"I'm sorry, let me start again," Mom says, wiping a tear from the corner of her eye. "Our dog,

Oops, Doggy Dog!

Toto Garibaldi—actually he is more like my son—has always adored our neighbor's dog, Buffy. But he has been prevented from having any normal social contact with the object of his affection. However, I guess dogs, like humans . . . well, you know the story of Romeo and Juliet?" Mom asks, turning and staring directly at Judge Fowler.

"Mrs. Garibaldi, I'm going to have to ask you to refrain from submitting information that is not relevant to the case." Judge Fowler's face is frozen like a clay pigeon.

Ooh, that's foul. I can't believe he dissed Mom like that! Now I know how he got his name. Foul . . . Fowler . . . Fowlest!

"Yes, your honor. Pardon me." Mom puts the tissue back in her purse. "Well, Toto found the opportunity to visit Buffy in the hallway one day, when Mrs. Brubaker was getting some furniture delivered from Africa. My husband was trying to help her, you see. My daughter and I were in Los Angeles at the time, and were unaware of this dalliance."

"'Dalliance'?" Judge Fowler repeats, raising his eyebrows.

"I mean, the courtship was consummated during their hallway rendezvous," Mom says, trying to be delicate about it.

"Do you mean that your dog mated with Mrs. Brubaker's?"

"Yes, that's what I mean," Mom says, fanning herself in relief that he got the point. "Mrs. Brubaker later brought it to our attention that Buffy was pregnant, and told us she had no intention of giving us any of the puppies."

"Is that it?" Judge Fowler says abruptly. "All right. Now the defendant may state her case."

I can tell Judge Fowler is in a hurry. I wonder how many cases he has to hear in one day.

Mrs. Brubaker clears her throat and turns her sourpuss face to Judge Fowler. Ignoring us, she starts in on her sob story. "I have taken great pains to make sure that Buffy is protected in my house. She is a pedigreed bichon frise, with lineage that can be traced back to France. I was hoping to find a suitable male—with similar lineage—to mate with my Buffy, but then Toto got her pregnant without my permission."

Mrs. Brubaker stops abruptly, pulls a tissue out of her purse, then bawls like a baby crocodile. Now I'm not sure who is the bigger drama queen, Mrs. Brubaker or my mom. My heart sinks as I realize we're never gonna win. Mrs. Brubaker is making it sound like Toto attacked Buffy! Judge Fowler is gonna feel sorry for *her*, not us!

We all sit quietly, waiting for Mrs. Brubaker to finish. Even the court stenographer has stopped typing on his machine.

"And I just don't see why I should have to give them a puppy!" snaps Mrs. Brubaker.

"How many puppies are in the litter?" Judge Fowler asks.

"Oh! Well, six—but one of them seems sickly," Mrs. Brubaker says, fighting back more tears.

"Thank you," Judge Fowler says, writing something down, then raising his head again. "That will be all. I will notify both of you of my decision."

Mom and I look at each other, not sure if we're supposed to get up, but Mrs. Brubaker beats us to it. She jumps up like there's a fire, clutching her purse tightly, and heads for the door.

I guess Mom can tell by the expression on my face that I'm disappointed. She reaches over and gives me a hug.

"We're not gonna win," I moan. "You're not gonna be a grandmother . . . yet."

"We'll see about that!" Mom says, seething. "She won't get away with this. Not if there's any justice in this world."

I bite my tongue hard. I want to say that there isn't any justice in this world. If there was, we'd have half the puppies, the Cheetah Girls would have a record deal, and Eddie Lizard would call me on the phone!

But for once, I let Mom have the last word.

Chapter 9

Usually, I'm excited about going to Drinka Champagne's Conservatory on Saturdays, but today, I'd rather slink back under my cheetah sheets and hide all day. I drag my behind getting dressed, praying under my breath that a cheetah fairy is gonna come any minute and solve my problems by: 1) Making Eddie Lizard grovel at my feet so I don't have to throw a fit when I see him, or 2) Making Aqua grovel at my feet so we can squash our beef jerky.

I call Chuchie on my Miss Wiggy cell phone, to make sure she would wait for me in Drinka's lobby. That way, I won't have to deal with this situation by myself.

"Why can't I just meet you upstairs in the studio, *mija*?" Chuchie asks, puzzled.

I've been trying not spell out the drama, but I

guess I have to, since Chuchie is acting like a dog with a bone who just won't leave it alone.

"You know Eddie Lizard hasn't called me all week!" I snap.

"Maybe he had to go with his father to unhex somebody. You know, like an emergency, *está bien*?"

"Yeah, well, when I get hold of him, he's gonna need some unhexing himself!" I say, then get embarrassed, because my real feelings are showing through.

"You really like him, *mija*!" Chuchie says, poking fun at me.

"No! I don't," I stammer, lying. "Oh, just meet me in the lobby, Chuchie, will you? Stop asking so many stupid questions!"

Chuchie is wearing lots of little hair clamps all over her head, which makes her look like a Christmas tree without the bulbs. "You think you have enough clips in your hair?" I ask when I see her waiting for me in Drinka's lobby. Leave it to Chuchie to overdo everything. "At least you're not wearing that masquerade makeup."

"What happened?" Chuchie says, embarrassed. "You don't like my hair?

"No, it looks cute, but you could have left some of the clamps for a rainy day."

"Did you get the puppy?" she asks, her eyes widening like Ring Dings.

"Oh—I forgot. I gotta find out what next business day means," I say as we get in the elevator.

"What happened?"

"Never mind," I mutter, my heart pounding hard. God, I hope Chuchie is right that Eddie Lizard isn't here, and is off somewhere on a witch-craft expedition with his father.

"Hey, Cheetah Girls!" Winnie, the receptionist, greets us warmly as we approach her desk.

"Hi, Winnie. Um, do you know what 'next business day' means?"

"Well, let's see, today is Saturday, so the next business day would be Monday."

My heart sinks. "Oh, I see. Well, Chuchie, I guess we have to wait until Monday to find out Judge Fowler's ruling on the Buffy situation." I can't believe I have to wait that long! I've been waiting for days and days already!

Winnie smiles at me, then pushes the attendance sheet across the desk for us to sign.

"You won't know until Monday, *mija*?" Chuchie asks.

I scan the list quickly—yikes, there it is! Eddie Lizard's sprawling signature. My heart sinks right down to my purple pedicure.

"I can't believe this!" I say, nudging Chuchie as we walk to the waiting area outside Studio One. Aqua, Angie, and Dorinda are already waiting there for us.

"Hey, Cheetah Girls," shouts out Danitra, this pink-haired singer. Her group used to be called Think Pink, until she found out there was another group with the same name. So now her group is temporarily nameless, and it seems like Danitra's always trying out new names on everyone she sees.

"What do you think of Stinky Pink?" she asks, eager for my response. But I barely hear her. I'm too busy gaspitating at the sight of Eddie Lizard, who has just walked up behind her.

"You don't like it?" Danitra asks, reading the expression on my face wrong.

"No, it's not that," I stammer, trying to focus on Danitra instead of on my buckling legs, which feel like they're gonna give out any second.

Chuchie hangs on to my arm because she knows that I'm losing it. Obviously, Eddie hasn't been out of town at all. He's just been avoiding me. I can't believe he has the nerve to show his face here. How could he play me like this?

"I think Stinky Pink sounds smelly," Chuchie blurts out.

"We almost bought pink wigs to wear for our studio session with Mouse Almighty," Dorinda the peacemaker chimes in.

Danitra's face turns crimson, and her eyes look like they're shooting darts. "What do you mean?"

Aqua and Angie look straight at me, like, "See, we told you it wasn't a good idea!"

"What's wrong?" Chuchie stammers. "We just thought it would be fun."

Oh, I get Danitra's drift—she thinks we were trying to bite her flavor! "You know pink hair is my group's signature," she says. "How would you like it if we started wearing cheetah clothes, huh?"

"We didn't *buy* the wigs," I point out, avoiding Aqua's stare. I guess she was right about the wig situation, in more ways than one.

"Hey, Galleria," Eddie Lizard says, like a lizard squirming out of quicksand, living up to his namesake. Obviously, he's totally oblivious to the beef jerky surrounding him.

"Oh, hi," I say, feeling my cheeks burning like barbecue coals, and praying he doesn't notice how red they are.

Well, two can play the same game. I proceed to ignore Eddie Lizard, and keep talking to Danitra instead. "We're not trying to bite your flavor, Danitra, okay?"

Danitra throws more pink shade at me, but I pretend I don't notice—even though I want to read her from head to toe. I mean, who does she think she is? The Supremes making a comeback? Pleez! At least the Cheetah Girls are recording a demo tape. What is her group doing, besides thinking or stinking pink?

Then I notice that Aqua is staring at Eddie Lizard like a gooney bird. I get a sudden attack of the green-eyed monster. She'd better not try to talk to him—not now. Not after what he did to me! I throw Aqua a look that the Wicked Witch of the West would have been proud of, but the Southern belle doesn't even flinch. Aqua just keeps staring at Eddie, and then, believe it or not, actually starts talking to him!

I scurry inside Studio One, just to get away from them. Chanel follows me like a puppy dog.

"Hey, Galleria, wait up!" Dorinda says, trying to catch up with us. "You awright?"

"Yeah, I'm cooler than a fan," I sniff. I'm not gonna let Eddie Lizard wreck my flow.

Drinka Champagne comes into the studio and says hi to all of us. She is wearing a hot-pink jumpsuit today, with a matching shawl. "That's right, y'all, I'm thinking pink," she says, laughing at Danitra, who blushes. What a coinky-dinky! I guess

Danitra isn't gonna accuse Drinka Champagne, the great disco queen, of biting her flavor!

Danitra cuts her eyes at me and smiles. I guess she wants to squash our beef jerky, which is more than I can say for Aqua, who stands next to Eddie during the entire vocal lesson! I can't believe she is tripping like this. I sneak a peek at Eddie from behind, and notice that he is wearing the same snakeskin pants and jacket he had on last week. I wonder if he has any other outfits to floss.

After class, even Danitra goes over to Eddie and starts giggling, batting her eyelashes, and running her fingers through her short pink hair. I feel my heart pounding like a jackhammer. Does every girl in the *whole class* like Eddie Lizard?

All during class, I tried so hard not to look at Eddie Lizard that now my head is pounding. "You got any aspirin?" I ask Dorinda, because she carries everything but the kitchen sink in her cheetah backpack.

"Yup," she says, looking at me concerned. "Hey, what happened with the Buffy lady?"

"Oh, we've gotta wait until Monday to see what the judge ruled," I explain. "You shoulda seen the performance Mrs. Brubaker put on in the courtroom—she deserved to win an Oscar Mayer wiener!"

"Word?" Dorinda chuckles. "So, do you think you won the case?"

"No, I don't think so."

"Don't say that, Bubbles!" Chuchie butts in. "You never know."

Involuntarily, my eyes dart over to Eddie Lizard, who is standing by the elevator talking to Aqua and Angie. Drinka Champagne walks over to them, and I can't help eavesdropping on the conversation. "So how is your father?" Drinka asks Eddie. "Back in the day, we made quite a couple, you know," she giggles to Aqua.

Is Drinka saying that she dated Eddie's father? I can't believe it! Eddie didn't tell me that. Now I'm starting to feel dizzy, nauseous, *and* kaflooied. Chuchie starts for the elevator, but I grab her arm and whisper, "Wait till they leave."

"What happened?" Chuchie asks, like a dodo bird. She frees her arm from my grip and keeps walking toward the elevator, but I refuse to budge. I'm not getting in that elevator with Eddie Lizard and Aqua.

Dorinda, at least, peeps the situation, and waits with me. "Maybe we could think of something else to add flava to our look," she offers.

"Yeah, maybe, Do'," I say absentmindedly, because I'm still trying to eavesdrop on the chatter before they all pile in to the elevator. "I'm not even sweating that anymore."

"I could think of something, if you want me to," she says, shrugging her Munchkin-tiny shoulders.

"I can't believe Eddie Lizard had the nerve to show up today!" I blurt out, totally cutting off Dorinda's flow.

"I heard that," Dorinda says, nodding her head.

I stand like a statue, staring at the poster of Drinka Champagne in the hallway. It's a blown-up photo from her legendary Sippin' and Tippin' world tour. In it, Drinka is wearing a metal chain outfit, and is being held up by six muscled men who are naked except for their suede loincloths. "Can you believe Drinka went out with Doktor Lizard?"

"Word?" Dorinda asks in disbelief—or maybe she's in awe of my divette detective skills. We stand there uncomfortably for a few more minutes, until Winnie the receptionist starts looking at us. "Everything okay, girls?" she asks, concerned.

"Yes, Ms. Winnie," I respond, then turn to Do' Re Mi and say, "It's time to jet."

"Why don't you just talk to him?" she asks me once we get in the elevator.

"No way, José. This is not an MP—it's an HP—

his problem, you know what I'm saying? Come on, let's go to Micky D's."

"You sure?" Dorinda asks.

"Absolutely. No way am I in the mood for any drama from the Huggy Bear twins."

But when we get downstairs, Eddie Lizard is waiting with Chuchie. I feel a sting in my chest. Aqua and Angie didn't even wait for us. They are definitely not trying to squash our beef jerky. I look at Chuchie, but she just smiles nervously.

"Galleria, can I talk to you for a sec?" Eddie asks quietly.

I want to scream, "No!" but I hear a tiny voice inside me say, "Okay." So while Dorinda walks ahead with Chuchie, I just stand there, waiting to hear whatever comes out of Eddie Lizard's mouth.

"Listen, I'm sorry I didn't call you this week, but, um, things got a little hectic," he starts in, smiling at me and fluttering his long, pretty eyelashes. "My bad."

He's got that right. What a weaselly explanation. As much as I want to hit the slimy Lizard over the head with my cheetah backpack, I know I can't. Suddenly, I feel tears welling up in my eyes. "Oh, quench the noise!" I blurt out.

Eddie looks at me, shocked. "You're upset?"

I glare at him, then blurt out, "Thomas Edison

definitely didn't invent your lightbulb, 'cuz it's too dim!"

"Okay, well, I'm sorry," Eddie says, shoving his hands in his pockets. "You know, we come from different worlds, you and me."

I stare back at him, like, "What brought on this *Star Trek* moment?"

"There's a lot you don't know about me—about us," he stammers.

"You mean, besides the fact that your father is a witch doctor?" I ask sarcastically. "What else could there be?"

"He's three hundred years old," Eddie says.

My jaw drops, and for a second, I'm totally speechless. "So?" I finally say. "How old are *you*? One hundred?"

"Uh, no," Eddie chuckles. "See, there's stuff like that you don't know."

"And I don't care, either."

"Well, anyway, I wanted to tell you. So I guess I'll see you around?"

"Yeah, see ya 'round like a doughnut," I say, smirking and fighting back tears. I run off to catch up with my crew before I burst out crying. That stupid Eddie Lizard! I hope he crawls back into whatever snake pit he came from!

Chapter 10

The next morning, I'm awakened by the rub of a leg other than my own. I let out a shriek. Then I realize that it's Chuchie's leg, sprawled all the way over on my side of the bed. Thank gooseness Chuchie and Dorinda spent the night with me, I think as I flop my head back down on my pillow.

There is no sense in getting up now, because it's Sunday, and I'm feeling really depressed. Then I remember that Dorinda is sleeping on the couch, so it would be rude to let her stay out there with just my mom and dad, who are banging around in the kitchen already. "Move, Miss Cuchifrita," I moan, disentangling myself from her wayward limb.

"Is Dorinda here?" Chuchie says, popping her head off the pillow, looking goofy because her eyes are only half open.

"She's on the couch, slouch. Now get up!"

Daddy has made us a true continental Bolognese breakfast. I think it's his own personal version, because I don't remember seeing anyone in Italy eating this much in the morning. "I'm so proud of you, *cara*," he says, "for stopping to chew that terrible gum—and you, too, Chanel!"

"Thank you for making us breakfast," Chuchie coos, slurping up the syrup on her tutti-frutti waffles, made from Dad's homemade recipe. They're made from buckwheat flour blended with heavy cream and chunks of strawberries, blueberries, and bananas—yum!

"This is really good," Dorinda says, finally looking up from her plate after inhaling the food like a vacuum.

I stare glumly at my untouched breakfast, thinking about Eddie Lizard, and how he dissed me so *hard*. I complain to my mom about it.

"Welcome to the real world, darling," Mom says, looking over at my grouchy face. I hope she doesn't start giving me her told-you-so speech, but I have to admit she was right. She knew there was something slithery about Eddie Lizard, who has turned out to be a frog in a snakeskin suit after all.

"I just don't understand why he did this," I moan out loud, even though I promised not to talk about Eddie Lizard again as long as I live.

115

"You've just experienced the most popular dish that's not on the Chinese menu," Mom says, speaking in her usual riddles. "Hot, cold, and *sour* soup. They chase, then they disappear like cockroaches in the night. Or in his case—"

"I know, Mom," I say, cutting her off. "Hey, did you know that Doktor Lizard dated Drinka Champagne back in the day?"

"More like *aghast from the past* is what I heard," Mom says, like a Missy Know-it-all, sipping her double latte cappuccino with a cinnamon twist like it's filled with gold. "Turns out he was also married to Mrs. Depooter, one of my very best customers. You know, the one who always has to have tassels, pom-poms, or trapezes hanging from her backside!"

"I can't believe he went out with Mrs. Depooter!" I say.

"Darling, when you're three hundred years old, you can leave behind quite a trail!" Mom says matter-of-factly.

"Mom, you don't believe that hukalaka hookie, do you?" I ask in disbelief, staring at Dad for backup.

"Bubbles, how can you say that!?" Chuchie shrieks. She believes in *brujería*, Santería, and other witchcraft shenanigans, just like the twins do.

Right about now, though, Aqua and Angie are probably at church, singing "Hallelujah!" Not that I care.

"Well, I guess Aqua and Angie aren't gonna set their father up with Drinka Champagne," I say, shaking my head. "Not after they hear this latest drama."

"A former disco queen would be a walk in the park after that high priestess he was dating," Mom says wisely. "He's better off without Abala Shaballa, just like you're better off without Eddie Lizard."

"You didn't want me dating Eddie because you think I'm too young," I blurt out accusingly. "That's why you didn't like him."

"I didn't tell Eddie Lizard not to call, if that's what you're thinking," Mom humphs, throwing a glance at Dad. "I think he figured out how to do that all by himself."

Suddenly, like an idiot, I start crying.

"*Cara*, what's the matter?" Daddy says, running over to me. He hates to see me cry.

"I really liked him, Daddy," I sob into his arms, bawling like a big baby.

Everybody gets real quiet while I finish my stupid boo-hoo attack. Then, just as I'm sniffing back the last tears, the doorbell rings.

117

"I'll get it," Dad says, racing to the door. When he looks through the peephole, he lets out a gasp and mutters, "*Non lo credo*. I don't believe it. Come see with your own eyes, *cara*."

I jump up excited, wondering if it's Eddie Lizard standing there, with the biggest bouquet of flowers he could find in the florist's shop. I feel my heart pounding as I look into the peephole.

It's not Eddie Lizard—what was I thinking?—but it's something almost as good. I gasp in happy surprise, and hug Dad, giggling. He covers my mouth as he flings open the door and lets out a hearty, "*Buon giorno*, Esther!"

"Oh, um, good morning, Franco and, um, Galleria," Mrs. Brubaker says, clutching a big woven basket covered with a white blanket. "May I come in?"

"Of course," Daddy exclaims, stepping aside to let Mrs. Brubaker enter.

I can't believe Mrs. Brubaker has the nerve to come over just to show us Buffy's puppies! One cuddle, and I'll be hooked on a new pet, if you get my drift. I mean, it's not fair! I try to smile at Mrs. Brubaker, like I don't want to whack her and snatch the basket away from her.

"Would you like some Italian continental breakfast, Esther?" Daddy asks cheerfully.

"Oh, no, thank you. Well, a cup of your coffee would be wonderful."

"Have something to eat. Maybe some grits?" Mom asks.

"Well, I'll try one," Mrs. Brubaker says.

I try not to laugh. Obviously, Mrs. Brubaker has never had grits before. I see a tiny smile curling up in the corner of Mom's mouth. "Honey, put a little of everything on a plate for Esther."

Toto runs out of the kitchen and makes a beeline for Mrs. Brubaker. "Down, Toto!" I hiss at him, causing him to stop in his tracks.

"How are you, Dorothea?" Mrs. Brubaker asks Mom, sitting down and carefully holding the basket in place on her lap, like it's a pot of gold.

"I'm fine, darling, how are you?" Mom answers, looking up from her paper like everything is hunky-dory, even though I know she probably wants to smush a bagel with cream cheese right on Mrs. Brubaker's nose.

"Listen, I've been thinking about this whole mess, and I've made a decision," Mrs. Brubaker says. "I'd like you to see the puppies. I mean, they're all quite adorable."

"Yes, I'm sure they are," Mom cuts in.

Mrs. Brubaker takes the blanket off the basket,

and Chuchie lets out a big gasp. "Ooh, they're so cute I'm going to faint!"

"Yes, they are. I hope you don't mind, but I've only brought along three," Mrs. Brubaker says.

I stand patiently by Mrs. Brubaker's chair, waiting for her to finish her stupid spiel so I can get my grubby little paws on the furballs. I look at the one with the darkest black eyes and my heart starts to melt. I don't know if I'm gonna be able to let them go back to Mrs. Brubaker's safari apartment.

"Well, I hope this ends our nasty little business," Mrs. Brubaker continues. "I mean, you didn't have to take me to court, or act like such a—never mind."

"It wasn't an act, darling, trust me!" Mom snaps back. "And you're not doing us any favor by simply letting us sneak a peek!"

"What more do you want?" Mrs. Brubaker shrieks, like she's on the brink of losing it. "I can't possibly let you have more than three, Dorothea, you're being unreasonable!"

More than three?

"Are you letting us *keep* them?" I ask, practically out of breath because my heart is pounding so hard.

"Why, yes—that's what I've been trying to *tell* you," Mrs. Brubaker says in her usual grumpy fashion.

"Oh, Esther, I'm sorry," Mom says, getting up. "We thought you were merely parading the pups in our faces so we'd keel over from an attack of Gucci envy!" I can tell from the glint in Mom's eyes that she is as relieved as I am. Daddy, too. He grabs me by the shoulders and squeezes me.

"Esther, were you afraid the judge would rule in our favor?" Mom asks.

"Heavens, no!" Mrs. Brubaker says, getting huffy again. "I just think it was deplorable that you resorted to such measures!"

Deplorable? I wonder what *that* means. Probably "disgusting" or maybe even "radikkio." Whatever it means, I don't want Mrs. Brubaker getting so upset that she takes Buffy's "puffies" back to her apartment!

"Mrs. Brubaker, you made us really, really happy," I say, trying to take the basket from her.

"Well, Galleria, I can't give you the basket!" Mrs. Brubaker says, clasping the handle tightly.

"But—but you just said!" I stammer. I *knew* Mrs. Brubaker was pulling another hoax-arama! I stare at the top of her bright red hair, wondering if she's really a sea dragon—just add water and she'll sprout wings!

"I know what I said, but you can't have the basket!" Mrs. Brubaker says excitedly. "I got it on my last trip to Thailand. You'll have to get your own."

Oh, *now* I get her drift! "Oh, I'm sorry, Mrs. Brubaker," I apologize. "I thought you meant—well, never mind."

"Oooooo," Chuchie says, rushing over to put her paws on a pup.

"No, *I'll* get it, Chuchie," I snap, nudging her out of the way. I gently pick up a puppy and give it to Daddy. His whole face lights up as he plays with the white, furry ball of fluff who's so little he almost fits in the palm of Daddy's hand.

"They're so little, Dad," I coo. "Look, Toto, look at your babies!"

"Don't worry, they'll grow—sooner than you'd like," warns Mrs. Brubaker.

I pick up another puppy, and bend down so that Toto can look at his offspring. The puppy tenses up in my hand and makes a whining noise. "Ooh, look, this one has a bigger head than the other one! Don't be afraid, Biggie," I tell him, rubbing his nose in my face. Toto starts barking like crazy. "No, Toto, you can't touch him yet. Not till he's a little older."

"Can I at least hold the other one? *Por favor!*" Chuchie whines.

"Of course, Chanel," Mom says. "Just don't run off and make a purse out of her fur!"

"How do you know it's a she from there?" I ask Mom.

"She's right," Mrs. Brubaker says. "Those two are boys, and that one's the girl."

"Can I have this one?" Chuchie begs, smothering the poor puppy against her chest.

"Let's not decide that right now, Chanel, or your mother is going to get a restraining order against me," Mom jokes. She's right. That's all we would need is another "Battle of the Divas."

"Let Dorinda have him, Bubbles!" Chuchie says excitedly.

I suddenly realize that Do' hasn't said a word this whole time. Now I see it's because she's been biting her lip, not letting herself even hope for a pet of her own. I look at her pleading eyes, and decide it's time to do the right thing.

"I see somebody is wagging their tail," I smile, handing Dorinda her prize pooch.

"Can he be my dog *and* yours?" Chuchie asks, snuggling up to Dorinda.

"Of course, Chuchie—you can come over and raise the woof anytime you want!" Dorinda says, overflowing with puppy love. "I don't mind sharing. At my house, we have to share everything anyway!"

Poor Dorinda, I think to myself. She always has

to share things. But I have to admit, she doesn't seem to mind. Maybe I'm just spoiled, being an only child and all. But the thought of her ten foster brothers and sisters pawing over Toto's puppy makes me shiver.

"What are we gonna name him?" Chuchie asks excitedly. But before Dorinda can say anything, Chuchie blurts out, "Let's name him Nobu." Nobu is Auntie Juanita's favorite Japanese restaurant in Soho, and it's owned by Robert De Niro, whom Auntie Juanita has had a crush on since I can remember.

"Word—that's cool," Dorinda says, holding her fluffball like he's a baby.

"So, how is your singing group?" Mrs. Brubaker asks, sipping her cappuccino like one of those society ladies with monogrammed hankies. "Oh, Franco, this coffee is divine. You really must tell me your secret."

"It will never leave my lips!" Daddy says, grinning from ear to ear.

I guess Mrs. Brubaker doesn't really want to know about my singing group, but I decide I'm gonna tell her anyway. "We're recording a demo."

"What, Galleria?" Mrs. Brubaker asks absent-mindedly. Her pink lipstick has come off, and some of it is smudged in the corner of her mouth, but I don't think it's a good idea to tell her.

"You know, the Cheetah Girls are recording songs for the record company to listen to," I explain.

"Oh, I see," Mrs. Brubaker says, nodding her head, then touching one of the pearl clasp earrings she always wears. "Well, now that everything's settled, I'd better be going."

Nobody tries to talk her out of it. And the minute the door closes behind her, Mom huffs, "What a dog and *phony* show!"

Chuchie, Dorinda, and I jump up and down, screaming for joy. Daddy hugs us all, then wags his finger at me, "*Cara*, you can only keep one puppy!"

"Dad!" I whine, then look at Mom, and realize this is one battle I'll never win.

"Can I use the phone, *Madrina*?" Chuchie interrupts.

"Chanel, you don't have to ask. This is your home, too," Mom says, coddling the third puppy in her lap.

Chanel goes into the kitchen, and soon I hear her talking on the phone. She's probably trying to convince Auntie Juanita to let her have a dog, I figure. Ha! Teaching a chimpanzee to sashay down a runway would be a whole lot easier.

"Bubbles, *here*!" Chuchie says, handing me the receiver.

"I don't want to talk to her," I whisper.

"Take it!" Chuchie demands, shoving the receiver in my face.

I take a deep breath and get ready for some puppy drama with Auntie Juanita. I'm so surprised when I hear Aqua's voice that I clam up like I swallowed a canary—even though I was jumping up and down like a Chucky doll just a second ago.

"Congratulations," Aqua says, but I can tell by the sound in her voice that she's just as uncomfortable as I am. "We heard you got the puppies."

"Oh. Yeah," I say, realizing that Chuchie is trying to play peacemaker with this pronto little move of hers. Oh, well. Too late to get out of it now.

"What are you gonna call them?" Aqua asks.

"Well, I'm only keeping one," I tell her, "and I'm gonna name him . . . *Ragu*."

"Oh, that's real nice," Aqua chuckles. "Like the spaghetti sauce, huh? And, um, what are you gonna do with the other ones?"

"Well, Dorinda's getting one. That's really Chuchie's dog, of course, but it can't live with her, because, well, you know, Auntie Juanita."

"I hear that," Aqua says. She chuckles for a second, then stops, and there's a long silence. I

126

ponder what to say next, because I don't want to hurt Aqua's feelings.

Chuchie mouths at me, *Make up with her!*

I want to tell Chuchie to zip her lip, but Mom is looking right at me.

I pause for a few more seconds, then blurt out, "Do you and Angie want one of the pooches?" I stare at the receiver in disbelief at what I just said. I decide right then and there to swear off Dad's cappuccinos. Obviously, they're making me punchy!

"Yes! We'd love to have a dog! Porgy and Bess are mighty lonely when we're gone all day," Aqua says, sounding like her bubbly, gushy old self. Porgy and Bess are the twins' beloved guinea pigs.

"Well, don't you have to ask your father?" I ask, trying to figure a way out of this dill pickle. But how can I do that when I've already made the offer?

"Hold on," Aqua tells me, then screams to Angie, "Galleria's giving us one of the puppies! Go ask Daddy if we can have one!"

All of a sudden, Chuchie comes over and grabs the phone. "Can he be, like, my dog, too?" she asks, giggling into the receiver.

I can't believe how shameless Chuchie is! First she asks Dorinda, and now Aqua and Angie!

Judging by the huge grin on her face, I guess Aqua has said okay.

I grab the phone back from Chuchie, and Aqua tells me, "Daddy said we can have one!" she shrieks in my ear. "We'll be right over like a four-leaf clover!"

It makes me chuckle that Aqua is talking in rhymes, trying to sound like me. You know what they say—imitation is the sincerest form of flattery. And I do feel flattered. It shows me that Aqua really does like me, in spite of everything that's happened.

On the spot, I decide to squash our beef jerky once and for all. "Um, Aqua? I'm sorry about all the stuff. The wigs and stuff. And I guess you know about Eddie. . . ."

"Thank you, Miss Galleria, but all's forgiven. And now I gotta get off the phone so we can come on over and get our dog!"

"Awright, chicklet," I chuckle, happy that we're back to being real crew again. Who needs Eddie Lizard? The Cheetah Girls are going back into the studio to finish off the demo that's gonna get us our big record deal!

"Come on over," I tell Aqua. "It's time for the Cheetah Girls to raise the woof!"

Oops, Doggy Dog!

So you think you're fly
Just by looking at the sky
Well think again
'Cuz the Cheetah Girls are
Raising the woof
No, we ain't Mother Hen
Or Chicken Little
Stuck in the middle
Of your latest riddle

Now you know that the Cheetah Girls
Got more than curls
We'e got the swerve, the nerve
To be in the mix and up to tricks
Hah! These days we're down with Snoop
And scooping up puppy poop

Oops, doggy dog!
Oops, doggy dog!
Oops, watch your claws
I'll scratch your back
If you scratch mine

That's right, y'all
We're in the house awright
With Toto who put a Mojo
On little Buffy in fluffy fox next door
And now there's more
As a matter of fact they're numbering
Five in the litter
So don't be bitter
That we got three
That's right, y'all, we got it going on
Till the break of dawn
Hit it, Chuchie, it's time to raise the woof

Oops, doggy dog!
Oops, doggy dog!
Oops, watch your claws
I'll scratch your back
If you scratch mine

Chuchie did you feed Nobu?
Bubbles, did you feed Ragu?
That's Miss Ragu, to you!

The Cheetah Girls Glossary

Back in the day: Before you were born.

Beef jerky: Static. Fight.

Bocheenchando: Spanish slang for "gossiping."

Boo-hoo attack: Crying jag.

Bozo: A jerk. Or a boy who thinks he's *all that*, but isn't.

Bring in the noise: To perform, sing, dance, celebrate.

Cara: Italian for "precious one" (girls only; for boys, it's *caro*).

Chicklets: Friends, girl members of your posse.

Compromise: When you try to work out a solution instead of being stubborn about having your way, 'cuz real life isn't like a Burger King commercial!

Crushed and mushed: When you have a crush on someone and can't get over it.

Dill pickle: A juicy cucumber soaked in vinegar. Or, a messy situation.

Dissed: Disrespected. As in, "I can't believe she dissed me like that."

Down for the twirl: Up for whatever it takes to make your dreams come true in the jiggy jungle.

Drama and kaflamma: Drama times two. A whole big mess. A real dramatic situation that gets out of hand.

Duckets: Money. Coins.

Flackeroni: Static.

Flossin' and bossin': Showing off *and* trippin' at the same time.

Gaspitating: Getting nervous or upset about something. As in, "I'm gaspitating that Eddie hasn't called me today."

Gooney bird: Someone who is gaga over a boy or girl. As in, "Shaniqua was staring at that new boy in school like a gooney bird."

Goospitating: Going gaga for someone or something.

HP: His problem.

Hukalaka-hookie: Wack nonsense. As in, "That sounds like a whole bunch of hukalaka-hookie if you ask me."

Jointski: The joint. Da bomb.

Kaflooied: Upset.

Kizzie fit: When someone gets jiggety or out of control.

Lollygaggers: People who move too slowly, or don't get with the program.

Mad flava: Supa-dupa-fabbie-poo-ness. As in, "That song has mad flava."

Madrina: Spanish for "Godmother."

Meow-rageous: Out of control. Outrageous.

Mija: Spanish word of endearment, like *darling, honeybunch, precious one.*

MP: My problem. As in, "That's not an MP, okay?"

My bad: My fault.

Petulant: Huffy. Pouty.

Pronto: Right quick. Fast. As in, "Get on the Batphone pronto and find out where the party is." Also, an Italian salutation for answering the phone. *"Pronto, chi parla?"* which means, "Hello, who's calling?"

Quench the noise: Stop fibbing. Stop faking. As in, "I know you were at the movies, so why don't you quench the noise?"

Radikkio: Ridiculous. As in, "Don't be radikkio."

Read: To tell someone off. As in, "Don't let me read you, Miss Quadrilya, because you'll never recover!"

Scoopology: The art of dishing.

Snorkle: To say something snotty. As in, "Why you snorkling at me?"

Squash the noise: Kill the noise. End something abruptly. Change the station. As in, "I hate that record, please squash the noise."

Straight off the cuff: Unedited. Speaking your mind. As in, "Shavonne just says things straight off the cuff; that's why I like her."

Supa-dupa: Extra. As in, "These wings are supa-dupa crispy, yo."

Thank gooseness: Thank goodness.

Throw shade: Give someone a dirty look.

Total eclipse: When the sun is completely overshadowed by the moon. Or, when your emotions are so overpowering, you want to freak out on somebody. As in, "He was so shady, I almost went total eclipse on him."

Vindicate: To justify. Or to feel like you got somebody good for dissing you.

Bow-wow Wow!

To the ferocious onscreen Cheetah Girls, Kiely
Williams (Aquanette), Adrienne Bailon (Chanel),
and Sabrina Bryan (Dorinda), who are truly
flexing their growl power. Stay tight, *mamacitas*!

Chapter 1

I don't mean to be *tan molesto*—sooo annoying— and ruin the puppy party for everybody. But all of a sudden I burst out crying like a whacked-out piñata that lost all its red hots. I'm sorry, but I just can't stop the tears, *las lágrimas*! Bubbles thinks I'm doing it on purpose. I can tell because her nostrils are flaring out. Her puffy cheeks are starting to fill up like she's going to turn into Puff the Magic Dragon and breathe fire on my frizzies any minute. But what do I have to celebrate, anyway? *She's* the one getting to keep the cutest poochie out of Buffy's litter. *Es la verdad.* It's true. Ragu is staring at me with his black little eyes and I just want to stuff him in my cheetah backpack and hit the door like a mad matador. Like Bubbles needs another white fluffy meatball—*una otra*. She already has Toto, who is the only star on the Upper

The Cheetah Girls

East Side, where they live—especially now that he prances around in cheetah coats and hats (which I helped pick out, *está bien*?).

So what do I have? Okay, so I have the Cheetah Girls and I should be happy that I—poor *pobrecita* Chanel "Chuchie" Simmons—am one of the five wannabe divettes-in-training who are destined to sing and dance to peeps around the world, *en todo el mundo*. That's what Bubbles says, anyway, to anyone who will listen to her talk about our dreams. Well, right now, I wish someone would listen to me. I want my own puppy—*ahora mismo!* No, I take that back. I want five puppies—and to live in my own Cheetah castle too, so nobody, *nadie*, can tell me what to do ever again!

The Cheetah Girls, of course, are: my-super-bossy-best-friend Galleria "Bubbles" Garibaldi; the Texas Rangers Aquanette and Anginette Walker, who keep our backup vocals *tan coolio*; Dorinda "Do'Re Mi" Rogers, the best dancer in our crew; and last but not least, Chanel "Chuchie" Cuchifrita, Ballerina Simmons, the mushy *señorita*. (Just so you know, Cristalle is my Confirmation name because I'm Catholic—and Coco is my *real* middle name but I never use it.)

"Look at Toto, yo," heckles Dorinda, trying to make everybody forget about my piñata episode.

All of a sudden, Toto flies into the living room from the kitchen like he just got shot out of a doggy cannon, then jumps on top of Ragu, humping him to the beat of a salsa conga drum. *Ba.Da.Da.Da.Ba.Da.Da.Da.* Now my tears are dripping on the fluffy cheetah carpet in the living room. How embarrassing!

"Toto looks so big next to Ragu," Angie says, popping on her gum.

"Supersize-me, that's Toto," Galleria riffs. "He's pound-for-pound pure smoochie pooch."

By now, you may be wondering what is up—*por qué* all this puppy talk? Well, here is the whole yappy soap opera: While the Cheetah Girls were in Hollywood performing in the New Talent Showcase for Def Duck Records, Galleria's dad (and my favorite godfather), Mr. Francobollo Garibaldi, let Toto hump Mrs. Brubaker's dog, Buffy. *Qué pasó?* That's right. Toto got Buffy pregnant. Not that Mrs. Brubaker noticed until Buffy started waddling in her apartment and tripped over her scary leather baby hippopotamus footstool. (Poor Buffy is not even allowed to go out for a walk because Mrs. Brubaker has her paper-trained.) Well, Mrs. Brubaker almost had a canary herself when she found out that Toto was the father of Buffy's litter. Then, just for spite, she wouldn't let Galleria have any of the puppies. Well, Galleria's mom, who is my godmother, *la mía* Madrina, and the Cheetah Girls manager, put a cheetah chompdown on the situation right away. That's right, Mrs. Dorothea Garibaldi filed a lawsuit in family court and—you guessed it—won half the litter in the custody battle!

"Can Ragu go outside and play yet?" Dorinda asks, hypnotized by Ragu's eyes too.

"No way, Do', he has to get his shots first," Bubbles says, picking up Ragu and holding him in her arms like he is a baby *she* just delivered! *"My little baby waby has the cutest little pawsy wawsy!"* Bubbles coos in singsong fashion like a cuckoo bird.

Ay, por favor, please don't let Bubbles run and grab her Kitty Kat notebook so she can start scribbling lyrics for a new Cheetah Girls song—because that lyric is whack-a-doodle-do. *Qué terrible!* Okay, so maybe I am *un poco celosa*—a little jealous. *Who do I have waiting for me at home?* Nobody, *nadie*, but my Snuggly Wiggly stuffed pooch that my Abuela Florita gave me for Christmas last year as a joke because she knows how much I want a dog. (Mamí won't let me have one because she says she's allergic to them, but Abuela says it isn't true. Mamí is just being selfish.) Of course, I also live with my ten-year-old brother, Pucci the gadget boy. (Pucci is always glued to some stupid computer game, except when he's bothering me or sneaking into my room to steal things when I'm not home.) Even Pucci has a pet, though—an African pygmy hedgehog named Mr. Cuckoo. Bubbles and I bought Mr. Pygmy for Pucci's last birthday (but Pucci thought of the stupid name all by himself). *Gracias* gooseness, Pucci is over Daddy's house a lot these days. The place where Pucci is taking karate lessons is uptown, near Daddy's, so he doesn't have to bother me all the time.

"Toto, stop trying to smother him with your rumpshaker!" Galleria screams, grabbing Toto off Ragu. She never yelled at Toto like that before. From the way she is treating him already, I can tell Ragu is gonna be the new Prince Pooch on 67th Street.

"I can't believe Kadeesha had the nerve to tell us what peeps are saying at school about us," Dorinda blurts out, obviously still upset about the latest Cheetah Girls Telemundo soap opera. Now there is a rumor going around our school, Fashion Industries East, that the uptown crews think the Cheetah Girls are corny and are a bunch of powder puff wannabes because we lost the Apollo

Amateur Hour contest to those way-too-crispy rappers Stak Chedda. They don't know the truth—that the Cheetah Girls should have won that contest.

Aqua and Angie throw each other a look. And I know what that look means. Because they are twins, they can read each other's minds. Suddenly Aqua blurts out, "We didn't want to say nothing, y'all, but that rumor ain't just at your school."

"Yeah," adds Angie, "everybody at our school is saying the same thing."

"Well, when we get our record deal—let's see what everybody will have to say about our street 'cred,' then," Bubbles says, poking her mouth out like she does when she's really angry.

Aqua and Angie look at each other, puzzled. Sometimes the twins don't understand when we talk because they are from Houston and have their own way of saying things.

"I heard that," Dorinda says, nodding her head. "If we didn't have street cred then Def Duck Records wouldn't even be trying to nibble at our kibble and bits."

Now Angie and Aqua burst out laughing, but I didn't. I don't think it's funny that everything Dorinda and Bubbles say now has to do with dogs!

Uncle Franco, who has been in the kitchen

making us dinner, bursts into the living room. "How are my amaretto cookies?" Uncle Franco asks, beaming at Aqua and Angie, who look like twin pumpkins holding a puppy. But they just stare back at Uncle Franco, giving him that dumbfounded look they do so well, then Angie quickly blurts out, "We didn't get any."

"No, *cara*, the two of you are my amaretto cookies!" he says, laughing loudly like he always does, moving his hands around a lot, then giving them both a bear hug. Uncle Franco, my godfather, is from Bologna, Italy. He always talks with his hands (and sometimes his feet too). "I haven't seen you—ah, since the Mariah Carey concert—*insomma*, anyway, you girls aren't fighting anymore, no?"

Bubbles throws Uncle Franco a little smirk because she didn't know that he knew about the slippery Eddie Lizard situation. (Madrina must have told him.) Eddie Lizard is this really cute boy who goes to Drinka Champagne Conservatory, where we take our vocal and dance classes on Saturdays. Let's just say both Galleria and Aqua liked the same creepy crawler who turned out to be a snake in the grass. (Every time the phone rings, though, Bubbles jumps up because she secretly hopes Lizard will call, but he doesn't.)

Uncle Franco runs into the kitchen and comes

back with the only thing Aqua and Angie love more than horror movies—food. "I got the mozzarella from the Ottamanelli Market this morning—just for my two amaretto cookies!" Uncle Franco says, standing over them with a serving tray filled with his fresh-out-of-the-oven chunky cheese balls. *E buono, no?*

Now my mouth is watering too, but I can't eat. I feel so fat now that I have my crutches off and I haven't exercised for four weeks. (I broke my ankle at an audition for the Ballet Hispánico school. It was *qué terrible!*) I have secretly been on my own carrot diet. (I mean, if they were good enough for Bugs Bunny, then they are good enough for me. Tee-hee-hee.)

"I'm surprised Galleria hasn't invited the whole neighborhood over for a puppy parade," Madrina shouts from the dining room table. I guess I'm mad because Bubbles called Aqua and Angie over today to join the puppy party and show off Ragu. She didn't even ask me if it was okay to give the twins the last puppy. I know Mamí won't let me have one, but she could have asked me, right? "Chanel, come on, darling, could you please stop crying. Come take some cheetah tissues for your issues—and perk up for round two."

I ignore Madrina because I am too busy

watching Aqua as she takes the first bite out of Uncle Franco's chunky cheese ball. *Ay, qué delicioso*, if Aqua and Angie could take a bite out of crime like they do those cheese balls, New York would be the safest place in *todo el mundo*! Uncle Franco always fries his cheese balls just right—they never get too soggy or too burnt. It's a secret recipe he got from his mother.

"Gimme one, Daddy!" Galleria teases as Uncle Franco dances around with the tray.

"Darling, I can't believe you're eating one—you always complain about the melted mozzarella getting stuck in your braces," Madrina says, beaming.

"Yeah, well, I'm practicing!" Galleria says, smiling and showing off her metal mouth. "I can't wait till Monday. I'm gonna be in there like swimwear!" After school on Monday, Bubbles is getting her braces off. She gets to have everything. No more braces—and a puppy too.

"Here, Galleria, take mine!" Aqua squeals in delight. Looking at these two lovebirds, you would never know that Aqua and Bubbles were still chomping on the beef jerky about Eddie Lizard—before Mrs. Brubaker came over and surrendered the puppies.

As if reading my mind, which Bubbles does all the time, she blurts out to Aqua and Angie, "I can't believe your dad is letting you keep a pooch, smooch," but darts her eyes over at me. "He must still be under that spell Abala Shaballa put on him because he sure is awfully 'howdy doody' these days!"

It was lucky for Mr. Walker that we even knew Doktor Lizard (he's Eddie Lizard's dad and the first hoodoo practitioner we ever met). But, if it wasn't for me, the twins would have never found out that their daddy was under a spell in the first place. See, Esmeralda, the Spanish housekeeper from the apartment next door, was with the twins when they found their dad unconscious in bed surrounded by *brujería*—witchcraft—potions. They couldn't understand what Esmeralda was trying to tell them because she doesn't speak English, so the twins hopped on the cell phone so I could translate. Doktor Lizard came right to the hospital and saved Mr. Walker from that terrible hexarama drama. But judging from the way the twins are acting now, you wouldn't even know that I helped. *Es verdad*, it's true. They don't seem grateful at all. All they care about is their new puppy—and how many cheese balls they can stuff in their mouths. (Aqua is up to five and Angie has devoured four!)

"Galleria, you're a mess," Angie says, smirking,

nodding, and popping cheese balls through her juicy lips.

"We can't believe it either!" Aqua sighs, popping a cheese ball into her mouth. "He is usually so strict about everything, especially who comes into our house making a mess."

"Well, there won't be any mess. This is one dog who will be walking the streets of New York by four months, 'cuz we know Daddy ain't gonna stand for all that paper-training too long!" Angie pipes in.

"Dag on, let me hold her now, Aqua!" Angie squeals, trying to get her paws on their new puppy. She plops the puppy in her lap like the animal is a ham-and-cheese sandwich on her plate she's about to devour.

"Daddy said we have to keep her in our room," Aqua announces to her, handing over the new prize to her twin sister. "And he is not going to walk her—ever—so we have to really work out our schedule now."

I can't believe my ears. I just want to scream, *Parate*, already! Stop it, please. Well, I guess the secret is really out—we all know now who really is the strictest parent in our bunch. Mine. *Es verdad*—it's true—Juanita Domingo Simmons wins the grand prize!

"Where is your mother now, Chanel?" Angie asks gingerly, because I guess she is tired of pretending that I am not there.

"With Mr. Tycoon," I mumble under my breath. "I think they went to Nobu." *Call me on my celly-jelly if you need me.* That's what she told me when she went to meet him. Hah! She's never there when I need her. I can picture Mamí at Nobu now—wearing one of my too-tight tops and giggling like a schoolgirl and sucking up sushi with Mr. Tycoon, cooing, "Oh, I couldn't—okay, just one more." Mamí is always borrowing clothes from me without asking. I mean, I know she's trying to impress Mr. Tycoon with how hip and *coolio* she is. But what about what I want? No, we never talk about that. All we talk about is what Mamí wants: Mamí wants me be a fashion buyer instead of a singer. Mamí wants me to stay at home and not see Papi's girlfriend, Princess Pamela, because she thinks she's a witch—*una bruja*. (It is not true. Princess Pamela was born with a veil over her eye, which means she has the gift of sight. She is a psychic.) Mamí wants me to pick out clothes for her to wear and she doesn't want me to have a dog because *she* is allergic to them.

"Chanel, darling, we've put out an APB police bulletin for Juanita—as soon as we hear from her,

I'll give her my drill. If it worked on that sourpuss in family court, maybe it'll work wonders with Juanita and she'll let you have a puppy. After all, it seems she has found a "lapdog" in the likes of Mr. Tycoon, so maybe she can spread a few milk biscuits around," Madrina says, chuckling, trying to make me feel better. However, I start crying a waterfall of tears until Madrina adds, sighing, "I appreciate the free carpet cleaning Chanel, but you *really* didn't have to!"

"But there aren't any more puppies!" I blurt out, my mouth trembling.

"Oh, don't you worry, I promise you this—if Juanita says you can have a puppy, then I will get one more from Mrs. Brubaker—if I have to hang her from her overplucked eyebrows myself."

"Whatever you say, *Madrina*," I mumble, still looking down at the carpet.

"Oh, come on, Chanel, this was supposed to be fun for you girls—if I didn't know better I'd think I was at a wake for the death of miniskirts."

"Chanel, come on, help us name our dog," Aqua says, laying on that Southern drawl like she does when she's trying to be super nice, but then she opens her eyes wide because she realizes that she shouldn't have said anything.

I don't want to name her stupid dog, *está bien*?

"You did a dope job naming my puppy," Dorinda says, trying to be nice.

Yo no lo creo, I can't believe it—even Dorinda's foster mom said she could keep one of the puppies. So what, she let me name him Nobu after Mamí's favorite restaurant. I *hate* sushi! Oh, but Nobu is sooo cute. He looks almost identical to Ragu, but he has an even cuter little nose.

"Chanel, you can come over and play with Nobu whenever you want," Dorinda says, trying to smoothe down my frizzies, which are all over the place. Today, I look like one of those voodoo dolls—all hair and a big tummy!

"I know, Dorinda," I say, whining. But who is she kidding; once she gets home, there are eleven foster brothers and sisters waiting to paw him to death. Nobu isn't gonna need me to pet him and love him.

Now my stomach feels like it has a whole lot of spicy cinnamon Red Hots doing the cha-cha inside to their own beat. One, two, cha-cha-cha. Three, four, hit the door. I hold my stomach, which does look like a little pouch all of a sudden, and rock back and forth. "*Ay, mija*, I don't care what Dr. Reuben says, I'm going to exercise. I'm fat. *Una gordita!*" I say in utter distress.

Dr. Reuben said I can't exercise for at least one

more month so my ankle can really heal. But I have to do something to slow my jelly-roll, *está bien*. Now, I don't know what's worse—walking on crutches, or being fat! At least I got more attention when I was on crutches. Now nobody cares about my feelings—especially Galleria.

"Chuchie, could you pleez save it for the opera!" Galleria hisses under her breath so her mother, who is my godmother, doesn't hear her being mean to me as usual.

"Come to think of it, Chanel, you're not eating," Madrina says, getting really concerned.

"I'm not hungry," I mumble, finally getting up off my knees and going over to Madrina to get a cheetah tissue. I blow my nose.

"That's fabulous, darling, just like a fire engine blowing its horn," Madrina says, her hand extended, waiting to take my cheetah tissue filled with snot.

"I don't think *Mamí* is going to call," I whisper to Madrina so Bubbles doesn't hear me.

"I know, Chanel, but we don't have to take care of this today. You have my word—I'm gonna fight for you like Martin Luther King walking forty miles in Selma, Alabama, for the Civil Rights Movement. Don't forget, now it's my job to see that my talent gets what they deserve," she says, winking at me.

Now I start to giggle. Madrina is so *dramática*! I sigh and take a deep breath, which makes my stomach feel a little better. Drinka Champagne would be proud of me. She always makes us focus on our breathing in vocal classes. I know Madrina will really try to talk Mamí into letting me have a puppy. The Cheetah Girls are so lucky. I mean, how many singing groups have someone like Madrina for their manager watching their back?

"Puff may know how to huff but nobody stands in my way when I want something for my talent," Madrina says, putting her arms around me. "Nobody—*especially* not Juanita. Now be on time tomorrow."

Now that the Christmas season is around the corner, I have to work Sundays at Madrina's boutique in Soho near my house—Toto in New York . . . Fun in Diva Sizes. (See, I maxed out Mamí's credit card when I was mad at her, so now I have to put back every single ducket in the bucket, *esta bien.*)

"One little cheese ball for my Cuchifrita?" Uncle Franco says, holding one out on a fork.

"No, thank you!" I say, my mouth watering like Niagra Falls. All I care about right now is staying on my carrot diet and helping the Cheetah Girls pounce—big-time.

Chapter 2

Walking from the subway exit on Prince Street, I feel the Red Hots coming back for more cha-cha lessons in my tummy. And now my legs feel like the plate of Uncle Franco's *linguini con vongole*. As I turn the corner on Wooster Street to walk to my house I start to feel dizzy too. *Ay, Dios mío*, now all I need is to start with the tears again—in front of all these people! This man with a tummy fatter than Santa Claus is walking in the opposite direction. I can't help looking because he isn't wearing a shirt. *Ay, Dios, mío*—it looks like he's delivering triplets! I stop and lean against a NO PARKING sign, then stare like a rag doll into the Datz So Phat Boutique store window directly across from it. *Ay, qué linda*. There is a pink T-shirt with a cute pussycat outlined in rhinestone right on the front. It is so *la dopa*. I wish I could buy it, but I can't. *No lo puedo.* I'm out of Benjies for a while. Most of the money I make from working in Madrina's boutique I have to give to Mamí to pay her back for all the things I charged on her credit card. I hate it. *Lo odio!* And my allowance is not enough to buy anything nice like the Datz So Phat pussycat tee. I can just pay for stuff I need, like S.N.A.P.S. cosmetics Mango Tango glitter.

People are walking by me but, *gracias* gooseness, nobody is really paying attention to me just standing here like an orphan. I keep staring into the Datz So Phat store window. Now I'm staring at the five-foot poster of Zimora Chin that's in the store window. Zimora is the *tan coolio* model who owns Datz So Phat Boutique. She is so pretty. She has slanty, exotic eyes and juicy lips like Aqua and Angie. Suddenly, a lightbulb goes off in my head. If I looked like Zimora, I know the Cheetah Girls would get a record deal with Def Duck Records. Fantasizing, I see the president of Def Duck Records—in my daydream he is short, bald, and wears a red suit with a yellow tie and big rhinestone-trimmed glasses—banging on my loft apartment door. He is really nervous. I open the door and I'm wearing a pink leopard dress trimmed with pink feather boa that matches the pen he pulls out of his pocket for me to sign the record contract. Por favor, *Chanel, please sign. Por favor! We love you! Don't tell Galleria, but without you, there would be no Cheetah Girls!*

I stare at Zimora's poster some more. She is wearing a white bikini and her stomach is so flat. That's it! I'm going to eat carrots until my stomach looks just like hers.

"Miss, are you okay?"

I am so startled that someone is talking to me, I lose my balance and hit the left side of my head, *la mia cabeza,* on the pole below the sign. *No, I'm not okay,* I want to scream, but I just say politely, "I'm okay," rubbing the boo-boo on my left temple.

"You looked like you were gonna topple over, there!" the PEZ-head lady says, letting out a squeal. She has a really high-pitched voice like a hyena. I pass by her every day. She has a card table set up on the sidewalk with stuffed animals that have PEZ candy dispensers sticking out of their heads. "You know what I do when life gets too cuckoo? I just pop some candy from a PEZ dispenser right into my big mouth. I tell ya, they're better than vitamins! Come look. Come on, it doesn't cost ya to look, cutie pie."

"No, that's all right," I say, embarrassed because I couldn't buy her PEZ dispensers even if I wanted to. All I have is five dollars. Pucci calls her the PEZ-head lady.

"I'm okay, really," I repeat to her and start walking away quickly. I pass a few more street vendors—including my favorite, Lacey Stacey, who makes this really cool mesh jewelry from Mexican silver—but I make sure not to look at her today so I don't get tempted. When I turn the corner on Mercer Street and walk near my building, I start coughing from all the dust. There is always a lot of construction going on in my neighborhood, but right now they are tearing down the building next door to mine and there are a lot of big men pounding with supersize drills and hammers and breathing fire from this big machine (okay, so it's called an electrical torch). I can't take it! I stare at the hollow half-broken building piled high with rubble inside where the Pickle Pit Stop used to be. When I was younger, Mr. Briney, the owner, who is this really big man with a twirly mustache, used to greet me the same way every time he saw me. "A pickle a day keeps the doctor away. So what can I do for you, little lady?" Sometimes Pucci would say, "Let's go see Mr. Briney's hiney." (That was Pucci's way of saying to Mamí, "Let's go get a pickle.") Now I feel so sad that I didn't get a chance to say good-bye to

Mr. Briney. It just seemed like the store closed overnight.

All of a sudden, my feet start walking without me like they're stuck on a Ouija board or something! Mamí hasn't called me yet on my cell to see where I am. No way, José, am I going home yet. I let my feet walk me to Spring Street. *Por favor*, please let Princess Pamela be there. Even though her hair salon is probably closed by now, there must be a lot of people walking around who want to get their fortune told. My heart leaps when I see the red neon sign in the window of Princess Pamela's Psychic Palace. There is no one in the front of the store, but I am sure I see shadows behind the red crystal-bead curtains that divide the store. I try to open the door, but it is locked. I tap gently on the glass, but no one answers. Disappointed, I turn to walk away, when I hear the crystal beads jingle and Princess Pamela hurries toward the front door.

Unlocking the door, Princess Pamela whispers, "My little Chanel, I'm *verrry* surprised to see you."

By the way her big brown eyes are twinkling at me, I don't think Princess Pamela is upset, so I coo at her, "I just wanted to see you."

"*Astepta un moment*—wait one minute. I have a *verry* important client inside," Princess Pamela says, clutching her red shawl with bright blue flowers close to her chest, then shooing me inside to sit on the red velvet couch while I wait for her to finish. I look around at all the photographs of hair-styles on the wall. Boot-i-full! as Princess Pamela would say in her thick Romanian accent. I helped Princess Pamela come up with some of the hair-styles. Princess Pamela and my dad have been together since I was nine years old, and Daddy, who used to be in construction, even helped build all three of her stores himself. (The other two stores are Princess Pamela's Pampering Palace and Princess Pamela's Pound Cake Palace. Both of them are on 210th Street and Broadway.)

Suddenly I hear the customer crying *really* loudly from behind the curtains. "He said he would take me to an island for our honeymoon. He can't even afford Coney Island!" she says, cry-ing really loud.

I try not to look at the customer when she comes from behind the curtains so she won't get embar-rassed. While Princess Pamela is talking to her some more, I sneak a peek. Her eyes are very puffy and sad, but now she smiles back at me. "This is my stepdaughter, Chanel," Princess Pamela says proudly to the lady as she ushers her out. Wow, Princess Pamela does love me. I wish she was my mother. Then I could have a puppy, be a singer, and open a hair salon right next door called Miss Cuchifrita's Curlz.

"My little Chanel, what are you doing here?" Princess Pamela says, grabbing my cheeks and jiggling me out of my bad thoughts.

"There is all this construction stuff—I can't take the nose—I mean the *noise*," I moan feebly.

Ah, yes, poor Mr. Briney, he have to go back to Mykonos," Princess Pamela says, nodding.

"Mykonos?"

"In Greece," Princess Pamela explains patiently, then lets out a troubled sigh. "I hear he had to go back home because the store rents are too high now in New York. Always here, the landlords try to suck the blood. At least in my country they are honest about it." (Princess Pamela is from Transylvania, home of Count Dracula.)

Stroking the long fringes on Princess Pamela's red pashmina shawl, I can't resist asking, "What did he do with all the pickles?"

"He pack them in his suitcase, of course," Princess Pamela says, her brown eyes twinkling with mischief like they always do when she is with me, but I notice they are puffy too. I know it's really hard running three stores. Suddenly, I get another terrible thought. Her eyes are puffy because she is fighting with Daddy. I remember when Mamí's eyes used to look like that all the time. Then Daddy moved out. But maybe that was because Mamí threw his clothes out the bedroom window. She even hit this lady over the head with a pair of his Oxford wingtipped shoes. (By accident, *esta bien*. The lady just happened to be walking by.)

"I must go back home, too—to Romania," Princess Pamela says, rubbing her eyes.

I'm right. She doesn't love Daddy anymore! Suddenly, my heart sinks. I don't want her to leave. Since Daddy left, I never see him as much anymore. Please don't let Princess Pamela leave. *Por favor, Dios!*

Seeing the worried look on my face, Princess Pamela gently strokes my frizzies, then says, "Don't worry, my little Chanel. Thousands of people—*émigrés*—from my country are flying to Bucharest next weekend. They will come to assemble, to lobby for property restitution laws," Princess Pamela says slowly because she is trying to make me understand. I am too embarrassed to ask her what she is talking about, because I don't want her to think I'm stupid.

Princess Pamela sees the expression on my face and explains her situation some more. "We are not just fighting for what the greedy *apparatchiks* took from our families. How can I explain? Everywhere in Eastern Europe, the governments have already made the laws. If the Romanian government does not do the same thing, then Romania won't stand a chance to be admitted in the European Union. Now you understand?"

I stare blankly at Princess Pamela. "What is the Union? Is it like Western Union where you go get money somebody sends you?"

"Well, no. It's more like—lemme see. You know how you are in the Cheetah Girls? Well, the five of you sing better together. It is better than one, no? Well, if all the countries in Europe join the EU, then they will be more strong, and they can use the same money—no more liras, the leu, which is the currency we use in Romania. "

"*Yo entiendo*. I understand. You are just watching your back, going for yours," I say, chuckling. "That's how we put it, anyway."

"Oh, I like that. I'm going for yours," Princess Pamela says excitedly. She loves when I teach her stuff.

"No, no—when you say it about yourself, you say, 'I'm going for mine,' otherwise it sounds like you're trying to steal something!"

"Yes, yes, of course. Okay, *beeneh*, enough with

my problems. Now you tell me the truth, my little Chanel, why are you *really* here?" Princess Pamela says, staring deeply into my eyes as if she is trying to hypnotize me without her crystal ball. "You could get into trouble if your mother knew you came to see me."

I tell Princess Pamela the whole story about the custody battle for Buffy's puppies and going into the studio with Mouse Almighty to record songs for a demo and how we're waiting forever, then all of a sudden, I break into tears and, that's right, another birthday piñata loses its Red Hots. Now I really can't stop crying because I feel safe with Princess Pamela.

"Oh, my little Chanel. You have your whole life ahead of you. If the Cheetah Girls are meant to be, they will be. It does not matter about the Mouse Little. No one can stop you," Princess Pamela says, holding me tight in her arms.

I burst out laughing, then correct her, "Mouse Almighty!"

"Whatever," Princess Pamela says, waving her graceful hand, which has a sparkly ring on every finger. She has the most boot-i-full jewelry. Once she gave me diamond stud earrings from Tiffany's which, I wear whenever Mamí is not around. "And don't worry about the puppy either.

You will get one," Princess Pamela says firmly.

Now my eyes get really wide with excitement because Princess Pamela's predictions really come true. *Es la verdad.* It's true. People come from all over the world just to get a reading from Princess Pamela. Even Papi told me she is a world-famous psychic.

"I see a furry creature with—how do you say again?" Princess Pamela asks, scrunching up her face so I can understand.

"Whiskers?" I ask, giggling.

"Right, *beeneh*, good—little whiskers coming up to your pillow, rubbing against your face—but he is trying sooo hard to get close to your heart," Princess Pamela says, tickling my chin with her fingers.

"But *Mamí* will never let me have a puppy," I whine, wrapping my arms tighter around Princess Pamela. "And how do you know it's a he?"

"Don't you worry, my little Chanel, her heart will soften. You will have your puppy," Princess Pamela says, kissing my cheek. "And to answer your question, the force in which he tries to get next to you tells me his energy is masculine."

"I hope you're right. About both things," I say, eyeballing the room that always makes me feel so warm. I feel a twinge of guilt that I am not wearing the boot-i-full Tiffany diamond stud earrings that Princess Pamela gave me, but I have hidden them in my closet for now so Mamí can't find them. Gazing next to the vase on the coffee table, I notice a big white book for the first time, *Property Restitution in Romania*. I feel so proud of Princess Pamela for fighting the government to help Romania be a better place for everybody.

"How about some shoobys?" Princess Pamela says. "I just made a fresh batch," she said, referring to her favorite pastry.

"No, thank you!" I say, unwrapping my arms from around Princess Pamela, who runs into the back to her kitchen. As much as I love Princess Pamela's pastry concoctions from Romania, I have to stick to my diet. I won't touch one if she brings them out here. Yawning, I reach into my cheetah backpack to check my Miss Wiggy cell phone.

"Aaaay!" I let out a loud shriek when I see the 1 MISSED CALL prompt on my cell phone. I hate when an incoming call goes right into voice mail without the phone ringing. I bet you it's Mamí. Nervously tapping my foot against the couch, I listen to the message. It *is* Mamí. A chill runs up my back as I listen to Mamí's message: *"Where are you? Dottie told me you already left. I'll see you when I get home."*

"Princess Pamela, I have to go!" I scream, shoving Miss Wiggy back into my bag.

"What happened, Chanel?" she says, running back into the room. But by the look on my face she already knows.

"I'll tell your daddy you said hello. You know Pucci is spending the night."

Good, I think to myself. I hope he never comes home. Who needs him.

"*La reverdere!*" Princess Pamela says, shoving the shoobys into my backpack.

Chapter
3

When I get home, I am so grateful that Mamí isn't there yet. Sneaking past the *giganto* life-size poster of Mamí from her modeling days, I hightail it to my bedroom, then change into my pink cheetah pajamas and slip on my fluffy pink rabbit slippers with the floppy ears. (I wanted them in cheetah, but they didn't have any.) Kneeling down, I start to pray, "Por favor, Dios, *please God, help me become a better person and think of other people instead of thinking about myself all the time. Please don't let* Mamí *come home and yell at me. Please let me forgive Bubbles for acting like a* babosa *today. Please let Princess Pamela help Romania. Okay, I'm sorry, I'm doing it again. God, do whatever you want. I'm sorry for giving you so many instructions. Amen.*"

When I hear the elevator door open, I realize that I flew home just in the nick of time. Mamí walks

168

into our loft apartment and yells, "Anybody home?" By the sound of her voice, I can tell she is in a good mood. *Gracias* gooseness. Maybe Robert DeNiro was at Nobu's tonight and told Mamí that she is still the prettiest girl in the room. Since DeNiro's the owner, Mamí is always hoping he is there when she goes. I know Mamí has a crush—*un coco*—on him since she was a model and met him at Studio 54. Back in the day, Studio 54 was the most famous disco in the world. She says he told her that she was the best dancer in the club, but I'm sure she is exaggerating.

"I'm here!" I shout out in the dark.

I quickly pull a book from my bookshelf, then plop down on my bed and pretend that I'm reading it. Daddy gave me the book for my birthday and I feel guilty that I haven't had time to read it yet. I know it's probably better than the boring book he got Pucci for his birthday (*Harry Henpecker's Guide to Geography*), because the cover is decorated with sparkles and the girls are wearing *tan coolio* outfits.

I was right about Mamí's sneaky ways. As she stands in the archway of my bedroom, pulling her hair up in a ponytail, I notice she is wearing my leopard top with the sash in the back and the "hippie" flared sleeves.

"Sorry I borrowed one of your tops again, but I wanted to look 'tight.' We went to Nobu," Mamí says, but I know she isn't *really* apologizing.

"*Está bien*. It's okay, *Mamí*," I respond, but I don't mean it either. (This is a little game we play with each other all the time.)

"Can you clean the bathroom tomorrow before you go to the store?" Mamí asks. "Okay," I say, mumbling like Barbie from Bozoland. You know the kind of doll that doesn't talk back. She doesn't sweat either. She doesn't eat too much. She's *perfecto*! But as hard as I try, I can't stop acting disappointed. "Um, did you talk to *Madrina* about the puppies?"

Mamí takes a deep sigh—the kind she takes when she gets really annoyed—*tan molesta*—with me. "I don't want to talk about it right now, Chanel. *Está bien*?"

"You don't have to talk about it—just tell me. Can I have a puppy, please?" I say whining.

"NO."

"What do you mean no? I never—"

"I mean the opposite of yes! How many times do I have to tell you the same answer! Hah? *Dígame*," Mamí says, prodding me. "You should be happy that I let you go to the studio to record the demo with the Cheetah Girls. But it's never enough with you. I give you a little—*un poco*—but you abuse everything. Just like you did with my credit card!"

I try really hard to be Barbie from Bozoland again, but I can't help it. "Ever since you met Mr. Tycoon, nothing else matters. I don't matter! We never spend time together anymore. That's why I need a puppy—so there is somebody waiting for ME when I get home!!!!"

Mamí stands there staring at me like she's going to perform *brujería* on me any second and stick pins into me to make me disappear. *Uh-oh.* I think I went too far.

"Finally I meet someone who likes me for me— not because I'm a model or I'm pretty. And you can't be happy for me?" Mamí says, and she is starting to tremble. "And, for your information, Mr. Tycoon has asked me to move to Paris. I told him I would let him know by the end of the week. I don't want to hear anymore about the stupid puppy. *Sí. Es bueno.* Paris will be good for us!"

Mamí storms off, then screams down the hall-way, "And you'd better clean the bathroom in the morning!"

Yo no lo creo. I can't believe it. How could she even think about moving to Paris? She really does-n't care about my dreams. I work so hard—going to school, rehearsing after school, and working in Madrina's store. Lying on the bed like a frozen Popsicle, I keep obsessing about all the things Mamí said. How could she say that about Daddy only liking her because she was pretty and a model?

I jump out of bed to log into the Phat Planet chat room so the Cheetah Girls can talk, but then I decide I don't want to. Bubbles, Dorinda, Aqua, and Angie are probably too busy playing with their puppies to talk to me anyway! I hold my Snuggles-and-Kisses stuffed dog real hard, and fight back the tears.

Cleaning the bathroom would not be that hard except I have to wipe *all* the oodles and oodles of Mamí's gooky hair stuff—there's hair spray, mousse, gel, spritzing lotion, coloring pomade, shining potion—it never ends! I'm surprised that Mamí's hair doesn't get confused by all the stuff she puts in it. (Okay, I use a little too, but not like she does.) Wiping the aerosol can of Suddenly Blond hair shine booster (yes, sometimes, Mamí, is suddenly blond), I realize, I can't be mean to Mamí today, because she won't give me money to get my hair straightened! I get so nervous that I drop the can and it suddenly starts spritzing on my leg. *Ay, Dios!* I hear the music blasting from the kitchen. Ever since Mamí started dating Mr. Tycoon she has been playing French music—the singer has a really low voice and sounds like she has a stuffed nose or something. *La Vie en Rose. La Vie en Rose.*

At least one thing hasn't changed—Mamí still drinks her cup of Spanish *café con leche* in the morning. She likes Café Bustelo, which is so strong, I can smell it all the way in the bathroom. *Gracias* gooseness, I finally finish cleaning the bathroom. I rub Mango Potion lotion on my hands (yes, it's Mamí's) then drag myself into the kitchen.

"What are you listening to?" I ask Mamí, to show her that I don't want to fight anymore.

"Edith Piaf," she says, sipping her coffee and ignoring me.

I don't know who Edith Piaf is, but she is probably someone famous in Paris, so I just blurt out the truth, "Mamí, I need to go to the hairdresser."

"If I give you money to go, will you shut up about this puppy already?" Mamí retorts.

"*Sí*," I say, but I know the truth inside. I would rather walk around looking like the Cookie Monster than give up the chance to get a puppy.

"Don't even think about going to that *bruja* to get your hair done, *esta bien*?" Mami says, handing me the money. I know she is talking about Princess Pamela, so I keep my lips closed like they are shut with Krazy Glue.

Walking to Madrina's boutique from my house, I stop to buy a big bag of raw carrots at Little Kim's Deli (not that Li'l Kim) on Grand Street. I pretend I don't notice the big fat sausage hanging over the counter, which looks like it's going to attack me. Paying for the carrots, I decide that tonight when I get home I'm going to start exercising even though Dr. Reuben said I should stay off my feet until my ankle heals. Well, my ankle feels fine and I want to make sure I'm as skinny as Zimora by the time we meet the record executives at Def Duck. I wish I could wave my magic wand and make myself tall like Zimora, but I can't. *Qué lástima*. I'm just a shrimpy like Bubbles and Dorinda. (Aqua and Angie are just a little taller than us but they are still short too.)

As soon as I get to the store, Madrina asks me to go get her a Caribbean Sunrise smoothie and offers to get me one. "I'm not hungry," I lie. All the way to the store, Once Upon a Tart, my mouth waters thinking about the coconut, strawberries, banana, yogurt, and pineapple juice concoction that Madrina and I usually drink together at the store. When I return with her smoothie, Madrina is steaming some cheetah bustiers and putting them on hangers.

"You look nice," I tell her, admiring her big leopard skirt with red leopard flowers trimming the hem. It's one of her original designs, but I wonder how she found leopard pumps that match with big red leopard flowers in the front, because Madrina doesn't design shoes. But that's Madrina—everything always matches. Now I feel embarrassed for eating the carrots because Madrina makes diva-size clothes and she thinks big is better.

"How is that construction going on by your house?" Madrina asks me.

"Noisy," I say, shrugging my shoulder.

"I found out the developers have already sold the lot to Banana Republic," Madrina says, annoyed. "You'd think they'd run out of bananas by now!"

I understand what Madrina is trying to say. Her boutique is *adobo down* and SoHo is supposed to be all about—*sabor*—and those big stores like Banana Republic don't have any original flavor. Kinda like the Cheetah Girls. We're one hundred percent *adobo down*—original flavor.

"I could help you with the steaming!" I say, volunteering because I know Madrina has a million things to do.

"You sure?" she asks hesitantly. "Good—I can

get to invoicing. By the way, Chanel, you know I did my best trying to talk Juanita into Operation: Puppy Patrol, but she's so stubborn. Getting an English bulldog to budge from a tea party would have been easier."

"*Sí, Madrina,* I know. *Yo se.* But at least she said I can go to Pepto's on Tuesday."

Pepto B. is Madrina's and Kahlua Alexander's hairdresser. He owns a trendy hair salon called Churl, It's You! He even arranged for us to meet Kahlua and she hooked us up with the Def Duck Record peeps.

"Oh, are you going to be another Diva with a Weava?" Madrina asks jokingly.

I know she is only playing with me. She knows Mamí would never let me get extensions. It's too expensive. Madrina let Bubbles get a weave when we performed for the Kats and Kittys Halloween Bash. I was a little jealous. *Un poco.* "No. I'm gonna get my hair straightened."

"Why?" she asks, surprised. You have such beautiful wild and wooly hair—it goes with your Cheetah Girls image!"

"I know, but it's gonna look nice, you'll see, " I say, wincing because I'm too embarrassed to tell Madrina the real reason why I'm getting my hair straightened—Zimora.

Bow-wow Wow!

"I think you girls should have gone with the pink wig routine myself, but oh, well, whatever makes you swell, Miss Chanel," Madrina says, dragging out a stack of papers from behind the accessories bureau.

"We liked the wig idea, but Aqua and Angie didn't want to wear them," I say quickly. I don't want Madrina to think we don't listen to her ideas. Bubbles found some wigs in Ricky's Urban Groove, but Aqua and Angie looked like they had a bottle of Pepto-Bismol stuck on their heads! (Mine looked really cute and so did Dorinda's.)

"Galleria will probably want to get her hair done, too," Madrina says, sipping her Caribbean Sunrise smoothie. "Ayyy, disgusting! Honey, you go and tell Pedro that the sun has set on this con- coction and he'd better use fresh strawberries instead of rotten ones."

I run back to Once Upon a Tart, then run back to the store and start steaming the bustiers.

By one o'clock, the steam had caused my frizzies to stick to my face.

"How are you doing back there, Miss Chanel?" Madrina yells from the front of the store.

"Okay," I say, not wanting to let her down. She probably would have finished everything by now, but as slow as I am, I'll be here all day sweating like Cinderella!

Chen Chen, the seamstress who does the in-store alterations for customers (the clothes are made in a factory in Brooklyn that Uncle Franco operates), comes from the back. "You okay?" she asks me. I nod my head, yes. Even Toto hops off his cheetah bed in the store window and comes over to rub his chubby furry body against my leg.

"Hi, Toto!" I kneel down to pet him for a second. I bet Bubbles is sitting home playing goo-goo ga-ga with her new puppy, Ragu.

The door chimes and another customer comes in. I jump up and get back to work. One of the customers comes toward the back and is peering in the accessories section. She smiles at me and I get a real creepy feeling. I mean, she kinda looks like a cross between Marceau the mime and Mystique the slithery mutant from the X-Men comic books. I wonder how she got her eyebrows so high and her skin to look so pasty white. Maybe she dusted her face with flour instead of pressed powder. "I'm looking for a leopard turban—a cloth one," the mutant mime lady says to me in a snobby voice.

"I don't think we have one," I say, trying to help.

"Well, why not? You have leopard everything else," she says, getting huffy puffy, then shooing me away like I don't know what I'm talking about.

"Can I help you, darling?" Madrina asks, coming to my rescue.

"Yes, I want a leopard turban—in a nice soft cotton Lycra."

"What on earth for?" Madrina asks. "That look went out with *Ali Baba and the Forty Thieves*. Why don't you try wrapping your hair with a nice leopard silk sash?"

I think Madrina is trying to tell the lady that wearing a turban is old school, but she always has a funny way of saying things. "Oh," the lady says, giving it some thought.

Toto runs up to Madrina and gets on his hind legs for her to pet him. He always does that in front of customers.

"Oh, look at him running to his master," the mutant lady says, smiling like a phony baloney.

"Darling, he's not a runaway slave," Madrina says, chuckling. Then she hands the lady a leopard silk sash. "Trust me, you'll get a lot more mileage out of this little number than the Arabian Nights contraption you had in mind."

"Well, if you say so," the mutant lady says, following Madrina to the front of the store. As she's leaving, Madrina says to her, "Darling, while you're down here in SoHo, go over and see Miss

Tanika at the MAC makeup store on Spring Street. Tell her Dorothea sent you. Miss Tanika is a magician with brow pencils and pressed powder."

"Oh, thank you, I will," the lady says.

Madrina watches the lady go down the block, then snorts, "She certainly was aghast from the past, wasn't she? The Grim Reaper has a warmer smile."

All of a sudden, the phone rings and the door buzzer *bling*s at the same time. Madrina picks up the phone and presses the door buzzer. Bubbles flings the door open. What is she doing here? I wonder.

"Well, well, Miss Chanel, the shopaholic in action," she says, smirking at me. She has Ragu wrapped in her arms in a cheetah doggie blankie.

I throw her a startled look. I want to blurt out, "Well, well, Miss Galleria, you're named after a shopping mall in Houston and that's why you're a cheetaholic!"

"Look, Chuchie, I'm sorry I behaved like a vending machine yesterday. You know, out of order. And I'm sorry that Auntie Juanita won't let you have a puppy," Bubbles says, hoisting Ragu to her chest. "What's going on with your hair, *mamacita*?"

"I'm working so I don't have time to worry about my hair," I blurt out, then walk to the back of the store, to finish steaming the new clothes. If Bubbles came here to show off Ragu again, she can put him in a puppy parade for all I care!

Of course Bubbles follows me to the back. "And Princess Pamela says I'm going to get a puppy!" I blurt out, dragging the steamer farther to the back.

"Hmm. Princess Pamela and her predictions. I hope she didn't charge you for that one," Bubbles says, pooh-poohing what my dad's girlfriend told me.

I throw Bubbles another nasty look.

"Come on, Chanel, let's just squash this thing like disco. Let it go. It's over," Bubbles says. "I came here to tell you the latest chat from the Phat."

"What happened?"

"I just found out a way we can get back our street cred with the peeps uptown," Bubbles says, dangling the carrot.

I just keep steaming the bustier and act like I'm not interested. I'm tired of Bubbles and her ideas— especially when they don't involve me getting a puppy!

"I found out on Phat Planet last night that the Harlem School of the Arts is having a Can We Get a Groove? competition for its 35th-year-anniversary fund-raiser." Bubbles continues, ignoring me. "I mean, while we're waiting for Mouse Almighty to get us into the studio again, we could be out there living *la vida loca*."

I still don't answer Bubbles and keep pressing the bustier like I'm looking for gold.

"Where were you yesterday, by the way?" Bubbles asks, annoyed.

"What happened?" I ask, puzzled.

"Why weren't you in the chat room last night? You know we were supposed to have a Cheetah Girls council meeting, right?"

"I was fighting with *Mamí*, so I didn't have time to go online," I say, exasperated. "She says we're moving to Paris!"

"Hold the phone. She said what?"

"Well, she said she doesn't want me to be in the Cheetah Girls—and she wants to move to Paris."

"She must have been drinking some supa crispy Chardonnay at Nobu's and it went straight to her head," Bubbles says.

"*Mamí* wouldn't leave *Abuela* behind, would she?" I ask, puzzled. My abuela Florita lives in Washington Heights, where Mamí grew up.

"Right," Bubbles says. "Listen up, buttercup. If we win the first prize in this competition, then finish the demo for the album, Juanita will have to squash the noise about Paris, right?"

I don't say anything because I am tired right

now of getting my hopes up about everything.

"I did mention there is a prize just waiting for us to get our paws on, didn't I?" Bubbles says, smirking.

"Really?" I ask, breaking out into a smile, then wiping the sweat from my forehead with the back of my hand.

"Would I pull a *señorita*'s slinky chain?" Bubbles says, taking out a cheetah tissue from her cheetah backpack. "And use this, please. You look like a ragamuffin on the run."

"So what are the prizes?" I say, grabbing the tissue because I'm anxious to hear.

"It's a goody bag situation from their sponsors. Let's see, there's a two-hundred-dollar gift certificate to the Girlie Show boutique, one hundred dollars' worth of S.N.A.P.S. cosmetics, gift certificates to Radio Shack, Maroon's Restaurant, and Barnes and Noble bookstore—I forget how much for each. Oh, and a one-year scholarship for the after-school program at the Harlem School of the Arts, of course," Bubbles says proudly.

"Well, it's not Prada, but it's not *nada* either!" I say, blowing the hair out of my face.

"That steam is killing my dreams. Can you turn it off for *un segundo, mamacita*?" Bubbles asks me.

"I'm finished anyway," I say, turning the dial off

on the steamer. "Well, I have to ask *Mamí* first."

"No way, José. Let our manager handle that," Bubbles says, smiling.

She's right. Madrina should talk to Mamí about anything that has to do with our career. That's what a manager is for, right? "*Mamí* gave me money to get my hair straightened," I tell Bubbles.

"To Pepto's right?" Bubbles asks.

"*Si.*"

"I wanna go too!" Bubbles says, then does the Roadrunner to the front of the store to talk to Madrina, who is just getting off the phone with an impatient customer.

"Some of these women need to get a life—not another outfit!" Madrina says, putting down the receiver. "Galleria, what happened? Don't tell me you got skirt-jacked!" Madrina says, looking at Bubbles's tiny pleated cheetah micromini in horror.

"Nothing happened, Mom," Galleria says, rolling her eyes.

"Don't you think you're taking the schoolgirl look a little too far?"

"Mom, you know it's the latest style—everybody's wearing them," Bubbles says, ignoring Madrina's protest.

"As far as I'm concerned, no one should wear a

skirt that's only one inch longer than a ruler. I can't wait till this apology-for-a-skirt joins its cousin— neon yellow lip gloss—in the fashion cemetery."

"Mom, save your breath for last. Chuchie is getting her hair—"

Madrina cuts her off. "Yes, calm down, Galleria. You can go—on two conditions."

"Condition one?"

"You extend the moratorium on Biggies bubble gum for one more week."

"Hold up. Another week without bubble gum? Are you trying to kill the economy?" Bubbles spurts.

"Like Gloria Gaynor, the bubble gum industry will survive," Madrina says firmly.

"Okay—what's condition number two?" Bubbles says, now visibly upset that she can't resume the glory in her nickname.

"If I give you money to get your hair straightened, then you have to put that skirt in the back of the closet until it grows—or you do," Madrina says adamantly.

"Okay," Bubbles says, knowing she has been defeated.

"And, by the way, you shouldn't be bringing Ragu here," Madrina says, annoyed.

"Don't worry, Mom, he's hiding in his blankie—

and I'm gonna go right back home. I just wanted to tell Chuchie—and ask you—about us performing in this talent show on Saturday."

Another talent show?" Madrina asks, her eyebrows raising over her glasses.

"Mom, we're sitting around waiting for Mouse Almighty to get us into the studio again—I mean, I'm going cheetah crazy!" Bubbles says, tapping her feet impatiently. "All he cares about right now is finishing Kahlua's album."

"Well, darling, you have to understand that she is everybody's favorite platinum pussycat right now. Your album hasn't even gone 'tin' yet."

But we don't have an album!" Bubbles blurts out.

"That's the facto exacto," Madrina says, sewing cheetah sequin flowers onto a bustier.

"Did I tell you what one of the prizes is?" Bubbles says, dangling the bait. "A gift certificate to Maroon's Restaurant."

"Well, why didn't you say that in the first place?" Madrina says, smiling. Maroon's is her favorite Caribbean and soul food restaurant. After eating a piece of their red velvet cake, Madrina says she can conquer the world. "Yes, the talent show will be good for you. Yes, I'll talk to Juanita. Yes, I'll make sure the Cheetah Girls are entered into the competition. Now take Ragu home and don't leave him alone or give him a bone!"

"Thank you, Mom," Bubbles says, excited, then pulls my arm for me to walk her out of the store. "Come on, Chuchie, walk me outside and let the 'Riddler' do her work!"

Chapter 4

In school, Bubbles is always—*siempre*—the leader of our crew, grabbing (all the attention) or gabbing (about the Cheetah Girls game plan) to any of the Fashion Industries East peeps who'll listen—which is mostly everybody ever since the Cheetah Girls were flown to Hollywood to perform in the Def Duck Records New Talent Showcase. I'm not bragging, but we have gotten more hookups than all the other peeps at school (even the seniors) and that is why some of them are *muy celoso*—very jealous—of the Cheetah Girls "growl power," since we're only freshmen.

Today, though, I can't tell who is gabbing more—Dorinda or Bubbles. I am so sick of both of them munching on everything. I know it's probably because I haven't eaten lunch and the only thing I have to munch on are my stupid carrots, but I just want to scream at both of them, *Cáyate la boca!* Shut your traps, *está bien.*

It's finally three o'clock and the three of us are standing by the lockers, when we run into Daisy Duarte. She is wearing a pair of pink suede UGG boots. I want a pair of those too because they are *tan coolio.* "I love your boots!" I moan to Daisy.

"They are my early Christmas present from *Papi,*" she says, smiling. Daisy is Dominican and her parents are divorced like mine, so we have a lot in common. But Bubbles cuts right in and starts talking about her braces. Then Dorinda starts in with the puppy tales from the projects! "Word, as soon as I opened the door to my house, *everybody* was ready to pounce on me—and trying to get at Nobu," Dorinda says, chuckling, recalling her first day bringing Nobu home. "Kenya tried to put Nobu in the toilet to give him a bath! Topwe snuck into the kitchen and put some Cheerios and milk in a bowl. He was worried that Nobu would get hungry or something. And Corky was crying because we wouldn't let Nobu sleep in *his* room. It was cheetah crazy yesterday at my house!" Corky, Kenya, and Topwe, of course, are three of Dorinda's eleven foster brothers and sisters who she lives with in the Cornwall Projects on 116th Street.

I start to feel sooo jealous again—*tan celosa otra*

vez—about Dorinda's pooch that I blurt out to her, "How is Gaye?" just so she can change the channel, *está bien*. Gaye is Dorinda's newest foster sister. Even though their apartment is already too crowded, Mrs. Bosco agreed to take Gaye in because she was abandoned in a park. (And that's how we got the hookup for the Mariah Carey concert at Madison Square Garden. See, when the Charm Bracelet diva heard about Gaye in the newspapers, she donated concert tickets to the foster care agency.)

"Oh, she didn't go near Nobu. I think she was kinda scared of him," Dorinda says, chuckling.

I feel my cheeks getting *caliente*. I didn't ask Dorinda about Nobu. I asked her about Gaye. No more—*no mas*! I keep quiet because nobody is listening to me anyway. Daisy just keeps nodding her head (kinda like a puppy too) until Dorinda says, "Chanel, that's foul your mom won't let you keep a puppy, but you can come over anytime to see Nobu, okay?"

"*Yo se*. I know," I say, trying to smile. I am so embarrassed that she said that in front of Daisy! And no way, José, would I come over her house to steal affection from her puppy.

Now Bubbles makes it even worse. "Tell Daisy about Princess Pamela's prediction. '*Ooooooo*—there is a furry creature waiting to cuddle with you!' "

Now my cheeks are burning, but I pretend like I'm not embarrassed. Besides, Daisy is Dominican like me, so she understands things like *brujería* and doesn't make fun of it like Bubbles does. I fix Bubbles's wagon, though, because I tell Daisy in Spanish. She is so nice, she nods her head and says, "I hope you get one, *mija*."

Daisy tells us she has to hurry up and get to her babysitting job, but now Bubbles is going on about the Can We Get a Groove? competition on Saturday night.

Kadeesha Ruffin and her crew, who are the only girls on the school's basketball team, pile next to our lockers. Kadeesha is always eavesdropping on Bubbles. All of a sudden, she goes into her locker and pulls out a book, then says really loudly, "Yo, did y'all write this?" She is pointing at the cover of the book that everybody at school is reading after school, *Confessions of a Backup Singer* by Anonymous. "Oops, that's right, y'all ain't got a record deal yet. Well, you'd betta be taking notes 'cuz this is what y'all gonna be doing *real* soon— *backing up*."

Of course, Kadeesha and her cronies, including Backstabba (who stole her nickname from the lead singer of Karma's Children), exchange some more snickers and woof-woofs. Then she turns and gives *me* a look like, "Yeah, I think you're whack. What?"

I turn away quickly because I really don't like them. There is nothing we hate worse than people who are copycats. Peeps can make fun of us all they want, but we, the Cheetah Girls, are original. *Pura vida.*

"Yeah, well, maybe you should pick up a copy of *Full Court Press-On* because that's what you'll be doing after you graduate," Bubbles blurts out. "Fixing your broken nails during halftime at the *playground.*"

Backstabba flings her arm full of tick-tacky rubber bracelets in Bubbles's face but Bubbles doesn't flinch. "Yeah, well, get ready for the cheetah chomp down—coming real soon."

"Yeah, well, betta hurry over to Mickey D's and try their new special. I think you'll dig it—a jerk sandwich," Bubbles riffs.

Derek and Mackerel scurry in our direction to bite on the beef jerky. "Oh, snaps, the Cheetah Girls are at it again," says Derek Ulysses Hambone with his crony Mackerel Johnson in tow. "Guess you could say they always got more pounce to the ounce." The Red Snapper, which is the official nickname we gave Derek, is also a design major like Dorinda and has a giganto crush on Bubbles.

Mackerel is kinda cute, but I never pay him any attention because he is really shy. Today, though, he smiles at me before he shoves his hands into his oversized jeans pockets. I look down at the floor because he makes me uncomfortable.

Derek leans on the locker next to Bubbles. "Hambone, what're you holding, because we have to bounce. I'm off to the ortho—"

"Oh, trust, we know," Hambone says, putting his hands together over his mouth like he is Principal Daly holding his megaphone and about to make an announcement to the students: "ATTENTION, ALL GIRLIES AND BOYZEES. WE HAVE A CHEETAH GIRLS UPDATE LIVE FROM THE SERENGETI CONSERVATION CAMP. GAL-LERIA GARIBALDI, THEIR STYLING FELINE LEADER, WILL BE MORE FEROCIOUS THAN EVER COME TOMORROW WHEN HER METAL JAWS ARE REMOVED. THAT'S RIGHT. THIS IS AN ALL-POINTS BULLETIN ALERT. WATCH OUT—'CUZ NOW THE CHEETAH GIRLS ARE 'BOUT TO UNLEASH THE NOISE—*FOSHIZ-ZLE.*"

"Well, thank you for doing what you do best— *hamming* it up!" Bubbles says, slamming her locker shut. "Now if you'll excuse us, we have to make the next stop on our busy itinerary."

"What, you're not going to invite us to watch you get down at the Can We Get a Groove? competition on Saturday?" Derek asks, flashing his gold tooth. Bubbles looks at Derek, impressed.

"Oh, trust, the bathroom walls have ears," Mackerel chimes in. "Not that it would be too hard getting the Cheetah Girls' full *itinerary* around here—considering you announce it every half hour." Even I snicker at that remark (because it's true).

Bubbles throws Mackerel a look like he's in choppy waters.

"Oops," Mackerel says, doing *our* Cheetah Girls handshake with Hambone.

"Oh, you two are so cutie patootie," Bubbles says, smirking, "you should have a wedding ceremony and wear matching *fins*. As for Saturday, if you've got the duckets to pay at the door, then I guess you will be seeing us perform. What can I say? It's a free country."

"Thank you for that heartwarming speech, Miss America—trust, we'll be there in the front row," Hambone says, clutching his Starter jacket. "Oh, and we'll be rolling up first thing tomorrow mornin'. Can't wait to see those shiny fangs— oops, I mean teeth—out of prison."

"Whoa, ease up, cowboy—gotta have a cup of

cappuccino before I stomach the likes of you that early. Can we start that rodeo around noon?" Bubbles says, looking at the gold tooth in Derek's mouth. "Oh, and maybe it's time for you to take a cue—why don't you let go of a little *precious* metal yourself, huh, Mr. Duh?"

Derek just stands there looking goo-goo-eyed. Sometimes I don't think he catches Bubbles's drift. "Whatever makes you clever, Cheetah Girl," Derek says, waving good-bye at us like his arms are fins.

"Oh, Do', I have been hanging on to these forever," Bubbles says, turning her back on Derek and opening her locker again. "Daddy got them duplicated!" Now Bubbles whips out pictures of all of us with Mariah Carey in her dressing room after the concert. "Everybody gets one, but, Do', you get three so you can give one to Tiffany."

Dorinda is the official keeper of the Cheetah Girls scrapbook, and Tiffany is Dorinda's adopted sister who came to the concert with us. "Oh, Tiffany is gonna go gaga for this! Good looking out, Galleria," Dorinda says, placing the photos in her backpack like they are gold.

"Can a brother get a peek too?" Derek says, peering over Bubbles's shoulder.

Bubbles probably pulled the photos out just to impress Derek and Mackerel. They were sooo green with Gucci envy that we got to go to the Mariah concert in the first place.

Bubbles just ignores Derek and goes on about Mariah in the photos. "Wow, she really *is* tall—she doesn't seem that much shorter than Mom. She is definitely wearing Dolce head to toe."

"Word?" Dorinda says, scrunching up her nose.

"Her shoes—they must have five-inch heels. They have to be Dolce."

"Oh, right," Dorinda says, nodding, then hoisting up her backpack. "I gotta go take care of Nobu before they fry him for lunch."

Bubbles grabs my arm (which I hate) and starts walking us down the corridor to the exit so we can get to her orthodontist appointment.

We are waiting in Dr. Gold's office for over an hour, so I start tapping my feet out of nervousness.

"Chuchie, you seem jumpy, bumpy," Bubbles says, flipping through a *Cosmo Girl* magazine.

I know I should tell her about my secret plan, but I don't want her to try and stop me. Bubbles is my best friend, but sometimes she thinks she knows everything. (I mean, she has a nice figure and it looks good on her. But when I gain weight, I just look like a toothpick with an olive in the middle, *está bien*.)

The office phone rings. "Galleria, it's your

mother on the phone," Ornella, the receptionist, says, handing Bubbles the receiver.

Mom, why didn't you hit me on Miss Wiggy?" Bubbles asks impatiently. "Don't worry, I told you I'll have Ornella call you as soon as we finish. Did we get in? Wow, really? Okay. Okay. Bye. Oh, all right, Mom!" Bubbles hands the receiver back to Ornella.

"My mom feels bad she couldn't get away from the store to be here—that's why she's calling," Bubbles explains to Ornella, who just nods her head and smiles politely. I know Bubbles is embarrassed that Madrina called to check up on her.

"Mom says we're in there like swimwear for the competition on Saturday," Bubbles says excitedly, leaning on the receptionist's counter and fiddling with her cheetah applejack cap. Bubbles is so happy that she will be performing without her braces finally. Bubbles looks at Ornella again and explains to her about the Can We Get a Groove? competition.

"That's really nice," Ornella says, beaming at both of us. She has really big white teeth and a pretty brown complexion like Aqua and Angie. I wonder what country she is from, but I don't want to be rude and ask her.

All of a sudden, Bubbles whips out her Kitty Kat notebook, the one she uses just for writing songs.

"Wow, I got a new drift—Bow-wow Wow!" she exclaims, then starts scribbling in the notebook, humming a melody to herself, which sounds a lot like Snoop Dog's song. (It's obvious that Bubbles has puppy on the brain all the time now.)

"Are you left-handed?" Ornella asks Bubbles, her big brown eyes opening even wider.

"Yes, I am," Bubbles says, nodding, and still scribbling.

"In my country that means you come from royal blood," explains Ornella.

"Really?" asks Bubbles. "What country is that—'cuz I should move there!"

"Well, I'm actually from Gabon—but I was born in a village called Medoumou," Ornella explains. "Off the coast of West Africa."

"Maybe when we're famous, we'll get to perform there," Bubbles says excitedly. "We're gonna try and go to every place on the planet!"

"Well that sounds like a plan," Ornella says politely.

"My dad is from Bologna," Bubbles says proudly. "So I speak Italian too."

Ornella nods her head and keeps smiling.

"Do you think it's gonna hurt?" Bubbles asks.

"Wearing braces is the hard part," Ornella says calmly. "Getting them off is easy."

"Good, because I can't wait!!" Bubbles says, tapping the pen on the counter to the "Bow-wow Wow!" melody.

A woman wearing a long white cape and pajama pants comes from the back and stands at the receptionist counter. It's a good thing Madrina isn't here because she would want to send the lady's *Star Wars: The Final Frontier* outfit to the fashion cemetery and bury it along with leopard turbans and yellow lipstick, *está bien*.

"How's my favorite Cheetah Girl!" Dr. Gold shouts, coming from the back and giving Galleria a hug, then taking her arm. "Come on back into my den of torture!"

Galleria looks back at me, then says with a snicker, "Hang tight, Chuchie. And don't forget to read my horoscope."

Why did Bubbles ask me to read her horoscope? Aqua always does that, not me.

Ornella finally looks at me and smiles. "She certainly is excited, isn't she?"

I wanted to say, Yeah, *all the time*, but I just smile back at Ornella and say, "Yeah."

"Do you two perform together?" Ornella asks innocently.

Even though I feel my cheeks sting, I try to act like the question doesn't bother me. Bubbles didn't tell her I was part of the Cheetah Girls. "Yeah," I explain, "Bubbles and I started the group together."

"The two of you must look really cute on stage together," Ornella says. I know she is trying to be nice, but I have to correct her.

"Bubbles and I started singing together—like when we were six or something. But now we have a group—the Cheetah Girls. There are five of us."

The phone rings again and Ornella answers it. I sneak into my cheetah backpack and take out my bag of carrots and start chomping on them.

"Oh, I'm sorry, but you can't eat in here," Ornella says nicely.

Now I really feel like day-old nachos—not so fresh!

Suddenly Bubbles comes from the back by herself and she is smiling like she just won the Miss America contest. "Wow, I can't believe how your teeth look!" I say, surprised because she doesn't really look like herself without her braces. Now I feel insecure. Maybe I should have gotten braces too?

"Can you believe it, *mamacita*?" Bubbles says, grinning ear to ear. "Now we're definitely ready for Freddy. Come Saturday night, winner takes all!"

Chapter 5

Even though it's supa chilly, the Fashion Industries East peeps are crowding the sidewalk outside of our big ugly school. They never stop blowing cold air out of their mouths and tap dancing in their galoshes and fancy UGG boots to keep their feet toasty.

"Wait up, yo," Dorinda says, running to catch up with us. She takes a different subway than we do and we always meet outside. "Bow-wow-wow!" Bubbles snickers when she sees Dorinda's new brown knit cap with a big white bichon frise appliqué stuck right in front.

"I made it last night," Dorinda giggles, touching the adorable doodad she made out of a piece of white felt, then sewed onto a plain knit cap. "Nobu tried to lick it!"

"Hook me up, Do'," Bubbles exclaims. "Make

me one. I'll give you my tan cap to put it on."

I want one too, but I keep my *boca* closed and just smile at Dorinda like, *Oh, you are so cutie patootie.*

"Okay, I'll make you one on one condition," Dorinda starts in.

"Wow, you're beginning to sound more like my mother every day," Bubbles says, raising her eyebrows.

"Well, you have to tell me exactly what is a bichon frise—because Twinkie won't let me sleep until I tell her every last detail," Dorinda chuckles. Twinkie is also one of Dorinda's foster sisters.

"Okay, where do we begin? Um, nobody knows where the breed comes from exactly, but they were definitely a favorite among the royal families, starting from around the fifteenth century," Bubbles says like a know-it-all. I didn't even know she knew that much about anything other than writing songs. "They made the perfect lapdogs for kings of choice but don't think the bumpin' bichon isn't always turning out a few surprises. Today in Norway they have found out that bichons can be trained to round up sheep. How do you like that, Little Bo Peep?"

"Twinkie will be happy. I'll tell Nobu too when he's older," Dorinda chuckles proudly.

"Oh, and just tell Twinkie they are happy, snappy dogs who like sausages and lots of kisses!" adds Bubbles. She never wears lipstick to school, but today she put on her new tube of S.N.A.P.S. lipstick Getdown Brown, and her lips look really juicy. "Aren't you going to say anything, Do'?"

"My bad! Wow, your teeth look amazing!" Dorinda says, putting her arms around Bubbles as we walk into the middle of the block.

True to his Red Snapper words, Derek is standing practically in the middle of the street to scope our arrival. He has on his usual supersize-me Starter jacket in that ugly khaki color. For design majors, Derek and Mackerel are kinda boring in the style department. They just dress like everybody else. Unlike us, the Cheetah Girls, who are always *adobo down*. Today, *la gente*—peeps—are really checking out our flavor. That's probably because Derek makes a high-pitched noise like an animal on the prowl when he sees Bubbles.

"Get ready for a cheetah takeover!" Derek cackles like a jackal. I can't believe that Bubbles breaks out in a big grin instead of acting mad like she usually does when Derek is macking her. *Ay, Dios mío.* Now that Bubbles has her braces off, she is going to get all the attention. I snap out of my *celoso* thoughts when I notice that Kadeesha and

Backstabba are rolling their eyes in our direction. Even Keisha Jackson's eyes are turning green with Gucci envy. Keisha is another pest in our homeroom class, and right from the start she never really liked Bubbles.

I start feeling Red Hots in my tummy again, but luckily, LaRonda Evans gives Bubbles a shout-out that everybody can hear, "Hey, Galleria. You look *cheetah-licious!*" LaRonda is in Dorinda's homeroom class. (Dorinda even invited LaRonda to the Mariah Carey concert, so she is supa cool with us now.)

"Feeling *cheetah-licious*," Bubbles riffs back, breaking into another big smile.

"Hi, LaRonda," I say, but she ignores me because she is too busy gagging at Bubbles without her braces. "Wow, did it hurt?"

"A little—but nothing I couldn't handle. After five years of heavy metal, there is nothing like the taste of freedom!"

I can't believe Bubbles. I remember when she first got her braces, she was crying like a baby until Madrina took us to Mr. Sniddles Ice Cream Parlor and let Bubbles eat two double-scoop Mallomars ice cream cones! (I only had one. *Te juro.*)

Dorinda looks at me and shrugs her tiny little shoulders like, "Datz Bubbles for ya." Dorinda does look so cute with Nobu on her head, but nobody says anything about her new cap because they are too busy goospitating about Bubbles's new teeth.

Derek wheedles his way next to Bubbles and I can tell he really is goospitating. Mackerel looks at me, then digs his hands into his pockets. Maybe I should be nice to him. Nobody else pays attention to me. "Are you coming Saturday to see us perform?" I ask him nervously. I start pulling at my hair in front, trying to straighten it, but I can't feel the strands through my pink woolly mitten. Mackerel looks at me like he's startled that I'm speaking to him.

"Um, yeah, we are definitely going," he replies, shuffling his feet. "You gonna be singing some new songs?"

I wonder if he means, did Bubbles write a new song. All of a sudden, I hear myself saying, "Well, we're working on a new song now that I'm writing too."

"Oh, word?"

I can tell by the way Mackerel responds that he is impressed.

"Um, yeah—Bow-wow-Wow," I add quickly, then look over nervously at Bubbles to make sure she didn't hear. But she is too busy eating up all the attention from peeps at school to hear what I'm saying. Shuffling my feet to keep them warm, I start wondering, What is wrong with *una pequeña mentira*. A little fib-eroni, huh?

"Yeah, I do write some of the songs too. We co-wrote the song 'It's Raining Benjamins' together," I say boldly. That part is true, even though Bubbles doesn't want to give me credit for writing the song because she says that I didn't contribute enough. (I don't understand why she's getting so technical about the percentage; it's not like we're collecting publishing royalties or something.)

"Oh, yeah, that's the song y'all performed in Hollywood?" Mackerel says.

Wow, now I'm impressed. I didn't know he paid so much attention to the Cheetah Girls' every smooth move. I try not to stare at Mackerel, but he is kinda cute. He is Bubbles's complexion and has cute freckles. If he would just fix the big gap in his front teeth he would be so much cuter. My mind starts working again. Maybe I should suggest that he goes to Bubbles's dentist?

"*Sí*, that's the song!" I say quickly, so I can shake away thoughts of insulting Mackerel. Bubbles is looking over at us now, so I'm careful about what I say. Mackerel just stands there staring at me, anyway. "Is Mackerel your real name?" I blurt out.

"Yup. My father used to go fishing for Spanish mackerel down in Florida," Mackerel explains. "My mom says even my yellow freckles look like their spots."

"I have an aunt who lives in Miami," I say excitedly.

"Word? You ever heard of Plantation Island?"

"No," I reply, embarrassed because I haven't. Now that makes two places in two days I never heard of—Plantation Island, Florida, and Gabon, West Africa.

"Well, we lived near there. Lots of water. I do love to swim—maybe I am like the king mack, you know."

I just stare blankly at Mackerel because I thought he said he was named after the Spanish mackerel. But maybe it's like having relatives; you're all part of the same family even though some of the names are different.

As if reading my mind, Mackerel quickly adds, "That's, like, another species. I guess if I had a choice I would have named myself after the king mackerel. But I didn't," he adds, chuckling. "Personally, I think the king mack is flyer looking. It has this purplish blue color that shimmers under water. Um, you can see them real up close because they always swim right under the surface. I'd go fishing with my father sometimes. Um, yeah, there's a lot of other mackerel species too."

Now I know Mackerel is nervous because he is babbling and that isn't his style at all. Wow, I didn't know that Mackerel was so smart. Twirling my hair through my mittens, I can't help thinking, Maybe he won't like me when he finds out I'm not as smart as he is!

"Maybe we should hang out sometimes," Mackerel says. "Um, what are you doing after school today? Um, I can—I wanna roll over to China Fun before practice."

After school, Mackerel and Derek play basketball a lot at the YMCA on 63rd Street, which is near Aqua and Angie's school. I ponder his proposition, but I know I can't go to China Fun, because I will be tempted by all those crispy egg rolls, pork fried rice, and juicy dumplings.

Quickly I ponder a solution. "We could go to Papaya King?" I offer, "but I have to be at, um— somewhere at five o'clock." I don't want to tell Mackerel that I am going to the beauty parlor to get my hair straightened.

"Yeah, that's cool. I'll hook up with you then," Mackerel says, satisfied with our game plan.

Finally, Bubbles is finished gabbing with everybody so we can get to homeroom on time, but she is still interested in my conversation with Mackerel. "I saw you macking with the Mackerel. You must be hooked!"

"No, I'm not," I protest. I'm not going to tell Bubbles what we talked about because it may sound stupid. I have to tell her that I'm meeting him, so I blurt out, "We're gonna go to Papaya King after school."

Bubbles threw me that look like I'm a bobo head. "You can't meet him. You know Pepto B. gets queasy if we're late for our blow-dryer date!"

"But we don't have to be there till five o'clock." I protest. "You and Derek can come with us. Then we can go to—"

"What are you now, my social planner?" Bubbles says, putting on her smirk face. "The only place I'd ever go with Mr. Duh is to the dentist for a gold-digging outing!"

"Okay, so I'll go by myself," I stammer. I'll show Bubbles she isn't the only one who can get someone to like her. I bet if Eddie Lizard called right now and said he wanted to meet her after school, she would drop me like a soggy egg roll—and just tell me to wait for her at Pepto B.'s like a puppy dog!

"Okay, you can meet him, but you're not going by yourself. I'm coming with you," Bubbles says, like she is my mother! I hate when Bubbles does that. "I'll sit at a table with Derek—but you owe me *double* big-time, *mamacita*!

"What happened?" I ask, puzzled. "Double big time?"

"Oh, you don't think I'm helping you with your Italian homework at lunchtime because I have nothing better to do? Do you, Chuchie?" Bubbles asks adamantly. "I'd rather be doing something useful like painting my toenails in my favorite Pow! shade nail polish in a grungy school restroom stall than helping you with a subject I already know. Know what I'm saying?"

"*Está bien.* Okay, Bubbles," I stammer. I wish I didn't need Bubbles's help with my Italian home-work, but I do because I hate it. My Italian teacher, Mr. Lepidotteri, doesn't cut me any slack. Boy, if my homework weren't due today at last period, I would tell Bubbles to stuff mozzarella up her nose, but I can't. *Yo no puedo.*

"See you lunchtime," I say cheerfully as we walk down the hallway.

Leave it to Mamí to ruin my first date with Mackerel. Right when I'm leaving school, she calls me on Miss Wiggy to tell me that I have to pick Pucci up from his karate lessons after school.

"*Parate*, Chanel! Stop it and just do what I tell you to do," Mamí screams into the phone receiver.

I slam my Miss Wiggy cell phone closed and fight back the tears.

"What did she say?" Bubbles asks, concerned.

"The meeting with her book editor got pushed up so we have to go to the Tae Kwon do Center on 100th Street and pick up Pucci," I answer, pouting. I know Mamí is trying to get a deal for a new book about the rise and fall of oil tycoons and their girlfriends, called *It's Raining Tycoons*. "I hate her!"

"How do you spell relief?" Bubbles says, letting out a sigh. "I sure didn't want to get that up close and personal with Derek's 'gold rush' anyway. Guess we're back to you owing me big-time—just once."

It's just like Bubbles to always think of herself. What about me?

"Are you gonna come with us?" Bubbles asks Dorinda as we walk to the subway.

"I don't have any come-with money. And I gotta get home to help with the kids—and Nobu," Dorinda says.

"Oh, come on, Do', remember how much fun we had that time we went to Churl, It's You! We could become like a beauty parlor quartet!" Bubbles says, trying to get her way. The last time we went to Churl, It's You! we sang a song for Kahlua Alexander. She was in town to star in the movie *Platinum Pussycats*, and she only trusts Pepto B. to put in her extensions.

"Quartet is four?" Dorinda asks, puzzled, squinching up her tiny nose.

"I know that, Do', but I'm just riffing off barber shop quartet," Bubbles explains. "Come on, please. Aqua and Angie are gonna meet us there. We'll be better than any Sixties act could be—the Cheetah Girls in all their spots?"

"All right, I guess it's cool. I can just hang," Dorinda says, giving in but looking a little worried. Bubbles hands the Missy Wiggy cell phone to Dorinda so she can call her foster mother, Mrs. Bosco.

I wish I had the money to pay for Dorinda to get her hair done too. For true. *Es la verdad*. (When I charged all the stuff on Mamí's credit card, I bought Dorinda a *tan coolio* outfit for our meeting with Jackal Johnson, a big Willie record manager who turned out to be crooked.)

"Wait a *segundo*," Bubbles says, looking puzzled. "That means, we won't have time to take Pucci down to your house, so we have to take him with us to Pepto's?"

We give each other a look like, Oh, no, not again.

See, they hate Pucci at Churl, It's You! The last time he was there, he was showing off the stupid scooter Mamí brought him from Paris and crashed into the popcorn machine. The hairstylists were picking up kernels for days afterward. "Well, at least he won't have Flammerstein & Schwimmer with him, so what could possibly go wrong?" Bubbles says, shoving her hands in her cheetah mittens.

"What am I supposed to do about meeting Mackerel?" I ask, biting my lower lip.

"He'll get over it," Bubbles says, waving her hand like she just don't care. Then she starts looking at me funny. "Chuchie, are you using Auntie Juanita's makeup again?"

"Why?" I stammer.

"You look kinda orange," Bubbles says, unsure of what is wrong with my complexion. "Doesn't she, Do'?"

I can tell Dorinda doesn't want to say anything wrong because she gets real quiet, then blurts out, "Um, your face does look a little different, Chanel."

"No, it doesn't," I say, brushing them off.

I get lost in my thoughts as we walk toward the subway station. What am I going to tell Mackerel? Maybe he's going think I didn't want to go out with him?

Bubbles grabs my arm so we can walk faster, but I look around quickly to see if I spot Mackerel and Derek, but I don't. How bozo. When I want to see him he's not anywhere. Stopping at the corner of 25th Street, I start thinking more cuckoo thoughts. Maybe he didn't really want to go out with me? He was just being nice. Nobody wants to go out with me. They only like Bubbles! All of a sudden, I lose my balance and fall off the curb, right in front of a fast-moving yellow taxi.

"Chuchie!" Galleria screams, yanking me out of the street and back on the sidewalk. "That taxi almost took you straight to ER. And I don't mean the show, hello?"

"*Lo siento.* I'm sorry," I mumble, flustered.

Bubbles looks at me like I'm a puppy in need of a hug. "Don't tell me you're sorry. Tell yourself, Miss Cuchifrita. What is wrong with you?"

"Nothing. *Nada!*" I protest and this time I'm not telling *un pequeño* fib-eroni. Everthing is wrong. *Todo está whacko!*

"Are you okay, Chanel?" Dorinda asks.

"Yes."

"Are you okay, miss?" asks a big man with big Mr. Magoo glasses.

"Yes," I say, fighting back the tears. I don't want to start crying right on the sidewalk. I tell the man,

"Thank you for helping," and smile at the other people watching us. I'm sooo embarrassed.

"Come on, Miss Cuchifrito," Bubbles says, holding my arm, then looking at the people who are still staring at us. "She's all right."

Walking me carefully down into the subway, Bubbles riffs, "Man, that is the one thing I love about the Big Apple. There is always somebody there to pick you up when you fall down like a rag doll on the sidewalk!"

Chapter 6

Pucci thinks he looks *tan coolio* in his white starched karate outfit. "I got a yellow belt today!" Pucci exclaims to Bubbles outside of Churl, It's You! hair salon. I don't care what Pucci got. I just wish he was somewhere else right now instead of with me. Dorinda and I stare starry-eyed inside the salon's box window. We could gaze at the sparkly pink neon sign with the floating brown mannequin heads covered in pink, blue, yellow, green, and purple wigs all day.

"I think your mom was right; maybe we should have gotten wigs for our act," Dorinda says, still totally mesmerized by the window display.

"Wait till she sees me with straightened hair. Then she'll realize we are headed 'straight' for a gold record," Bubbles says, heckling. I can't believe

216

Bubbles. Now she's acting like getting our hair straightened was *her* idea?

"I said I got a yellow belt today," Pucci screams louder at Bubbles, pulling her sleeve.

"I know. I'm not surprised, because you're the man, Pucci," Bubbles says, holding the door of the salon open for him. The musical chimes go off, and a recording starts playing: *"Churl, It's You! Work the blue! Think pink like I do! Get sheen with green! We love—guess who!"*

"That is so goofy," Pucci says, making fun of the salon's jingle.

"Look, big man, you'll be a black belt in no time," Bubbles says, still pumping up Pucci.

"Uh-uh. I can't get one until I'm sixteen!" Pucci protests.

"Word?" Dorinda asks. I know she is supa curious about kung fu moves, because she is the most daring of all of us—gymnastics, Rollerblading, boxing—Dorinda digs it all.

We are standing at the receptionist's desk waiting for Fantasia, the purple-haired receptionist to get off the phone. "You got the top and the pants? You are too Fubu for me, girl. Hmm. Hmm. I signed up for singing lessons—shoot I was Fantasia before that heffa knew how to burp. All right, but tell me quick. I got customers waiting."

Bubbles looks at me and whispers, "Wasn't Fantasia's hair red the last time we were here?"

I nod my head, *Sí*.

It must be so coolio to be able to change your hair color whenever you want. That's what I'm gonna do too when I have my own hair salon. Bubbles keeps smiling at Fantasia who has become very popular now because of that other Fantasia from *American Idol*. (Now this Fantasia wants to be a singer too.)

The door opens again and the musical chimes kick in. It's Aqua and Angie. Pucci giggles, then tugs Bubbles by the shirt, "How come the car got a stomachache?" he asks, telling one of his stupid jokes.

"Because you were driving?' queries Bubbles.

"No, silly, because it had too much gas!" Pucci says, snorting like a pig. The customer standing next to us looks up and smiles at him, then pulls out a checkbook and leans against the counter to write.

Pucci blurts out at Aqua and Angie, "Doesn't *loco* Coco's face look like the color of a Halloween pumpkin? *Una calabazza*." Now the same customer looks up to quickly glance at *me*. Suddenly, I feel *totally* self-conscious. I wish poot-butt Pucci would just move into the Tae Kwon do Center so I would *never* have to see him again!

"You do have a little, well, different color, Miss Chanel. You okay?" Aqua asks, concerned. By now I know I am a different color because my cheeks are red.

"Aqua, let me show you what I learned today in karate class!" Pucci says, then kicks his leg into second position at a forty-five-degree angle, knocking over the bowl of plastic clips onto the shiny black-and-white linoleum floor.

"Oh, no. Tell me I'm not having déjà vu. Not today," Fantasia moans, putting down the phone receiver and pointing her five-inch acrylic-tipped forefinger at us. "Girls, you've got to take the Bruce Lee wannabe back to the Seventies. Actually, I don't care where you take him, just get him outta here!"

Aqua and Angie start picking up the clips. "Lord, we are so sorry."

I start to stutter, "Pucci, *deja*—"

"I got this," Bubbles says, grabbing Pucci's arm and bending over to talk to him. "Pucci, we need you to slow your karate roll for a minute."

"Galleria, I'm sorry. He's got to go. But you know Toto is welcome here *anytime*. How is my baby boy?" Fantasia says, leaning in to Bubbles. "That cheetah coat y'all had on him was major! You should make him part of your act."

"We are," Bubbles says, smiling and restraining Pucci.

What does Bubbles mean, *We are?* I wonder.

"We've got puppies now too," Dorinda chirps in. "Nobu and Ragu."

"I can't wait to meet them," Fantasia says, holding a finger out to the other customer as if to say, Hold your horses, I'll be right with you.

"So, what do you say, big man?" Bubbles says, staring down at Pucci.

"You need things. I need things," Pucci says, grinning with his buck teeth.

"I'll give you fifty cents for every half hour you chill against your will," declares Bubbles, the master negotiator.

"How much is my time worth to you?" asks Pucci.

"I'll give you an extra dollar," I blurt out. Then I reach into my cheetah backpack to get my wallet and pull a carrot out of my baggie, chomping quickly to squash the urge to straighten Pucci instead of my hair.

Bubbles looks at Fantasia and says, "We're cool now."

"Ka-ching. Nice doing business with you, Cheetah Girls," Pucci says, setting the timer on his Techno Marine watch, then sitting down to play with his Game Boy.

We sit down next to Pucci to make sure he keeps his promise. Aqua turns to look into the wall mirror and begins fussing with her hair. "I'm so glad y'all decided to come here today because my hair's a mess!"

"If you ask me, they can't do *nada* for you here— this is a beauty shop, not a magic shop!" Pucci heckles.

"Pooch, I thought we had a business arrangement," Bubbles whispers.

"Yup, we do," Pucci says, nodding, "but maybe it's time to negotiate my profit participation."

Bubbles restrains Pucci, then whispers, "Only if we negotiate how much time I keep your head under a heated dryer."

"Okeydokey. I think I'm satisfied with our present arrangement," Pucci says, zipping his lips.

"Good, Mr. Financial Wizard, because you're costing me a tube of S.N.A.P.S. lipstick—and I get very grumpy without the extras," Bubbles hisses at Pucci.

"Should I get popcorn for us?" Dorinda asks, squirming in her seat. "Or maybe cotton candy?"

"Both," says Bubbles. "This bubble gum jones is really breaking my spirit."

"Your jaws must miss the exercise too!" Aqua

says, chuckling while Angie snickers under her breath.

That's about the only exercise Bubbles ever gets! I want to blurt out. Even though I'm starving, I strengthen my resolve not to eat the yummy pink popcorn or sweet pink cotton candy that Dorinda brings back. Bubbles may think she knows everything about how to help the Cheetah Girls get a record deal, but she doesn't.

"I'll go put Kahlua in heavy rotation," Bubbles says, jumping up and walking over to the big pink metallic jukebox to play hits from our favorite platinum pussycat. I close my eyes and imagine her working with Mouse Almighty in the recording studio. There she is giggling, playing with the headphones, going over the lyrics with her favorite producer. One day that could be us. *Por favor, Dios. Por favor.*

Finally, Pepto B. prances from the back of the salon. He still has a platinum blond Afro and is wearing a pink shirt. His eyes light up when he sees Bubbles. "Dorothea tells me the Cheetah Girls are gonna lose their curls today. Say it ain't so!"

"That's right, Pepto. B.," Bubbles says, giving him a hug. "It's time to take our act STRAIGHT to the top!"

We plop down in the chairs in the back and like Mini-Me robots our eyes become glued to the television monitor screens directly above our heads. Pepto B. plays music videos on the monitors all day—some of them are even old school ones, not just the latest ones like they show on BET, VH1, and MTV.

"Okay, girls, let's twist again like we did last summer," Pepto B. says, putting a pink plastic bib apron on top of Bubbles's cheetah top.

"What?" Aqua asks, looking puzzled.

"You girls don't know who Chubby Checker was? I thought Ms. Dorothea was schooling you on the classics," Pepto B. says, smacking his lips. "I'm gonna have to read Ms. Dorothea, like, the *Billboard* Top 100 Singles Chart."

"We do have Seventies Appreciation Night once a month and know all about the groups that were climbing the charts," Bubbles tries to explain.

"Honey, Chubby didn't climb the charts—he was too fat and rich. He sat his big ole butt right there at the top of the charts and looked down at everybody else trying to scramble up, okay?" Pepto B. retorts.

Aqua clears her throat and says, "I'll make sure we watch his videos."

"You do that," Pepto B. says, studying Bubbles's

reflection in the mirror, then swirls her in the chair till he sees Pucci in his sight.

"And, Jim Kelly, you'd better save those karate moves for *Black Belt Jones* or you and I are going to have a problem, okay?" Pepto B. says, eyeballing Pucci. "Knowing Hollywood, they're going to be filming the sequel any second, so you might want to practice those moves—at an audition."

Aqua and Angie look at Pepto B., then snicker quietly. "You girls do know about that classic film from the Seventies, don't you?" Pepto B. asks.

We all nod our head in unison even though I'm sure none of us has ever heard of Jim Kelly. Dorinda smiles and pulls a book out of her cheetah backpack, then notices that Pepto B. is trying to see what she is reading. "I checked it out of the library. I mean, I thought I should read it and see what is says," she says, embarrassed, trying to hide the cover.

"*Confessions of a Backup Dancer*?" Pepto B. says, raising his eyes. "Y'all a little young for that, aren't you?"

"Everybody in school is reading it," Dorinda says in her defense.

"At our school too," Aqua and Angie say in unison.

"It's research—um, like, Seventies Appreciation

Night—except it's the real deal about right now," Bubbles says, squirming in her chair. "We need to know this kinda stuff if we're going to become stars."

"What you need to know you'll find out soon enough," Pepto B. huffs, then comments on the music video showing on the monitor.

"Now that outfit is a slinkster!" he says, looking at the pink fur cape draped over the new pop singer Stone Alone.

The second thing we love about coming to Pepto B.'s salon is getting all the latest *chisme*—gossip about our competition. (Well, they would be our competition if we had a record deal.)

"So spill the refried beans, Mr. Pepto B.," Bubbles says, egging him on.

Pepto B. looks around quickly, then lowers his voice. "Ms. Chutney Dallas was in here last week and she wanted me to pull a donkey out of a hat or some such miracle on her head. She went to one of them—now, excuse me, Chanel—Dominican weavers uptown behind my back and her hair was a mess. You know the type of hairstylist I'm talking about—they should be practicing *brujería* instead of cosmetology, because they turn a silk ear into a sow's purse instead of the other way around."

We all hang on to Pepto B.'s every word so we can keep up because he talks really fast. "Well, Ms. Chutney came up in here and her hair looked like a DON'T instead of a DO, so I told my key stylist Lyah to take care of Ms. Chutney because my lowly Wilfred Academy cosmetology degree can only go so far. After all, I'm a hairstylist, not a *magician*."

Pucci chuckles loudly at that one. Bubbles throws him a look and whispers to him, "The clock is still ticking and I know you don't want a licking."

"That's too bad her album didn't sell—I liked that one song, "Don't Make Me Over," Dorinda says, looking up from her book.

"Yeah, well, don't take her advice, honey, or you'll end up signing nothing but bad checks!" Pepto B. quips.

Bubbles looks at Pepto B., then smiles because she finally catches his drift.

"That's right—that check Ms. Chutney Dallas gave the salon bounced from here to Hiroshima," Pepto B. says, taking a deep breath, "but, you know, 'she's special.'"

That's Pepto B.'s way of saying "she's cuckoo." Aside from Madrina, Pepto B. has the most interesting way of talking of all the grown-ups we know.

Pepto B. claps his hands together and says,

"Okay, your turn. Tell me, what's going on with the Cheetah Girls?"

Bubbles tells him everything about what has been happening, including the rumors uptown about the Cheetah Girls being corny and whack ever since we lost the Apollo Amateur Hour to a couple of bozos.

"Oh, we're not having that!" Pepto B. says, smoothing the relaxer on Bubbles head first, then mine. "You girls are gonna give those wannabe divettes something to talk about till they're fifty, right?"

"Right!" we all say in unison.

"Does it burn?" Dorinda asks, staring at the chemical relaxer that is slobbered on top of Bubbles's and my head.

"You never had a relaxer before?" Aqua asks, surprised.

"Nope—never did."

"Well, you're not missing anything," Bubbles pipes up. I know she is still trying to make sure that Dorinda doesn't feel bad about not getting her hair done.

"Okay, Texas Rangers—it's your turn," Pepto B. says, motioning for Aqua and Angie to sit in the chairs.

"Miss Dorinda, you sitting there reading. Why

don't you give us a tune?" Pepto B. says, smoothing the relaxer on my head now.

Dorinda squirms in the pink swivel chair.

"You're not starting to believe all that nonsense, are you? Pepto B. asks, challenging Dorinda to pump it up.

Dorinda starts singing words to the song, "Bow-wow Wow!"

"Why you getting sooo sooo wicked
Just 'cuz we issued you a ticket
To the tune of forty-five RPM live
Right down to the honey beehive
And while you were trying to put the bite
     on our groove
We were busy making the moves
And singing Bow-wow Wow!
Yippee Ayy, Pay Day
Bow-wow Wow!
Yippee Ayy, Pay Day
That's coming our way.

"That's all we got so far," Dorinda says, stopping abruptly, then grinning that impish grin, which puts dimples in her cheeks.

"How come Dorinda knows the words to the song and I don't?" I ask, puzzled.

"We were just riffing with it on Phat Planet the other night. You know, when we were online. You pulled a Houdini, remember?" counters Bubbles.

I don't know if it's the chemicals or if it's because I'm really mad at Bubbles, but now my head feels like a roof on fire.

"Chuchie, stop pouting. We can practice it at rehearsal tomorrow. You'll love this song. All we gotta do is bark in between verses." Bubbles starts making barking sounds like Toto.

"*Está bien*, Bubbles. Maybe you can teach that to Toto too," I blurt out.

"Oh, I forgot to tell you, he's gonna be in the show on Saturday. I taught him how to dance!" Bubbles says, giggling.

"No, you didn't," Pepto B. says, rolling his eyes. "You are shameless. You'll do anything to get that gold record on your wall. I'm not mad at you, though."

Well I am! I want to scream. Bubbles is always doing things without telling me. I mean, I love Toto, but putting him on stage while we're performing. That's really taking growl power a bark too far if you ask me!

By the way Dorinda looks at me so-o-o sheepishly, I can tell that she already knew about this puppyfest even though she blurts out, "I just found out about it too. Bubbles says he's a really good dancer."

"I thought you were the best dancer in our crew," I say, staring at Dorinda.

"Don't worry, Chuch, that's what we needed in our act—a pooch. Mommy is gonna make him a little skirt for Saturday too," Bubbles says, like she is no longer asking for my advice.

"A skirt?" Pucci says, looking up from his Game Boy. Now Angie and Aqua stare at him so he shuts up.

"Well, it's a little tutu—like what Chuchie wears for ballet—and it's got little leopard ribbons floating all around," Bubbles explains. She always tries to be nonchalant when she knows I'm ready to whack her like a piñata.

I can't stop pouting. Bubbles and Pepto B. keep chatting away and I pretend I'm not listening. Dorinda keeps reading her book and looks over at me and smiles every now and then.

"Wow, your hair looks *major*," Dorinda says when Pepto B. finishes blow-drying me. I look in the mirror and I smile, but I still don't say anything. He has parted my hair on the side and my hair is sort of covering my right eye.

"You remind me of Aaliyah with your hair like that," one of the customer says, looking at me and smiling. I nod my head back at her because she is right. Aaliyah was one of our favorite singers. We loved Aaliyah too and used to practice some of her dance moves. We cried the whole day when she was killed in the plane crash.

"The world will never be the same without Miss A.," Pepto B. sighs, then turns the ends of my hair under. I look in the mirror again and I can't help smiling at my reflection. Pepto B. fusses with Bubbles's hair some more. "The center part works for you, Miss Galleria—because it gives your face more balance," he explains, fixing a few wisps in front. I look over quickly at Bubbles, but she isn't looking at me. She is too busy looking at herself in the mirror.

"Are you gonna come on Saturday?" Dorinda asks Pepto B. when he bends over to give Dorinda a hug.

"Honey, if I'm not worn out from all the heads, I'll be there or be square," Pepto B. says, then starts twisting like Chubby Checker. "Y'all should throw that in your act. A little shimmy never hurt any career that I know of."

"We'll take it under consideration," Pucci says, puffing up his chest like he's our manager.

"The only thing I want you to consider is the door!" Pepto B. says, ushering Pucci to the front.

"Pucci faces the glass door and waits for us while we pay at the receptionist counter. And don't get any ideas about that glass—if I hear a shatter, they'll be lots of chatter—that's right, guess who, I'll sue you!"

When we get outside, Bubbles grabs my arm. "Just in case you start falling off sidewalks again."

"I can walk by myself," I protest.

Bubbles ignores me, then coos, "Good move with the new do."

I let out a big sigh. At least Bubbles thinks some of my ideas are good.

Dorinda grabs my other arm. "I think the peeps uptown are definitely going to be digging the dos!"

"Yeah, well, if they DON'T, then things are gonna get hairy once again in Harlem and I'm not talking about what's on our heads," Bubbles says, taking a deep sigh. I can tell she remembers our awful experience losing at the Apollo Amateur Hour.

"But this time we've got a lot more to worry about than the Sandman yanking us offstage," Aqua says, her forehead etched with worry lines.

"That's right, we've got to defend our precious rep," Angie chimes in. "We didn't come all the way up here to have someone tell us that singing in church choir isn't worth anything!"

"Can I get an AMEN on that one?" shouts Bubbles. "Ayiight, see you cheetahs at rehearsal after school tomorrow."

Chapter 7

It's so hard for me to keep secrets from Bubbles because she is my best friend, but the way she has been acting lately makes it much easier, *está bien*. So even though I'm dying to tell her that I can't wait until Mackerel sees me with my new straight hairdo today, I keep my *boca grande* closed. We're standing together outside school and I take off my red mittens even though my hands are cold, because I want to smooth my hair when Mackerel comes. The first person we run into today, though, is Daisy Duarte, who coos, "I'm getting a puppy too! I'm going to call him Bandito."

"What kind are you getting?" Dorinda asks, excited for Daisy.

"A Havanese terrier," Daisy says.

"Oh, I never heard of a dog like that, " Dorinda responds.

Bow-wow Wow!

I want to scream, *I hope he's ugly!*

Daisy kills that thought with a BB gun because she coos, "Ooh, he is sooo cute," then whips out a picture of an adorable brown-and-white puppy with a mushy face. "They're bred in Havana, and *Mamí* knows one of the breeders, so we got a really good deal."

Now I'm beginning to wonder, How come Daisy gets a puppy all of a sudden? Dorinda is still goo-gooing over the picture. "How come you named him Bandito?"

"Because he stole my heart from the moment I saw him," Daisy says, giggling.

Oh, how corny! I want to blurt out, but I don't say anything because I'm not too good at faking it all the time, *está bien.* Daisy must notice how upset I am, because all of a sudden she shuts up about the puppy and exclaims, "Wow, you look *muy bonita,* Chanel!" Then she looks at Bubbles and adds, "You too, *mamacita.*"

But Bubbles is too busy checking out Catalina Versace's new outfit. See, every morning, peeps at Fashion Industries East are always eyeballing everybody's outfits and today is no exception—especially since Catalina is a new transfer student from Pasadena Tech (that's right, right near Hollywood where we performed). Everybody at school is saying that she is a granddaughter of the cousin of designer Gianni Versace, but we think it's a hoax-arama. (I mean, my name is Chanel, but I'm not related to the late, great designer Coco Chanel, *está bien*?)

"I heard her father is a plumber and they live in Weehawken, New Jersey," Bubbles says, shaking her head at the silly rumors.

"Yeah, but she always brings it," Dorinda says, gazing at Catalina's purple bell-bottom hip-huggers with a dangling gold charm belt and white T-shirt etched with rhinestone letters that says, "So Many Boys, So Little Time."

"Yeah, well, tell her that the Seventies is that way," Bubbles says, pointing in the other direction.

Eyeing the T-shirt again, Dorinda heckles, "Catalina's *busy* schedule is going to clear real soon if she stays here at Fashion Industries." I know what she means because most of the students at Fashion Industries East High School are girls and the few boy students are, um, kinda "gay and sway," as Madrina would say. They even wear mascara to school. *Es la verdad*. It's true!

"It's not hard to see why Red Snapper and Mackerel moved here from Motor City," Bubbles says, like she's a reporter or something. "They get to be big fish in a very little pond."

"Is that a Prada skirt Catalina is wearing? She's sleeping on her brand," Dorinda adds, chuckling. I know she is making fun of me because my motto is "Prada or Nada." (Even though Mamí has made sure I'm stuck with the *nada* part for a long, long time until I pay off every penny I charged on her credit card.)

"Well, I wouldn't know, Dorinda, because I am not down with O.P.P." I say, smirking.

"O.P.P.?"

"Other People's Prada!" I say, trying to keep my feet warm by tap dancing in my red suede boots with the fringes up the side.

"Yeah, well, we'd better get down with D.W.D. right about now because they're on the move," Bubbles says sarcastically. I don't understand what Bubbles means but I turn and see Mackerel and Derek walking in our direction. Suddenly, my heart starts skipping to its own salsa beat. *Ay, Dios*, please don't let Mackerel be mad at me for leaving him alone with all those juicy hot dogs. (I'm trying to make jokes because I'm nervous, *está bien*.) I take my frozen left hand and try to smooth down my hair in the front so it falls over my right eye, but my hand is so cold I almost poke myself in the eye! I can feel his big brown eyes staring at me.

"Wazzup, Cheetah Girl? Okay, I'm digging the

look, snook. Yeah, I like you with a little less fur on your head," Derek says, nodding in approval at Bubbles's hair.

Mackerel moves closer to me and huffs, "I was holding down Papaya King waiting for you. A brother can't get any respect—what?"

Oh, no, I realize. Mackerel is *caliente* mad at me.

"Hold up the bait on that right hook, all right, Mackerel," Bubbles cuts in. Now I'm getting more embarrassed. Why is Bubbles always acting like she is my mother and wrote a note for me for school or something? "We had a major appointment to pounce on yesterday, so we had to bounce. You understand."

"Yeah, what appointment?" Mackerel asks, like he isn't satisfied with Bubbles's corny explanation.

I start to talk, but Bubbles interrupts me. "The Cheetah Girls were in the hot chair, that's all I'm saying, okay?"

"More like hot rollers, if you ask me," Derek chimes in. "Stevie Wonder could see the Cheetah Girls changed their spots. Oh, hold up," Derek says, holding his hand like a phone. "Excuse me, Miss Galleria—it's *National Geographic* magazine calling for an exclusive on the Cheetah Girls change-up."

"Yeah, well we exclusively belong to ourselves,

so tell them they'll have to catch us in action uptown on Saturday night," Bubbles retorts, "like everybody else."

"You know if you were feeling that way about the situation, you coulda told me," Mackerel says. "But if you want to make it up to me, we can hook up later."

"Um, we have rehearsal," I say, my heart pounding.

"I got 'chu. Working on your song?" Mackerel asks me in a loud voice.

Oh, no! Now my head freezes like a piña colada FrozeFruit Bar. Bubbles looks puzzled, but I quickly blurt out, "I can see you Saturday at the thing—at the competition," I say, my eyes pleading.

"Nah, I got plans to—I'll probably be going fishing or something—you know in the pond in Central Park," Mackerel says sarcastically. "*Catch* you later."

"Yeah, well, if you're slow you miss 'The Show,' if you *catch* my drift, Mackerel," Bubbles chimes in, then turns to Derek. "I hope you won't let your fishing buddy drag you to an icy pond on Saturday."

"Nah, nah, I'll be there—no doubt," Derek says, smiling goofily at Bubbles.

I don't understand. Why is it everybody always ends up liking Bubbles!

"Come on, Chuchie. I can't take the heat from Mr. Drezform again," Bubbles says, dragging my arm. Bubbles is right. We can't be late for homeroom class. I fight back the tears again. Derek and Hambone are right behind us. As we run inside, LaRonda shouts out, "Your hair looks dope!"

Walking to homeroom class, I realize Mackerel didn't even say anything about my hair. "Bubbles, what did you mean by D.W.D.?" I ask sheepishly.

"Dealing With Dunces," she riffs back. "But you shouldn't be sweating it, Chuchie. We've got bigger fish to fry—like rehearsing it to the max so we can win that competition on Saturday. Hey, what did Mackerel mean by you working on a song?"

"*Nada*. He is confused," I say, squirming. "He forgot that you write the songs."

I can feel Mackerel is still right behind me as we move into class, and suddenly he blurts out to me sarcastically, "Good luck with your songwriting."

"Songwriting?" Bubbles asks, like she's ready to pounce on me.

I can't tell Bubbles about my fib-eroni or she will fry me like *plátanos*.

"I, um, told Mackerel I was gonna help you write Bow-wow-Wow, maybe," I blurt out.

"What?" Bubbles says, her eyes getting so big, they look like they're going to explode like a piñata any minute!

"We'll talk about that later," Bubbles hisses, then plops down in her seat in homeroom. I push my hair behind my ear so I can see. It's only eight thirty in the morning and already I can't wait till school is over today!

Bubbles acts weird to me all day at school, but I'm so glad she doesn't ask me anything else about the song. I don't care about "Bow-wow Wow!," puppies, poodles, or noodles. I just want to get out of school so I don't have to keep avoiding Mackerel. We're all meeting at my house at four o'clock to rehearse and do a run-through for the competition. We always rehearse at my house since Mamí had an exercise studio built into the loft. It is completely surrounded by mirrors and has a really good sound system, so it makes it perfect for rehearsing. Bubbles said she had to go home first, and I didn't even ask her why.

Dorinda comes with me to my house. Aqua and Angie will be coming here directly from school. "I'm so glad Pucci will be at Little League practice until later," I say, walking toward the red Formica counter island directly outside the kitchen.

"*Mamí* is going to pick him up. Honestly, I wish he would spend the night at *Papi*'s and not come home."

"Word. I know it gets hectic. It's like that in my house too," Dorinda says, moving Pucci's scooter out of the way so she can sit in one of the swivel red chairs at the counter.

Now I feel stupid for complaining. I only have to deal with one poot-butt brother but Dorinda has to deal with eleven brothers and sisters. I open the refrigerator to see what I can give Dorinda. As usual there is a case of Burpy soda, which Mamí lets Pucci order from an Internet store. I'll fix his poot-butt. "Want a Burpy, *mamacita*?"

"Um, yeah," Dorinda says, shrugging her shoulders.

"Purple Durple, Sloppy Boppy, or Pinky Winky?" I ask her. The Burpy soda flavors have stupid names, which is probably why Pucci likes them.

"You can never go wrong with 'thinking pink'— or winking it, I guess," Dorinda says, chuckling. I know she is making fun of Danitra, who is in our vocal classes at Drinka Champagne's and has a group that changes its name from thinking or stinking pink depending on the week. As a matter of fact, now I think Danitra is going to try flying solo. That makes me wonder about the peeps at

Drinka's. "I wonder if anybody else from Drinka's is competing on Saturday?"

"Probably," Dorinda says, slurping up her soda while I chomp on my carrot stash. "I'm sorry that you didn't get a puppy. I really am," Dorinda tells me quietly.

"I know you are," I say, chomping even harder on my carrots. I wish Dorinda would stop talking about the stupid puppies, already. *Ay, Dios mio.*

"Chanel, I didn't want to say anything, but how come you're always eating carrots now?" Dorinda asks sheepishly.

"What happened?" I stammer. "It's just from my diet."

"Um, what diet, Chanel?" Dorinda asks, squinching up her nose and squirming on her stool.

"You promise not to tell Bubbles?" I ask before I spill the refried beans to Dorinda. But I know I can trust Dorinda. It's not her fault that Bubbles gave her a puppy and not me. "I'm trying to lose five pounds by Saturday. You know, my tummy is too big from not exercising while my ankle was broken!"

"Um, I don't think that's such a good idea," Dorinda says quietly.

I look at Dorinda like, What do you know. You're skinny! You don't even have a tummy! "Just don't say anything to Bubbles, okay?"

Dorinda doesn't say anything. Suddenly I get scared because I realize she is not going to keep the promise.

"You promised!" I blurt out.

"No, I didn't, Chanel," Dorinda stammers. "I, um, didn't say anything."

I try to stare at Dorinda the way Bubbles stares at me when she is *caliente* mad, but I can't do it. Not to Dorinda.

The doorbell rings, but I don't move to press the buzzer. I just keep staring at Dorinda. The doorbell rings again. I run to answer the door. It's Aqua and Angie. While we wait for them to come up in the elevator, I start babbling to Dorinda. "You can't tell Bubbles. She is mad at me for telling Mackerel I wrote the Bow-wow song."

"I know," Dorinda says, looking down at her feet. "She is really mad."

Uh-oh. Now I know for sure that Bubbles is going to go off on me. She didn't believe my fiberoni after all. "What did she say?" I ask, drilling Dorinda.

"I'm not saying *nada*, okay," Dorinda says defensively, obviously imitating me. "You two can squash that beef jerky on your own."

I can't fight with Dorinda too. Aqua and Angie are ringing the elevator bell now. I run to open the elevator door and they step into the loft.

"Dag on, I don't know how you're dealing with all that noise outside," Aqua says, wiping imaginary dust from the shoulder of her coat. The twins are very fussy about dirt, just like I am, and there is plenty of it outside with all the construction.

"I know. I can't wait until they build the building already!" I moan.

"Well, from the looks of it, we'll be getting a record deal before they put up that dag on building!" Angie chimes in.

"It looks so scary, all gutted out like that—like a haunted house or something," Aqua goes on.

Then Angie changes the subject. "We should have known that JuJuBeans Quinnonez is going to be in all her glory on Saturday." Aqua rolls her eyes in disgust. JuJu is an annoying wannabe divette who goes to Performing Arts Annex with Aqua and Angie.

"She thinks she is going to be the next Mariah Carey, but she can't even 'carry' a tune!" says Angie.

The two of them look at each other, then Angie says, "She's the one who was spreading the rumor about us being corny since we lost the Apollo Amateur Hour."

"Now she says she's going to beat us on Saturday," Aqua adds.

"Well, tell them to bring it on," Dorinda says, greeting the twins with a hug.

"How is Nobu?" Angie asks.

"Yesterday he took a roll of toilet paper and pulled it around the whole apartment," Dorinda says, laughing like she does when she starts her puppy tales from the projects. "Mrs. Bosco says she is going to have to start charging him money for incidentals." All of a sudden, Dorinda starts blushing, then she explains, "Um, see, when Mrs. Bosco fills out the expense report for the agency, she has to write down all the extra stuff she bought so they can reimburse her. That's what she means by incidentals."

"Oh, I understand," Aqua says, nodding. "Where is Miss Galleria? I can't wait to see her without those braces!"

"Oh, everybody at school is sweating her now," Dorinda tells them without a trace of Gucci envy like I have. Now I feel bad. How come Dorinda isn't jealous of Bubbles the way I am?

The doorbell rings again and this time it's Bubbles.

"Oooh, look who's here!" Angie coos, running over to Toto. He is wearing his leopard coat and hat. I wonder why Bubbles brought him to our rehearsal.

"Where's Ragu?" Angie asks, laughing.

"Oh, well, he won't be having any more outings right now," Bubbles explains. "My mom had a coronary that I took him out of the house before he got his shots, like he's going to catch some voodoo vampire disease or something."

Aqua laughs at Bubbles's joke too. I'm glad to see at least the two of them are so chummy again. I think they both still have a crush—*un coco*—on Eddie Lizard even though they're pretending they don't. (He played a corpse in the movie *Vampire Voodoo Voyage*—one of the twins' favorite horror movies. *Cuatro* yuks.)

"What is Toto doing here?" I finally ask Bubbles.

"I told you, Chuchie, he is going to be in the show on Saturday with us," Bubbles says matter-of-factly. "We can use all the help we can get."

"What happened?" I stammer, wondering what Bubbles means by us needing help.

"Wait till you see the dance I taught him," Bubbles coos to Aqua and Angie.

Toto runs up to me and starts licking my leg, but I ignore him.

"Okay, cheetahs, let's stop gabbing and get to rehearsal, so we have it down like cold turkey," Bubbles explains. "That means you too, Toto!'

"You're right. Let's get this rodeo on the road,"

Aqua says, stretching her arms over her head.

"Okay, I figure we should open the same way we did for the Kats and Kittys Klub Halloween Bash because that number was supa dupa crispy," Bubbles explains. "Then—"

"You mean we get to perform more than one song?" Aqua asks, interrupting Bubbles's rundown.

"No, we don't—it was just how I was breaking it down," Bubbles explains. "We're only performing one number because it's not our show, *está bien?* We're gonna perform 'Wannabe Stars' because that's a crowd-pleaser and Pepto B. got me thinking—you know where we do our growl power sign and dip in the chorus, we could add a twist *and* a bend-over shake-a-tail feather routine like we saw in the Ike and Tina Turner video, remember?"

"Well, let's see it all together," Aqua says, unsure. Bubbles just smiles and does the routine, step by step. I guess she's used to the fact that it always takes a little more—*un poco mas*—to herd the twins into the corral like cheetah cattle.

"Wow, I'm digging that," Dorinda says, excited. She jumps up and does the routine and she looks so adorable doing it.

"Chuchie?" Bubbles asks, turning toward me.

"You down for the twirl. Or are you still thinking about lyrics for Bow-wow-Wow?"

Dorinda winces like, "Ding, ding, ding. Round's over."

But I just ignore Bubbles and ask, "Where does Toto come in?"

"Don't worry about that," Bubbles says, annoyed. "Let's just do a run-through first and when we hit the music, we'll let him come on in."

"*Está bien*," I say, sighing. I realize that nothing I say can stop Bubbles from turning the Cheetah Girls into a circus act.

But I should have known that there was nothing Toto can do to make me mad. As soon as we do our run-through for "Wannabe Stars in the Jiggy Jungle," Toto runs toward us and starts twirling around on his two legs. Bubbles sees the look on my face and can't resist rubbing it in. "I told you he'll bring the house down. Hearts will melt and deals will be made. Trust me."

I burst out giggling because Toto looks so funny dancing.

"Go, Toto. Go, Toto. Go, Toto!" we start chanting in unison.

"You must have bribed him with sausauges or something to get him to do that twirl," Aqua says, shaking her head. "I know you, Miss

Galleria, you will stop at nothing to get your way."

"Let's just say Snausages did enter the picture," Galleria says, hugging Toto while he is still standing on his two legs. "But I knew my little brother would do his part to help us wiggle our way to the top, top, top!"

Chapter 8

$\mathcal{S}$peaking of little brothers, Pucci is home and talking really loud to Mamí in the kitchen. The aroma of Spanish food is also filling up the loft, which means Mamí is cooking tonight, probably to show off for the Cheetah Girls. Or maybe she is trying to make up for me having to pick up Pucci from karate classes yesterday.

"Has Auntie Juanita said anything yet about that move to Paris?" Bubbles whispers even though Mamí can't hear us in the exercise studio.

"No, not yet," I moan back.

"Um, we're finished rehearsing, right?" Aqua asks, smacking her lips because she is hungry. (I can hear her stomach grumbling. Or maybe it's mine!)

"Um, yeah, it's a done deal-io," Bubbles says, like she's the boss. Toto must know rehearsal is over too because he runs to the kitchen. "Go get yours, boo!"

"*Mami* won't mind if you stay for dinner," I tell the Cheetah Girls. I want them to stay.

"No, Daddy told us to be at the dinner table on time," Angie explains nervously. Their dad, Mr. Walker, is a really good cook and he likes for them to eat dinner together as a family. (Their mother still lives in Houston.)

"Believe you me, nothing I would like better than to sample your mother's food," Aqua says, smacking her juicy lips again, "but, um, Galleria, should we, um, you know?"

I feel my heart racing again. What is Bubbles up to now?

Sure enough, Bubbles turns to me and say, "Chuchie, we're performing on Saturday—"

"What happened?" I stammer before Bubbles even finishes her sentence.

"Don't you notice anything?" Bubbles asks me, getting annoyed.

"You got your braces off?" I answer, but now I am squirming.

"No, not my braces, but the fact that you're turning into a pumpkin—and I'm not talking about Cinderella, okay?" Bubbles blurts out. "What is going on with you?"

"It's from the carrots," I blurt out because I know Dorinda is going to spill the refried beans anyway to Bubbles.

"How many carrots are you eating?" Aqua asks, concerned.

"It's not how many—it's how little she is eating of anything else," Bubbles says, figuring out my secret like Pet Detective Snausage. "Am I right?"

"Um, no, um, yeah," I say, bowing my head. "I have to lose weight. That's why I didn't tell you, because you wouldn't understand!"

"Chuchie, you're skinny—what's wrong with you?" Bubbles asks me adamantly.

"I just need to lose a few pounds—my tummy is big," I stutter.

"Look on the color wheel, Chuchie—orange is not your hue," Bubbles spurts out. "And you're stomach is cute. You're hallucinating, okay."

I look at Dorinda, my eyes pleading for her to help me, but she won't look at me. I am so-o-o embarrassed that I walk out of the studio and into the kitchen, plopping into a chair at the table. I'm not going to eat anything, but I'll show them.

Pucci slams his G.I. Joe on the table.

"Pucci—put away your doll," I hiss at him.

"It's not a doll. It's an action figure!" he hisses back.

"*Parate*. Stop it, you two," Mamí says, putting *arroz con pollo* on a plate. "Is everyone staying for dinner?"

I don't answer. Bubbles and the rest of the Cheetah Girls stand by the counter outside the kitchen.

"Hi, Auntie Juanita," Bubbles says, smiling. "We can't stay for dinner, but I just wanted to say hi and we'll see you on Saturday?"

"Yes, I'll be there—and so will Luc," Mamí says proudly. My face burns. Mamí didn't tell me she was bringing Mr. Tycoon to the competition. He makes me so nervous. I don't think he likes me at all. And now he is trying to drag us to Paris. I hate him!

Mamí dishes up another serving of *arroz con pollo* and puts it in front of Pucci. "*Pobre* Pucci, you had to sit in that hair salon with all those girls."

"That's okay. I know how to turn a sow's ear into a silk purse," Pucci says, patting his pockets, then snapping his fingers. I know he is imitating Pepto B. and so does Mamí because she laughs like he's so clever. I just stare back at Pucci and keep my mouth shut. I wish I could turn him into a pig purse; then I could drop him down a sewer!

"How is the book coming?" Bubbles asks Mamí spotting the big pile of papers on the counter.

"It's coming—with or without me," Mamí says, shaking her head.

"Bubbles, what happened when the skunk wrote a book?" Pucci asks, smirking.

"I don't know, Pooch—it turned out to be a *stinkeroo*?" Bubbles asks giggling.

"Ha-ha-ha!" Pucci says, then trumps her. "No. It became a best *smeller*!"

"Pooch, your jokes are always so, well, appetizing," Bubbles says, watching me to see if I'm going to eat anything. "Okay, we gotta bounce." I wave at Bubbles, like, "Bye, Bye," then just move the food around on my plate. I knew Bubbles wouldn't say anything in front of Mamí because she'd be too afraid Mamí wouldn't let me perform on Saturday and ruin everything for the Cheetah Girls. Tee-hee-hee. I know that Bubbles wants that Girlie Show Boutique gift certificate so bad her paws are itching. I sit tensely in my chair, waiting for Mamí to say something about Paris, but she doesn't. Mamí is too busy reading the papers in front of her to notice if I'm eating or not. But all of a sudden, Mamí looks up at me and blurts out, "Are you wearing my makeup again?"

"No, *Mamí*, I'm not! No, I haven't. I'm not," I exclaimed, praying she doesn't keep snooping on me.

"How come you look so orange. *Por qué?*"

"Bubbles got this new bronzing lotion, so I was trying it," I say, telling a fib-eroni.

"I told you you look like a scarecrow," Pucci says, laughing.

I stare at Pucci real hard, wishing he would disappear.

"You two eat, then study," Mamí says, getting distracted. "Luc is taking me to the opera, but I will be checking up on you at intermission. *Ay, Dios mío*, Chanel—even your fingers are orange!"

"Oh, that—we were doing a project in school," I blurt out, putting my hands in my lap.

"You still finger painting?" Pucci grunts, then shoves some rice and beans in his big mouth. "Even I don't do that in school anymore!"

"Okay, I have to get dressed," Mamí says.

I stare at Pucci really hard, then whisper, "Don't even think about bothering me tonight, *para nada, está bien?*"

"I'm calling Daddy, anyway. I don't have time to be bothered with you, *loco Coco!*" Pucci says, jumping up from the table without putting his plate in the sink.

I run after Pucci and grab him by the collar. "All right, get off me!" he grunts, then jabs me in the stomach. "But you're washing the dishes."

"I know that," I whine. Pucci only has to wash the dishes once a week, usually on Saturdays while I have to do everything else. Pucci runs out of the kitchen and into the den. I quickly take my plate and throw the food in the garbage can before I'm tempted to eat it. Then I put Saran wrap on all the leftovers and stick them in the refrigerator. *Ay, Dios*, the yellow rice and beans look sooo good. I stand there staring at it through the Saran wrap, fantasizing about putting my face in the bowl and eating it like a pig in a trough. Pucci's loud laughter snaps me back to reality. He is on the phone. I walk on my tiptoes by the study so I can sneak a listen, but Pucci slams the door shut as soon as he sees me. Maybe Pucci has a girlfriend. No way, José. Who would like him? I'm sure the girls at school think he is just as annoying as I do. Walking to the bathroom, I start to think about Mackerel. I wish he wasn't mad at me. I feel so bad that I made him wait for me at Papaya King while I was picking up stupid Pucci at the Tae Kwon do Center. If only Mamí knew how she messed things up for me. Now that nobody is around to bother me, I want to see what my face looks like in the mirror. I close the bathroom door behind me and stand there for a few seconds before I turn on the light. *Ay, Dios mío!* Bubbles was right. I do look like a pumpkin. *A big fat pumpkin*, I shriek to myself while pinching a bulge around my tummy. I start to feel dizzy and light-headed again, so I decide to go lie down on my bed until I feel better. But only for a little while I tell myself, because I have so much homework to do for math class. I pull off my clothes and throw them on my Mono monkey footstool because I am too tired to hang them up. I take my pink cheetah pajamas out of the bureau drawer and quickly put them on. Leaving the light on, I close my bedroom door and make sure it's locked so Pucci can't bother me anymore. Then I plop down on my canopy bed like a lazy rag doll. As I start drifting off to sleep, I fantasize about my favorite daydream. The Cheetah Girls are finally performing in Madison Square Garden. The fans are screaming, *"We love you Cheetah Girls. Growl Power Forever and Forever!!"* Then thousands of fans all dressed in cheetah outfits, start throwing stuffed cheetahs onto the stage until the whole stage is covered with small furry stuffed animals. . . .

I don't know how long I've been sleeping, but I feel something itching my face. I slowly wake up and go to scratch my face when I feel something furry nestled in my hair. My heart freezes as I look up and see a mouse staring straight at me.

"Aiyyyyyyyyyyyyyyy!" I scream at the top of my lungs and jump up straight in my bed like a vampire in his coffin. "Pucci! Pucci, come here!"

The mouse runs into a corner and I can't see it anymore and I start sobbing uncontrollably. Pucci is jiggling the doorknob and knocking loudly on my door. I hear him screaming, "What's wrong?"

"Open the door, Pucci!" I yell, slobbering all over myself. I am too scared to move from my bed. "Pucci, open the door." Suddenly I remember that I had locked the door, and I wrap the duvet around my body because I feel naked and I don't want anything to jump out and bite me. I'm so scared, I walk like a mummy toward the door.

"Chanel! Chanel!" Pucci screams through the door.

I reach the door and open it. Pucci just stares at me like I have finally become *loco Coco* for real.

"Did you see a ghost?" Pucci asks, his eyes widening.

"A mouse tried to eat me!" I scream, crying again.

"Where is it?" Pucci asks, pushing me out of the way and coming into my room.

"I don't know—he didn't tell me where he was going!" I shout, slobbering.

Pucci gets on his hands and knees and starts looking for the mouse. I walk as fast as I can in my mummy outfit out of my bedroom and go sit on the island counter. I don't want my feet touching the ground anymore. I start rocking back and forth, frightened to death. Suddenly, I realize that I still feel dizzy like I did before I took a nap. I stop rocking and sit still.

Pucci runs out of my bedroom and stops in front of me, trying to catch his breath. I can tell that he has something really bad to tell me.

"Chanel, there is more than one mouse in your room," he says. I can tell for once that Pucci is not playing with me.

"They are having a party in your room—I swear—there are three of them hopping around in your closet!" Pucci says, still trying to catch his breath.

I start crying again.

"Don't worry, Chanel—they ran when they saw me."

"Oh, that really makes me feel a lot better, Pucci!" I scream, spitting on my brother by mistake.

"Please stop the weather report," Pucci moans. "I know what to do."

"What?" I scream.

Pucci doesn't answer me and runs into the kitchen. He opens the cupboard and takes out the big jar of Jif peanut butter.

"Are you crazy, Pucci?" I scream louder. "What are you going to do—give them food for their party, *baboso*! Huh?"

"No, I'm making mousetraps," Pucci explains.

I am sooo scared, I can't move. I watch while Pucci cuts up pieces of plastic, then puts his model craft glue on it and peanut butter in the middle.

"This is gonna work, I'm telling you," Pucci says.

"I'm not moving," I say, wrapping my duvet tighter around myself. I'm sleeping here on the counter. I lay down on my side and try to make a pillow out of part of my duvet.

"Don't worry, Chanel," Pucci says. "This is gonna work."

Suddenly, I realize that maybe we should call Mamí on her cell phone. "Call *Mamí*," I yell at Pucci.

"No," Pucci says. "I'm gonna put the traps down."

I am too tired to argue with Pucci. I lay my head down on the counter and listen as Pucci patters around the loft, putting down his homemade mousetraps all over the loft. I feel my heart pounding loudly, *What if the mice come back and bring their friends once they smell the peanut butter?*

When I hear the elevator door open, I realize it is the first time in a long time that I am glad that Mamí is home. I was so scared that I couldn't fall asleep. Pucci runs to Mamí and tells her everything. "You wait until I call that construction company tomorrow!" Mamí yells. "I was worried about this—there are always a lot of mice around when there's major construction and buildings being torn down."

I wonder why Mamí didn't tell us that before we had uninvited guests with whiskers throwing a party in our house. "Chanel, go to bed. We'll take care of this tomorrow."

"I can't," I moan.

"You can sleep in my bed," Pucci says.

I am so tired, I don't even care if I have to sleep in Pucci's bed. I am not sleeping in mine, that is for sure.

Pucci runs to his room and takes his blanket and pillow, and plops on the couch. I lie down on his bed and try to drift into sleep. Suddenly, I hear a scratching sound and I jump up screaming. Pucci runs into the room. "It's okay, Chanel. It's just Cuckoo Cougar!"

I forgot all about poor little Cuckoo, the African pygmy hedgehog that I bought Pucci for his birthday. He is tucked away in a cage under the desk. I start crying again and pull the blanket over my head.

"Don't worry, Chanel," Pucci says. "That mouse will be singing its last lullaby in peanut butter heaven." Pucci runs out of his room and I can't help but laugh to myself. I forgot how funny Pucci is. When we were younger, I used to laugh at him all the time. Now I know why he calls me *"loco Coco,"* because I really do act like a cuckoo bird sometimes.

Chapter 9

When I tell Bubbles about my unexpected visit from the mouse and his family (even though I didn't see the relatives, I believe Pucci for once), she feels sorry for me. "Auntie Juanita is right. They probably were living in pickle jars in the basement of that store for years before they had to run for cover," she says, chuckling, then puts her arms around me. "I guess Princess Pamela was right too—you finally met the furry creature who is trying to paw its way into your life."

"I almost got bit by a mouse and you say something mean to me?" I say, my mouth trembling.

"Chanel, mice don't bite—for real," Dorinda says, stroking my shoulder.

"What am I going to do about my math homework?" I ask, suddenly realizing that I'll be stuffed in a pickle jar if I miss any more math assignments.

"We'll do it at lunchtime together," Bubbles says quickly, then looks at Dorinda to back her up.

"Yup, we got you covered," Dorinda says, nodding.

I look at both of them, surprised that they would give up lunch for me.

If things couldn't be any worse, Derek and Mackerel see me crying and come right over, but Bubbles puts up her hand and blurts out, "Put it on pause, *please*."

"Ayiight, but Daisy D. told us you put out a cheetah distress signal. We wuz just looking out," Mackerel says with an attitude, looking at me. I try to wipe away my tears, but everybody at school knows I've been crying.

"We got the situation under control, but thanks for the lookout," Dorinda says, being nice. She is always nice to Mackerel and Derek, even though they usually ignore her.

After lunch, I feel so much better because Dorinda really helped me with my homework. She is so smart. I still feel dizzy, but I don't say anything to Bubbles and Dorinda as we walk to dance class, which we all take together. I also decide I am *not* going home later, no matter what Mamí says.

"What did she say?" Bubbles asks me as I put down the cell phone after talking with Mamí.

"She said the construction company is going to send in an exterminator for the whole building," I explain. See, Mamí owns the loft so it's not like she can call a super for anything, like Madrina can. Mamí has to take care of everything herself and now that Daddy isn't there, nothing gets taken care of, *está bien*? I look over at Dorinda and realize I shouldn't complain. Her whole building is smelly and disgusting and I bet the super doesn't do anything but watch the *cucarachas* play tic-tac-toe all day. *Cuatro* yuks.

Walking into the gym locker room, I tell Bubbles and Dorinda, "I'm not going home tonight."

"Of course, you're not," Bubbles says firmly. "The only 'Mouse' we want to be in the house with is Mouse Almighty, and since he has forsaken us for a platinum pussycat named after a liqueur, we plan on staying mouse-less for a while, anyway."

"Can I stay at your house tonight?" I ask Bubbles.

"You don't have to ask, Miss Cuchifrito. As long as you don't pull any pirouette moves and pull a muscle, the couch is yours," Bubbles says, then giggles. "I'm only kidding. Consider it an official sleepover."

Inside, I get excited. Now I'll get to play with Ragu and Toto as long as I want. Suddenly, I feel like a *babosa* for being mad at Bubbles. If she wasn't my friend, I don't know what I would do.

Dorinda changes into her tights. I watch her carefully because I wish I was skinny like she is. As I go to put my foot in my tights, I lose my balance and bang into the locker.

"You awright?" Dorinda asks.

I rest my head against the locker for a second, then quickly say, "No, I'm okay. I just lost my balance. I was thinking about the stupid mouse again. His eyes were so black!"

Dorinda and Bubbles are so curious that they forget about my dizzy spell. "You could really see his eyes?" Dorinda asks in disbelief, her own almond-shaped brown eyes widening like she is watching a horror movie.

"Yeah, I saw them," I say, nodding my head and wiggling into my tights. "I'll never forget those beady, greedy eyes." I catch a glimpse of myself in the long mirror and see that my tummy is a little flatter. Now I feel giddy because my carrot diet is working.

Dance class is our favorite class of the week at school, and we always stand in the back so we can watch each other's moves carefully. Today we have a substitute teacher, Mrs. Driscoll, and she is really working us hard. "One, two, three," she says as we do our combinations, which seem harder than usual. As a matter of fact, my whole body is shaking. Turning on the jazz step, my legs feel like spaghetti, and suddenly, I feel myself falling on the gymnasium floor.

"Chuchie!!" Bubbles screams, but she sounds like she is a million miles away.

When I open my eyes, I am lying on a cot in the school nurse's office. Mrs. Coates, the school nurse, comes right over. "Chanel, don't be alarmed. You fainted," she says in her soothing voice. I hear Bubbles talking in the background, but I can't see her. "Can we see her now. She's awake, I saw her," Bubbles is saying to someone. I hold my head up and see that Bubbles is talking to Darrell, the school security guard.

"Auntie Juanita is on her way," Bubbles whispers loudly across the room, motioning to me with her hands. Now I see that Dorinda is right beside her.

"Could you please just have a seat for a second," Mrs. Coates says firmly to Bubbles and Dorinda.

I fight back the tears, because suddenly I realize what I have secretly known for a while. There is probably something really wrong with me and Mrs. Coates is going to tell me. They are probably going to take me to one of those special hospitals where they take really sick, terminally ill patients who can't go home anymore. The tears start streaming down my face. That's what I get for saying I didn't want to go home anymore. *Now I'm not going home for real.*

Mrs. Coates stands by me and waits for me to stop crying. "Chanel," she says gently.

I can't answer Mrs. Coates because I am crying so hard. She stands there patiently, adjusting my intravenous bottle on its stand.

"Chanel, I need to ask you a few questions," Mrs. Coates says, standing over me.

I nod "yes."

"Upon examination, it seems you are completely dehydrated and carbohydrate deficient. The intravenous is feeding you glucose." Mrs. Coates says. "What have you been eating?"

I wonder what carbohydrate deficient means, but I just take a deep sigh and tell Mrs. Coates the truth, "Carrots. Nothing but carrots."

"That's what I thought from the color on your fingers," Mrs. Coates says, shaking her head. "Why would you do something like that?"

"I just wanted to lose weight," I explain, sobbing.

"That is not the way to go about it," Mrs. Coates stays sternly. "Your mother has been contacted and will be here shortly. She will be instructed to feed you lots of carbohydrates."

"Carbohydrates?" I ask.

"You're going to have to eat pasta, bread—in other words, young lady, anything but carrots for the next few days," Mrs. Coates adds. "Do you understand?"

"Yes," I say. "Do I have to go to a special hospital or something?"

"No. You keep this up, however, and you'll end up in an eating disorder clinic. Do you understand?"

"Yes, I understand. If I don't eat food, then I will have to go to a place where they force you to eat, right?" I respond to Mrs. Coates.

"That's a dramatic way of putting it, but yes, your food intake would be monitored very closely," Mrs. Coates explains.

No way, José! I want to scream. I don't want to go home, but I don't want to have to stay in some sort of creepy hospital and be force-fed.

"Okay, you can come over for a few minutes," Mrs. Coates says, motioning to Bubbles and Dorinda.

"Okay, Bugs Bunny, we're going to my house to

eat, and you know what that means—pasta till it comes out your nose," Bubbles says firmly. I feel so ashamed that I fainted and ended up causing everyone problems.

"I'm sorry, Bubbles," I say, and the tears start streaming down my face.

Bubbles looks at me in the same way she did when I charged up Mamí's credit card and got caught—like I'm a basket case *babosa*.

"Why did you do it?" Bubbles asks, and I can tell she really wants to know.

"I thought if I looked like Zimora Chin we could get a record deal quicker," I say, laughing, because now I can hear how silly I sound. "That's why I got my hair straightened too."

"Wow. I don't get you, Chuchie. I know you have a weakness for carats—but not this kind," Bubbles says, turning to Dorinda who just shrugs her shoulders. At first, I don't get what Bubbles means, then I understand. She is talking about the diamond stud earrings that Princess Pamela gave me from Tiffany's.

"How do you make up these things in that piñata head of yours?"

"Well, you're kinda bossy, Bubbles, and I never feel like I'm doing anything right," I blurt out to my best friend.

271

"Chuchie, everything I do is to make sure that *our* dreams come true," Bubbles whispers to me so that Dorinda doesn't hear. "And besides, you're kinda sneaky!"

"No, I'm not!" I wince, but I know it's true. It seems like I'm always keeping secrets.

"Okay, I take it back," Bubbles says smiling and holding my hand. "You're *very* sneaky!"

"I know," I sigh, defeated. Then I ask the question that I've been avoiding. "But what is going to happen about the competition?"

"I don't know," Bubbles says, shaking her head sadly.

The door opens and Mamí walks in. Now I know the answer to that question. She's not going to let us go on Saturday. I know Mamí.

As Mamí walks toward me, I notice she is wearing makeup and a pink knit cap. When I look closer, I realize that it is my pink knit cap, but I don't say anything. Mamí looks so pretty. Bubbles is really nice to Mamí and tries to make it sound like I fainted because I was upset by the mouse, but Mrs. Coates comes over and puts an end to that fake medical report.

"Your daughter was severely dehydrated from lack of sufficient caloric intake." Mrs. Coates goes on explaining to Mamí the extent of my incident.

"But you can take her home and contact your physician should there be any further complications."

Further complications? I wonder what Mrs. Coates means by that, but I don't ask. Bubbles helps me up from the gurney. I expect Mamí to yell at me, but she is very calm and talks to Bubbles in a normal voice.

"Dottie is waiting for us," Mamí says to Bubbles. I wonder if Mamí is going to spend the night in our "mouse house" or if she is going to spend the night at Mr. Tycoon's.

"I feel okay, now," I tell Mamí so she doesn't worry about me.

Mamí just smiles at me and doesn't say anything. She looks at my hands and I know just what she's thinking. As we're leaving, I want to ask Mrs. Coates why Bugs Bunny didn't have orange fingers too.

"I got your clothes from the gym locker," Bubbles says, carrying my backpack for me. "I wish you could stay with us tonight, too, Do'." Dorinda piles into the taxi after Bubbles because Mamí insists that we drop off Dorinda before we head to the Upper East Side. Dorinda doesn't protest.

"Um, see you tomorrow," Dorinda says when

we reach 116th Street in front of the Cornwall Projects, where she lives. I'm so glad she said that, in case Mamí had any ideas about me staying home from school tomorrow. No way I want to miss school tomorrow so peeps can keep talking about me fainting in dance class.

When we get to Madrina's, I run to her for a big hug. "I'm so sorry, *Madrina*," I whisper into her ear.

Mamí and Madrina go into the kitchen together and we can hear them talking loudly all the way in the living room.

"I knew her fingers were orange for a reason," Mamí moans.

"So what do you want, Juanita," Madrina says, raising her voice, "a Cracker Jack prize? I wouldn't worry about the carrots if I were you. It's time to stop pretending everything is okay between you and your daughter."

Bubbles and I look at each other like, someone call the referee, please.

"Okay," Bubbles says, jumping up. "Daddy's on his way home, but we don't have to wait for him to cook. I know how to throw down too."

"I don't think you should go in the kitchen," I say, wincing. But Bubbles doesn't listen to me. She waltzes right into the kitchen and I can hear her fumbling in the cupboards. "Oops," Bubbles says, dropping something on the kitchen floor. "Sorry, Mr. Rigatoni, but your services won't be needed tonight. Mr. Fettuccine is the flour of the hour."

I can tell that Mamí and Madrina are ignoring Bubbles because they keep talking for a few more minutes before they come out into the living room. I hope Madrina talked Mamí into letting us perform on Saturday. *Por favor, Dios.*

While Bubbles is boiling the fettuccine, Uncle Franco comes home. I see his face, and that's when I realize how embarrassed I am. Uncle Franco always cooks for us and I feel bad for lying to him about eating his food last Sunday. Or I should say not eating his food. He puts his arms out for me to hug him and says, "If you wanted me to cook for you again—all you had to do was ask, *cara*. You didn't have to faint for it."

"I'm sorry, Uncle Franco," I say, whining. Mamí is staring at me, then she takes a deep breath. "I have to meet the exterminator in half an hour."

"Listen, Juanita, you can go ahead now. If anything happens, I'll call you, but she'll be fine here," Madrina says. I am so relieved that I am spending the night here. Waiting for dinner, I start to think maybe Madrina is right: there is something wrong between Mamí and me. I guess it isn't normal that

I hate her sometimes. I bet she calls Daddy and tells him what happened. I hate to disappoint Daddy—again.

I make sure to eat all the fettuccine carbonara on my plate, then ask for a second helping.

"Wow, take it easy, greasy," Bubbles says, smiling at me.

"I guess I didn't realize I was so hungry until now," I say, smiling nervously.

"Maybe that's a blessing, Chanel," Madrina says, delicately putting the fettuccine on her fork. "I always realize I'm hungry an hour before my stomach does."

After we finish eating and are watching television, I decide to get the nerve up to ask Madrina the question we all want to know. "Are we going to perform on Saturday in the competition?" I ask, unbuttoning my pants so my stomach can breathe.

Madrina takes forever to answer. "I'm gonna make you the same deal I made Bubbles. If I see one carrot within one block of you, you can kiss that Girlie Show Boutique certificate good-bye!"

Bubbles jumps up from the couch and hugs me tight, then gives me a Cheetah Girls handshake. "Come on, Chuchie, let's twist again like we did last summer!'

Chapter 10

By Saturday morning I feel stronger than Superwoman, Batgirl, and Catwoman all rolled into one cheetah *mamacita*. Mamí doesn't put up a fight at all about me going to Drinka Champagne's for my vocal classes, or competing later in the competition. She seems kinda different today, and I'm so embarrassed about the incident at school. I mean, it's been a long time since she had to come pick me up from school like I was little kid with a tummyache.

"You should let me handle it!" Pucci yells at Mamí. He is kinda upset with Mamí, though, for letting the exterminator remove all of his glue traps.

"He wanted to see if his peanut butter mouse-traps would work," I tell Danitra and some of the other peeps at Drinka's.

Today, of course, everybody at Drinka's is

amped up about the competition later. "Mostly everybody is coming," squeals Danitra, who is the only other student besides Fabulina Fredericks who took the competition bait.

"Honey, I don't need any more dance classes!" exclaims Malcolm Extra, who waves his hand when asked why he didn't enter the competition. He is a supa chilly falsetto singer who also goes to Performing Arts with Aqua and Angie.

"You girls are gonna have to be ferocious today," Winnie the receptionist yells to us as she walks into the vocal studio. I guess she means all of us, not just the Cheetah Girls I realize, disappointed. (We think Winnie really likes us the best of all the students.)

"We know. We're gonna have to really bring it today," Dorinda whispers to our crew. I can tell by the scrunchies on her forehead that she is worried and nervous at the same time, just like I am.

"We were so worried about you, Miss Chanel," Aqua says as we take our place in vocal class. "If you ever pull a stunt like that again, I swear we are going to enter you in the Urban Rodeo Contest in Houston and see how long you last on that mechanical bronco!"

"I know," I say, wincing. "Just call me *basta*, pasta from now on, *está bien*?"

"Uh-oh, SpaghettiOs," Bubbles says under her

breath when she sees that oh-so-slippery Eddie Lizard. I can tell just by the way she looks at him that I am right. She still has a crush—*tiene un coco*—on Eddie Lizard! At least Aqua pretends she doesn't see him. Bubbles runs over to talk to Eddie Lizard like someone shot her out of a cannonball. I try not to act like I care. I guess it does make me sad, though, that Mackerel isn't going to come see us perform at the Harlem School competition.

"It would take a mighty storm to keep that Hambone character away from Bubbles," Aqua chuckles, still pretending she doesn't see Eddie Lizard. Aqua met Derek and Mackerel at the Mad Millenium Fashion Show we all went to at Times Square. Derek was in the show and he invited us. "I thought he was gonna fall in the punch bowl and go swimming," exclaims Aqua, smacking her lips.

I don't say anything because it's obvious that Mackerel wouldn't do the same thing for me.

It's not until we're backstage in the dressing room at the Harlem School of the Arts competition that I get the nerve up to ask Bubbles what she was talking about to Eddie Lizard today. "Oh, he says he's coming to see us perform," Bubbles says, a satisfied smirk on her face.

"What are you going to do, Miss Galleria, with

two suitors coming to fill your glass with punch?" Aqua asks curiously while she changes into her red cheetah dress. (I'm so glad Madrina talked us into wearing red for the competition because it matches the Christmas decorations all around the auditorium.)

"I don't know—keep them on separate sides of the room, I guess," Bubbles coos back, like her dance card is always full. There are two dressing areas in the back—one for boy acts and one for the girls—but there is no privacy because it is just a big, communal space, so we have to stand in front of each other while we're changing.

"I can't believe Monie hooked you up," I say, gushing over Dorinda's straight hairstyle. Dorinda's older foster sister who she calls Monie the meanie behind her back has finally decided to go to beauty school and become a hairstylist. Dorinda became her first subject, or your could say, first victim, judging by all the burn marks Dorinda has. *Pobrecita* Dorinda pulls back her bangs to show us the burn marks from the hot comb on her temple.

"Did it hurt?" I ask.

"Probably not anymore than that gunk that Pepto B. put on your head," Dorinda says, smoothing down her hair. "Nothing wrong with a few battle scars."

"Lord knows the Cheetah Girls sure have enough of them," Angie says, nodding her head like she is testifying in church.

All of a sudden, Dorinda, who is facing us, gets a look on her face like she has just seen the Sandman practicing with his hook.

Galleria, don't look, but we've got a situation," Dorinda says.

Bubbles turns her head immediately, and so do the rest of us.

"Tell me I'm not having déjà vu," Bubbles says, imitating Fantasia from Pepto B.'s.

"Tell me I'm not seeing double," Aqua says, staring with her mouth open at the girl group on the other side of the dressing room. The four girls, who are about our age, are all decked out in brown cheetah tube tops and miniskirts! Of course, they are staring at us too now. As a matter of fact, they are radiating supa attitude in our direction.

"Who are they?" Dorinda asks nervously. And we're all wondering the same thing—out of what jungle did the fake wannabe cheetahs crawl?

"Mom will handle this situation," Bubbles says, biting her lip while trying to keep her nostrils from flaring which means she is *caliente* mad. The five of us stand there like mummies waiting for Madrina to come back into the dressing room. She told us she would be waiting in the front for Uncle Franco to park the car. It could take him a long time to find a parking space in this neighborhood.

Danitra runs over with Fabulina Fredericks, who is huffing and puffing like she just ran track. "You are not going to believe this."

"Trust me, we'll believe anything 'cuz this has just turned into another 'Nightmare on Elm Street,'" Aqua says. A lightbulb goes off in my piñata head. Now I know what Bubbles meant by déjà vu. She was talking about the nightmare we went through at the Apollo Amateur Hour contest. I feel a chill running through my body, remembering that horrible "aghast from the past," as Madrina would say.

"The name of their group is the Fabulations," Fabulina says in disbelief. "They are true haters!" We all stand there like deer caught in the headlights instead of cheetahs. Fabulina stomps her foot and folds her arms across her chest. "I'm ready to lose it. I don't think I'm going to perform."

"Oh, I get it now. They don't care whose flavor they're biting—just as long as they're biting," Bubbles says, nodding her head in a daze. "Maybe we shouldn't perform either."

Aqua and Angie stop changing into their outfits and sit down on the aluminum chairs with their hands in their laps like they are about to start a prayer vigil in church.

"Um, what are we gonna do?" Dorinda asks, squirming in her chair.

"Everybody just chill—'cuz we may just have to blow this Popsicle stand," Bubbles says, her eyes dancing all over the place as she tries to figure out our next move.

Finally, Madrina walks into the dressing room with Toto, and everybody turns to stare at her because she is six feet tall and decked out in cheetah from toe to head, including her big furry (fake) cheetah hat. "Oh, dear, what do we have here?" Madrina says out loud, almost as if she is talking to herself. Madrina stops dead in her cheetah tracks and stares in disbelief at the bite-happy fake wannabe Cheetah Girls. Even Toto rests on his haunches and stares at the pathetic girls.

"Young ladies, can I have a word with you or your management?" Madrina asks them, staring at the girl closest to her who is wearing black rubber earrings that look more hula than hoop, *está bien*. All of a sudden, the girls start acting like they swallowed a bag of canaries.

"Hmm. Hmm. Where's all that serious attitude they were radiating before, I wonder?" Bubbles says to Fabulina. "Gone like *cucarachas* running from a Roach Motel eviction notice, that's where."

Even Fabulina puts her hands on her hips, waiting for Madrina to get this rodeo started.

"Could someone pass the pumice stone, please," Fabulina says, as the roughest-looking girl in the bunch who has ashy knees walks over to Madrina.

"Whom am I speaking to?" Madrina asks the girl who is trying hard to look up at Madrina.

"Cassandra," she mumbles.

"Well, Cassandra, may I ask who your costume designer is?"

Cassandra gives Madrina a very puzzled look.

"Exactly—that's what I thought," Madrina responds. "What about your manager?"

Cassandra gives Madrina another puzzled look.

"Okay, so some of us don't know our ABCs. Let me try another approach. Do you know who we are?" Madrina asks, pointing over to the five of us.

"Yeah—I guess," Cassandra says, sucking her mouth. "They the girls that lost the *Amateur* Hour contest at the Apollo?"

"That's right—so why would you want to be wearing outfits that represent the theme of our group instead of wearing something that represents the theme of yours. On that note, may I suggest chokers with dangling fangs?" Madrina says, getting huffy.

"'Cuz we didn't know they would be here, that's why," Cassandra says, getting huffy back at Madrina.

"I see, said the blind man—and obviously blind girls," Madrina says, shaking her head at Cassandra and her crew like they're anything but faboo. "You know what I think? You girls need to rethink your image and right now would be as good a time as any to get started."

"What you mean rethink?" shouts the one with the supersize-me hoop earrings. "I know you don't mean we should change our outfits!"

Fabulina can't hold herself back anymore. She stands next to Madrina and blurts out, "We mean you need to change the name of your group—and your whole safari situation."

"We're not having it," says the hoop-ty girl.

By now the other acts in the dressing room—Sonia Santes, the Smugaboos, the Twilights, and JuJu Quinnonez—are watching us like a Pay Per View boxing match. "I'll be right back, girls. Somebody is going to lose their spots over this," Madrina says. The Fabulations start pacing up and down in the dressing room and whispering among themselves. We hang tight. Nervous but very tight.

"Everytime we come uptown, somebody is trying to start some mess with us," Aqua says, shaking her head. "I don't understand. Are we jinxed or something?"

"Aqua, take the pins out of the voodoo doll, okay? Staying downtown is not going to solve our problems," Bubbles says, waving her hands. "There's always going be some drama and kaflamma, and right about now that just happens to be these, um . . ." Galleria pauses as if she is trying to think of the right word.

"Heffas," Aqua butts in. "Just call them what they are. Plain ole heffas."

Madrina returns with Ms. Coley, the talent coordinator for the competition. We watch as she carefully explains everything. "Frankly, I don't understand how you could let this happen," Madrina adds politely.

"Okay, girls," Ms. Coley says, turning to all of us. "This talent show is for a very good cause. At the Harlem School of the Arts we nurture performing artists unique self-expression."

"Unique self-expression?" Madrina says in disbelief. "These girls are shameless copycats. And from the looks of their scraggly ragtag outfits, I'd say they aren't even good at that!"

"Oh, I'm about to go off on Mama Bear over there," cuts in the hoop-ty girl who calls herself Sonaysha.

"Young lady, if you continue in this fashion, then I will have to ask your group to leave," Ms. Coley says bluntly.

The room gets eerily quiet.

"As I was saying, all artists have the right to find their own unique voice—and image. At the Harlem School of the Arts our mission is to nurture those choices. We are here today to provide an opportunity to all the talent in this room to find that unique self-expression," Ms. Coley says adamantly. "Am I making myself clear?"

We all look at Ms. Coley with a blank stare.

"I will tape up the lineup for the competition in each of the dressing rooms," Ms. Coley says, taping sheets to the wall. "I suggest that each of you reads the lineup sheet so that you will know the order of the competition. If there is any more disturbance in this room, you'll be asked to leave."

After Ms. Coley leaves the room, Bubbles asks Madrina, "Mom, what do you think we should do?"

"Well," Madrina says, pausing for what seems like forever, "in the immortal words of James Brown, Tina Turner, and every performer who has ever had to subject themselves to the chitlin' circuit just to get some respect, I say, The show must go on!"

We stand there, silent for *un segundo*—a long moment—trying to take in what Madrina just said.

"I don't care about this stupid performance anymore," Bubbles says, pouting. "And Aqua is right too. Every time we come uptown, we're getting static. We should stay downtown so peeps can stop swiping our porridge!"

Now my stomach is upset, but I don't say anything. "I have to go to the bathroom," I say, wincing as I run to the toilet. Just what I need—all of a sudden I have a bad case of the "runnies."

Let's just say I'm in the bathroom for more than a minute trying to get my runnies situation under control. All of a sudden, I hear Bubbles knocking on the restroom stall. "Chuchie, you okay in there?" she asks, concerned, like maybe I'm sneaking carrots again or something.

"I have the runnies—that's all, Bubbles, I swear. *Te juro*," I say, whining.

I don't tell Bubbles that I don't want to come out of the restroom. I just want to hide in here forever!

"Can you believe this drama? I can't believe Eddie Lizard is coming—of all the times he is coming to see us perform," Bubbles says moaning through the stall door. *I knew it.* Bubbles *still* has a crush on Eddie Lizard. "Why does he have to come tonight?"

I get scared by the tone of Bubbles's voice. "You don't think we're gonna lose, do you?" I ask, but I really don't want to know the answer for real.

"I don't know what to think anymore—not tonight anyway," Bubbles says, tapping the melody to "Wannabe Stars in the Jiggy Jungle" on the stall door. "You should be glad that Mackerel isn't coming."

"Yeah, I know," I say, even though I still feel disappointed about him dissing me like that in front of everybody at school.

"You know I was kinda jealous of him goospitating over you all of a sudden," Bubbles admits.

"I know," I say, smiling to myself, then flushing the toilet. "Sorry for the stinky poo." Taking my Yves Saint Bernard cologne out, I spray around the stall. Bubbles doesn't answer me because she has run to the stall next to me and it sounds like she's throwing up.

"Bubbles!" I shriek, standing on the toilet seat so I can peek into the stall next to me to see what she is doing. "What happened?"

Bubbles is bent over the toilet throwing up. "Should I go get *Madrina*?" I ask, scared. Bubbles is never sick. I am always the one who is sick.

"No!" she yells adamantly. "I'm fine. God, this sucks!" Bubbles jumps up and kicks the side of the restroom stall. Then all of a sudden, she starts balling her eyes out like a baby. I don't know what to do. I'm freaking out. My head feels dizzy and I think I'm going to faint. Bubbles sits down on the toilet seat and grabs lots of toilet paper and starts blowing her nose. I rest my head on the stall so that I can keep calm. "Bubbles, you were right about Princess Pamela. She didn't know what she was talking about—about the furry creature and everything," I say, moaning. "Maybe *this* is a sign—you know what's happening to us—and maybe we should listen. I mean, we don't have to be in a singing group. We could open a pet store like we wanted to before or a beauty parlor for people—and pets together."

All of a sudden, Bubbles starts laughing through all her slobbering. "You always make me laugh, Chuchie."

"But this could be horrible if we go out there and perform," I say, pleading with Bubbles because I'm really afraid. But Bubbles isn't listening to me.

"Sorry for what I said about Princess Pamela, by the way," Bubbles says, smirking. "Maybe her crystal ball just got a little cloudy or something. I know she really loves you."

"Yeah," I say. Now I feel my eyes starting to water.

"Please, Chuchie, don't start with the Niagara Falls display again—please!" Bubbles says, looking at me straight in the face. "Come on, let's just do this. We can twist again like we did last summer!"

Every time Bubbles says that, it makes me laugh.

Chapter 11

We all try not to freak out that the Fabulations are scheduled to perform before the Cheetah Girls. "There's never a Sandman around when you really need one," Aqua says, like she's talking to a church choir.

"You look *fabulous*," Madrina says to each of us as we hold hands to say our Cheetah Girls prayer. "No, *you* look fabulous!" Angie says to Madrina, and starts laughing hysterically. I guess we are all really nervous now. When we say the line in our prayer, "May we summon the growl power of all the divas who came before us right here, right now," we look at each other hard because we know that we really mean it now.

One of Ms. Coley's assistants ushers us out of the dressing room and into the backstage area to stand in position. When the assistant positions the

Fabulation fakes nearest to the curtain because it's their turn to perform, Aqua pretends to poke her finger into her left eyeball and moans, "This ought to be a real *eye opener*."

"It sounds like it's really crowded in the audience," Dorinda says, getting amped. So far some of the acts have been really good, so the show isn't as corny as we thought it was going to be. In other words, it's not just full of imitators like the Fabulations.

The crowd roars as the master of ceremonies, Show Bizza, takes the microphone onstage and proceeds to announce the Fabulations. He is a rapper from the Bronx who had one hit record back in the Nineties called "Datz a Hoot."

"Hailing from my hometown—that's right—the Boogie Down ain't just a borough y'all—the Bronx—these four freshman from Soundview High are here to tell us all about the tribulations of being downright fabulous. Please welcome our next contestants in the Can We Get a Groove? competition at the fabulous Harlem School of the Arts—THE FABULATIONS!"

We all put our hands together and do a fake clap in unison, then sneer out loud. The track music to Britney Spears's "Oops, I Did It Again" pipes up loudly and we look at each other in disgust. "It figures—taking bites wherever they can," Bubbles says, nodding at us like, *What are we sweating? We've got this comp on lockdown.*

It turns out that Sonaysa is the lead singer of the group because she leads the vocals. "Oops, I did it again, I broke all the rules, then stole your heart. I guess I'm just too fabulous!"

We burst into fits of giggles because we are soo relieved that the Fabulations are just that—"Something made up out of plain nothing!" Aqua says, shaking her head in disbelief. "We're gonna go out there and tear it up, you hear me?"

It turns out that we're not the only ones laughing at the Fabulations' amateurish act. (There is nothing other groups hate more than singers who use other singers' material in competition shows.) As we look around backstage, we see some of the other acts laughing too. So far, our biggest competition turns out to be Danitra. "It's a good thing she left all that pink stuff behind and came out solo," Bubbles riffs. It's true. Danitra seems to be finding her own groove, as Drinka Champagne would say. I'm proud of Danitra for not being a copycat like the silly girls on stage right now.

Madrina stands right by the stage so she can let Toto run on at the right moment to do his little dance number. "Keep your eye on the prize," she yells at us as we hit the stage. The best and worst part about performing is the moment you hit the stage and see the audience. My stomach is doing the salsa, but this time in a good way because I don't feel sick anymore. As we sing our favorite number, "Wannabe Stars in the Jiggy Jungle," I can tell that the audience is digging our flavor. Right on the chorus, Toto runs onto the stage and does his twirling dance number. The audience loses it! They start clapping hysterically. I look over at Bubbles and smile. She was right—Toto could take us straight to the top. All of a sudden, I start thinking about our world tour—Toto comes onstage in a little cape studded with rhinestones. I see the poster for our world tour—Toto is right in the middle of us wearing his little cheetah hat draped in diamonds.

As we take our bows, I am grinning from ear to ear. Right there standing on the stage I realize, Who cares if we win the competition? Or even if we get a record deal. The fun part is performing. There is nothing else like that. *Nada, está bien*?

Finally, the moment we have been waiting for arrives. After the last act performs (two rappers named the Buddha Boys whose raps were weak), Show Bizza comes onstage to announce the winners of the "Can We Get a Groove?" competition. I take back everything I said before. Now all I care about is that we win this competition! I start to pray and grab Dorinda's hand, "Please, God, let us win and I'll never ask you for anything again," I say, giggling, "until tomorrow—*manana!*"

Show Bizza prowls on the stage in his black tailcoat, zoot pants and top hat. "Now that was a show—am I right?" Show Bizza asks the audience, spreading his arms wide like a scarecrow on a post. "We had a little safari action—okay, a lot of that," he says, pausing so the audience gets a laugh at our expense. "We had some spiritual riffs, a dancing dog, okay, and a few hyenas." The audience bursts out laughing again. I feel a chill go through my body—like was the hyena part supposed to be about us too? I look at Aqua who just shakes her head like, Don't mind that.

"And most of all," Show Bizza continues, "we had a lot of fun and gave some of the young talent in our community a chance to shine on scholarship time if they're lucky—am I right?" Show Bizza nods his head at the audience.

"Okay, in third place—winning a Radio Shack certificate and dinner for two at Red Lobster, we have," Show Bizza says, fumbling while he tries to take the paper out of the envelope. "Please bear with an old school player like myself. What's that say—I'm just joking—all right—the winner is those Brooklyn tap dancers—Smugaboo!"

The audience claps while we hold each other's hands tighter. I try not to glance over at the Fabulations, but I can't help it. I'm not the only one, either—Fabulina is staring down Cassandra like, "Lunch time is coming up!"

"Our second-place winner is—from make-money Manny-Hanny—DANITRA!" Show Bizza shouts.

Aqua lets out a sigh. "Thank you, God, for not letting JuJu win. Now keep up the good work!"

We all giggle hysterically as we wait for Show Bizza to announce the grand prize winner.

"And taking first place in our competition which is celebrating the 35th-year-anniversary of the Harlem School of the Arts. By the way, can you believe it's been that long?" Show Bizza asks, waiting for the audience to answer, but they shout out, "Come on, bring it!" Show Bizza starts laughing. "I'm just playing with y'all—all right, the winner is." He stares at the paper in his hand for a long time like he can't see, then shouts, "Now we know who's not a wannabe up in here."

We look at each other and pause like petrified cheetahs waiting for Show Bizza to break it out.

"Okay, well, truthfully, the other groups didn't stand a chance once my man Toto hit the stage."

I burst into tears and cover my face before Show Bizza even finishes.

"You believe that dog? He had a rump shaker cuter than half the girls I've dated!" Show Bizza shouts, cracking himself up. "Well he's a top dog now—come on out here, you dirty dog. Oh, and bring THE CHEETAH GIRLS!"

Bubbles shoots out her right arm and cups her paw, doing our Growl Power sign. "YES! I TOLD YOU WE WERE POISED FOR THE NOISE!"

Meanwhile, Madrina shoves Toto into Bubbles's arms and pushes us out onstage.

I can't stop crying and I can't even see where I'm going, so Dorinda grabs my arm to make sure I don't trip over anything. The more the audience claps, the more I keep crying. Bubbles lets Toto get down on the stage and takes the envelope from Show Bizza. He gives her a hug. Toto does another little dance and the audience goes wild.

As soon as we get backstage and into the dressing room, Madrina says, "What did I tell you girls—real talent always shines through."

"I guess they'll be changing their spots real soon," Aqua says, quietly looking over at the Fabulations.

"And their name too, I hope," Angie shouts loudly so they can hear.

"And their profession," Madrina chimes in.

"Guess what, Miss Chanel?" Aqua says proudly, turning to Aqua for approval. "We have decided to name our puppy Coco in your honor."

"Oh, that is so *coolio*," I coo, and this time I really mean it. Even though I am still sad about not getting a puppy, I am happy that Aqua and Angie have one, and now they've named it after my middle name.

"That's tight," Dorinda says, nodding her approval. We all quickly change into our clothes and head to the reception area so we can celebrate our latest Cheetah Girls victory.

"What's the word on the street now!" Bubbles yells out as we approach. "I'll tell you what it is—get ready for a global getdown!" As we enter the reception area, all our peeps from Drinka Champagne come running up to us, yelping and screaming.

"Cheetah Girls—that was dee-luxe!" screams Malcolm Extra, throwing his arms around us.

I notice Bubbles really eyeing the room, and I know what she is doing. "Have you seen Eddie Lizard?" she asks Malcolm, who heckles, "He ain't been slinking around here, that's for sure. I haven't seen him since class this afternoon."

Bubbles tries to hide it, but her face falls like an avalanche. Just as quickly, I see disappointment flicker into Bubbles's eyes and I turn around to see Derek and Mackerel. My heart stops. *I can't believe he came!*

"What's up, *señorita*?" Mackerel says, trying not to smile.

I can't help smiling and shouting at him, "I'm sorry about the other day!"

"Oh, I got that—no ruffle," Mackerel says, embarrassed that he let me see him get mad.

All of a sudden, Pucci pushes Mackerel and the other peeps out of the way, introducing himself loudly. "I'm Spida Man. The Cheetah Girls' manager!"

"Hey, pooch, what you got in that bag?" Bubbles says, giggling at my little brother. "Dig the threads, by the way."

"Chanel—I got something for you!" he says excitedly.

"What, Pucci," I say, beaming at my little brother, who looks so handsome in the burgundy velvet suit that Madrina bought him for his birthday.

"I told you my mousetrap works. Look inside, one of the mouse got stuck on one!" Pucci says proudly, shoving the paper bag in my face.

I let out a scream and push the paper bag away. Mackerel and Derek burst out laughing. "That's right, little man. Show 'em how to exterminate a situation."

"I'm just kidding," Pucci says, smirking up a storm. "Go ahead—look in the bag!"

"Pucci, if this is one of your jokes," I warn my brother, grabbing the bag slowly, "it will be the last one you pull before you're locked away in reform school."

I open the bag and look inside, puzzled. "A doggy bone?" Shaking my head, I beam at my brother. "Thanks, Pucci. I'll save it for breakfast, if that's all right with you?"

"You don't have to, *loco Coco*! Somebody else is going to eat it," Pucci says, laughing.

I laugh back at my brother because I finally get his jokes. He must be talking about the mouse in my bedroom. "Right, Pucci."

"Is he really your manager?" Mackerel asks, chuckling.

"No, Bubbles's mother is," I say, pointing to Madrina.

"I'm sorry about jamming you up with your girl," Mackerel confesses, but I don't get it.

"What happened?" I ask.

"You know—that songwriting thing," Mackerel

continues, shoving his hands in his pocket. "See, Derek told me about the beef you two had with writing songs together."

"Oh, you knew about that?" I ask, finally realizing that Mackerel had set me up when he let the cat out of the bag at school the other day. "Well, sometimes I tell fib-eronis. So now you know my little secret."

"Well, I kinda knew that already," Mackerel says, chuckling uncontrollably. My face turns such a bright shade of red and I can feel my skin radiating. "But you're real cool or else I wouldn't be messing with you."

I feel a tap on my shoulder and turn around. "Surprise!" Pucci screams, shouting at the top of his lungs.

I am speechless. Mamí is standing in front of me holding Nobu. I can't believe she would hold a dog. She never even held Toto.

"Is Mrs. Bosco here?" I ask Mamí, taking Nobu from her arms.

"Oh, yeah, I think she is over there," Mamí answers.

"I'm so glad you like Nobu," I coo, beaming at Mamí.

"This is not Nobu," Mamí says, smiling.

"Oh, who is it then?" I ask, snuggling my nose to

the puppy. "I know it's not Ragu—his eyes are darker."

"He's yours—you name him what you want," Mamí says proudly.

"I told you, *loco Coco*, somebody else was going to be eating the bone!" Pucci shouts, proud of himself for keeping a secret. I wonder how long he has known about this.

I start crying and Bubbles comes over quickly. "Who is this?" she exclaims, grabbing the puppy from my arms. "Omigod, Mrs. Brubaker gave us another puppy!"

"No," Mamí explains, "I bought him from a breeder in Long Island. I figure we should leave Mrs. Brubaker and her brood alone for a while."

Bubbles screams louder than I do and everyone comes over to see what the "show" after the show is all about.

"What are you going to name him?" Dorinda asks me excitedly.

"Well, let me see, designer names are part of my family's tradition," I say, looking at Mamí proudly. "First came Chanel, then came Pucci. Please welcome the newest and cutest member of the Simmons family—Mr. Prada!"

Everyone gathered around us starts clapping.

"Guess you're not down with O.P.P. anymore

for real," Bubbles shouts out, then whispers in my ear, "Guess Princess Pamela was right after all too." We give each other a Cheetah Girls handshake on that one.

"Thank you, *Mamí*," I say, crying, and I give her a hug.

"I'm proud of you," Mamí says, beaming into my eyes. "And so is Luc." Turning, I notice Mr. Tycoon in the background. He bows his head at me. "I told him we're not moving to Paris. If he wants me, he has to come to New York because your dreams are important to me too."

I hold Prada tight in my arms and look up at everybody, crying. "What did I tell you, Prada or *nada*—for life!"

Bow-wow Wow!

Haters always getting sooo, sooo wicked
Just 'cuz we issued the much needed ticket
To the tune of forty-five RPM amped live
Right down to the ducket beehive
And while you were trying to put the bite
on our groove
We were busy making cheetah-licious moves
And singing Bow-wow Wow
Yippee Ayy Pay Day
Bow-wow Wow
Yippee Ayy Pay Day
The duckets are coming our way.

Bow-wow-wow
Yippie yay, yippie yay
Bow-wow-wow
Yippie yay yippie yay

That's right y'all to all the haters
We got to reveal the game plan
So face the factos
There's no way of knowing

Which direction the Cheetah Girls are going
But you can set your compass
To the obvious factos
Just get a sniff or whiff of our
Get-paid situation 'cuz
We'll be going where all the dogs
Are barking about our business.

And they'll be singing
Bow-wow Wow
Yippee Yay Yippee Yay
Bow-wow Wow
Yippee Yay Yippee Yay
The Cheetah Girls always get their payday

Bow-wow Wow
Yippee Yay
Bow-wow Wow
Yippee Yay

It's a hootenanny hooray!
For the Cheetah Girls and their splendid-ferocity

Bow-wow-Wow
Yippee Yay Payday . . .
Bow-wow Wow
Yippee Yay Yippee Yay!

The Cheetah Girls Glossary

Adobo down: Mad flavor. As in, Alicia Keys's new jammy is *adobo* down.

Babosa: Spanish for bobo-head, idiot.

Bad case of the runnies: Diarrhea.

Bite-happy: Someone who steals someone else's flavor.

Bite your tongue (but don't eat it): Now would be a good time to shut your trap. Like when you are definitely tripping over your own words.

Boca grande: Spanish for "big mouth." As in, Why don't you shut your *boca grande* for a change and some coins?

Bring it: Come prepared. Don't slouch.

Caliente mad: Madder than regular mad. More like red-hot pissed off.

Cheddar cheese meltdown: When you start freaking out about things all at once.

Cheetah chompdown: Handling a situation. Handling your business. Stepping to the plate when something isn't right or isn't working out.

Cheetah-olic: Someone who is a shopaholic like Chanel, but buys everything that is cheetahlicious like Galleria.

Chitlin' circuit: Back in the day, performers had to

play real dives and holes in the wall. It was known as the "chitterling circuit" in honor of the pig's intestines that was once a favored staple in soul food cuisine.

Cuatro yuks: When someone or something is four times disgusting.

Cucarachas: Cockroaches.

Cutie patootie: When someone or something is soooo adorable. As in, Nobu is such a cutie patootie, I could just kiss him to death!

Dangle the bait: Get what you want. As in, she always knows how to dangle the bait.

Déjà vu: French word pronounced like *Day-jah voo*. It's that spooky sensation you get when you feel like you've been there, done that before.

Drama and kaflamma: Drama times two.

Fabulation: The tribulations of being fabulous.

Feeling kinda way: When you have a change of heart. Feeling wayward. As in, I'm feeling kinda way about the situation.

Foshizzle: For sure.

Frizzies: Curly hair like Galleria's and Chanel's.

Goospitating: Ogling and licking your chops over someone or something. As in, Derek is always goospitating over Bubbles.

Gracias, gooseness: Thank goodness.

Growl power: The brains, heart, and courage that

every true Cheetah Girl possesses to make her dreams come true in the jiggy jungle.

Huffy puffy: When you're so busy talking down to someone like they are stupid and you're better than they are that you get out of breath.

Itinerary: Schedule. As in, "Check my calendar, darling—see if the meeting with the guidance counselor is on my itinerary."

Jiggy jungle: That magical place inside of every dangerous, scary, crowded city where you can make your dreams come true. The jiggy jungle is the only place where every cheetah has its day.

Loco: Spanish for cuckoo.

Macking: When you're really trying to get someone's attention. As in, "Stop macking me. Get up off me, yo!"

Madrina: Spanish word for "godmother."

Major: Tight. Faboo. Dope.

Mamacita: Term of endearment to use with crew members only. When a boy you don't know says it to you, then it's whack and disrespectful.

Mija: Spanish term of endearment. Means "sweetie," "honey."

Mucho attention: A piñata-full of "props." A lot of attention.

No ruffle: Don't sweat it. It's nothing. As in, "I know you're sorry. No ruffle."

Off the chain: Dope. Tight. Coolio. Fabulous.

O.P.P.: Other People's Prada. As in, I am not down with O.P.P. I'm gonna save my duckets and get my own!

Piñata: A decorated animal made from papier-mâché, filled inside with candies and gifts, that is hung from the ceiling to be broken with sticks by blindfolded kiddies as part of Christmas or birthday celebrations.

Poochie wooch: The cutest, most adorable dog. Kinda like Toto.

Pulling a Houdini: Pulling a disappearing act.

Scrunchies: Wrinkles like on the forehead.

She's special: She's cuckoo. As in, Katrina wore yellow shorts to school today even though it was snowing, but you know, she's special.

Slow your jellyroll: Slow down. Take notice. Watch what you're saying.

Street cred: Credibility in the 'hood with your peeps. If you have street cred, then your product or act is tight. The opposite of being corny or whack.

Supersize-me: Riff off the movie. Means bigger than average. A whammy jammy size.

Tan coolio: Spanish for "so cool," "that's tight, *ayiight*."

Wait a segundo: Wait a second.

What'chu holding: Hurry up, tell me what you want 'cuz I gotta bounce.

Bring It On!

Let me holla at my ferocious friend
Tonya Pinkins,
who is always calling out the shameless hyenas
while looking out for the bona fide cheetahs
in the jiggy jungle.
You're simply growlicious, girlita!

Chapter 1

$\mathcal{S}$aturday is definitely the most dig-able day of the week because I get to go to the Drinka Champagne Conservatory for vocal classes with my crew, the Cheetah Girls. But Sunday is the only time in my crazy-busy week that I get to indulge in my three favorite things: 1) listen to hip-hop music 2) spend time with my favorite foster sister Twinkie and foster brother Corky 3) fantasize about, then sketch some of the cheetah-licious outfits I'm going to make for the Cheetah Girls when we have the duckets to afford my designing skills.

Lying in my twin-size bed on the supa-lumpy mattress, I close my eyes for a second so I can imagine the Cheetah Girls performing at a supersize place like Madison Square Garden with *thousands* of peeps in the audience. Yeah, I see it. The five of us descend from the ceiling propped up on a ten-foot-long glittery papier-mâché cheetah. We are dressed in Dorinda Designs—cheetah fur capes over cutout leather hip huggers and halter tops studded with serious sparklies—Austrian crystals shaped like flower petals, bugle beads sewn by hand, okay? When the big, sleek cheetah touches the stage floor, we hop off—swirling and twirling so the supa-bright klieg lights bounce off the sparklies, causing the audience to go cheetah crazy!

I know I'm dreaming, but one day I'm gonna get the op to make costumes for us, even if we end up on the chitlin' circuit (second-banana nightclubs all around America where second-banana singers performed back in the day, to keep duckets in their buckets). All I know is, we'll be the best-dressed girl group the chitlin' circuit has ever seen.

"*Dorinda*, I don't have any more clean underwear," my sister Chantelle yelps, interrupting my fantasy flow. "When you gonna do the laundry?"

I should have known my ten-year-old sister would find a way to snap me out of my daydreams so early in the morning. See, I share my bedroom with my foster sisters Chantelle and Monie. Luckily, Monie, who is seventeen, has been spending a lot of time at her boyfriend Hector's house on the weekends. I know I shouldn't be tripping about Chantelle whining—but she knows I don't do the laundry until after we eat breakfast. And she's not the only one who depends on me.

"Are you coming, Cheetah bear?" Twinkie giggles and peeks her head in my bedroom.

"I'll be right there, Twinkie bear," I call back. Like I said, Chantelle is not the only one who depends on me. Everybody in my family does. And now that I'm in the Cheetah Girls, I'm doubly busy because my crew depends on me too. I'm not flossing: for example, I'm the best dancer in my crew, so I'm sort of the unofficial choreographer for all the Cheetah Girls' dance moves. Oh, my bad. Let me tell you who the Cheetah Girls are: we are the fiercest singing group in the jiggy jungle, according to Galleria "Bubbles" Garibaldi, the real leader of the group. There's also Chanel "Chuchie" Simmons, Aquanette and Anginette Walker and, the youngest member, yours truly, Dorinda "Do´ Re Mi" Rogers.

Sitting straight up in my bed, I glance at Chantelle, who is plopped down on the floor—naked from the waist down—with all her clothes in front of her piled up in a big heap. Miss No-bloomers has even left the bottom two drawers of our bureau open, like a thirsty dog with his tongue hanging out.

"I know you're going to put your clothes back in the drawers, right?"

"I was looking for clean underwear, I told you!" Chantelle whines, not moving off the floor.

"Not in your shirts and tops drawer!" I counter.

"I thought maybe they was there," Chantelle protests. "Sometimes you put stuff in the wrong drawer."

"No, I don't," I reply, but calmly, because I know what Chantelle was *really* thinking—that I should have given her one of the prizes that the Cheetah Girls won at the Harlem School of the Arts talent show competition. Backstage after the show last Saturday, Chantelle grabbed my goodies bag and blurted out: "I want a prize, too!" Mrs. Bosco put a clamp down on that situation, though. She told me right in front of my ten foster brothers and sisters that I can't give away any of my prizes (which included a one-year scholarship to the Harlem School of the Arts after-school programs, dinner for six at Maroon's restaurant, as well as shoportunity gift certificates from Barnes and Noble, Radio Shack, and the Girlie Show Boutique).

Staring at the big pile of magazines messily stacked next to Chantelle's bed, I start to feel bad that I can't buy her more *Sistarella* and *Word Up!* magazines for her collection. (There is nothing Chantelle loves more than to sit on her bed and flip through grown-up magazines like she's in college

instead of third grade!) But Mrs. Bosco was right—
"The Cheetah Girls earned those prizes and the
Cheetah Girls should enjoy them." And I'm definitely gonna be doing that tomorrow after school:
me and my crew are going to the Girlie Show
Boutique to cash in on the shoportunity of a lifetime, you know what I'm saying? I'm probably
going to be doing cartwheels when I walk into that
store! Right now, though, I walk over Chantelle's
big pile of clothing and open the top drawer of the
bureau to pick out a sweater. Holding up my khaki
ribbed turtleneck sweater, I notice a big hole right
in the front. I stick it back into the drawer, because
I don't want to deal with that holey drama right
now. See, here's the real deal: ever since I was five
years old, Mrs. Bosco has been bringing home
bags of secondhand clothes, while we're supposed
to pretend that they're new, even though most of
them have stains or holes in them. I used to fall for
that when I was little, but not anymore. One day,
even my five-year-old sister Kenya, blurted out, "I
don't want no more holey clothes."

Suddenly I get a cute idea. I could put a brown
poodle appliqué on the sweater to cover the hole.
Yeah, that'll work. Nah, maybe not. I already put a
white poodle appliqué on my gray knit cap last
week. I don't want peeps to start wondering if I'm

a dogcatcher working for the ASPCA. See, everybody knows that the Cheetah Girls are obsessed with dogs (only the cute, fluffy ones, though!). The bichon frise dog has become the Cheetah Girls' mascot because Galleria has a white bichon frise named Toto. Luckily, frisky Toto impregnated Buffy, who belongs to her nasty neighbor, Mrs. Brubaker. As a result, the Cheetah Girls hit puppy payday: we won half of Buffy's litter after Ms. Dorothea, Galleria's mom and our manager, took Mrs. Brubaker to court to fight for custody. Of course, Chanel wasn't allowed to take a puppy, because her mom, Ms. Juanita, wasn't having it. (Ms. Juanita claimed she was allergic to dogs, even though bichon frise dogs are hypoallergenic.) But Ms. Juanita should have known that Chanel would get her way: for a whole week, Chanel walked around with her bottom lip stuck out so far she looked like a cuckoo bird. Ms. Juanita finally caved in and bought Chanel a bichon frise puppy from Dolly Dog Breeders in Hempstead, Long Island. Now cute little Prada is in the mix with Toto; my puppy, Nobu; Aqua and Angie's puppy, Coco (in honor of Chanel's middle name); and Galleria's puppy, Ragu. And to top everything off, Galleria even wrote a song for our victory: "Bow-wow Wow."

Bow-wow Wow—that gives me another *sweet*

idea: I can give the rest of the Cheetah Girls poodle appliquéd knit caps—for their Christmas presents. Then we'll be the fluffy five for the holidays. "Bow-wow Wow, Yippee Yippee Yay, Yay," I start humming cheerfully while looking for less holey sweaters in my drawer. I pull my brown long-sleeved T-shirt out and examine it for boo-boos. After it passes inspection, I close my bureau drawer real tight, just in case Chantelle gets any more messy ideas for our room. Now my mind is really percolating. Maybe I could make a felt flower appliqué decorated with sequined petals? Yeah, that would look tight, too. I start getting excited again and pull on my junior size–five blue jeans. (Yeah, that's right, I'm shrimpy. So shrimpy that Chantelle and me wear the same size jeans even though she is two years younger. But she is not allowed to wear my clothes because then I would really go off.)

Now Miss No-bloomers is sitting with her legs crossed Indian style like she's on *I Dream of Jeannie* waiting for Aladdin to rub the lamp.

"You could at least put your denim skirt on." I shake my head. Why am I stressing? Chantelle shouldn't be so upset that I'm not giving her any of my gift certificates. See, I definitely need to buy some books for school and some clothes without holes in them. And I'm definitely looking forward to that tasty meal at Maroon's restaurant, with my crew and Mr. and Mrs. Garibaldi.

As if she's reading my thoughts, Chantelle turns up the volume on her complaining machine: "I wish my birthday was coming up so I could get some presents," she moans loudly, like I'm supposed to feel sorry for her.

"Okay, so I won a few prizes *and* my thirteenth birthday is next Saturday," I say, trying to reason with Chantelle. "I got your message."

"*I got your message,*" Chantelle mimics, then throws out a not-so-bright idea: "I'm gonna start my own singing group."

I bite my tongue to keep from blurting out, "Please don't start singing now." After all, it's not Chantelle's fault that she sings like a hyena having a hiccup attack. Instead, I tune her out and think about the colors of felt I'm going to use to make the flower appliqués—peach, brown, plum—they would make a nice contrast against my khaki sweater. But before I get too creative, I check my supply box to see what color felt pieces I have left. These days, I'm guarding my design supplies like diamonds in the rough, because I don't have duckets to buy more, and they're dwindling fast. Plus, I know that Chantelle has been swiping some of my supplies. That's why I started storing them in my locked metal file cabinet (even though I think she knows where the key is hidden, because sometimes I'll go into the drawer and notice things have been messed with).

As I step into my black Mad Monster combat boots, I fantasize about walking into the fabric stores on 38th Street and 7th Avenue and going to town—buying all the fabric and supplies my heart desires. See, aside from being in the Cheetah Girls and performing all over the world, I dream about having my own dopelicious boutique stocked with Dorinda Designs—just like Ms. Dorothea does. She has a beautiful boutique—Toto in New York . . . Fun in Diva Sizes on West Broadway in Soho, which is really far south from where I live. I've only been to Ms. Dorothea's store a few times, but I think about it all the time. Chanel is the lucky one: she works there on Sundays so she can pay back her mother for going to town with her credit card a few months ago. (None of us knew what Chanel was doing, but sometimes she can be sneaky like that.) Anyway, you've got to see this store: it's decorated in leopard, with pink, orange, and lime-green wall panels. Then there are all these glitter-flecked pink, orange, and red flowers hanging off the ceiling, mirrors, and wall panels.

The Cheetah Girls

The whole setup is definitely off the cheetah meter.

"Okay, Chantelle, I'm going to make breakfast, so you can sit there all day in front of that pile of clothes like it's Magic Mountain," I warn my messy sister, who goes out of her way to make sure that her side of the room always looks like the Salvation Army.

"If it was *Magic* Mountain, then there would be underwear underneath it, Dorinda," Chantelle says, poking her lip out.

"After breakfast, I'll do the laundry already, okay?" I let out an annoyed sigh.

She doesn't answer me, so I just walk out of the room to go take care of my new puppy. Ever since Nobu's arrival, Nestor, Corky, Arba, Topwe, and Twinkie sit at the kitchen table every morning, waiting for me to open the wooden gate at the kitchen entrance so they can watch me feed Nobu and play with him for a little while before we eat breakfast. The only one who isn't panting for Nobu is my youngest foster sister, Gaye. She is definitely afraid of him. So every morning, Mrs. Bosco lets Gaye come into her bedroom so they can spend a little time together alone.

I don't understand how anybody could be afraid of supa-cuddly Nobu. I get so excited every time I open the kitchen gate and see his precious little face. Nobu, who is lying on his little blanket, jumps right up when he sees me. "What's up, pup?" I giggle and nuzzle his face. Ms. Dorothea said to keep Nobu in his own little space until he is four months old so he can get used to being with us. So I guess the kitchen is his room until he is old enough to stay with me. I put Nobu back down on the blanket so I can throw the soiled Wee Wee Pad in the garbarge, then spray Lysol on the floor and wipe it clean before I put down a fresh Wee Wee Pad. (Nobu also can't go outside to do his business until he's had all his vaccination shots.) Even though Mrs. Bosco doesn't like the idea of Nobu peeing in the kitchen, she is happy that I got a free puppy. A bichon frise puppy from the pet store or a private breeder would cost at least $650. Meanwhile, I was so happy about getting my own puppy and feeling so bad for Chanel when she was puppy-less that I let her name him. (I'm telling you, Scrooge would have broke down if he had seen that sad face!) Chanel chose the name Nobu—after her mother's favorite Japanese restaurant, where all the Big Willies eat raw octopus for fifty dollars a plate.

"I sure hope you live up to your namesake," I coo to Nobu. "But I know you're gonna be a Big Willie, too." I go into the cabinet to get his tube of

Nutri-Cal paste. My favorite part of feeding Nobu is letting him lick a nice, fat dollop of the vitamin-packed brown gooey stuff off my finger twice a day. His little tongue always tickles my fingers. Ms. Dorothea says the paste is supposed to give him a shiny fur coat and help him grow strong. I sure hope so, because Nobu seems so little—like me. When I was younger, it bothered me a lot to be so tiny because peeps was always messing with me. Now at least I go to a high school (Fashion Industries East) where peeps are more interested in dressing skills than fighting ones.

Now that Nobu is here, though, it seems like everybody is fighting over *him*: my foster brothers—Twinkie, Nestor, Topwe, and Corky—are pushing each other right outside the kitchen gate, jockeying over who is going to pet Nobu first. (I don't allow them to play with Nobu all at once, because I know my tiny pooch would get over-whelmed.)

"You went first the last time!" six-year-old Corky yells out. Corky is my favorite brother—he has a big head of ringlets and the prettiest hazel eyes.

"Can I play with him now?" Topwe whines, though he knows better. They know my routine—clean up the poop, feed him his paste, put out fresh water and his dry puppy dog food mixed with a little hot water, and let him eat it before *anybody* gets to pet him.

"Okay, time for the wolves to come in." I chuckle and pet Nobu's head. I always watch while everybody plays with him, to make sure he doesn't get hurt—especially with Kenya, because she treats Nobu like he is a stuffed toy or something.

"Corky comes first," I order, since nobody can agree.

"Corky comes first!" Twinkie shouts out. Twinkie's real name is Rita, but we call her Twinkie because she has a big pile of fuzzy blond hair on her head that looks yummy enough to eat like a Twinkie. She is such a trip. She likes to act like a Mini Me, repeating everything I say.

Corky comes inside and I hand Nobu over to him. "He's so tiny. Is he gonna grow?" Corky asks, giggling.

"I think so," I answer, staring at Corky as he pets Nobu. When I look at Corky and Nobu, I *know* there is a God. Who else could have created such cuteness and perfection? Other times, though, I don't think there is a God, because of all the foul things going on—like Gaye's mother abandoning her on a playground. Why would anybody do such a mean thing if there were a God?

"How do you say his name again?" Corky asks.

"Nobu?"

"No, not that—his other name?" repeats Corky.

Now I know what he's asking me. "Oh, you mean his breed name," I answer, chuckling. "*Bichon frise.*"

Corky tries to say it, but he fumbles over the French name. Ms. Dorothea told us that back in the day, bichon frises were bred as lapdogs for royal families. I could see Nobu sitting on some fancy king's lap, just chilling.

Corky gives up trying to pronounce Nobu's breed name, and asks pleadingly: "Can I go see the singing frogs today?" Corky is as obsessed with frogs as the Cheetah Girls are with dogs. I wish I could take him to the planetarium, but I can't. Not with all the chores and homework I have to do today.

"I'm sorry, Corkster, but not today, okay?" I say sadly. I hate turning Corky down for anything. Suddenly, we hear a loud bang outside in the street. I hear the kids running to the window to see what is happening. I pick up Nobu, and his little body is trembling. "Well, I hope you like being in such a big family, otherwise you're going to be shaking and quaking all the time," I coo, snuggling my nose up to Nobu's.

"Can I do that?" Corky asks.

"Yeah, go ahead," I say.

"Yeah, go ahead. We can't go see the frogs today!" Twinkie shouts out, mimicking me again. "Can I play with him now? I made him a name tag!"

"Okay, Miss Twinkie Dink, it's your turn now," I say, motioning for her to come in. Corky doesn't want to leave, so I have to nudge him out of the kitchen. Twinkie proudly shows me a square piece of plastic with a bone drawn on it. She made it out of Shrinky Dink and even put a hole in the corner so it could fit on a dog collar.

"That is so cute," I say. Twinkie loves the shrinky dink kit I got her for her birthday. Nobu looks at me with his shiny black eyes. I wish I knew what he was thinking. Maybe he wonders where his mother is, like I do sometimes.

"I'm making you a birthday present!" Twinkie announces.

"You don't have to," I say. I know I should be looking forward to my birthday, but I'm not. It just reminds me that I haven't told my crew yet that I'm only twelve going on thirteen. I don't know how the Cheetah Girls are going to react when they find out—but I have a feeling I might become an endangered species, if you know what I'm saying.

"Well, I'm making you a present anyway, you cheetah bubblehead!" Twinkie shrieks, getting a little giddy. Then she picks up one of Nobu's mini milk bone biscuits and throws it. Nobu jumps and runs after it. Twinkie giggles hysterically.

After all the kids take turns playing with Nobu, I kick them all out of the kitchen so I can fix breakfast. "Awright, everybody out," I say firmly.

"Come on, Dorinda, can't we play with him some more?" Kenya whines.

"Awright, everybody out!" Twinkie shouts, dragging Kenya out of the kitchen.

"You know I have to make breakfast—unless everybody wants to go on a diet," I say matter-of-factly while I start making breakfast. "We can start right now, if you want."

"You want to go on a diet? Then sit down!" Twinkie says sharply.

Mrs. Bosco cooks all week, so on Sundays I give her a break—at least for breakfast, anyway. Usually I make bacon and eggs with toast, or sometimes I make fried apples with cheese and potatoes. Today I'm going to make Twinkie's favorite—waffles with fried bologna, ham, or salami on the side.

I put a bowl of Ritz crackers and the orange juice container on the table so everybody can get their drink on while I'm cooking breakfast.

"I want the 'Make-It-Bake-It' Kit for Christmas,"

Kenya says, like she's placing her order with Santa Claus. Ever since we passed by the stationery store and saw the jewelry and charms crafts kit in the window, that is all she can talk about.

"I threw a ball and Nobu caught it!" Twinkie brags to Nestor.

"No, you didn't—that was a stupid dog biscuit—and he ate it!" says Chantelle.

I go back to the kitchen to whip up the waffle batter. I start fantasizing about Christmas dinner. I know Mrs. Bosco probably would like for me to eat Christmas dinner here, but I want to go over Galleria's house. Her father, Mr. Garibaldi, can really throw down—like the gourmet chefs you see on television.

"I don't want potatoes!" Kenya yells from the kitchen table.

"We're not having potatoes today," I yell back, looking in the refrigerator at all the cold cuts. I always cook the one that has a little brown around the edges and is about to dry up. The bologna looks okay so I put it back on the shelf, then open the package of ham. Yeah, the ham is definitely getting browner by the minute, but it's still kicking (that means it's not totally rancid and unedible). Now I push Nobu's blanket farther away from the stove, because I like to fry the ham until it's popping in the frying pan and I don't want Nobu to get stung in the face by hot, flying grease.

I hear Mrs. Bosco and Gaye come into the living room and sit down on the couch to watch cartoons together (the couch is covered with plastic slipcovers that creak loudly when someone sits down). "Can I watch cartoons, too?" Corky asks.

"No," I tell him, because I know that Mrs. Bosco wants to sit with Gaye alone. Gaye just sits there and doesn't say anything. They are watching *The Kernels*, this cartoon about a family made out of popcorn. I can hear Mrs. Bosco trying to explain the show to Gaye, but she doesn't say one word.

While we're eating breakfast, Twinkie talks enough for everybody. "Can we put fifty candles on Dorinda's birthday cake?" she asks excitedly.

"She ain't that old." Mrs. Bosco chuckles.

"No—but I wanna watch Dorinda blow them out like a big cheetah bear!" explains Twinkie.

"Awright, but Smokey gonna be on your tail— Lord, it sounds like you trying to start a forest fire," Mrs. Bosco says.

Twinkie laughs so hard she causes a chain reaction and we all start laughing. Even Gaye finally broke down and cracked a smile. Breakfast turned out to be a real Kodak moment.

Chapter 2

After breakfast, I turn the dial on the radio to Whammy Jam 99, my favorite hip-hop station, so I can begin my laundry routine. First, I gather all the dirty clothes out of the hampers, throw them in a big pile in my bedroom, then separate everything into two groups—light and dark—before stuffing them into laundry bags and heading to the laundry room in the basement. Twinkie loves this routine as much as I do, because we get our groove on, too.

When the tight new single "Yeah, I'm Chinese" by the rapper Jin comes on the radio, Twinkie starts rapping along to the song. "Y'all gonna learn Chinese when the punks come at 'cha, y'all gonna speak Chinese!"

I join Twinkie in her rap attack because Jin is one of my favorite new rappers. He has real serious freestyle flow, so it's not surprising he was getting a lot of play on the street when he didn't even have a record deal. Jin just hung tight, making beats in his family's basement in Chinatown till he got his—a record deal with Ruff Ryder Records.

Pulling one of Topwe's sweatshirts out of the pile, my stomach starts to turn, because it's covered with vomit stains. "Ooh, that's disgusting," I moan, squinching up my face as I blast the stains with the stain remover and ball up the sweatshirt so it gets a good pre-soaking. My brother Topwe is infected with the HIV virus (he ended up in foster care when his mother died from a drug overdose). Now that it's cold outside, he gets sick constantly because he hates bundling up. I take a deep sigh because I'm gonna have to say something to Topwe, and he gets so upset when anybody tells him he is doing something wrong.

"Yuk, that's disgusting," Twinkie says, wiping her hands like she touched the shirt.

"You're gonna be Chinese! You're gonna speak Chinese. You're gonna pass the peas!" I start rapping so she'll follow me. I check the pockets of Kenya's corduroy jumper, and sure enough, there is an empty M&M's wrapper. I shake my head.

"Ooh, she stole candy," Twinkie says, throwing the wrapper in the garbage can. I don't respond because I don't know how Kenya gets the candy. But her kindergarten teacher has called here twice because some of the kids in her class have accused her of stealing their snack money.

Twinkie starts rapping to the song again, spitting in my face.

"Say the weather, don't spray it!" I moan back at her.

Finishing up the laundry piles, I start thinking about the Cheetah Girls getting a record deal. Winning the Harlem School of the Arts competition was definitely the move. See, we can't afford to lose our street cred before we get a record deal—because then we will be a done deal-io. Even Jin had a hard time keeping the hype going because Ruff Ryder Records took so long to put his record out even after he got signed to the label. I mean, Jin had fans from Chinatown to Compton—just waiting for his product to drop—but they couldn't get their hands on nothing. God, I hope that doesn't happen to the Cheetah Girls.

"Awright, Twinkie Dink, put all the other piles in separate bags and I'll see you in a minute," I tell her.

"Please, can I come with you?" Twinkie begs.

"Only if you're gonna be Chinese," I riff back at her.

Twinkie squeals, then drags the bag to the hallway and opens the door, "Yes, I'm gonna be Chinese!"

Our neighbor Mrs. Gallstone is locking her door at the same time we come into the hallway. "What y'all carrying on about. Y'all going to the Chinese laundry?"

Twinkie giggles hysterically.

"No, we're going to the basement," I chuckle.

"We're going to the basement," Twinkie repeats.

Coming out of the elevator in the basement and walking toward the laundry room, I decide that if the Cheetah Girls do become famous, I'm definitely going to become real friendly with the peeps in the Chinese laundry, you know what I'm saying? Suddenly, I hear a loud banging noise coming from inside the laundry room, then I hear our neighbor Ms. Keisha groan, "You dag on good-for-nothings pain in my butt!"

"Uh-oh." Twinkie winces.

Uh-oh is right. Ms. Keisha is probably yelling at her kids, Pookie and Tamela. At least that's one good thing about living with Mrs. Bosco—she would never embarrass us in front of other people like that. Once, Ms. Keisha even hit Pookie upside the head with her bedroom slipper out in the courtyard. We were so embarrassed for him, but Twinkie pointed out that it wasn't such a bad thing. "Ms. Keisha's slipper is made out of sponge and Pookie's head is so hard!" Walking inside the laundry room, though, we realize that Ms. Keisha was talking to herself, because she is alone. That can only mean one thing:

"Are *all* the machines broken?" I ask, but I already know the answer.

"They're all broke and that's no joke," Ms. Keisha snaps back. As usual, she is wearing a headful of pink rollers tied with a pink scarf, and a pink terry-cloth bathrobe. Sometimes on Sundays, Ms. Keisha will spend the whole day in her bathrobe, hanging out in the courtyard or out her window, depending on the weather.

I roll my eyes. Twinkie rolls her eyes, too. Now we'll have to go to the laundry room in the basement of Building C.

"I hate going over there," Twinkie moans, plopping down the laundry bag for a second so we can catch our breath. There are three buildings in the Cornwall Projects, where we live. We live in Building A and secretly call Building C *Peeville* because the elevators and stairwells stink even worse than the ones in our building. I think more people cook in our building, because sometimes you can actually smell good things, like bacon, corn bread, collard greens, and other aromas waft-ing through the air. Ms. Keisha told us there are a lot more people on public assistance (welfare) in Building C—and a lot more drug addicts and winos, too. Ms. Keisha is also on public assis-tance, but the only bad habit she has is gossiping all day.

"Pookie, get in here and help me!" Ms. Keisha yells. Unlike most of the kids in our building, Pookie and Tamela hang outside in the courtyard even when it's cold.

All of a sudden, one of our strange neighbors, Mr. Horn, barges into the laundry room. He has a slick, teased-up pompadour hairdo like James Brown or Elvis Presley, and big yellow teeth that look like fangs because they're so crooked and crowded together. Mr. Horn even dresses like singers from back in the day—today he is wearing a brown short-sleeved alpaca knit sweater and skinny sharkskin pants in a metallic brown shade. But what really trips me out are all the tiger tattoos crawling down his arms. I wonder if he has tattoos crawling over his whole body. Before Mr. Horn can even put his basket down, Ms. Keisha lets him know the machines are broken. Mr. Horn's bulging eyes dart around like a frog, then he picks up his laundry quickly and bolts out.

"You know he buys ten, twenty pounds of ground beef at the Piggly Wiggly supermarket every week?" Ms. Keisha asks me, but doesn't wait for an answer. "Mmm hmm. Chancia told me. He buy the old packages of meat, too. Don't care none. Always asking if they have any meat gone bad he can buy."

"Maybe he's a vampire," I respond as I fiddle with the dials on all the washing machines. I don't mean to insult Ms. Keisha, but I just want to make sure all the machines have definitely croaked before Twinkie and me head over to Peeville.

"Yeah, well, even if he wore a long black cape and slept in a coffin I wouldn't pay him no mind. Something else about him just ain't right," Ms. Keisha says, nodding her head like she's a private detective about to fill out a case report. "But don't you worry, I'm gonna find the thorn in Mr. Horn's game plan. You can bet on that."

I'd definitely put the odds on Ms. Keisha finding out something shady. She could outsniff the pet detective even with her sinus condition, if you ask me.

"I'll go knock on Mr. Hammer's door afterward and tell him the machines are broken," I announce to Ms. Keisha. Mr. Hammer is our super, and we're not supposed to bother him on Sundays, but I figure it's worth a try. Mr. Hammer is always really cool with me. Once, somebody threw a computer out on the sidewalk, and Mr. Hammer fixed it up and gave it to me. Of course, Chantelle and Monie try to hog my computer.

"Well, there goes my day," gripes Ms. Keisha as we follow her down the hallway. We cut across the courtyard to Building C.

"I hate having to stay there," I reply. When we do our laundry in Building C, we can't leave it for a second because there are a lot of peeps with sticky fingers over there, if you know what I'm saying.

"I hate staying there, too," Twinkie says, squinching up her nose.

As soon as we open the door to the courtyard, the crisp chill hits our faces. I can't believe Pookie and "Walkie-Talkie" Tamela are posturing on the benches. Tamela, who is about Chantelle's age, earned her nickname because she talks a lot, like her mother, and today is no exception. She is blabbing away with our neighbors, Wanda, and her mother, Mrs. Bigge, who live in the same building we do.

"What y'all looking at? I told you to come help me with this!" Ms. Keisha sets her load of laundry on the ground.

"Dorinda, I got to talk to you!" Pookie says, running up to me.

"You better grab this bag before I *talk* upside your head!" Ms. Keisha warns Pookie.

Pookie is motioning with his eyes at a man in a gray wool overcoat who is standing in the corner of the courtyard all by himself. I've never seen him before. He isn't wearing a hat, and has lots of curly brown hair, but I can tell that he is kind of cold. Ms. Keisha stares at him too, then says out loud, "Who is that man?"

Pookie grabs his mother's coat and whispers loudly, "That is what I've been trying to tell Dorinda!"

"Tell Dorinda what?" Ms. Keisha asks suspiciously.

I feel a case of the bugaboo chillies hitting my stomach, and I try not to stare at the man, but I know something is wrong.

"That man asked me if I knew Corky," Pookie says, trying not to talk too loud.

"What's he want with Corky?" Ms. Keisha says, eyeing him.

"I dunno," I say. Who could this man be?

"I dunno," Twinkie repeats.

"I ain't afraid of him—let's go talk to him. He can't be standing around here," Ms. Keisha says.

Ms. Bigge and her daughter Wanda are looking at us, wondering what is going on. We walk over to the strange man, and he smiles politely.

"Can we help you?" Ms. Keisha asks.

"Are you Mrs. Bosco?" he asks nervously.

"No, I ain't, but I would like to know what you are doing hanging around here," Ms. Keisha responds.

"Um, I'm not trying to be rude or anything, but I just wanted to see my son, Corky, and where he lives, before he comes live with me, you know, maybe talk with Mrs. Bosco and thank her for everything," the man keeps babbling on.

"What you mean—before he come live with you? Ain't nobody said nothing about him living with you, as far as I heard," Ms. Keisha says, like she is correcting the man.

"Um, well, I have gotten custody of my son, but I don't think Mrs. Bosco knows yet—and I don't mean any harm, I just thought I could see where he lived," the man says apologetically.

"You're not Corky's father," Twinkie says, pouting.

"I beg your pardon, little girl?" the man says.

"We don't have a father—that's why we live with Mrs. Bosco," Twinkie says adamantly. "We don't have a mother. We don't have *anybody*."

I'm so embarrassed that Twinkie is telling some stranger our business. The man pauses as if he is trying to figure out what to say. I feel my heart sink into my combat boots. Now the man is staring at me, but I can't look at him. Maybe he is crazy, I realize suddenly.

"I'm sorry, but I just wanted to see where Corky lived, that's all. I didn't mean any harm," the stranger continues.

"You already said that," Ms. Keisha says with attitude.

"Um, Ms. Keisha, I'm going to go upstairs," I say, trying not to let my voice sound croaky, which it does. I grab Twinkie's hand and walk away, like a mummy in a fog.

Ms. Keisha yells after me, "Dorinda, what you want me to do with your laundry bag?"

"Oh," I say, embarrassed, "can you just put it in the laundry room and I'll get it in a minute?"

"Oh, I'll help you with that," the strange man says, reaching to pick up my laundry bag.

"No!" I yell out.

"We got it, Dorinda. Go on upstairs," Mrs. Bigge says, jumping up from the bench. Now everybody in the courtyard knows there is some drama going on, which means the whole building will know in a few hours.

The Cheetah Girls

My heart is pounding out of my chest as I run to the elevator bank. I dread having to tell Mrs. Bosco that some man who says he's Corky's father is hanging around downstairs. Even worse, I dread having to repeat what the man has told us about having custody. Twinkie and I press both the buttons like the boogeyman is after us. Up, down, whatever. Just please let the elevator come.

"Is he really Corky's father?" Twinkie asks, looking up at me, her eyes filled with fear.

"I don't know," I say, trying to hide the fact that my cheeks are flushed. I don't want Twinkie to know how upset I am. The man can't possibly be telling the truth. If Corky's father had won custody, our caseworker, Mrs. Tattle, would have told us about it. No way, José, can this be for real. This man is *tripping*.

"I don't know either," Twinkie says, shrugging her shoulders.

It seems like we're waiting forever for the elevator to come. Suddenly, I start to think about my sister Tiffany. Well, she is really my half sister (we have the same birth mother and different fathers), but she is adopted. Mrs. Tattle arranged for us to meet because Tiffany was looking for me. I didn't even know I had a real sister, half sister, whatever. "Why won't the elevator come when I need it?" I snarl, pressing the buttons repeatedly.

"Don't tell me the elevator is broken, too," Twinkie moans.

"The elevators are definitely on vacation," I say, stomping my foot. Twinkie stomps her foot too. Suddenly, I lose the courage to face Mrs. Bosco. If I tell her what that man said, it's only going to upset her, and if her high blood pressure acts up, it could make her sick again. Three months ago, Mrs. Bosco suffered a mild stroke and stayed in the hospital for two weeks. I stand there frozen. I don't know what to do. But if I don't tell her, and secretly leave a message for Mrs. Tattle to call immediately, I know that Ms. Keisha will flap her lips and the news will reach Mrs. Bosco anyway. Actually, I'm surprised that Ms. Keisha hadn't already heard about the strange man hanging around the courtyard.

"Come on, Dorinda," Twinkie says, grabbing my arm and motioning for us to climb the stairs.

I snap out of my daze and realize there's no point in waiting for an elevator that will never come. Twinkie and I climb the six flights of stairs to our apartment. When we reach our door, I am panting so hard I have to stop and catch my breath. Twinkie takes my keys out of my hands and opens the front door. I hear Mrs. Bosco in the kitchen. It sounds like she is washing the dishes even though she is not supposed to. Chantelle is supposed to wash the dishes on Sunday mornings. I look over at Chantelle sitting on the couch and I radiate serious attitude, but she is staring a hole into the television, trying not to look at me.

"The one job you have to do on Sundays and you can't even do that," I say. I just want to go over to the couch and shake Chantelle like a rag doll, wearing an Afro wig but I can't. Twinkie has already unlatched the wooden gate and run into the kitchen and is babbling away at Mrs. Bosco. I don't even stop her. "What?" I hear Mrs. Bosco ask.

"You're washing the dishes tonight, that's all I'm saying," I say gruffly to Chantelle. Even though she doesn't look at me, I know she hears me, because her eyes are twitching from all that pretending. I slowly walk into the kitchen. "Um, you're not supposed to be washing those dishes," I say politely to Mrs. Bosco.

"Never mind that—what is this nonsense Rita is talking about?" Mrs. Bosco says, scrubbing a plate with a Brillo pad. She's not even wearing her rubber gloves to protect her hands. (Mrs. Bosco is supposed to protect her hands because she has psoriasis—a nasty condition that makes her skin get scaly, kinda like a snake shedding its skin.

I recount the whole story of what happened in the courtyard. At first she just scowls and says, "Some people ain't got nothing better to do than mess up other people's lives." Then her hands start shaking and the plate she's holding drops to the linoleum floor, shattering in big shards. Nobu jumps off his blanket and hides behind the garbage can. I can see his little white butt and tail sticking out.

"Come here, Nobu." I crouch by the garbage can and wait for him to come out by himself. After a few more seconds, I gently grab him, then cuddle him like a baby to make him stop shaking. Mrs. Bosco stands there like a chess player contemplating her next move.

Twinkie hears someone talking in the hallway and runs to the door.

Oh, God, please don't let this man come to our apartment.

Chapter 3

"It's Mr. Bosco!" Twinkie hollers, letting me know not to be afraid. She waits until he opens the door with the key, because she is not allowed to open the door for anyone. Now I hear the keys jingling outside. Maybe he was talking to one of the neighbors.

"Don't say nothing to him," Mrs. Bosco calls out to Twinkie, her hands still shaking.

I make eye contact with Twinkie as she stands by the door, and put my finger over my mouth. She puts her finger over her mouth and nods her head to let me know that she understands. Luckily for us, Mr. Bosco is very slow. Usually he is really tired by the time he comes home. He works as a security guard on the graveyard shift—three A.M. to eleven A.M.

"We'll deal with this mess. Let him go sleep,"

Mrs. Bosco explains to me. Mr. Bosco has his routine—he always goes straight to the bedroom once he gets home from work. We can hear him watching the television before he passes out.

"Hi, Mr. Bosco!" Nestor yells as he runs into the kitchen.

"How ya doing, shorty," Mr. Bosco says, looking down at Nestor. Mr. Bosco is a really big man and he coughs a lot from smoking. He lets out a big grin, then heads right to the bedroom and closes the door.

Mrs. Bosco stands there for another few seconds, then wipes her mouth with the back of her hand. She instructs me to go call Mrs. Tattle. She ain't gonna be there, but leave a message for her."

"Okay," I say, but I don't move, because I don't want to leave Mrs. Bosco by herself.

"Go on, Dorinda. I'm not going to keel over or nothing," Mrs. Bosco says. "Just let me catch my breath." Sure enough, Mrs. Bosco starts wheezing, then the hacking coughing starts up. I stand there helpless.

"Go on!" Twinkie says, staring up at me.

I walk into the alcove to get the pad where I write down all the phone numbers for Mrs. Bosco's business. See, Mrs. Bosco is illiterate. She can't read or write. She pretends that we don't know she is illiterate, but we all know. Suddenly, I drop the whole pile of papers and bills and letters all over the floor. Twinkie runs over and helps me pick up the papers. "Go play with Corky," I whisper to Twinkie. "But don't you say one word about this to him. You promise?"

"You gonna let me be in the Cheetah Girls?" Twinkie asks earnestly.

I don't even smile. "Just go play with Corky." Twinkie nods and runs to knock on Corky's door.

I finally find Mrs. Tattle's phone number. Shaking, I dial Mrs. Tattle's office. Of course I get the voice mail for the Administration of Children's Service, Division of Foster Care. To stop my voice from cracking, I have to pause every second, then I decide to keep it brief. "Um, this is Dorinda. Mrs. Bosco needs you to call here. Please call."

I hope that I sounded okay. I hang up the phone and run back to Mrs. Bosco. She is sitting down in a kitchen chair. I know she is trying to hide how upset she is. "I'm tired of fighting with these people," she mumbles under her breath, then puts her hand on her forehead and massages her temples. I sit down and stare at her. "Y'all go on with your business today, but make sure Corky don't leave this house," Mrs. Bosco instructs me.

"But what about, um, Corky's—I mean, the

man?" I say. "I have to go back and do the laundry."

"Don't pay him no mind. He can stand there until he turns into Frosty the Snowman, for all I care," Mrs. Bosco says, then starts coughing again. This time I can hear her swallow the phlegm in her throat. I grab her some tissues so she can spit it out. I fight back the tears. I want to call Galleria, and even talk to Ms. Dorothea, but I just go back to the table and sit with Mrs. Bosco.

"He got some nerve showing up here. He want to thank me," she says. I can tell that Mrs. Bosco is really upset, because her voice is getting wobbly. "He lucky I don't go down those stairs and crack his knucklehead open."

I hear commotion in Corky's room. "I don't want to stay in my room!" Corky screams at Twinkie, who is trying to push Corky back into his room. The two have gotten into a fight and Nestor is trying to help Twinkie.

"Get off me!" Corky lets out a piercing sream that sends Nobu hiding behind the garbage can again. I reach down to pick him up. This is definitely too much noise for my poor little Nobu.

"You left a message?" Mrs. Bosco asks me.

I nod.

"Then we talk about this later," she instructs me,

walking out of the kitchen. "Y'all come out here in the living room," she commands Twinkie, Nestor, and Corky.

"She pushed me!" Corky whines.

"Rita, come on over here," Mrs. Bosco says. When the kids are gathered around, Mrs. Bosco tries to explain to them: "I'm not feeling well today so I need for y'all to stay in the house in case I need for you to help me. Y'all understand?"

"We understand." Twinkie nods, knowing that Mrs. Bosco is telling a fib-eroni.

I decide to go into Corky's room and sit with him for hours. This means the rest of my day will definitely be ruined. All I can think about is Corky's father hanging around downstairs, like the candyman waiting to snag us with his hook. I'm sure Ms. Keisha has already told all our neighbors about the whole drama and kaflamma, and is watching Corky's father out her window like an eagle ready to swoop down on its prey.

But I'm not bad-mouthing Ms. Keisha anymore, because she did our laundry for us and had Pookie and Tamela bring it to our apartment. No way was I going back down to the laundry room in Building C. I can't imagine walking into the courtyard and seeing that strange man standing there. At about five o'clock Ms. Keisha knocks on our door, and

I answer it. "The coast is clear," she informs me.

"I can't believe he stood out there that long," I respond, shaking my head.

I'm so glad we were able to keep Corky inside all day, but he knows something is wrong, because he's bouncing off the walls like an astronaut lost in space.

"Y'all should have called the police," Ms. Keisha says, sucking her teeth. "But he gone now."

"Who gone?" Nestor asks, jumping up from the couch.

"Nobody. Go sit down," I say gently. But Nestor knows something is up.

"Eunice there?" Ms. Keisha asks through the crack in the door. I wish Ms. Keisha didn't talk so loud all the time, like she's got a built-in bullhorn.

"Um, she is lying down," I whisper quietly, hoping she'll take a hint. Mrs. Bosco has been in her room for most of the afternoon.

"Well, tell her if she need anything else, I'm here, all right, Dorinda?" Ms. Keisha says.

"Um, thank you for doing the laundry," I say, smiling. "I owe you."

"I won't let you forget either," Ms. Keisha says, winking.

"I know." I chuckle. Closing the door and locking all five of the locks, I still don't feel safe. It don't matter if Corky's father has left, I'm still scared. As a matter of fact, for the rest of the evening, every time there is a loud noise, I flinch like a scarecrow. By dinnertime, Mr. Bosco has gotten up from bed, and I hear Mrs. Bosco talking to him behind their door. She is probably telling him the whole situation. Even though I know Mr. Bosco isn't going to work tonight, I still feel scared.

"Ain't nothing to do till morning, Eunice," I hear him telling Mrs. Bosco.

Corky is listening, too. He keeps watching me, waiting for me to tell him something. So does Kenya.

"Somebody got in trouble?" she asks. I'm not surprised by her question, because that somebody is usually her.

"Just go play, Kenya," I tell her.

Kenya drags her feet and heads for her room. I wasn't trying to be mean to her, but I really have to talk to my crew. It's times like these I wish I had a phone in my room. Instead, I head to my room and hop on the Internet and let the Cheetah Girls know that I need to talk. I ask if we can assemble in the Phat Planet chatroom at nine o'clock. Then I get out my schoolbooks so I can do my Spanish and math homework.

Mrs. Bosco finally comes out to fix dinner. She

has turned on the television in the living room again.

"Look, Dorinda, it's the tiger special!" Arba says excitedly, pointing to the television.

"No, it isn't," says Nestor. "It's the cheetah special."

I glance over at the television to see what they're talking about. The voice-over announces, "Operation: Save the Big Cats."

"Oh, it's a special about *all* the big cats," I explain to them.

"What are big cats?" Arba asks, twirling around in her chair.

"Tigers, jaguars, lions, cheetahs, leopards, bobcats," I rattle off a few of my favorite wildcats.

"Cheetahs!" Arba yells out.

"Yes, cheetahs, I said that—and cougars," I say, mesmerized by the image on the television. Since I've been in the Cheetah Girls I've become fascinated by the Animal Channel specials. I'm sure Galleria and Ms. Dorothea are probably watching, too, since there isn't an animal program they don't know about.

"Oh, that's scary!" Nestor says, staring at the grizzly sight—three lions eating a baby giraffe they just killed and "cracking the ribs to suck out its vital organs," explains the narrator.

"I can't watch this," I mumble to myself. I'm already too creeped out by the man who hung around in the courtyard all day.

"Look at the hyena!" Corky says, giggling.

"No, that's a jackal," I explain, watching the sneaky predator wait for a few scraps of leftover giraffe meat.

"The jackal that'll make you cackle!" Corky bursts out, riffing off one of the verses of the Cheetah Girls song "Wannabe Stars in the Jiggy Jungle" that we sang at the competition last Saturday. Tears well up instantly in my eyes. He is so smart and funny. How can he go live with his father now? I know the foster care system is screwed up, but they can't do that. Can they? I mean, the man was trying to be nice, but how can he just show up here like this?

"That's right, Corky," I say, going into the kitchen to help Mrs. Bosco. If I watch any more of the wild cat special, I'll lose it.

Putting the plates out on the dining room table, I suppress the urge to ask Mrs. Bosco what she knows about Corky's mother and father. I don't want to bother her with any more drama today. I know she is upset, because she didn't even play her gospel music all day, like she usually does. Mrs. Bosco loves anything by Mahalia Jackson and

Shirley Caesar—gospel singers from back in the day. She also plays a lot of old-school soul stuff, like Al Green, Otis Redding, and Bill Withers. When I go back into the kitchen to get the silverware, Mrs. Bosco asks quietly, "What did that Ms. Keisha have to say?"

I guess she heard Ms. Keisha at the door earlier.

"She said Corky's father left," I say, trying to keep the situation "lite FM," as Galleria would say. That means not causing more static.

"I bet Ms. Keisha made it sound like she chased the man off," Mrs. Bosco adds, humming to herself.

"Um, yeah, something like that," I say, smiling.

"Make sure you lock that top lock on the door tonight," Mrs. Bosco tells me. "No telling what creepy crawler is out there trying to bother people."

I chuckle at Mrs. Bosco's joke, but now I'm even more scared than I was before.

"And would y'all turn down that television, please—we about to eat dinner," demands Mrs. Bosco while she pats the top layer of cheese on the macaroni-and-cheese casserole she is about to put back in the oven. She always likes to give it a second cheese round, then she puts it in the bottom of the oven for a little extra toasting.

The Cheetah Girls

Ignoring Ms. Bosco's command, somebody has turned up the volume instead of down on the television. Now we can hear the narrator's booming voice all the way in the kitchen.

"What do we know about ferocious wild cats? Cheetahs will travel six hundred square miles to capture their prey. A jaguar can swim the Panama Canal, eating fish along the way. Tigers can weigh up to five hundred seventy-six pounds, and can eat up to ninety pounds of meat a day. Despite the man-eating lore that surrounds these big cats, they are generally able to live in close proximity to humans without disturbing them."

"What on earth are y'all watching?" Mrs. Bosco asks, wiping the sweat on her forehead with a napkin.

"Oh, it's this special on wild cats," I tell her while putting the meat loaf on the serving plate. Even though I feel bad that people are killing off wild cats, I shudder at the thought of being attacked by one.

"Ain't nothing wrong with wild cats—they just doing what nature intended for them to do. It's people you got to watch out for," Mrs. Bosco says, rubbing her forehead. I know what Mrs. Bosco is trying to say—that people can be foul sometimes.

"I'll go turn down the television," I announce,

then head into the living room to do the dirty deed. Of course, pulling teeth would be easier than pulling all the kids away from the television so we can eat dinner.

"Growl!!" Topwe says, howling like a lion at the table.

"That's enough, Topwe," Mrs. Bosco says. "You just got over a cold—no need for you to carry on like you in the circus, young man."

"I want to be in the circus!" Nestor yells out.

"I'm gonna be a lion tamer when I grow up," Corky says, nodding his head, then clapping his hands together. "And feed my lions frogs."

"I thought you liked frogs," I say.

"They gonna like frogs, too," Corky says, smiling.

Suddenly, I feel like I'm going to start crying again, so I put my head down—but I should have known Kenya wouldn't miss a trick.

"Why you crying, Dorinda?" she asks, poking fun at me. "You scared of the lions?"

"I'm scared of the lions," Nestor says, unfolding his napkin and putting it on his lap.

I don't answer because I don't want them to hear my voice cracking.

Everybody gets real quiet. I see them looking at each other like they all know what is going on. I look right at Twinkie and she gives me a look like, "I didn't say nothing." And I'm sure she didn't, because with this many brothers and sisters, if somebody knew something they would have blabbed their mouths already.

Now Mr. Bosco comes to sit at the kitchen table. Whenever he is home, he sits at the head of the table like he's the king of the jungle, which I guess he is in his house.

"Come sit next to me," Mr. Bosco says to Corky. Corky's whole face lights up, like he is really special. Nestor seems annoyed because he usually gets to sit next to Mr. Bosco at the dining room table.

"What you up to today?" Mr. Bosco asks Corky, running his hands through Corky's curls.

"I almost got ate by a tiger on the television!" he shouts out, making Twinkie and Arba giggle.

"Well, you'd better change the channel the next time, before he get to your leg," Mr. Bosco chuckles. "Legs don't come easy."

"They had a cheetah, too, like Dorinda!" Twinkie pipes up. "And they were swimming like Dorinda too—eating the fish!"

"That wasn't a cheetah—that was the jaguar they said swam across the Panama Canal," Chantelle says matter-of-factly.

Suddenly, I realize maybe it's a good thing

Chantelle reads all those *Sistarella* magazines because she remembers things and repeats it verbatim. And she was actually nice to me today, once she got a pair of clean underwear to put on.

"Oh, how did your show go?" Mr. Bosco asks, looking at me like he's sorry he didn't ask before.

"The Cheetah Girls won first place."

"Should have known that," Mr. Bosco says, chuckling, then shovels food in his mouth like he has to hurry up and go put out a forest fire somewhere.

I think about the fifty candles Twinkie wants to put on my birthday cake. I wonder if Mr. Bosco remembers my birthday is coming up.

Mr. Bosco helps Corky cut his meat loaf into smaller pieces. Nestor keeps eyeing them like, "What's up?" Meanwhile, Mrs. Bosco is trying to help Gaye eat her food. Gaye is definitely a fussy eater. She won't touch her macaroni and cheese, and spits out the meat loaf right onto her plate. Shawn stares at Gaye like she has lost her mind. As usual, though, he doesn't say anything. Mrs. Bosco is being real patient with Gaye, who is the most difficult child we have ever had to live with. Finally, Mrs. Bosco gives up trying to feed her. I feel sad that our Kodak moment from earlier is definitely over.

"Who's ready for dessert?" Mrs. Bosco asks.

Everybody screams, and Mrs. Bosco goes and gets the ice cream from the freezer. Gaye's eyes don't even light up when Mrs. Bosco hands her a cup, but at least it is the only thing she eats with no problem. On top of everything else, Mrs. Bosco has to start taking Gaye to a state-appointed child psychologist next week.

After dinner, I try real hard to concentrate on my homework, but I'm not feeling it. All I want to do is talk to my crew. Monie finally comes home and plops herself onto her bed in our room. I can tell by the way she says hello to me that she is upset about having to come home. Even though Monie is seventeen, Mrs. Bosco laid down the law: she has to be home at nine o'clock on school nights and Sunday nights as long as she lives here. Monie wants to be able to spend the night at Hector's house, but Mrs. Bosco isn't having it. I guess you could say the two of them aren't exactly getting along these days like mellow Jell-O.

I glance over at Monie propped on her bed and debate whether I should tell her about the Corky situation. I decide not to. She probably doesn't want to be bothered right now, so I leave her alone. Instead, I log on and go into the Phat Planet chat room so I can talk to my crew.

Assembling like cheetahs on the prowl, the five of us are finally all logged on. Of course, Galleria starts right in about the Operation: Save the Wild Cat Special.

Galleria: I don't care what they say, cheetahs are *not* an endangered species, because we're in the house!

Chanel: That's right, *mija*— and everybody should stop messing with us, because we're territorial!

Aqua: I bet you now everybody is scared of us—after last Saturday. At least uptown, anyway.

Of course, she is talking about our first-prize slam dunk at the "Can We Get A Groove" competition at the Harlem School of the Arts.

Angie: Well, we're still gonna have to deal with that heffa JuJu Quinnonez come tomorrow.

The Cheetah Girls

The twins have two computers in their bedroom.

> Galleria: Well, tell her to
> bring it on! 'cuz cheetahs are
> ferocious if you mess with
> us. And it's not like we're
> going around attacking
> peeps!!
>
> Dorinda: Listen, I have to
> talk to y'all.

I don't mean to break up their cheetah chatter, but I'm desperate.

> Chanel: Well talk, *mija*.

I look over my shoulder to see if Monie is watching me, but she isn't. She is lying on her side and is probably sleeping, even though she hasn't taken off her clothes. I carefully explain the whole Corky situation to my crew.

> Galleria: That sucks! Can't
> Mrs. Bosco get a lawyer or
> something to fight back?

```
Dorinda: Mrs. Bosco can't afford
any lawyer. She just deals with
the agency, but they're just
always pulling messed-up stuff.
```

I try to explain to my crew how hard it is for Mrs. Bosco to deal with those people down at the Administration of Children's Services.

```
Galleria: Too bad we can't go to
see the Wizard of Oz and get some
really good advice.
```

That makes me chuckle. *The Wizard of Oz* is Bubbles's favorite story. She even has ruby slipper stickers and magnets all over her room.

```
Dorinda: I guess tomorrow will
tell what the deal-io is. I
hope that man was just some
loony tune who is out of order
like a vending machine.
```

```
Bubbles: Hasta lasagna.
```

After Bubbles signs off, I log off, then I sit frozen on my bed. I feel too spooked to get undressed and take a shower. It doesn't help that they shut the heat off in the building at night. Shuddering, I lay down on my bed, fully dressed, and hide under the covers. I have a dream that a big fat tiger with sparkly dark yellow eyes walks into my bedroom and stares at me while I'm sleeping. I can't move because I am so scared that he is going to bite me. I try to scream but nothing comes out of my mouth. It's as if my tongue is frozen. I try to think loud thoughts so maybe he'll hear me by telepathy: "I know you weigh five hundred seventy-six pounds, because I just saw a television special on you, but check this: I don't have any ground beef under my bed, so why don't you bounce and go bother somebody else!" But the scary tiger just sits there staring at me and licking his chops.

When I wake up in the morning I have been perspiring so much, my face is covered with sweat. I jump straight up out of my bed because I'm afraid I'm gonna see that tiger sitting there—waiting for me to serve him breakfast. "Shoot," I want to tell him, "you're a day late and a dollar short, buddy, 'cause I only cook breakfast on *Sundays*!"

Chapter 4

Computer science class can't end fast enough today. I am squirming in my chair waiting for the bell to ring for lunch period.

"Don't forget, the first computer ENIAC was created in 1942—but kids back then didn't have the advantages you have. You can use the computer to do your homework!" Mr. Leone shouts as we bolt out of class like a herd of cattle. "So no excuses, no typos—get the assignment in on time—on Wednesday!"

Sprinting down the stairs to the cafeteria, I run into LaRonda, one of my favorite peeps from math class. "You got any more ticket hookups?" LaRonda jokes.

"Nah, I got nothing for you but love." I chuckle.

See, Mariah Carey heard about Gaye on the

news and had her record company supply Mrs. Bosco with free tickets to her concert. Of course, Mrs. Bosco put me in charge of the tickets, and I hooked up the rest of the Cheetah Girls, and LaRonda, because she's cool. I feel bad that I can't hook LaRonda up with another whammy jam, but right now I *have* to meet Galleria so I can use her cell phone to call Mrs. Bosco. No way am I waiting till after school to get an update on the Corky drama deal-io.

"I gotta bounce," I tell LaRonda as I jet down the stairs.

Bubbles is the first one out of the cafeteria. As usual she breaks into one of her riffs before I can snag her Miss Wiggy cell phone.

"Shoportunity is knocking—just three hours away!" Galleria says, grinning from ear to ear. Then she looks at me strangely, like I'm a walrus wearing a chiffon tutu at a pumpkin ball. "Do', you have a hole in your sweater, hello?"

"Oh, my bad," I grumble, looking down at the hole smack in the middle of my turtleneck. I was in such a trance this morning, I didn't even realize that I was putting on the same stupid ribbed khaki sweater that I avoided putting on yesterday. What a trip: why didn't somebody in my house pull my sleeve about my holey situation. I hate it when peeps aren't looking out for me. I mean, I'm always looking out for *them*.

Galleria is still staring at me like I've committed a fashion crime. I scan down to see what's putting the craw in her paw, but I can't figure it out.

"Do' Re Mi—why are you hording all the Frosted Mini-Wheats?" Galleria asks sarcastically.

"What?" I ask, puzzled.

"In your scalp," Galleria says, wiping dandruff flecks off my sweater.

"Oh, my bad *bad*," I say. Now I'm doubly embarrassed. With all the Corky drama yesterday, I was too freaked out to take a shower and wash my hair, so now I'm on my eighth day of dandruff disaster. (I only wash my hair once a week.)

Before I can ask Galleria to let me use her cell phone, she has peeped Chanel walking toward us with Mackerel and the Red Snapper in tow.

"So what's next, Cheetah Girls?" Derek asks, grinning and showing off his shiny gold tooth.

"What's next?" Galleria responds blankly. "Um, let's see. Lunch, and we're going alone?"

"Oh, it's like that? Well, I guess I can't tell you about *our* latest venture." Derek puts on his mystery man pose, which involves stroking the faint peach fuzz on his chin while raising his left eyebrow and squinting.

"Oh, *dígalo*—tell us!" Chanel protests, fluttering her eyelashes like a lovebird.

"Awright. Y'all are staring at the tightest spoken-word group to hit the mike," reveals Mackerel.

"Where are they?" Galleria asks, puzzled.

"Get wise—we're right in front of your eyes," Derek informs us.

"Now all we gotta do is find a venue where we can kick our floetry," Mackerel adds proudly.

"Oh, you're looking for a 'venue'?" asks Galleria. "May I suggest the Batcave? We hear it's available for performers who are, well, 'winging it.'"

"Okay, you get the last laugh now, Cheetah Girl—but wait till you hear our flow. Then you'll see that we got the skills to pay the bills, just like you do," Derek replies, amused by Bubbles.

Galleria smiles faintly at Derek, then scans him up and down—from his stonewashed jean jacket covered with racing car stickers, down to his chubby Adidas with the laces untied. "Well, let's just hope your rap attacks are better than your whack designs."

"So who's writing your lyrics?" Chanel asks before Galleria and Derek start sparring with shearing scissors.

"Unlike the Cheetah Girls—ours is more of a *collaborative* effort," Derek says proudly, like he has finally scored in the snaps department. Chanel winces because Derek's snap means that everybody in school knows about Chanel and Galleria's major beef jerky when it comes to writing songs together. They almost beat each other up with umbrellas over the one song they wrote together, "It's Raining Benjamins."

"What's the name of your group?" Chanel giggles. "Oh, *espérate*, wait! I know—*yo se*—Dynamic Duo?" Dynamic Duo is the nickname we gave Derek and Mackerel behind their backs.

"Mackerel and the Red Snapper," Derek announces.

"Now, that's what you call turning lemons into lemonade, I guess," Galleria says, shaking her head. "Oops, now I'm getting thirsty. Guess it's time to hit the Burger Box."

"Roger that, ready to move out," Derek chuckles, following us.

"Chuchie, pass me my bat spray!" Galleria stomps off so fast, we have to run after her.

Galleria's stomp still doesn't stop Derek and Mackerel from following us. They break into a silly rendition of "Somewhere Over the Rainbow." Chanel starts giggling because it is actually pretty funny. "You sound like penguins on laughing gas!" she quips.

Galleria spins around. "If I click my heels three times, will you two disappear?"

"See you in Kansas, shortie!" Derek mumbles, and they walk off, probably to Wok 'N Roll, which is their favorite lunchtime spot.

Once they're gone, I finally blurt out to Chanel, "Please, I gotta use the phone!"

"Oh, here, *mamacita*!" Chanel says, all hyped up. She passes me her Miss Wiggy cell phone like it's a magic wand. There is nothing like a shopping trip to get Chuchie on the supa-giddy tip. Galleria, on the other hand, seems annoyed about something.

"Mackerel was all over you like a rash," Galleria huffs to Chanel.

"What happened?" stutters Chanel.

While we're waiting on line at the Burger Box to place our order, I dial my home number. I am so nervous, I can hear my heart pounding. Meanwhile, Chuchie and Galleria are going at it like they're still in designer diapers.

"Don't try it, Chuchie—they aren't spoken-word artists!" Galleria insists. "I bet you they can't even put three letters together like, D.U.H." (DUH are Derek's initials—Derek Ulysses Hambone.) When the semester first started, Derek even had his initials shaved into the back of his head. Thank goodness he let that whack attack grow out.

"Would you like the Red Snapper if he didn't have a gold tooth?" Chanel asks coyly.

"Only if he had a gold finger instead!" Galleria says, then stares at Chanel like, Snap out of it!

"What's up with you, Do'?" Chanel asks while ogling the menu board. "Oh, my bad—you're trying to find out—I know. Sorry."

I keep my ear glued to the phone so I don't lose the connection. On the second try, Mr. Bosco answers the phone in a gruff voice. My heart sinks even further. "Hi, Mr. Bosco," I say, and I try to probe him for info.

"Hang on," he says gruffly.

Now my heart is pounding all the way down into my Mad Monster boots. Mrs. Bosco gets on the phone and it sounds like someone has hit her in the chest, because her voice is really winded. "Yeah, I heard from Mrs. Tattle."

I wait for Mrs. Bosco to say something else, but she doesn't.

"Mrs. Bosco?" I repeat into the phone.

"Yeah, I'm here."

"Um, what did she say," I ask nervously.

"Those fools done given Corky's father custody," she says, like she is about to collapse. "Just waiting to hear now when they gonna take him."

I am so shocked by this news that my eyes start

to sting. Galleria and Chanel's drama radar has gone off, and they are standing right by me, waiting to hear what is going on. "Did you tell them he was hanging around outside?" I protest. I can't believe the foster-care people would give Corky to a stalker.

"They don't care, Dorinda. The man done got custody—and soon as they finish the paperwork— Corky's gone," Mrs. Bosco says, like she is defeated.

Tears start streaming down my face. I stay quiet because I don't want to upset Mrs. Bosco. I have never heard her voice sound like this before. Not the whole time I've lived there. Now I feel guilty about going shopping at the Girlie Show Boutique after school with my crew. "Um, I can come home right after school, if you want," I say, stuttering.

"No—you go on with your friends. Ain't nothing we can do now but pray for that boy," Mrs. Bosco says, like she's testifying. "'Cause Lord knows the people supposed to be running his life ain't got no good sense. Next thing I know they be calling talking about they giving Gaye back to her mother. No matter that the woman done abandoned her child in a playground till the police find her. They do anything long as they ain't got to do no more paperwork on something!"

I shudder at what Mrs. Bosco is saying. But she is right. *How could they give Corky back to his father. This just can't be happening.* I am so numb that I just blurt out to Mrs. Bosco, "Where is Corky's mother?"

"She long gone," Mrs. Bosco mumbles.

I don't know what Mrs. Bosco means by "long gone," but I decide not to ask her any more questions right now. "I'll see you later, okay?"

"Yes, pumpkin. Get yourself something nice. Y'all won that prize. Nobody can take that away from you."

Like a mummy in a trance, I hand the phone to Galleria because I've forgotten that it's Chanel's cell phone. Galleria gives Chanel back her phone.

"Have you ordered?" asks the woman behind us in the line, startling me out of my numbness.

"I got this," Galleria says, ordering for us. "Chuchie, take Do' to a table."

Chanel takes my arm as we walk to an empty table. I plop down into a chair and stare into space. All of a sudden, my mouth starts quivering uncontrollably as I lose it.

Chanel puts her arms around me. "Oh, *mija*, what happened?"

"They're gonna take Corky," I moan into her fluffy pink sweater.

Chanel holds me tight. I hear people mumbling around me. One of the voices I recognize—it's Daisy Duarte from school. She is whispering to Chanel, "What's wrong with her?"

Chanel answers Daisy in Spanish. Now I feel embarrassed. Galleria plunks down the trays for us. Eyeing the burgers covered in chili sauce, I realize that I'm definitely not hungry.

"They're taking Corky away," Chanel tells Galleria.

"They're giving him back to a man who hangs around playgrounds?" Galleria asks dramatically. Galleria pauses, then blurts out, "Mrs. Bosco should fight them."

I just stare at Galleria.

"Look, Do', if there is anything I learned from that custody battle with Mrs. Brubaker over Buffy's litter, it's this—anything is possible if you fight for what you believe in," Galleria says, trying to help me. But she just doesn't understand. She doesn't know anything about dealing with the foster-care system.

"It's not like that. All Ms.—I mean, all your mom had to do is file a claim in family court. It's not like foster care," I try to explain to Galleria.

"Then we had to go down there before the judge," Galleria adds quickly.

"I know—but you didn't need a lawyer or anything," I say.

"Oh—so tell Mrs. Bosco to get a lawyer," Galleria insists.

"She can't afford a lawyer—and she can't use those lawyers from ACS because they're working for the system," I explain.

"Well, there has to be something she can do," Galleria says, like she isn't trying to hear me. "Why does she have to do everything they tell her to do? We're calling my mom about this. This may not be official Cheetah Girls' business, but she knows everything."

Before I can stop Galleria, she has whipped out her cell phone and is calling Ms. Dorothea, which makes me feel uncomfortable. I don't want Ms. Dorothea to think that I told Galleria to call or anything. I can handle my own business.

"Mom—well tell her to hang on to her knickers. We've got a situation here," Galleria says firmly to whomever answered the phone.

"Mom, you gotta help us," Galleria insists, then recounts the whole story blow by blow to her. Ms. Dorothea says something that upsets Galleria. "I'm not interfering, Mom, I just want to know what you think!" Galleria yells at her mother excitedly. "Okay, okay. I'll tell her."

Galleria snaps her Miss Wiggy cell phone shut tight like a Venus flytrap.

"Mom says Mrs. Bosco should take legal action and get a lawyer," Galleria says.

"Well, that's not going to happen, because she can't afford a lawyer," I say, staring down at my plate of food. "She barely gets enough money from foster care to take care of us." Suddenly, I realize this is probably going to be the worst birthday I've ever had. I burst into tears thinking about it. "Corky is not going to be here for my birthday!"

"Whatever happens, we are spending your birthday together, *está bien*?" Chanel says, looking directly at me.

I know that the lunch period is almost over, and I feel bad for taking up all the time with this drama. "You'd better eat, Chanel."

"I am!" she says.

I didn't mean to make it sound like Chanel was trying to diet on the sneak tip again, like she did with that carrot diet disaster. But I guess she is still sensitive about it. Chanel fainted in gym class and turned orange from that escapade.

I pick up my chili burger and start eating, but it might as well be newspaper, for all I care. I've known Corky since he was a baby in diapers. I can't stand the thought of losing him.

"This really sucks, Do'," Chanel says, putting her arms through mine as we walk back to school. I nod my head and let my feet walk me to next period.

"Tell me the name of your ten brothers and sisters again," Galleria asks, like she's got an agenda.

"Um, lemme see," I say, pausing like I can't remember.

Chuchie chuckles. "I know their names! There's Chantelle, Twinkie, um, Monie—she's the mean one—and Topwe—his name is a vegetable in African something or other."

"Arba—I remember her name because it sounds like Abba." Galleria chuckles.

Abba is a big singing group from back in the day. I think they were from Sweden or someplace like that.

"Oh, Kenya, like can ya get a groove. Then Nestor—sounds like Nestle's Crunch—and Shawn, which rhymes with fawn." All of a sudden, Galleria whips out her Kitty Kat notebook—the one she uses for writing down lyrics for songs.

"What happened?" Chanel asks, amused.

"I'm just riffing," Galleria says. Her brain is obviously percolating on some project.

"Who else is there?"

"Gaye, she's staying with us until they find

another home for her—or maybe somebody in her family claims her," I add. "And, of course, my boo, Corky."

"I'm meditating on the situation," Galleria says, satisfied. "But let's go to class before we get expelled."

"Word," I moan. I wonder what Galleria is up to, but right now I feel too sad to think about it. Remember what I said earlier about God? Well, I take it back: God may love puppies and Big Bird—and probably Miss Wiggy—but God doesn't care at all about kids who end up in foster care.

Chapter 5

After school, I feel so guilty about not going straight home, my left eye starts twitching. But Mrs. Bosco is right. There is nothing I can do that will change the Corky drama, so why should I miss out on shopping with my crew?

"The whole situation is just so foul," I tell Chanel as we stand outside the Girlie Show Boutique waiting for Aqua and Angie to join us.

"When is he leaving?" Chanel asks, flapping her pink mitts together to keep warm.

"We don't know yet because they have to do the paperwork and everything," I explain sadly. To cheer myself up, I stare inside the store window, checking out the Girlie mannequin that is wearing pink metallic hip-huggers and a tight crop top with the words "The Girlie Show" scribbled across the front.

"Hey, y'all!" yells Aqua as she turns the corner.

"Watch out!" Angie screams, because Aqua almost trips over a dog leash belonging to a not-so-friendly-looking Doberman pinscher. The lady was walking so fast, the poor dog didn't have enough time to catch up to its owner.

"Where is the fire, that's all I'm asking," Aqua says, shaking her head at the lady as she walks up to the boutique and hugs Chanel.

"Coco says hi!" Galleria giggles to Aqua, referring to the adorable pooch the twins were awarded from the Buffy custody battle. For now, Coco is staying with Galleria until she is properly housebroken, because the twins father, Mr. Walker, wouldn't allow any *eau dé pee* scent in his kitchen.

"Prada said *buy!*" quips Chanel, whipping out the Girlie Show Boutique Shoportunity Card and waving it around, squealing.

"Calm down, Chuchie—you're screaming like a nutty contestant on *The Price Is Right!*" yelps Galleria.

"Well, I'm sorry, *mamacita*, but I feel like one, *está bien*?" counters Chanel.

"Will you please get Chanel inside before she goes into shopping *withdrawal*," Aqua says, laying on her Southern accent.

Galleria opens the hot-pink wrought-iron door of the Girlie Show Boutique for us like we're royalty. Walking in last, I take in the interior design like I'm on a mission. "Wow, this is tight," I say in awe, ogling the hot-pink-and-black interior of the store. "This is *definitely* a dope setup. No doubt." Of course, my boutique would have more orange, brown, and green shades in the interior—like a happy forest.

"This reminds me of Princess Pamela's place," Aqua says, pointing at the gigantic flashy disco ball hanging from the ceiling.

"Yeah," Chanel says, smiling. Princess Pamela is her stepmother. She lives with Chanel's Dad, and she owns three Princess Pamela joints in Manhattan. For a special treat, Chanel snagged us some free pampering sessions at Princess Pamela's Psychedelic Palace uptown. I really dug it—except for the little trick the Cheetah Girls pulled on me. They made the spa technician trap me in this cellulite contraption so they could sneak out and plan my adoption party at my house. No, I'm not adopted, because Mrs. Bosco didn't understand the procedure, okay? But the surprise adoption party made me feel special.

"Disco will never die!" Chanel says wistfully.

"Disco did die, Chuchie—right on the Billboard

charts, in 1980, so let it go, please," Galleria says, giggling, sounding more and more like our manager, Ms. Dorothea, every day.

A salesgirl wearing a pink flowered micro miniskirt, with a black fishnet crop top, walks up to us with a friendly smile. "Hi there, ladies, let me know if I can help you."

"We will!" Chanel says, all hyped up. She loves it when someone calls her a "lady."

"Hey, listen up, chicklets—let's remember that this is all about Dorinda, okay?" Galleria says, combing through the dress rack. "Oh! I got the beginning of a jammy. What do you think?" Galleria whips out her Kitty Kat notebook and turns to a page, then starts riffing: "Let me tell ya about a cheetah named Dorinda Do' Re Mi/She's bursting at the seams with her dreams and leads her own family posse/That's right y'all there's ten little Indians she tries to keep in line/Starting with Shawn the fawn who is on like popcorn even though he's shy and just turned nine/Then there's a little tottie tottie who blabbers like Abba but don't forget the R and to call her little Arba . . ."

"That's what you were doing in history class today?" Chanel asks, dumbfounded.

"Well, I got bored! Mr. Hunnicut needs to step up that patter on the Pilgrims," Galleria protests, closing the notebook. "But at least that's where I got the idea about the ten little Indians."

"What does the nursery rhyme have to do with the Mayflower settlers?" counters Aqua.

"Nothing, but that's how my mind works—it cross-pollinates, like a true artist," Galleria boasts, then switches gears again: "Okay, Do'—let's get something that really says, 'It's your birthday.' It's your birthday! We're gonna party like it's your birthday!"

"Oooh, what about this?" Aqua asks, pulling out a brown jumper decorated with a "Hello Kitty" pink appliqué on the front.

"Hello Kitty," Galleria says, looking at the jumper carefully, then sticking it back on the rack: "Good-bye, Kitty!"

"Look, I don't need an outfit for that, um—" I start in because I'm feeling embarrassed about all the attention on my birthday. I still haven't even told my crew that I'm only going to be thirteen!

"Sorry, Do', but your birthday is a done deal-io big deal," Galleria says, still rifling through the dress rack.

Chanel is the one, though, who finds the cuddly prize: "*Ay, Dios*—it's another puppy *chulo*!" she says, holding up a fuzzy pink cheetah sweater top with a white poodle appliqué in front.

The Cheetah Girls

"How come there's never anything with a bichon frise on it?" Galleria asks, squinching up her nose. "Don't they know that bichon frises and Cheetah Girls go together like corn on the cob!"

"Corn is born on the cob, Miss Galleria, it didn't just get up one morning and decide to get in cahoots with the yellow kernels!" Angie says, grimacing and eyeing the pink sweater like it's Pepto-Bismol.

"Well, you get my drift, Miss Aquanette," Galleria says, feeling the fuzz on the pink sweater. "Now this is something to bark about. Is this cheetah-licious or what?"

Galleria sees the look on Aqua's face and goes, "Uh, oh, don't tell me I'm having déjà vu again." She is imitating Fantasia, the receptionist at Churl, It's You!, the hair salon where they all went to get their hair straightened for the "Can We Get A Groove" competition. (I couldn't do it because I didn't have the duckets.)

"Oh, I got you," I say, finally realizing where Galleria is going with this scenario. Aqua and Angie weren't down with Galleria's last big idea—wearing pink wigs from Ricky's Urban Groove.

"I'm sorry, Galleria, but we were not brought up to think pink, okay?" Aqua says, defending herself and Angie.

386

"That's right, we're Texas girls, which means we're always ready to ride with our spurs on," adds Angie, accentuating her words with her juicy lips, which are extra shiny from the Very Berry lip gloss she usually wears.

"Well, now that you're in the Big Apple—why don't you consider forgetting about spurs, and hail taxis instead?" Galleria challenges, then puts on a majordomo pout.

Angie and Aqua give each other that "twin" look we are used to seeing (it involves a double set of eyeballing and neck rolling). "All right, we'll try it on—that is, if they have it in our size," Aqua says, scrutinizing the sweater like it's small enough to fit Pebbles from *The Flintstones*.

"This one here looks like it'll fit Dorinda, but not us," Angie says, holding up the fluffy pink sweater.

Galleria whips through the rack like a prize-fighter ready to go another round.

The flower-power salesgirl is on our tail again: "Can I help you ladies?" she asks.

"Yes," Galleria says. "Do you have this cheetah-licious sweater in a *bigger* size?"

"Do you mean large?" the girl asks, smiling.

"No—I mean *extra* large," quips Galleria.

Aqua rolls her eyes again.

"Um, yes, I'll go look for it," says the salesgirl. "I like that word—cheetah-licious!"

"That's us," retorts Galleria, and waits patiently for the salesgirl to return.

By now we notice that two girls stationed at the skirt rack have been eyeing us for a few minutes. "Omigod—are you the Cheetah Girls?"

"In the flesh—ready to pounce on a purchase," Gallleria says playfully.

"Omigod, we saw you in the talent show. You were awesome!" The blond girl in the hot-pink fur jacket giggles. She has a really cute Southern accent, like Aqua's and Angie's.

"Really?" Galleria asks, trying to place her.

"Yeah, you were so-o-o-o much better than those other girls in the cheetah outfits," says the blond girl in the blue fur jacket. "We were rooting for you."

She is referring to the Fabulation Girls, who were biting our cheetah flavor and performed at the "Can We Get A Groove" competition, too.

"Now we put a cheetah outfit on our dog, too!" exclaims the blond in the blue jacket.

"What kind of dog do you have?" Chanel asks excitedly.

"A pit bull," blondie-in-blue retorts.

"Oooh, how ferocious, *mija*," Chanel chuckles.

"We're up here staying with our dad until after

New Year's. Muffin, our dog, lives with him now," explains blondie-in-pink.

"We live with our dad—permanently," Aqua says, nodding her head as though they have something in common.

The girls nod back because they are talking about the same thing—having parents who are divorced.

"Where y'all from?" asks Angie.

"Um, Cartersville, Georgia—our dad's next door waiting for us to finish shopping. He hates shopping with us," blondie-in-pink laughs. "Oh, I'm Destinee and this is my sister, Savannah."

"Word, you two look like twins," I say, surprised. I wonder if they're singers, too. Maybe that's why they came to the talent show.

As if reading my mind, Destinee blurts out, "Maybe one day we'll be like you—I mean, we sing and all, but we aren't professional yet."

"Well, we aren't all that professional either," Aqua says, sucking her teeth.

Galleria pokes Aqua in the side like she's using a cattle prod.

"Don't mind her, she's having a bad day." Galleria giggles. "We are definitely down for the twirl. And we've been in the studio with Mouse Almighty, working on a demo."

"Omigod, he worked with Karma's Children, we *love* them!" Savannah says excitedly.

Aqua grimaces. Karma's Children is the hottest group from Houston, their hometown. "Yeah, we got to perform in the 'Houston Helps its Own' benefit," Angie explains.

"Omigod you got to perform with them?" Destinee asks in disbelief.

"Uh, no. But we were one of the opening acts," Galleria says, and now *she's* grimacing. After the Houston benefit, we tried everything except "abracadabra" in order to get backstage and snag an autograph and photo op with Karma's Children.

"That sweater is so-o-o adorable," Savannah says chirpily.

"Um—it's Dorinda's birthday, so we're getting an outfit for her party," Galleria says boldly.

My party? I feel my face getting warm.

"How old are you going to be?" Savannah asks.

Now I think I'm going to faint.

Well, I guess it's as good a time as any to stop with the fib-eronis. "Um, thirteen," I say without blinking.

Galleria, Chanel, Aqua, and Angie all turn their heads to look at me like they just got a bad case of whiplash.

"We can't wait till we're thirteen!" Destinee says.

"My birthday is in March. Savannah's in July."

We all stand there quiet for a long minute.

"Um, yeah, that sweater should look great on all of you," Savannah says, eyeing us more carefully. I can tell she is trying to figure out what's going on.

"The red cheetah outfits you wore were totally awesome—but you should wear pink onstage. That would be even more awesome. Well, that's what we think, anyway," Destinee says, shrugging her shoulders and glancing at Savannah, who nods her head in agreement.

"I guess we can learn to love pink cheetah," Aqua says, giving in.

"You can," Chanel says, nodding her head happily.

"I have the extra large for you," the salesgirl says, returning with two sweaters.

"Um, great," Galleria says, taking the sweaters. "We'll need *both* of them."

Now Angie smirks and starts combing through the racks.

"I guess we'd better hurry up," Savannah says.

"We'll see you later," adds Destinee. I can tell they are both real glad to get away from us.

"Thirteen, *mamacita*?" Chanel asks once the girls are out of earshot.

"Yup, I got skipped in junior high," I say,

nodding and looking for a size medium for Galleria.

My crew stays quiet for about two seconds, then Angie blurts out, "Found a small for Chanel."

"Here's a medium for Galleria." I look at Galleria and she just smiles, even though I *know* she wants to make a crack about me.

We take the sweaters to the dressing room, when suddenly Chanel spots pink cheetah fake-fur skirts. She lets out another loud squeal. "*Ay, Diós, Mío!*" The flared skirt has a poodle appliqué near the hemline.

This time Galleria just shakes her head and grabs the skirts. "Well, I guess if our singing career doesn't work out, we will certainly have the right outfits to announce our Divette Dogwalker Service, won't we?"

"Heh, Bubbles, that's a good idea!" Chanel says.

"Don't even think about it, Chuchie," Bubbles warns Chanel. "Just keep your eye on the prize, please. We'll make it. You'll see." She pushes Chanel into the dressing room while we find other empty stalls.

Once we all have on our outfits, Aqua still seems unsure of herself in the pink cheetah sweater and skirt.

"You look cheetah-licious, don't fight it," Galleria warns her.

Chanel, on the other hand, is delirious. "This sweater is so *Sex and the City*!"

Aqua shoots her a look.

"I saw one of the reruns on TNT," Chanel says coyly. "*Mamí* fell asleep."

"If we come home with anything like those heffas wear on that show, Daddy will have us 'outta the city' faster than you can say Delta Air Lines!" Angie gripes, her eyes wide with fear.

"Well, it's Dorinda's birthday," Angie says, smiling. "The neckline's not low or anything. It's all right, Aqua—it's kinda cute. Daddy will like it."

Even though Aqua is still not convinced, Galleria drags her to the cash register, with our poodly cheetah tops and skirts. Destinee and Savannah are already there, buying black satin hip-huggers and powder-blue angora sweaters. Chanel whips out our shoportunity card and hands it to the cashier.

"Oh, that's right, you won great prizes!" Destinee says. She pulls out a credit card and hands it to the cashier. "It's our dad's."

Chanel looks at the credit card like it's a lamb chop dripping with mint jelly. "That's what I love about America—credit!"

"Snap out of it, Chuchie," Galleria says, poking her. "You need credit like I need cellulite!"

"You mean *more* cellulite, *mija*, right?" Chanel giggles.

"Hey, here's our phone number at our dad's. If you perform anywhere else, let us know!" Destinee hands Chanel a card.

Chanel takes the card from her. "Wow, I like the way you spell your name!"

Suddenly I feel a pang of jealousy, or Gucci Envy, as Galleria calls it. It must be nice having your own card to hand out. I glance at the pretty card. It says "Destinee" in nice, pink, script letters.

"What kind of name is Chuchie?" Destinee asks, teasing.

"The kind of name someone named Destinee spelled with two 'es' shouldn't ask about," Galleria answers, teasing back.

"She's just kidding—I'm Dominican," Chuchie responds.

"And Puerto Rican," adds Galleria.

"And Cuban," Angie chimes in, nodding her head like, "Believe it."

"Wow," Destinee says, glancing at Savannah with a look that says, "Don't you love New York?"

When the girls leave, Chuchie snaps, "You were mean, Bubbles!"

"They loved it. Now they can go home and say

they had an authentic New York experience," Galleria says, waving one of the shoportunity gift certificates. Now Galleria turns to me, and I'm sure she's going to drop a wisecrack like a boom, but she surprises me: "Since it's your birthday, Do', we've decided that you get to keep the Barnes and Noble gift certificate for yourself."

"No way," I say, astounded.

"*Way*," Galleria says forcefully. "Since when do you get anything extra? Take it"

"Thanks," I say quietly and put the card in my cheetah backpack.

"Well, I think we're *all* going to look real nice in our new outfits," Aqua says, obviously patting herself on the back for going along with our pink cheetah plan.

"Sometimes life forces us in directions which we should have found ourselves," Galleria says matter-of-factly, patting Aqua on her shoulder.

"Word, that's deep," I say, nodding my head, then pondering the thought for a second.

"*Holy sardines!*" Galleria says, her eyes widening. "I knew there was a reason we were thinking pink. I just came up with the master whammy jammy idea."

We stand there, watching Galleria's facial expression.

The Cheetah Girls

"It's Dorinda's birthday, right, next Saturday?" she starts in.

"Yeah?" Aqua says.

"And Mrs. Bosco needs to get an attorney so she can kick some foster-care-agency butt, right?" Galleria continues.

We don't say anything to that one, but just look at each other puzzled.

"So, if we throw a Cheetah Girls fund-raising benefit," Galleria says excitedly, "we can raise enough money for Mrs. Bosco to get an attorney—and celebrate Dorinda's birthday—*and* show peeps that the Cheetah Girls have growl power to the max!"

"Now that sounds like a plan," Aqua says, nodding in approval.

I stand there speechless.

"Listen, Dorinda, nobody ever said you had to take this lying down," Aqua goes on.

I look at Aqua, startled.

"It's a Southern expression," Angie says, gently taking my arm.

"Um, I don't know," I say, my cheeks burning. "I think I'd better ask Mrs. Bosco first."

"Speaking of authority," retorts Galleria, then fumbles in her cheetah backpack and whips out her Miss Wiggy cell phone. By now, I know exactly how Galleria's mind works—like light-ning.

As soon as Ms. Dorothea answers the phone, Galleria tells her the idea. "Ah-hah. Ah-hah. Ah-hah." Galleria keeps nodding and looking at us.

"Done deal-io," Galleria says, looking at us like she is not going to take no for an answer. "Mom was on point. She said that we should invite all the Def Duck Records executives to the fund-raiser. And she is going to send out a massive e-mail inviting all her clients once we've made an electronic flyer!"

"Do' Re Mi—this is gonna be the best birthday you've ever had! You'll see. *Es la verdad*," Chanel whispers in my ear.

"I know exactly what we're calling it—the 'Bring It On!' benefit," Galleria says, thinking out loud. "'Cause we are definitely gonna bring it on. Nobody is ever gonna say the Cheetah Girls take shots from anybody. Am I right, Do' Re Mi?"

I don't respond. I can't because I'm too busy cry-ing. My crew forms a circle around me and we stand there hugging for a whole New York minute.

Chapter 6

When I get home, I'm still trying to figure out how to tell Mrs. Bosco about the fundraiser idea. What if she gets upset? I mean, I don't want to upset her more than she already is. One look at Mrs. Bosco's face sitting at the dining room table, with Gaye on her lap, tells me I'm right. Corky and Twinkie don't even smile when they see me. They are sitting in front of the television.

"Corky knows, Dorinda," Twinkie says, looking up at me with her red, swollen eyes. Now I realize that everybody has been crying. Twinkie doesn't even ask me what's in my shopping bag, so I know she's really upset. I put my shopping bag in my room—in the closet so Chantelle doesn't mess with it, then walk into the kitchen and take my dinner out of the oven. Whenever I'm late, Mrs. Bosco always puts aside a plate for me covered with tinfoil. I'm not even hungry, but I go to the dining room and sit down at the table.

All of a sudden, I just blurt out Galleria's idea for a fund-raiser, then hold my breath and wait for her response. "She even wants to call it 'The Bring It On!' benefit, I add for good measure, because I know that Mrs. Bosco really likes Bubbles for being so bossy and determined.

"You know what," Mrs. Bosco says, pushing up her bifocal glasses on her nose. "Y'all go 'head with your fund-raiser. This boy ain't leaving my house without a fight."

I look at Mrs. Bosco with tears in my eyes. Now I finally understand what Galleria meant by what she said: sometimes life does force you in directions. I think she really meant to say: life kicks you in the butt so you can stop dillydallying about a situation.

The next morning, when I take Corky, Twinkie, and Kenya to the bus stop on Malcolm X Boulevard and 118th Street, Twinkie turns to me with the saddest blue eyes, and asks: "Is my father gonna come get me, too?"

"No, Twinkie," I say firmly. "And I'll tell you a little secret, neither is Corky's father."

She throws her arms around me and whispers

in my ear, "Is the boogey man gonna get him?"

"No, the Cheetah Girls are." I chuckle.

Twinkie's eyes turn a brighter shade of blue. "Bye, Cheetah Bear!"

Today, I can't wait to go to school and tell my crew that the "Bring It On!" benefit is definitely on like popcorn. That reminds me about the latest riff Galleria is writing about all my foster brothers and sisters. Her lyrical flow is always working 24-7.

That's why I'm not surprised when I hook up with my crew by the school lockers and Galleria hits me up with the finished riff first thing. She whips out of a copy for me and shoves it in my hand: "Let me know what you think. I'm open to any *collaborative* input on this one," she says haughtily. I know she's referring to that drama that went down after Kats and Kittys with Derek and Mackerel.

"Since when, *mija*?" Chanel chides her. "*Dame uno*. Give me one, too!"

Just when I thought Galleria was about to surrender her self-appointed position as "boss of the beats," I realize it's déjà vu all over again.

"Um, I wasn't talking about you, Chuchie—this is Dorinda's groove, okay?" declares Galleria.

"Mrs. Bosco said let's roll with the benefit," I

chime in, trying to squash their never-ending songwriting beef jerky.

"Then we're on it, doggone it!" Galleria says excitedly.

We plan to meet after school to get started on all the millions of details that go into making a benefit jump off.

"I'm gonna call Princess Pamela and get her to donate stuff for the goody bags!" squeals Chanel, whipping out her cell phone.

"Just don't think you're gonna get your paws on the merch—it's for *paying* customers," yelps Galleria, referring to the peeps who are going to shell out twenty-five dollars a ticket for our fund-raising benefit.

"See you later," I yell out, while they continue to go at it.

"Don't forget—" Galleria calls out over her shoulder.

"What?" I ask nervously. Bubbles moves so fast, I can't keep up with all the details.

"Dorinda's Family Groove—check it out, give me notes later," orders Galleria.

"Oh, right," I say, nodding. Walking to my homeroom class, I take a peek at the song Galleria wrote for me, but when I start reading it, I feel myself getting weepy again.

As a matter of fact, tears start streaming down my face. I finally realize why I can never get mad at Bubbles. She may seem bossy sometimes and full of herself, but she is always on the real tip. She's not thinking about herself at all—she's thinking about everybody.

"Are you okay, Dorinda?" Daisy Duarte asks me, touching my shoulder.

"Yeah, I'm cool," I assure Daisy. "Real cool."

For the next four days, I really am cool, because I'm not just sitting around thinking about the Corky situation. I'm actually doing something— meeting at Galleria's apartment every day after school to help the Cheetah Girls pull together our "Bring It On!" benefit. You can't believe how hard we have been working to "set it off." My bad. I don't mean we're doing this whole thing by our- selves. All the peeps around us are pulling their weight—everybody—from Princess Pamela to Mrs. Walker (Aqua and Angie's mother, who lives in Houston) to Drinka Champagne, our vocal teacher, to Galleria's dad, Mr. Garibaldi. Every- body we can count on has stepped up to the plate and helped us. So now the fund-raiser is about to jump off this Saturday. So far, it's been like playing a game of Monopoly—making our moves carefully—and we are definitely ready to pass "Go!" on Saturday night. In my mind, I run over all the details and make a list of everyone who helped us:

1) Drinka Champagne is letting us use the Drinka Champagne Conservatory for the benefit—for a price we couldn't resist—*free*. Drinka even got one of her old school peeps, Deejay Frankie Feelgood, to volunteer his deejay services for our benefit. (I mean, if the benefit is called the "Bring It On!" benefit then we have to have some thumping beats, okay, to help everybody do just that.)

2) Ms. Dorothea has donated lots of cheetah fabric and is even letting her seamstress, Chen Chen (she does all the in-store alterations at Ms. Dorothea's boutique), make the table coverings and wall drapings for the benefit. Ms. Dorothea has also donated 200 cheetah shopping bags and tissue paper for our gift bags. "See, when peeps pay $25 for a fund-raising benefit, they always expect to walk away with a few goody bags," Ms. Dorothea schooled us.

3) Mr. Walker, Angie and Aqua's father, designed the invitation on his Master Whammy computer (he's a Big Willie in the marketing department of a roach spray company) and printed out 1,000 invitations with envelopes. (The invitations, of course, are cheetah-licious and have cheetah paw prints in the corners.)

4) Mrs. Walker, the twins' mother, whom I met in Houston when the Cheetah Girls were down there performing for the "Houston Helps Its Own" benefit, has gotten her company, Avon, to donate oodles of beauty products for the gift bags and shipped us three huge boxes through FedEx. (In return, we have listed Avon Cosmetics as one of the sponsors on the bottom of the invitation.)

5) Mr. Simmons is donating all the spicy food and soft drink beverages from his Return of the Killer Taco restaurants (and, of course, Return of the Killer Taco is also listed as one of the sponsors on the bottom of the invitation). Mr. Simmons would have also donated the paper plates, napkins, and stuff, but Ms. Dorothea does not think forest green goes

with our theme. She insisted we use *her* personal stash of leopard paper plates, cups, and napkins. (She is right, as usual.)

6) Princess Pamela has donated gift certificates to Princess Pamela's Poundcake Palace and Princess Pamela's Psychic Palace for the goody bags.

7) *Everybody*—that means Drinka Champagne, Ms. Dorothea, Mrs. Walker, Mr. Walker, Princess Pamela, and Mr. Simmons have given us their client and customer lists so we can send out massive e-mail invitations. Of course, we have also put up a notice on the bulletin boards at both our schools (Fashion Industries High and Performing Arts East), and, last but not least, the Kats and Kittys Klub (the nationwide teen social organization we all belong to) office is sending out e-mails to all its tri-state members.

8) Ms. Dorothea's boutique is also handling the RSVPs. She has a Mastercard and Visa hookup, so we can sell tickets over the phone. So far we have sold thirty tickets, which means we have already raised $750 before the event!

9) Last but not least, everyone is going to perform—that means the disco legend Drinka Champagne herself, peeps who go to school with us—the mighty Malcolm Extra; Danitra; Fredericka; and Mackerel and the Red Snapper. Even Ms. Simmons, Chanel's Mom, is going to treat guests to her whammy jammy belly dancing.

"Is Auntie Juanita going to wear an authentic belly dancing outfit?" Galleria asks, interrupting my personal shout-out list. "Tassels, veils, gold coins, the works?"

We are all unpacking the Avon beauty products from the FedEx boxes.

"*Sí, mamacita!*" Chanel says. "I saw her trying everything on in the exercise studio."

"I can't believe Auntie Juanita is going to be jingling, baby!" riffs Galleria, who is fiddling with the little flower-petal-shaped lip gloss pots. "Mom, how many tickets have we sold so far?"

"You asked me that five minutes ago. I told you—thirty," Ms. Dorothea says, writing down a "to do" list. "Don't worry. People always wait till the last minute to buy tickets—and some even wait for the privilege of paying extra at the door."

"This Flower Swirl lip gloss is the whammy

jammy," Galleria says, slicking on one of the Avon products.

"Which one?" Chanel asks.

"Watermelon, of course." Galleria giggles.

"That's enough, Galleria! The products are for the *paying* guests. Now start putting the products in the gift bags!" orders Ms. Dorothea, smacking Galleria's hand.

I chuckle to myself because it turns out that Galleria—not Chanel—is the one who has been trying to get whiffs of all the freebies for the goody bags. We are in Galleria's living room, which has been turned into the official Cheetah Girls office, if you ask me. I mean, there are papers and boxes everywhere. My job today is to e-mail invites to everyone on all the lists we have compiled. Trust me, it's a whole lot of people. I even invited my adopted sister, Tiffany, and her family, even though she was disappointed that I wouldn't let her perform in the benefit. But trust me, she's like my foster sister Chantelle—they both can't sing, okay?

"Dad, this one sounds like he can get the job done," Galleria says, showing her father an ad in the back of the *Village Voice* newspaper. Galleria's dad is searching for attorneys so we can be ready to roll after the benefit.

Galleria reads the attorney's ad: "Mr. Buttafony, Esquire. I SUE 4 U."

"Sounds like a rapper," I retort, scrutinizing the shady newspaper advertisement.

Mr. Garibaldi doesn't answer Galleria, but he nods his head, because he is on the phone. "Okay, that sounds very reasonable. Okay, *bene*, thank you. We will be calling you very soon!" he says excitedly, putting down the receiver.

Mr. Garibaldi has to find attorneys that specialize in custody cases and are familiar with the snaky ins and outs of the child welfare system.

"I think I found a very good lawyer for Mrs. Bosco!" Mr. Garibaldi says proudly. He furiously takes notes on his legal pad. "And she only wants a twelve-hundred-dollar retainer—the rest is payable after the court's decision."

"What's a retainer—you mean like my braces?" Galleria asks.

"No, *cara*—a retainer means you have to pay the lawyer half the legal fees up front so they can begin working on your case," Mr. Garibaldi explains.

"Is Mrs. Bosco going to have to go to court?" I ask, trembling.

"But of course, Dorinda—you have to be fighting like a crazy person in the boxing ring," Mr. Garibaldi says, waving his hands. "And that is what court is in *this* country—everybody tries to punch the opponent in the nose."

"And in the pocketbook," Ms. Dorothea says, kissing her husband on the cheek.

While Mr. Garibaldi tries to find a prizefighting attorney, Ms. Dorothea is busy working the phone, offering invitations to Big Willy peeps. I guess you could say Ms. Dorothea is making sure we have all our bases covered—mail, phone, and e-mail invitations so we have a full house on Saturday evening.

"I still think we should do 'Bow-wow Wow,'" Galleria says, still fighting with Chanel about the song we're going to perform. (We have rehearsed all of them.)

"No way, José," Chanel blurts out.

"Why not?" Galleria asks, smirking. She wants to perform our favorite song, "It's Raining Benjamins," but she and Chanel are still fighting over songwriting credits. (Chanel did cowrite about five percent of the song.) "How are we going to look performing the same song that we did at the Def Duck New Talent Showcase in Hollywood?"

"Like we know all the words?" responds Chanel, smirking back at Galleria.

"Okay, Chuchie—I'll make a compromise. We

perform "Wannabe Stars" again, because that's the only number Toto knows—but we're back in rehearsals next week, getting tight with Bow-wow, Wow, or I'm really gonna start *barking*."

"How come we don't perform the song you're writing now—since it's for Dorinda," counters Chanel.

"I didn't want to stress everybody out about rehearsal," Galleria says, looking at us for assurance.

"We can handle it," Angie says confidently.

"Okay, then, we'll be ready to do Dorinda's Family Groove for our encore," orders Galleria.

"What makes you think there will be an encore?" asks Chanel.

Galleria levels her don't-try-it look, and Chanel shuts up. I can just hear the peeps at the benefit shouting the very words we all want to hear: *"Encore, encore!"*

Chapter 7

I look at my watch and see that it's already six o'clock, but I'm not trying to stress it even though I have to get home by seven o'clock so I can take Chantelle out for a special surprise.

"You don't think twenty-five dollars is too much to charge for the benefit, do you?" Aqua asks nervously. "I mean, it's not like they're gonna get to see Mariah Carey sing, or something.

"What do you mean—it's even better. They are going to see the Cheetah Girls in their natural habitat!" Mr. Garibaldi says, waving his hands.

"That's right," Galleria agrees. "Remember those peeps paid fifty duckets in the bucket at the 'Houston Helps Its Own' benefit, and they didn't even get a gift bag!

"She's right," Angie says, nodding her head and licking an envelope. "Okay, these are ready to be mailed." Angie shoves all the sealed envelopes with stamps into a shopping bag.

"I'll go with you!" Chanel says, grabbing Toto's cheetah leash. "Toto needs another walk."

"Chuchie, you just walked him an hour ago!"

"I know, but he's big—so he needs a lot of walks!" Chuchie pouts. "I think Toto should be the host at the door. With that tongue panting, who wouldn't fork over twenty-five dollars?"

Meanwhile, Angie and Aqua are fighting over petting Coco. "I can't believe Daddy won't let you pee in our kitchen!" Angie coos to their precious puppy.

"That reminds me—change the Wee Wee Pad in the kitchen before I start sniffing," Ms. Dorothea huffs to the twins.

"Maybe we should invite those girls we met at the Girlie Show Boutique to perform in the benefit?" Angie queries, like she's amused by the idea.

"We've got enough peeps, don't we?" I ask.

"Nothing like a little Southern hospitality, that's what our momma always says," adds Aqua, getting up to go to the kitchen and take care of Coco's business.

"Well, start being hospitable—you call them!" Galleria says, passing her phone to Angie.

All of a sudden, Ms. Dorothea snaps her fingers

loudly. We look over at her while she is talking on the phone. Something is definitely going down.

"Can't wait to see you, Mr. Isaaks. Oh, yes, that is a cheetah-certified fact. Bye- bye!" Ms. Dorothea says, putting down the phone. Dramatically, Ms. Dorothea puts her hand to her chest like she is thanking God.

Mr. Isaaks, I repeat to myself. That name does sounds familiar.

"Miracle worker—latest job description added to my very lengthy resume," Mrs. Dorothea says, sitting back calmly. We wait with bated breath for her to tell us about her latest coup.

"What's the scoop?" Galleria asks.

"Darling—this is not a scoop, this is a double scoop with whipped cream, nuts, *and* a cherry on top," Ms. Dorothea says, satisfied.

We stare at Ms. Dorothea some more. Ms. Dorothea smiles at us some more. "Well, after fifty phone calls, I finally got the man who quacks—" she starts in, obviously smitten with her supa skills to pay the bills.

"Omigod, Def Duck Records!" Galleria screams, interrupting her mom with a round of squeals.

"Yes, Mr. Tom Isaaks—whom some of you may recall—the A & R quackster from Def Duck Records on the West Coast who was at your showcase in Hollywood—well, he is in town and has purchased a few measly tickets."

"How many tickets?" Galleria asks, her eyes as wide as ice-cream saucers.

"TEN TICKETS!" Ms. Dorothea screams, then reverts immediately back to her diva self. "He will be attending with Freddy Fudge, the A& R person we met at Def Duck who has put our project on pause, obviously. Well, anyway, his secretary is sending a messenger tomorrow with the check."

"Sending a messenger?" Chuchie asks, impressed.

"Yes—so suffice it to say, Def Duck Records will definitely be providing a presence at the Cheetah Girls 'Bring It On! benefit!" Ms. Dorothea says.

We all jump up and down—hugging, kissing, and squealing, like satisfied cheetahs.

"So how many tickets have we sold now?" Galleria asks.

"Galleria, if I didn't know better, I would swear you're in need of remedial math," Ms. Dorothea says. "Now, if I can just pull a Mouse out of a hat— or at least out of his studio—we may really be killing, sorry, animal conservationists, I mean, *caressing* two birds with one phone."

Ms. Dorothea ponders her strategy.

"Yeah, Mouse Almighty," Galleria says wistfully.

Ms. Dorothea picks up the receiver and starts

pressing numbers again. We all do our tasks while Ms. Dorothea calls Mouse Almighty—keeping one ear peeled for a mighty screech, or at least a peep. But we can tell by the way Ms. Dorothea puts the phone down that the platinum-record producer didn't take a nibble.

"Mouse Almighty's secretary informed me that he sends his regrets, because he will not be attending our benefit," Ms. Dorothea says, defeated. "There is no way he can leave the studio until he finishes all the tracks for Kahlua Alexander's album."

We all join Ms. Dorothea in putting on a solemn expression. If Mouse doesn't come, that means we may not even get to go back into the studio with him to finish our demo. And that is what really matters, despite all our cheetah chatter.

"Maybe he really has moved on—and this is just his nice way of telling us," Galleria says, pouting.

"Trust me—where there's cheese, a Mouse always comes around to nibble—eventually. You just have to wait and be patient," Ms. Dorothea says, waving away Galleria's doubts.

"Mom—you're just saying that," whines Galleria.

"No, I'm not. True talent isn't always rewarded, but my inability to take no for an answer will level the playing field," Ms. Dorothea says wisely.

The phone rings again, and we all freeze, waiting to hear what is jumping off now.

"Now, that is *fabulous!*" Ms. Dorothea gushes into the phone.

We all perk up again. It must be Mouse Almighty calling back to say he is feeling our cheetahness again.

"Who needs a Mouse when you've got a celebrity like Constellation Jones at your service!" Ms. Dorothea announces to us.

"She's coming?" Aqua asks, perking up.

"Better than chedda, darling. She is going to be our Mistress of Ceremonies for the evening!" Ms. Dorothea says, doubly pleased with her latest coup. Constellation Jones is one of Ms. Dorothea's best customers, and she happens to also be a cohost on the morning lifestyle television show, *Say, What!*

"Wow," Galleria says, impressed, but I know she is thinking the same thing I am. "How come Mouse Almighty isn't coming?"

"Okay, Galleria, would you please keep your *chins* up—"

"Mom!" Galleria exclaims, cutting off Ms. Dorothea. "That's not nice, so don't say it twice."

"I'm just kidding. But come on, you're acting like the goose that broke the golden egg, then slipped on the egg yolk," protests Ms. Dorothea.

Aqua and Angie look at each other. "Is that the same thing as looking a gift horse in the mouth?" Aqua asks with a quizzical expression.

"Never mind. But speaking of two chins, don't think for a second that finagling Constellation Jones into hosting our benefit isn't going to be cost me a few hens out of the henhouse," Ms. Dorothea says, waving her left arm, which is piled with cheetah bangles.

We all look at her, trying to figure out what she is trying to say.

"I've agreed to make her a complimentary ensemble," explains Ms. Dorothea.

"Complimentary?" Aqua asks.

"Free," Ms. Dorothea retorts.

"Ensemble?" Angie asks.

"That means an entire outfit. And in Constellation's case—dressing Queen Sarabi in *The Lion King* would be cheaper!" huffs Ms. Dorothea.

"Well, *hakuna matata*!" Galleria chuckles.

"Word," I chuckle back. "*Hakuna matata.*" No worries is right. At least not about who is going to be our Master whammy Mistress of Ceremonies, anyway.

"Okay, I'm out," I tell my crew, putting on my shabby winter coat, then tossing my cheetah backpack over my shoulder.

"You got any changes for your 'Groove'?" Galleria asks, raising an eyebrow.

"Nah, it's tight," I say, smiling.

"Well, learn it and love it," Galleria says proudly, kissing me good night.

I really do love "Dorinda's Family Groove," and it's going to be a whole lot of fun singing it with Twinkie when we do the laundry on Sunday again.

When I open the door to my apartment, Chantelle is sitting on the couch watching television. "Did you finish your homework?" I ask her. She nods her head.

"I have a surprise for you," I say quietly.

"What?" she says, looking up.

"Go put on your coat and shoes, and I'll tell you," I say, then go knock on Mrs. Bosco's door to see what's new with the Corky situation.

"Mrs. Bosco, it's me," I say, speaking through the door.

"Come on in, Dorinda," Mrs. Bosco says quietly.

I open the door and Mrs. Boscos is lying on her bed in her nightgown. She smiles at me and says, "Mrs. Tattle's coming to take him next Thursday. I haven't told him yet, though."

"Yeah, well, it's not going to happen," I say firmly. "We're selling tickets and ready to roll."

"I know that's right," Mrs. Bosco says, peering

over her bifocals to gaze at me. "I'm going to take Chantelle to Barnes and Noble with me," I inform her.

Mrs. Bosco smiles and nods her head. "That's real nice of you, Dorinda."

"Okay, bye," I say, shaking it off.

Meanwhile, I have never seen Chantelle get dressed so quickly before. She is bundled up like a paratrooper and standing by the door waiting for me. "Where we going?" she asks eagerly.

"You'll see," I say, then lead her out the door.

"Can I come?" screams Twinkie, barreling out of her bedroom.

I feel bad, but I know this is something I have to do for Chantelle. Everybody knows Twinkie and me are real tight. But I have to share a bedroom with Chantelle, and the less "Magic Mountain" piles I see on my bedroom floor, the happier we'll all be. "I'm sorry, Twinkie, but you have to stay here and watch out for Arba and Kenya," I say weakly.

"Kenya doesn't like me," Twinkie says defensively.

I refrain from telling her that Kenya doesn't really like anybody unless they give her presents.

"Yeah, but Arba does, and I need for you to watch out for her so Mrs. Bosco can look over

Gaye—and Corky," I say, making a face so Twinkie gets the drift.

"Awright," she says, defeated. She wipes her chocolate-smudged hands on her pink T-shirt.

I don't ask where she got the chocolate from, just gently say, "Could you go wash your mouth and hands now?"

Twinkie makes a mischievous face, which lets me know the chocolate didn't come from Mrs. Bosco. "Awright, see you later, Cheetah boogie girl!" she riffs.

There is no Barnes and Noble near my house, so we have to take the #1 train downtown to the one on Broadway and 86th Street.

"Everybody is so sad now," Chantelle tells me earnestly as we climb out of the train station.

"I know," I say, smiling back at her.

"Is my father gonna come and get me, too?" Chantelle asks out of the blue.

I wonder if she and Twinkie have been talking about this. I decide the best way to deal with this foster-care situation is to just keep it real. "I don't know, Chantelle," I tell her, holding her arm. "I don't know anything about your father."

Chantelle gets real quiet until we approach the entrance of Barnes and Noble. Her whole face lights up when I motion for her to walk through the revolving door. The trip was worth it just to see that. It reminds me that Chantelle is really cool most of the time—except when she has her tantrums.

As we approach the magazine rack, she becomes instantly absorbed—music magazines, the teen magazines and a few others—maybe she just really loves reading magazines, because they have pictures and words but they aren't the same as children's books. It must make her feel more grown-up.

After Chantelle has selected a huge pile of magazines, we go to the reading section and I tell her to plop down while I go browse at some of the fashion books. I need to do some serious stocking up on books for school: First, I need to snag a book on appliqués and trimmings. It might be nice to find a book on leather design, too. I'm taking the class next semester, so I might as well get a head start. Once I start looking at all the fashion books, I get so excited that I create a huge pile. Then I get nervous and divide the piles in two: the I'm-fiendish-for pile and the I'm-just-being-greedy pile. When I see how much the two books I want cost, I almost keel over—fifty dollars total for *Inside Fashion Design* and the *Collectors Book of Fashion*. Now I'm starting to get dizzy. I can't leave behind *Hats Off to Fashion!* because I know I want to design hats one day, too. Then I put down the hat book because I realize I should take *Trim, Trim, Trim It!* and *Leather, Pleather, and Lace.*

After one hour of going through all the books, I realize I still can't decide which ones to take, so I take a break and run over to make sure Chantelle is okay. She doesn't even look up when she sees me. Her nose is practically glued inside the fanzine magazine *Karma*—a magazine devoted to Karma's Children, the group from Houston that makes Aqua and Angie go green with Gucci Envy. Chantelle is staring at a spread of the singers wearing gold lamé cutout jumpsuits. "You okay?" I ask.

"I don't have anything nice to wear on Saturday," Chantelle sighs. She sounds like she is sixteen years old instead of ten. I feel bad because she is right—she doesn't have anything really nice to wear to the benefit on Saturday.

"You can wear my cheetah outfit," I say, smiling.

"Which one?" Chantelle asks, smirking.

"You know which one—the one you like—that Chanel bought for me."

"Really?" Chantelle asks, breaking out into a big smile.

"Really," I retort. "But don't get used to it. It's a once-in-a-lifetime offer that expires on Cinderella time—at the stroke of midnight on Saturday night."

Chantelle nods like she gets the drift. "Do you think you're really going to raise the money for Mrs. Bosco to get a lawyer so they don't take Corky away?" Chantelle asks matter-of-factly.

Nobody told Chantelle what the benefit was for exactly, but I should have known that Miss No-bloomers would have figured it out. Now I bet all the kids know what the benefit is really for. I had told them that it was to help Mrs. Bosco, that's all.

If she had asked me that question yesterday, I don't know what I would have said, but now I know the answer for sure. "We're on like popcorn!"

"Is it really going to help Corky stay?" Chantelle goes on.

Suddenly I feel defeated. We have been all hyped up about getting a lawyer so Mrs. Bosco can fight the Administration of Children's Services in court, but that doesn't mean we are going to win. It doesn't even mean we won't be wasting all these peeps' money. I pause before I answer Chantelle, then reply honestly, "No, it doesn't mean we are going to be able to keep Corky. It just means we're not giving up without a fight."

Chantelle looks at me like she already knew the answer.

"Okay," I say, changing the subject, "which magazines do you want to buy?"

Chantelle plops down a pile of ten magazines, and I give her a look like, "Don't try it—or *you* buy it."

"Okay." She winces. "Can I have these five?"

I add the prices of the five magazines together—twenty-two dollars. "Do you want to get a book, too?"

Chantelle nods.

"All right, how about if we get four magazines and you pick out one book."

"Awright," Chantelle says, walking over to the grown-up-book sections.

"That way," I say, nudging her to the children's-book section. "Don't look a gift horse in the mouth, okay?"

Chantelle drags her feet, then smiles and says, "I won't look any horse in the mouth, because I'm afraid of them." Then she surprises me by asking, "Can I get a book for Corky instead of for myself?"

"Of course," I say, hugging her. Now I know that she is more than just smart. One day I hope Chantelle figures out how *special* she is.

Chapter 8

Sometimes a week flies by fast, like a cheetah going eighty miles per hour. Other times a week crawls by, like a toad stuffed with Micky Dee's. I guess I don't have to tell you which one describes this week, huh? Saturday is finally here, and it's just one hour before we open the doors to our paying guests for our throwdown at the showdown. The Cheetah Girls, with the help of everybody around us, have been supa busy doing everything we can to make sure our "Bring It On!" benefit is a night we'll all remember. Even better, the foster-care agency has no idea that they are in for a fight. Mrs. Bosco has an appointment first thing Monday morning with Ms. Dropkin, a really nice attorney that Mr. Garibaldi found. From what Mrs. Bosco told me, she seems like she really cares about us winning custody of Corky.

As if reading my mind, Angie asks me, "What did the lawyer say to your foster mother?" Right now we're lining the two hundred gift bags for the guests in the reception area at Drinka Champagne Conservatory.

"She said that Mrs. Bosco has a really good chance—especially since Mr. Dorgle, Corky's father, didn't have visitation rights and never kept in touch," I explain. "Her fees are reasonable, too. And Mrs. Bosco liked her on the phone."

"That's real good," Aqua says, peeking in one of the bags. "You sure we can't take a few of these for ourselves?"

"I don't think so." I chuckle and pat the sweat beads on my temples.

"You're as nervous as I am!" Aqua says, surprised.

Aqua is right. I have the worse case of bugaboo chillies that I've ever had in my life! I mean, if you think performing onstage in front of a live audience for the first time is hard, then you should try hosting your own fund-raising benefit. Even with the five of us acting like the "hostesses with the cheetah mostest," this is still the scariest thing you can think of—never mind the fact that it's my birthday, too. (On the real tip, I will never forget turning thirteen as long as I live, okay?) The scary part is not raising the money we need: we have sold seventy advance tickets so far. And in less than an hour, we open the doors to Big Willies (and Little Willies), and will probably sell more. What makes the whole thing so scary is: 1) Before the event, you spend every other minute worrying if peeps are going to show up. 2) During the event, you know you're going to spend every other minute worrying if peeps are having a good time, or if they will secretly wish they could get their money back, and every time they see your face in the future, they are going to think about that twenty-five dollars they spent! 3) Your jaw is so tired from smiling and being nice to everybody *way* before the event so that you make sure that peeps will actually come. 4) During the event, you're going to spend every other minute hoping that none of the "talent" gets onstage and slips on their own banana peel, if you know what I'm saying. 5) In between all of the above, you're supposed to be having fun, but you're so tired because you haven't gotten enough sleep, that you start acting like one of those mechanical women in *The Stepford Wives*. 6) If you don't have fun at your own benefit, then you feel stupid, because that's one of the reasons you're doing it in the first place!

Now Drinka Champagne snaps me out of my list-making: "Girls, you are looking very cheetah-licious," she coos, and admires our matching pink cheetah outfits with the poodle appliqués. Drinka is wearing a cheetah jumpsuit in our honor, with cheetah mules stacked on stiletto heels so high I'm worried she is gonna topple over when she gets onstage to perform her 1972 number-one single, "Just Sippin' When I'm Not Tippin.'" (Somebody pinch me because I still can't believe that the miniqueen of disco is going to perform at the Cheetah Girls benefit!)

"Toodles to the poodles!" riffs Chanel, waving at Drinka from the deejay booth where she, Angie, Galleria, and Ms. Dorothea are working—covering the whole deejay area with cheetah fabric. And from the looks of all the giggling and sniggling, I think Chanel is also flirting with Deejay Frankie Feelgood, who is setting up all his crates of albums. I want to go over to check out his albums, but I'm on gift-bag duty (Galleria didn't trust Chanel). Deejay Frankie Feelgood has brought about ten crates of records—that's right, vinyl records from back in the day—to do some *serious* spinning before and after the live performances. I'm itching to get my fingers on some of his old school tracks, but I have to make sure we get everything set up before the guests arrive.

"Angie, come help us with the food!" I yell across the room. But she doesn't hear me because she is talking to Ms. Dorothea. I bend over to open the box with the paper items. I don't see Twinkie out of the corner of my eye until it is too late.

"Say Cheetah!" screams Twinkie, snapping a picture of me with my mouth pursed tensely. I have given most of my foster brothers and sisters their own tasks. My sister Monie and her boyfriend, Hector, are on coat-check duty.

Twinkie is on photo detail. That means she's in charge of taking all the photos that I will later put in the Cheetah Girls' scrapbook. I can tell that Twinkie is getting a little snap happy, and I don't want her wasting the film. "Twinkster, you need to put that on pause," I start in.

"What do you mean?" she asks, squinching her little nose.

"Twinkie, it's a disposable camera and there are only twenty-six shots—so I need you to take pictures, um—"

"I know—when you're not bending over and showing your cheetah bloomers!" Twinkie says, giggling hysterically.

"Right," I reply, tweaking her left cheek.

I glance over at the man of the hour—Corky—to

make sure he's okay. He looks really nice in his blue sweater and pants. He is holding Toto's leash real tight, even though Kenya is trying to pull Toto away from him. (Corky is on Toto detail tonight.) Kenya's only task tonight is to behave, and she is already dropping the ball, if you know what I'm saying.

At last, Malcolm Extra, Danitra, and Frederika Fabulina make their entrance. Right behind them is Gina Garfunkle and a few other peeps that take classes at Drinka Champagne Conservatory. All the peeps who are performing had rehearsals here earlier today, so they should be on point. And I'm not flossing, but it definitely looks like it's going to be a crowd-pleasing lineup. Now I'm starting to get excited because I realize the place is going to be jumping. I mean, not everybody is paying to get in the benefit, but at least it will be filled with peeps that know how to get a party started, if you know what I'm saying.

Screeeeeeeeeeech!! The annoying noise from the microphone is so piercing that Twinkie drops the camera and covers her ears. "I'm sorry, Dorinda!" she squeals nervously.

"That's okay," I say, putting out the stacks of plates and cups on the banquet table.

"Hey, hey, hey—read all about it!" says Malcolm

Extra, coming over and giving me a kiss. "The critics will be raving!"

Malcolm is being dramatic, I guess, so I just laugh.

"You need any help?" he asks.

"Nah, this situation is under control," I say nervously.

Chardonnay, who works for Chanel's father, Mr. Simmons, is putting the hot trays on the buffet tables now. She also puts little burners underneath the trays, to keep the food warmed.

"Yum, yum—gimme some," Malcolm Extra says, turning on his falsetto voice.

"Don't worry, we're getting our grub on real soon," I assure Malcolm.

Danitra comes over to and gives me a kiss. "If we didn't tell you before, then let me tell you now. We are so proud of you!" she coos.

I feel embarrassed because the benefit wasn't my idea, and I sure didn't do all this by myself, but I don't say anything except, "Thank you for helping us out."

"Are you kidding?" Danitra says, rolling her neck. "I'd sing at a Bar Mitzvah if they were giving out free bagels, okay?"

Malcolm, Frederika, and Danitra all do high fives on that one snap. "That's performing arts peeps for yooooou—we are always down for the *twiiiiiirl*, don't you know that, *Cheetha Giiiirrl!*" chimes Malcolm Extra, turning his riff into a song.

Now Destinee and Savannah are back, too. They were actually pretty good at rehearsal (they're going to sing the Karma's Children song, "We're Two Independent"). "Hi, Dorinda," Destinee says, giving me a hug. "Gosh, we are all wearing pink!" The two of them are wearing pink velvet jumpers and pink shearling UGG boots. I wish I could snag a pair of those, but that is wishful thinking. I introduce them to all the Drinka Champagne peeps, including Danitra—but she is being very rude—she doesn't even say hi to Destinee and Savannah—because she is goospitating over someone in the distance.

"Ooooooh, who are *those* tasty morsels!" Danitra coos, turning her head like a snapdragon.

I turn to see whom she is talking about. It's Derek and Mackerel. They couldn't come to the rehearsal earlier because they were competing in the YMCA Youth Program Basketball Tournament. It was okay, anyway, since they aren't using track music. "Oh, are you feeling the Mackerel and the Red Snapper?" I say, chuckling. I'm glad that they aren't wearing their usual Johnny Be Down or

Sean John ghetto getups. They actually look nice. Derek is wearing a purple iridescent shirt over a pair of black baggy dress pants. Even his shark-skin shoes are nice. Mackerel is wearing a red-and-black sweater over a pair of black pants and some combat boots. "The Red Snapper is hooked on Galleria, and Mackerel on Chanel," I explain to Danitra, but she isn't listening.

"The Mackerel and the who and the what?" Malcolm Extra giggles.

"Don't you remember they were at the "Can We Get a Groove" competition uptown?" explains Danitra, waving to Derek like, "Yoo-hoo, hottie! Over here!"

Derek walks over but he has a puzzled look on his face like, "Do I know you?" Mackerel parts company for a second to head over to the deejay booth, no doubt to talk to his crush Chanel. Chanel is still tacking up the glittery letters on top of the cheetah fabric that covers the deejay booth. The letters spell "Bring It On!"

"Wazzup, Dorinda," Derek says, acknowledging me for once. Then he smiles at Danitra, who is obviously goospitating over him.

"I saw you at the competition," Danitra says, without introducing herself.

Derek gives her a confused look, then

catches on. "Oh, right—at the Cheetah Girls chompdown," he says, chuckling. Then he realizes that Danitra was one of the performers. "Oh, yeah, you were dope, too."

"Yeah, I'm performing tonight, too," Danitra brags.

"Oh, yeah, so are we," Derek says, motioning to Mackerel.

"Well, bring it on," chirps Danitra. "By the way, how come you weren't at the rehearsal earlier then, huh?"

"We had a hoop situation to tend to," Derek says, bragging. "But anyway, pure spoken-word artistry is best displayed with just the artists and the microphone—on the stage, *alone*." Derek gestures dramatically to get his point across.

"The artist has spoken—hello!" butts in Malcolm Extra, in his singsongy voice.

They carry on with their repartee, while I get back to finishing the banquet table. Now I'm starting to sweat, because the room is getting crowded with all the talent. I know it's not the same as the guests, but I'm starting to feel the pressure building, you know what I'm saying?

"Okay, listen up, talent!" yells Drinka. "We need for all of you to take a good look at the lineup sheet and know your place. If you have any questions about the production setup, take that up with Marty now. And if you're changing into costumes to perform, everything should be in the dressing room now. Don't wait till the last minute, or I will grade you—even if you're fifty."

There is a loud chuckle around the room. Marty is the technical coordinator who is responsible for all the music and sound cues for the talent show. Meanwhile, Nestor, Chantelle, and Kenya come over to the banquet table to eye the tasty dishes. Kenya's skirt is caught up in her waistband. I motion to Chantelle to fix it. (Chantelle is on look-nice duty, and she is supposed to make sure that all the kids behave so that Mrs. Bosco can get a break.) I look over at Mrs. Bosco sitting on one of the folding chairs, with Gaye on her lap. Sure enough, Ms. Simmons is talking with her—and I can hear her trying to tell her that everything is going to be okay. I notice that Ms. Simmons is carrying a big duffel bag on her shoulder. "Chantelle, go tell Ms. Simmons to put her costume in the dressing room," I say, like a true talent coordinator.

"I guess this food should be good enough for the cattle!" says Chardonnay, taking a break now that she has put up all the covered pans of food on the banquet table.

"Is Mr. Simmons coming?" I ask her, wondering what Chanel's father is up to tonight. I know he works even harder than Ms. Dorothea and Mr. Garibaldi. Chanel is always complaining that she doesn't get to see him enough—especially since her mother, Ms. Juanita, hates his girlfriend, Princess Pamela.

"He'll probably be here before we finish, to help bring all the stuff back to the restaurant," Chardonnay says blandly. "The night manager done called in sick *again*."

I don't say anything else, because I don't think Chardonnay understands what I'm really asking. I shoot my eyes over at Chanel, who is having fun putting up the sign, and giggling with Mackerel, who is now helping her with the letters. I know it would mean a lot to Chanel if her father showed up and supported us. We're real happy, though, that he provided so much food for our benefit. Now I wonder if Princess Pamela is going to be here, too. Chanel loves her.

I glance over at Galleria, who is fixing the stage area with Ms. Dorothea. I motion for her to come over. She comes running. "Does Mrs. Simmons know if Princess Pamela is coming?" I whisper to her. "We don't want another showdown at the Okie Dokie Corral tonight." I'm referring, of course, to the drama we had in Houston. When we performed at the Urban Rodeo, we had a terrible run-in with a singing group from Oakland called the CMG (the Cash Money Girls), because they accused us of cribbing their lyrics. Obviously they were spoiled brats who needed their pacifiers, because they lost to us.

Galleria giggles, then shrugs her shoulders, "They're grown-ups. Let's hope they remember that when Auntie Juanita gets the urge to strangle Princess Pamela with one of her belly dancing scarves and Princess Pamela gets the urge to draw blood like Dracula!"

"Um, right," I say, giving her a Cheetah Girls handshake.

"Can you believe we did it?" Galleria says, gloating.

"No, I can't—yeah, I can," I say, correcting myself.

"The eats look thumpingly delicious," Galleria says, nodding her head in approval at the buffet spread.

"How do you know? The pans are covered," I ask her, chuckling.

Galleria looks at me like I should know better. "A cheetah never loses her sense of smell—don't ever forget that!"

Chapter 9

At last, every detail is taken care of, and we're ready to "Bring It On!" The five of us stand right behind the sign-in table, so we can greet peeps with a cheetahfied welcome. Winnie, the receptionist at Drinka Champagne's, has volunteered to take all the tickets and handle the money drawers. "Get paid, girls!" Winnie says, winking at us. She is even wearing a big cheetah flower in the lapel of her brown blazer in our honor. We all dig Miss Winnie because she has been feeling our flavor since jump street.

"Dag on, I feel like I'm in the Miss America Pageant!" Aqua says, panting heavy and waving at the guests who are finally coming in.

"I told you, thinking pink was the move—even for the Houston contingency of our group!" Galleria riffs at Aqua.

438

"Contingency?" Aqua says, smirking. "You sure are paying more attention in English class than we are, Miss Galleria."

"Well, you know my lyrical flow is *contingent* on increasing my vocab, Miz Aquanette!" Galleria chuckles, imitating Aqua by waving at the guests like she just won the Miss America Pageant, too.

"When we left he house tonight, Daddy asked us if we thought we had on enough poodles," snickers Angie, smoothing down her cheetah skirt.

"Well, I think we are changing our Daddy one spot at a time—and I can't wait till he lets Coco come home!" adds Aqua.

Our "Cheetah chatter" is interrupted by a group of incoming guests whom I don't recognize. After paying Winnie, they make their way in, and we give them our very best Cheetah Girls welcome. "Thank you for coming to our 'Bring It On!' benefit!" Chuchie says enthusiastically.

"Have we met before?" asks Galleria. That's the code word for "peeps we don't know approaching."

"Princess Pamela, yes?" the lady responds in a really thick accent.

"Oh, you know Princess Pamela!" squeals Chuchie with delight. "Is she coming?"

"She is, I'm sure. She is back," the lady

responds, nodding dramatically. Now I remember what Chuchie told us a few weeks ago. That Princess Pamela had gone back to Romania to fight for her family's property that was confiscated when the Communists took over. I guess my family is not the only one fighting with government agencies, if you know what I'm saying.

"Well, we're the Cheetah Girls," Galleria says politely. "Who are you?"

"Oh, I'm sorry! *Lo siento!*" Chuchie says, embarrassed. "I'm Chanel—Princess Pamela's, um—"

"We understand," the lady says. "We know who you are. I'm Pavlova Pratz, and this is my husband, Emil, and Rucsandra is our daughter."

"Nice to meet you!"' exclaims Chanel.

"You are her stepdaughter, yes? *Ah, beeneh.* She has told us so much about you, Mrs. Pratz says, beaming at Chanel. "She cares for you very much."

Chanel reaches out her arms to give Mrs. Pratz a hug, and whispers, "I can't wait to see her!"

"I like your outfits," Rucsandra says shyly. She is about ten years old and has on a pair of powder-blue UGG boots. Now I really want a pair.

"Those boots are popping up everywhere, like sheep," comments Galleria, like a fashion reporter, after the Pratz family heads to the coat-check area.

By now, peeps are piling in and we are greeting everybody. The room fills up with guests, and it looks like we've got quite a shindig going on. My whole face lights up when my sister Tiffany appears, with her parents in tow.

"Omigod, you look cheetah-licious, *mamacita*!" Tiffany barks loudly. Chanel giggles loudly at her. Tiffany is always trying to talk like, well, the Cheetah Girls, but it sounds supa funny coming out of her mouth. She gives me a big hug.

"Word. I like your perfume," I tell Tiffany, giving her shoulder an extra sniff. She smells like a fresh apple orchard.

"It's called 'Cheetah-licious,' by Canine Klein. Do you really like it?" Tiffany asks.

"Cheetah-licious?" I say, surprised, because we sure never heard of it.

"I'm just pulling your weave, *mamacita*!" Tiffany heckles like a hyena. "It's called 'Fresh.'"

"Oh, I got you," I say, my dimples stuck in smiling mode.

Now peeps are really piling in and Tiffany realizes that we are playing hostesses, so she says, "Oh, I'll see you later, Dorinda! Bye, Galleria, see you later, *mamacitas*!"

We are all still giggling after Tiffany leaves. She actually looks cute in her cheetah outfit.

441

"Wow, who are all these peeps?" I whisper to Chanel.

"I don't know. *Yo no sé, pero*, keep smiling!" orders Chuchie.

Looking around the room, I recognize some peeps from Fashion Industries, and the rest I don't who they are. Aqua seems to know a few of them, because they go to Performing Arts East. Of course, a lot of the guests are Ms. Dorothea's and Drinka Champagne's clients and friends.

All of a sudden, Deejay Frankie Feelgood starts kicking tracks—house music, which I'm not really into, but Galleria loves. "Omigod, I can't believe he's digging up Chicago house music," Bubbles bursts out.

"What is it?" Aqua asks.

"This is like Paradise Garage jammies from back in the day—I think it's Adonis. No, no—it's that group Kraze. I love them!" Galleria boasts. She does know a lot about house music because of Ms. Dorothea.

I have no idea what artists Galleria is talking about, but I know I'll be glad when Frankie changes up his rotation and hits us with some hip-hop tracks. Galleria and Chanel start getting their groove on a little, but we're still nervous because the Def Duck Record peeps haven't shown up yet.

Neither has Princess Pamela, which I think is a good thing. I don't want Mrs. Simmons and her to get into a beef jerky situation.

Drinka Champagne is running around like the disco diva of the hour. She really knows how to make sure peeps are having fun. I also can't help but notice how much she is flirting with the twins' father, Mr. Walker.

"She definitely has a crush on your father," comments Galleria.

"Yeah, well, I sure hope she asks our daddy out for a date." Aqua chuckles. "Even though we know he won't go!"

We all snicker at Aqua's prediction, as our Mistress of Ceremonies, Constellation Jones, makes her grand entrance. The whole room buzzes with her presence, but she is immediately whisked to the dressing room so she can get her diva makeup done by makeup artist Fave Rave (also a customer of Ms. Dorothea's) and have her hair done by Pepto B.—our favorite hairstylist.

Ms. Dorothea also runs to the dressing room area to make sure the "Say, What?" diva is happy with the gowns she has selected from Toto in New York . . . Fun in Diva Sizes. Mr. Garibaldi delivered a whole rack of gowns for Constellation Jones to choose from.

Finally, Galleria blurts out what we're all thinking: "Where are the Def Duck peeps? Could someone please put them in a boat with a faster paddle so they'll get here before we turn into cheetah pumpkins!"

As usual, Galleria is right. If the Def Duck Records executives come too late, we are definitely going to turn into—something.

"Well, maybe we should just strap ourselves in, because it looks like it's going to be a roller coaster ride tonight!" Galleria sighs, then announces: "I gotta grab some chips and a dip before I crunch my nails instead!"

Now the photographer that Drinka invited from the *Amsterdam News* shows up and takes a picture of us!

"You know how to spell our names, right?" Galleria asks him.

Chuchie pokes her in the side. Twinkie runs right up and shows the photographer her camera. "How come your camera is bigger than mine?" Twinkie asks him, giggling.

"Well, young lady, maybe you should take that up with Santa." The photographer chuckles, then excuses himself.

We all run over to the banquet table, because the food is finally being served and we are starving.

Everyone is drinking, eating, and having fun, so there is no reason for us to be on meet-and-greet duty at the door anymore.

Finally, Constellation Jones is ushered to the stage. We notice that the Def Duck Record peeps *still* haven't arrived. We wave at Pepto B. and Fave Rave, who are standing near the stage. Pepto B. throws us hugs and kisses. Ms. Dorothea is huddled at the side of the stage with the technical coordinator, Marty. Deejay Frankie Feelgood puts his tracks on pause, and peeps start clapping, so we all know the benefit is about to jump off.

"Good evening, everyone," Constellation Jones says, taking the microphone off the stand. She is wearing a sparkly, sequined leopard dress that trails on the floor like a diva mermaid gown.

"Ariel would be panting if she saw this tasty tuna number." Galleria chuckles. She is referring to Ariel, the little mermaid—one of Twinkie's favorite Disney characters. "That's a five thousand creation, fit for a dip in the Atlantica."

"Word?" I say, impressed. I notice that Fave Rave even glued sparkly sequins in the corners of Constellation's eyes. I nudge Galleria and put my finger to my eyes so that Galleria gets my drift.

She whispers in my ear, "I'm going batty over those!" She flutters her eyelashes like she's doing Morse code—imitating Drinka Champagne.

"I want each and every one of you to thank yourselves for coming out this evening. I mean it. Take your hand, *kiss* it, and say, 'Thank you!'" says Constellation Jones, flashing her million-dollar smile. "Now, I kiss my hand every morning that God sees fit for me to wake up. But that's just me, okay."

The crowd chuckles at her joke. The photographer from the *Amsterdam News* runs to the front of the stage, crouches, and starts snapping a million photos of Constellation Jones.

"But I'm asking you to say thank-you to yourselves for a different reason. I know you could be at home watching the *Sex and the City* rerun marathon," Constellation Jones banters, looking around at the audience. "Except for our younger divettes, of course—whom I'm sure would much rather be studying algebra on a Saturday night!" Constellation chuckles at her own joke. Galleria pokes Chanel in the back.

"But you're here because you care about the fate of one very special child—and because one woman has said, 'Uh-uh, you can't just pass our kids around like Popsicles. We care a little more about our kids than that. And we also care *who* is granted the authority to care for them'," continues

Constellation Jones. "If you don't know the woman I'm talking about—Mrs. Eunice Bosco, could you stand up, please?"

My heart stops. I can't believe that Constellation Jones is calling out Mrs. Bosco like that. Mrs. Bosco is so shy. I look around the room, searching for Mrs. Bosco, but I can't see her. All of a sudden, Mrs. Bosco stands up and everyone in the room claps. Mrs. Bosco smiles, then waves, and sits back down. Galleria grabs my hand and Chanel grabs my other one.

"Yes, Mrs. Eunice Bosco is going to fight the foster-care system. A foster-care system that arbitrarily decides the fate of children who can't make decisions for themselves," Constellation Jones says, getting serious. Everyone in the audience gets quiet. "Because of your contributions to the 'Bring It On!' benefit, we are going to give a mother and a child the chance to fight for their fate. Not let someone else decide."

Twinkie runs over to me and grabs my leg. "Is she talking about Corky?" Twinkie asks, whispering. I put my finger over my mouth for her to be quiet.

"I love kids so much, when my dear friend Dorothea Garibaldi—do y'all know this fabulous woman here?" Constellation Jones asks the crowd, pointing to Ms. Dorothea, who is still standing near the stage. "Well, if you don't know Ms. Dorothea, then you'd better ask someone, okay!"

The crowd starts cheering again. "This is the reason why I'm on television *every* morning looking as fabulous as all you size-two heffas out there! Look at this gown—but stand back, 'cause you can't have it—it's an original, like the diva who designed it!" Constellation Jones cracks herself up again. Now I can see why she is on television, because she sure knows how to "break it down."

The crowd cheers some more, and Ms. Dorothea throws air kisses with her hands to everyone in the audience.

"You'd better work, supermodel Mom!" Galleria screams.

"Okay, where was I—Lord, I get to testifying like I'm in church, and get carried away," reveals Constellation Jones, patting her forehead with a tissue. "Like I was saying, when Ms. Dorothea told me the purpose for this benefit, I was truly honored, because I stand for our children's welfare. So let's give a hand to those adorable Cheetah Girls and Ms. Dorothea for putting together this benefit that brought all of us together this evening."

As the crowd claps, Constellation Jones continues to talk, letting the audience know she could go till the break of dawn with her flow. "In case you don't know—one of the Cheetah Girls is Ms. Dorothea's daughter. Show us your growl power, Miss Galleria."

Galleria throws up her left arm and cups her hand to make the growl power sign for the crowd. "Growl power forever!" Galleria shouts.

"I understand that another one of the Cheetah Girls also lives with Mrs. Bosco. I'm sorry—" Constellation cups her hand to hear someone in the audience. "Yes, that's right—Dorinda—show us your growl power."

I cup my hand, too, and wave smiling around the room. Now I breath a sigh of relief because I'm so glad that Constellation Jones did not call me a foster child.

"Do' Re Mi is in the house!" screams Galleria. "And it's her birthday!"

"Happy birthday, darling," Constellation Jones says, congratulating me. "So, let's get busy with the fabulous lineup of talent here to entertain you. 'Cause you know we about to give you your money's worth. And there's also a fabulous deejay, if I can just remember his fabulous name."

"Frankie Feelgood!" Drinka Champagne screams from the crowd.

"Yes, now I know why I've been feeling so good

all evening," Constellation Jones moans in a deep voice. "Mr. Frankie is bringing me back to my youth, when I'd stay out all night getting my groove on instead of waking up at five o'clock in the morning to go to work. Oh—and y'all remember Drinka Champagne—Miss Sippin' and Tippin'? I know I'm aging myself, but that was one of the songs that kept me out all night. Oooh, I loved that song. "

While Constellation Jones keeps her chatter up for a few more minutes, I keep eyeing the room, hoping to catch one of the Def Duck executives making an entrance. I don't see anybody who looks like a Big Willie record executive, but I do see Princess Pamela in her bright red flowered shawl coming through the door. I elbow Chanel and motion with my eyes toward the door. Chanel claps her hands together like a kid and squeals, "Yeah—now we can Bring It On!"

Chapter 10

Finally, it looks like Constellation Jones is going to surrender the mike: "All right, let me get to the entertainment portion of this evening," she says, whipping out her stack of index cards. We glance over at Derek and Mackerel. It was Galleria's idea that they should be first in the lineup. "Throw some ice cubes into a hot frying pan and they're not going to last," she quipped when we made out the lineup list.

"Derek Ulysses Hambone originally hails from the motor city, Detroit, Michigan, while Mackerel Johnson grew up off the coast of Pensacola, Florida. That's near my hometown, too!" exclaims Constellation, flashing her teeth on overtime. I wonder if she had braces like Bubbles did, because her teeth are really perfect. "When they realized that they shared the same universal groove, the two Fashion Industries East freshman design majors joined forces, becoming the dynamic duo Mackerel and the Red Snapper. Here tonight to give you a logical—oh, I'm sorry—lyrical dose of this message—'Fashion is a Passion but Peace is Betta than Hair Grease.' Okay, darlings and darlings, please welcome to the stage, Mackerel and the Red Snapper!"

"Go, Mackerel!" Chanel hoots, rallying up support for her secret "boo." Chuchie catches Galleria's blank expression and quickly adds, "The first spot is always the hardest, *mija*!"

"That's right—hook it up, Red Snapper!" whistles Danitra from across the room.

Galleria throws us a look like, "Somebody hand her some ice cubes, too, please."

Mackerel and the Red Snapper grin from ear to ear as they step to the microphone. We all wait with bated breath to hear this lyrical flow.

"Your thigh-high boots are a mystery to me, but the color of your skin I never see," riffs Mackerel.

"It's you inside that makes me glide on a universal cloud, so don't make me shroud inside your goosed-down Starter Jacket," riffs Derek, doing a slick James Brown slide away from the mike.

The crowd goes wild. Danitra whistles from the back again. Now we're gagulating over Mackerel and the Red Snapper's lyrical skills. Galleria's mouth is open so wide, a tooth fairy could pay her a surprise visit.

"Who knew?" Chanel says, her eyes opening wide.

Aqua and Angie throw us a look like, "They're real good."

The Red Snapper and Mackerel continue dropping tasty lyrics: "You may wonder why I wear my lace-ups unlaced when I'm face-to-face with the reality of a world tied down by the color of *my* skin," riffs Red Snapper in a slow, melodic style. "Well, wonder this. Why does someone need a Wonderbra to bring *da* noise, when we're always poised—without the crutches. Lies. Alibis. Tries. For four hundred years?" riffs Mackerel, breaking out into an explosive cadence that makes the audience erupt again in rapid applause.

"That was tight," I say, clapping loudly. The five of us look at each other and shake our heads. It's definitely on tonight. When Mackerel and the Red Snapper leave the stage, Aqua sighs. "Whew. We got a good show tonight."

Constellation Jones applauds the rappers loudly. "Why doesn't my boyfriend talk to me like that?" After cracking herself up again, she announces Destinee and Savannah to the stage.

We are so hyped by the vibe in the room that we shimmy and shake to the Karma track, "We're Two Independent." After Destinee and Savannah finish their number—which is a little heavier on the giggles than it was during rehearsal—we are all pumped up to see Drinka Champagne.

Meanwhile, Danitra has sidled over to Derek like a silly groupie, and Galleria is not having it. "You should have been nicer to him, *mija*!" Chanel teases Bubbles.

"Okay, darlings and darlings, please welcome my girl, Miss Drinka Champagne," squeals Constellation Jones.

"Hold up, let's check this," I whisper to Chanel. This is the first time we've ever seen the fabulous Drinka Champagne perform live, even though we know the words to her hit single by heart.

"So you think you broke my heart and are coming back for a brand-new start. Well, mister—I'm just sippin' when I'm not tippin' out the door to look for Mister Right Now, so don't put up a fight!"

We all break out in uncontrollable giggles watching Drinka doing her disco number. She gyrates like the old-school disco dancers used to, and even breaks out into a split. "Go, Drinka. Go, Drinka!" we shout, clapping along. Watching

Drinka perform in front of older people, we can see that she really does have a lot of fans. I mean, you can tell some of the peeps are definitely going down memory lane for this old-school jammy. Even people who were acting all straight and narrow when they first got here are now shaking their groove thing to Drinka's beat! Even the Pratz family and Princess Pamela are grooving! I look around for Ms. Simmons, but she is probably in the back changing into her belly dancing costume. I notice that even Galleria's dad, Mr. Garibaldi, is waving his hands wildly in the air like he just don't care. Now the whole room is chanting, "Go, Drinka! Go, Drinka! Go, Drinka! Go, Drinka!"

Drinka finishes her song and does another split. "Now you can see, you ain't got the best of me cuz I'm still sippin' when I'm not tippin'!"

"I'm going to be singing that song all night," Aqua says, chuckling when Drinka leaves the stage. But we should have known Drinka would be back for more. The crowd screams for an encore. Drinka goes back onstage and does a rendition of her other hit single, "Champagne Bubbles of Love." Then Drinka squeals with joy into the mike, "Hello, people! I just want to say thank-you for twenty-five years of support. And, honey, I'm not faking, 'cause I'm still shaking it!

Just remember, Miss Drinka will never stop sippin' success until she meets her Maker!"

Constellation gets back onstage and seconds that motion. "I heard that. What I would give for that figure—Miss Drinka, you are poured into that jumpsuit, girl! I don't care what time I have to get up tomorrow morning, I swear I'm heading out to a disco. Let them fire me, girl. That's right—I'm going to grab all my girlfriends and say, 'Girls, it's time to hit the door so we can work the floor!'"

Constellation starts dancing, but her heel gets caught in her gown's mermaid train, so she stops and chuckles. "If I trip on this train I won't be sippin'—I'll be slippin', and Ms. Dorothea will read me four ways till Sunday. But we have someone who will provide you with all the entertainment you need. Ms. Juanita Simmons is a former Ford Model, who some of you may remember from back in the day. Well, honey, she hasn't changed a lick, and after you see her belly dancing, you'll agree. A fan of Middle Eastern dancing for the past five years, Ms. Simmons—whose daughter, by the way, is Chanel, one of the Cheetah Girls. Chanel show us your growl power!"

Chanel giggles and holds up her arm and cups her fist.

"Like I was saying, Ms. Simmons has practiced

Middle Eastern dancing as a form of exercise—and you will see, honey, it has paid off in spades. Darlings and darlings, please welcome, Ms. Juanita Simmons to the stage!"

Deejay Frankie Feelgood cues an exotic Egyptian music track—with a tight and tasty thumping beat. Ms. Simmons enters from stage left. She is wearing a purple belly dancing costume with gold sparkles and trim. Chanel is grinning ear to ear. We all clap our hands to the beat as she takes the stage. I stand there gagging at Ms. Juanita belly dancing—for real.

"That looks *real* hard," Angie says, her mouth hanging open.

It does look hard. Ms. Juanita told us that all the control is in the tummy. Well, she is definitely working her belly button. I guess she should know how: every time I've ever been to Chanel's loft, Ms. Juanita is in the studio, belly dancing up a storm. Right now, Ms. Simmons starts shaking the jingly bell things she has in her hands, and then starts twirling her hips at about ninety miles an hour—faster than a cheetah—I'm serious! If I didn't know Ms. Juanita was Chanel's Mom, I would think she was younger than she really is.

Now Chanel is staring over at Princess Pamela until they make eye contact. I can tell they're exchanging a few giggles together. Meanwhile, we are still sneaking peeks at the entrance, praying that the Def Duck Record executives will come any minute. All of a sudden, Ms. Simmons gets off the stage and makes her way through the crowd, belly dancing. Some of the guests start taking out dollar bills and sticking them into the waist of Ms. Simmons's harem pants. "Oh, that is real funny!" squeals Aqua. Ms. Simmons comes past us and wiggles her scarf in our face. We giggle like a pack of goofy cheetahs.

After Danitra, Malcolm Extra, and Fredericka Fabulina each perform their solo numbers, it's showtime for the Cheetah Girls. Ms. Dorothea comes running over to us and exclaims, "They're here!" We were so busy getting hyped about our performance, we stopped eyeing the entrance. I look over by the door, but it's too crowded to see any of the Def Duck Record executives.

"Right there," Galleria says, pointing at a group of people standing by the banquet table. "Bingo— that's them." I look again and then realize that the guy with the bald head is Tom Isaaks, the A&R executive from Def Duck Records. "Oh, he looks different," I mumble, realizing that he has shaved his head.

"Well, the difference is they're here, so I need

you girls to get up there and show your spots, okay?" Ms. Dorothea says, her face shiny from perspiration.

"Do we ever do it any other way?" riffs Galleria.

Constellation Jones takes the stage again and announces us. "Now, I told you before that the growl-licious girls you are about to hear are the ferocious force behind this benefit." Everybody in the crowd starts clapping. "That's right—they pulled this whole benefit together, with the help of a lot of other helping hands, including Ms. Dorothea. The five members of the Cheetah Girls came together through the Kats and Kittys Klub, a nationwide social organization for teens that provides skills in leadership, learning, and following your dreams. Here to demonstrate their growl power—which I have been told is the brains, heart, and courage that every true cheetah girl possesses to make her dreams come true in the jiggle jungle—Whew, did I say it right?" Constellation says. "Darlings and darlings, could you please welcome to the stage this year's Harlem School of the Arts first-place talent show competition winners, THE CHEETAH GIRLS!"

Ms. Dorothea is at the side of the stage holding Toto. We take our places and do the song that is a real crowd-pleaser, "Wannabe Stars in the Jiggy

Jungle." All of our Drinka Champagne Conservatory peeps and Kats and Kittys Klub peeps know the lyrics to the song and sing along with us:

"Some people walk with a panther
or strike a buffalo stance
that makes you wanna dance.
Other people flip the script
on the day of the jackal
that'll make you cackle.
But peeps like me
got the Cheetah Girls groove
that makes your body move
like wannabe stars in the jiggy jiggy jungle.
The jiggy jiggy jungle! The jiggy jiggy jungle! The jiggy jiggy jungle!

Ms. Dorothea releases Toto onto the stage and he does his little twirl on two legs. Just like at the Harlem School of the Arts competition, everyone loses it! They start cheering wildly. "Encore, encore," the audience screams when we leave the stage.

We run back out and Galleria takes the mike, "A true Cheetah Girl judges others by their character, not the color of their spots—that's what we've been trying to tell people with our groove. Well, one of the Cheetah Girls has character to the max." The crowd starts clapping. "Her name is Dorinda—Do' Re Mi to her cheetah crew. I wrote this song for you," Galleria says, turning to me, "about all the peeps who make up your family. A family that we feel is worth fighting for."

I feel my cheeks turning red, but I make myself smile.

"So, if everybody here will bear with us," Galleria says, whipping out pages and handing a song sheet to each of us, "we're gonna sing 'Dorinda's Family Groove' on the a cappella tip, checking out the music sheet if we lose our place, 'cause this is fresh from the cheetah farm where we produce lyrics, okay?"

"Work it out, Cheetah Girls!" screams Malcolm Extra who is near the front of the stage.

Striking our five-member posse pose, we let it rip:

> "Let me tell ya about a cheetah named Dorinda
> Do' Re Mi/She's bursting at the seams with her
> dreams and leads her own family posse/That's
> right y'all there's ten little Indians she tries to
> keep in line/Starting with Shawn the fawn who is
> on like popcorn even though he's shy and just
> turned nine/Then there's a little tottie tottie who

blabbers like Abba but don't forget the R and to call her little Arba/Because there's another shortie named Kenya who can do even more than her other—Can ya rhyme, can ya tell time, Can ya tie your own shoes/Yes I can, yes, yes, ma'am, cause I'm alive at FIVE/Figure that's all there is in this Cornwall house, then you're wrong about the long arms on Nestor the little man at NINE taking no jive/He can grab your attention, do his math and think so fast you're sipping Nestle's Quik/Then you can start getting thick with glee over the other brother Topwe/African born and set to adorn the world with his mighty strong blaze/Don't be amazed at what he can do just cause he's only EIGHT and up in your face/And if you're feeling sorry about the space situation just shelve it/Cause Monie's not in the middle of this whole entire family riddle/She's just at the top of her game, SEVENTEEN and lean and mighty mean if you slip up on a dis/So it's better to kiss their other sister Chantelle just around the bend and more than just TEN/Can you tell she's reading everybody from cover to cover and more than books/But maybe Corky is the real lover in this house because he's mighty cute but more than just looks/With his curly hair and cutie eyes, there's fun to be had at five cause he's got a same aged sister/Twinkie loves her shrinky dinkie more than other kids her same/So in the end you can see this is more than just a name game/It's much deeper, more profound than any smooth move/See we all know what it is—it's Dorinda's family groove!"

At the end of our performance, we do a Cheetah Girls handshake, then hug each other for a minute. Now I could kick myself: what I was so worried about? I'm hanging with my crew, so how could this not be the best birthday I've ever had in my life. Little did I know what I was in for.

After our performance, Constellation Jones does a closing speech, begging Mrs. Bosco to come up onstage. I can't believe it when Mrs. Bosco gets up from her seat and lets Ms. Dorothea help her onstage.

"Mrs. Bosco, I want you to know that our prayers are with you as you move forward in your fight for what you believe is right," Constellation says, giving her a hug. The photographer from the *Amsterdam News* crouches by the stage to snap a picture, but Mrs. Bosco shakes her head, "No, don't do that . . ."

Constellation Jones picks up on Mrs. Bosco's discomfort and tells the photographer to stop taking pictures. Stepping back to the mike, she says, "I want everyone to stay and enjoy the buffet, drinks, and snatch one of the fabulous goody bags on your way out. And make sure you watch my show, *Say, What?*, which airs every weekday at 11:00 A.M. Drinka, girl, you'd better come on and show us how to stir it up after forty Lordy! And Ms. Simmons—consider yourself a guest, too! Okay, good night, everyone. I think y'all will agree—we have definitely 'brought it on!' Am I right?"

All the guests cheer as Constellation leaves the stage. Now Ms. Dorothea runs up onstage and grabs the microphone to say, "On behalf of the Cheetah Girls and myself, we can't thank you enough. You are the New York 'darlings and darlings,' as Constellation would say, that we *love*. Now, if you will just be so gracious to join us in our birthday girl, Dorinda Rogers's celebration."

I almost gasp because I can't believe it when everybody starts singing "Happy Birthday!" Galleria looks at me and I can tell she had this planned all along. I never had a birthday party in my whole life. And now that I am finally having one, I want to disappear into the floor.

All of a sudden, Mr. Garibaldi comes from the back with a big cheetah cake, with thirteen lit candles, that says, "To the Number One Cheetah

Girl, Dorinda. Happy Birthday. We love you." The crowd parts as he walks over to me with it. Galleria pokes me. "Make a wish!"

I close my eyes real tight and I think about what I really wish for: *God, please let the Cheetah Girls get a record deal*. No, that doesn't feel right. Then I realize I know exactly what I want to wish for: *God, please don't let them take Corky away from us*.

I blow the candles out with all my might. Twinkie giggles.

After we stuff ourselves with cake, Ms. Dorothea grabs us to make a beeline for the Def Duck Record peeps. "Freddy, thank you for coming," Ms. Dorothea gushes to Freddy Fudge, the A&R executive who specializes in R&B artists in the East Coast office. I guess he must have sneaked in while we were performing, because I didn't see him before, and he is not the kind of person you miss in a crowd. Freddy Fudge has short, blond, fuzzy hair, like Pepto B., and a chocolate-brown complexion to match. Actually, they look like they could be brothers, if you ask me.

"You girls were *tight*," Freddy says enthusiastically. Then he takes Galleria's hand and places it in his. "We're still waiting for the demo from Mouse Almighty. I understand you're going back into the studio with him soon."

"Well, I don't know if he sent you a smoke signal communiqué from the rain forest, because we haven't heard anything from his tepee!" Ms. Dorothea says dramatically.

"Well, yes, he has to finish the Kahlua project," Freddy says, like he is being real careful selecting his words. "It's slated for release in the second quarter."

I don't know what he means by "second quarter," but Ms. Dorothea clears that mystery up real quick. "Oh, I see—next spring. Well, the winter will have thawed, the birds will be chirping, and we'll be wilting!"

Tom Isaaks, the West Coast A&R executive interrupts and congratulates us. "The addition of the dog—" he says, shaking his head. "What can I say—you girls just keep getting better and better."

"Thank you. *Gracias!*" coos Chanel.

Next, Haruko, Freddy's assistant, and Chunky Carter, one of the talent coordinators we met during our meeting at the Def Duck Records office in New York congratulate us too.

By now my jaw is hurting so much from smiling, I have to get something to drink to thaw it out. After we *schmooze* with the Def Duck peeps for another twenty minutes, the Cheetah Girls storm the banquet table because we're all feeling the same way—taxed to the max. "Wow, this is really off the hook!" I exclaim to my crew while trying to slurp down some soda.

"How much did we raise?" Galleria asks her Mom excitedly.

"We had two hundred twenty *paying* guests," Ms. Dorothea says, satisfied. "So let's just say that after expenses there will be more than enough for Mrs. Bosco to give that foster-care agency a run for their money."

"*Qué bueno!* That's good," Chuchie sighs, nodding her head, then meekly asks, "but that means we don't get any leftover goody bags, huh?"

We all cackle till we can't laugh anymore. Looking around at my crew, I smile like the most satisfied cheetah cub in the jiggy jungle. I knew I was right: it will be a long, long time before I ever forget my thirteenth birthday.

Chapter
11

Just like we planned, Mrs. Bosco met with Ms. Dropkin, the attorney, on Monday, and gave her $1,200 as a retainer fee. I'm not sure how much we raised, but let's just say, after her attorney fee, there were still a few duckets in our bucket. As for me, Do' Re Mi, I'm still walking around on cloud nine, and today is Friday. Even Mrs. Bosco seems different. It's almost as if she is back to her old self—smiling and getting around without limping. That's partly because, on Wednesday morning, we get the call we have all been waiting for. Ms. Dropkin served the Administration of Children's Services, with a motion to delay. In order to do that, she had to file an injunction against the agency, then she submitted a motion for Mrs. Bosco to be considered for adopting Corky *herself*.

"Now the real battle is gonna begin, but I'm

ready for those folks. They're not taking this child without a fight," Mrs. Bosco says, repeating herself. As if her ears are ringing, Mrs. Tattle, from the foster-care agency, calls. I can tell that she is giving Mrs. Bosco a real "horse-and-phony show" on the phone.

"Well, you should have asked me before you went and gave that man custody. Don't that seem logical to you?" Mrs. Bosco talked to Mrs. Tattle without backing down. "Uh-huh, but you ain't asked me nothing. You just went and did it, so I did what I had to do. Well, that is up to y'all. No, no. That's not gonna help, because we want to adopt him now. No, no, I'm not supposed to be even talking to you about it. Hmm. Hmm. That's what the lawyer said. So why don't you ask her instead of asking me. You never ask nobody nothing." Even though Mrs. Bosco is trying to keep her voice calm I can tell she is real upset, because she keeps repeating herself.

When Mrs. Bosco gets off the phone she says, "We ain't gonna let her stop us from celebrating. At least Corky ain't leaving here this week." Mrs. Bosco shakes her head. "Lord, that woman sure don't know what she's talking about. She trying to make it sound like I shouldn't have gotten a lawyer, because they would have tried to work it out with me. She must think I was born yesterday."

I wait a few minutes for Mrs. Bosco to calm down. "Go on, Dorinda, go take Corky and meet your friends.

"Awright," I say, grabbing my cheetah backpack off the couch. I'm meeting Chanel and Pucci at five o'clock at the American Museum of Natural History. They have a frog show that Corky and Twinkie have been dying to hop to. Like I said, there were a few extra duckets, so Mrs.Bosco made me take forty dollars of the money we raised from the benefit so I can take Corky and celebrate. I figure hanging out with a bunch of frogs is as good a place as any.

"You sure you don't want to go?" I ask Kenya again before I leave the house.

"No. I don't like any stupid frogs. I want ice cream," she says.

I hate to say it, but I'm secretly glad that Kenya isn't coming. I just don't have the energy to deal with her today. And besides, I want to make sure that Corky has a good time, since he is the one who deserves a special celebration.

When we get downstairs to the lobby of our building, we see several police standing around. My heart stops. *Oh, no, don't tell me they are here to take Corky.* For one second, I think about running, but I have already made eye contact with one of the police officers. I just stand there frozen, holding Corky's hand real tight. Suddenly, one of the police officers moves toward the elevator, and right behind him is Ms. Keisha. "Dorinda!" she whispers loudly.

Oh, no, I think. Maybe Ms. Keisha has opened her big mouth and now the police are coming to take Corky away! Why else would Ms. Keisha be acting so secretive and motioning for me to come over. But I just stand there, because I don't know what to do.

As Ms. Keisha is walking toward me, I glance up at the police officer again. Yup, something is definitely about to jump off.

"I told you there was something weird about Mr. Horn," Ms. Keisha starts in.

"What?" I ask, puzzled. I feel like someone has let the hot air out of my balloon. For once, I'm genuinely relieved and really interested in hearing what drama Ms. Keisha is about to drop.

"They done found a tiger in Mr. Horn's apartment! Ms. Keisha says, her eyes bulging like Mr. Horn's.

"What do you mean?" I ask, chuckling. Let's just say, Ms. Keisha is no stranger to tall tales.

"They got some specialists coming in to try to

sedate the thing so they can take it out of his apartment!" Ms. Keisha goes on, trying to make me understand the wild situation.

"A tiger!" Corky shouts out. "Where?" Corky tries to pull away from me, but I grab his hand real hard.

"They said that Mr. Horn showed up at some hospital with suspicious bite marks, saying he got into a fight with his cat, so they sent the police to his apartment and looked through his window with binoculars!" Ms. Keisha says, out of breath. "Now Mr. Horn done escaped from the hospital, and they don't know where he is—but they are going to get that tiger out of his apartment."

"I don't understand," I say, puzzled. "He's, um, on public assistance. How is he going to keep a tiger in his apartment? They weigh five hundred pounds, Ms. Keisha."

"This one probably weigh more than that, Dorinda. Crazy people don't worry about things like that!" Ms. Keisha says, getting agitated. "The man got a tiger sleeping in his bed, okay? For how long, who knows."

"I wanna see the tiger," Corky pleads loudly.

"You are going to see frogs—and you'd better be happy with that," I say, trying to hush Corky.

"I sure wish I could get in there and get some of

the red meat he be buying. I sure could use that instead of him wasting it on some tiger," Ms. Keisha says, shaking her head till her pink rollers are shaking, too.

Walking to the museum, I think about the whole deal. That poor tiger probably got fed up being fed that rancid meat from Piggy Wiggly—and more important—he was tired of not having any tiger cronies to hang with.

Unlike me. I have the Cheetah Girls and we will be a crew forever. Looking down at Corky, I realize that now I have a family, too—even if it isn't the family I would have imagined for myself.

"Are they gonna have butterflies there, too?" Twinkie asks me as we near the museum entrance on 79th Street and Central Park West.

"I hope so," I say. But tonight is, well, gentlemen's choice, I guess.

"I hope there's a lot of frogs!" Corky pipes up.

"There will be," I assure him. "This museum has the largest collection of frogs in the world."

"For real?" Corky says, stomping in his galoshes.

"Hi, Corky and Twinkie!" Pucci says, grinning and waving at us. Pucci is Chanel's younger brother.

I can't wait to tell Chanel the whole drama

about the tiger in Mr. Horn's apartment. She just howls in disbelief. "The Cheetah Girls beat won't bite, but tigers sure do. Everybody is going cuckoo!" she coos hysterically.

"Who, Cuckoo Couger?" Pucci asks. Cuckoo Cougar is the name of the African Pygmy hedgehog that Chanel and Galleria gave Pucci for his birthday. We burst out laughing again. "You're acting cuckoo—Coco Loco," Pucci says, shaking his head. When we get inside, Pucci gives Corky a drawing of a frog that he made for him.

"I like purple frogs," says Corky.

"You like *any* frogs," counters Pucci, shaking his head.

When we get inside, it turns out Pucci was right. Walking around looking at all the frogs in the vivariums, there isn't a color we don't see. Orange, brown, blue, red, green, purple . . . "I never even knew that frogs came in so many colors!" exclaims Chanel.

"Too bad they don't have a pink one—you'd like that," Pucci tells his sister.

"You're getting to know me so well," Chanel coos to her brother.

"I wanna take one home. Can I?" Pucci asks.

"Me too?" Corky asks.

Chanel's cell phone rings. She gasps because she

forgot to turn it off. "Sorry!" Chanel says, making a face at the people who are standing near us. Chanel hurriedly goes into her cheetah backpack and turns off her Miss Wiggy cell phone. "It was Bubbles," she whispers to me. "We'll call her back when we leave."

"She probably has a Red Snapper update." I chuckle.

After the dynamic duo's performance at the benefit, Bubbles has done a three-hundred-sixty-degree turn on the Snapper situation. "He is the bomb—kaboom!" riffs Chanel, imitating Galleria all too well.

"She is so-o-o-o cuckoo for him now. She has *un coco grande*, the biggest crush I've ever seen!" swears Chanel.

"Well, at least that Eddie Lizard is out of the situation," I retort, referring to Galleria's last crush. We were grateful that the voodoo weirdo disappeared like ice cubes in a frying pan. Last we heard, Eddie Lizard went back to Los Angeles with his father, Doktor Lizard, who was here curating a hoodoo exhibit for a museum, or something. I'm not going to front, Eddie's father really did help the twins' father out of a bad situation (his girlfriend, High Priestess Abala Shaballa Mogo Hexagone, put a love spell on him that he couldn't get rid of without the Doktor's help), but, "How can you like somebody who claims he's three hundred years old?" I ask Chanel jokingly.

"*Yo se.* I know, *mija*. But I can't believe that sneaky Lizard left without saying good-bye to anybody." Chanel says, gazing at a tank full of blue poison dart frogs.

"Wow, look at that frog fly!" Twinkie exclaims. I'm glad that she is getting excited by the frogs, too.

"Of course they can fly, Twinkie—that's a Costa Rican flying tree frog. It probably can salsa, too!" coos Chanel.

"Is Bubbles going to go out with Derek now?" I ask.

"Yeah—she's been waiting for him to ask her for a date. She won't ask him," explains Chanel.

"Why not?" I ask, surprised

"Because Danitra is all over him like a rash now—and she's jealous, that's why," Chanel says, giggling mischievously. Bubbles has to be the top cheetah, or she's not having it.

Corky pushes the buttons to all the frog calls.

"They're definitely not getting a record deal," I say, covering my ears from all the frog noises.

"Maybe we're not, either!" Chanel counters, voicing our worst fear.

Now Pucci has turned up the volume on the Madagascar frog calls. They sound even worse than the bullfrogs.

"It would have been dope if Mouse Almighty had come to the benefit," I sigh, feeling a little defeated about the whole situation.

"*Sí, pero*, the executives from Def Duck Records came. That has to mean something, *mija*, no, Do'? Chanel says, her eyes pleading.

"Yeah—that they felt guilty about leaving us hanging, and sorry for Mrs. Bosco's situation," I say honestly. "Donating two hundred fifty dollars for ten tickets is nothing to a Big Willy record company like that."

"*Sí*, you're right," Chanel says.

"But they were definitely digging our perform-ance," I say, perking back up. "It's got to count for something."

"Or a whole lot of nothing, as Bubbles would say," Chanel counters, giggling. Then she looks nervous. "I'd better call Bubbles back soon. She knows we're together and I don't want her think-ing we're mad at her or something."

"Yeah, we'd better break out soon—because I'm getting batty from these frog calls, anyway," I say, looking over at Corky, who is clapping his hands to the chorus of frog calls. "Gosh, I hope that tiger has left the building like Elvis, by the time we get home!"

"How could he afford to feed a tiger?" Chanel asks, shaking her head. "They eat more than Bubbles, Aqua, and Angie put together!

"People do crazy things," I say, repeating what Ms. Keisha told me.

Twinkie is pulling at my sweater for me to pay attention to her. "Look, Dorinda—it's a cheetah frog."

We laugh and look inside inside the glass display. Sure enough—"It does look like a cheetah, but it's a Florida Leopard Frog," I explain to her, reading the plaque on the wall.

"Oh, Mackerel probably knows about that one," Chanel coos, starry-eyed.

"Are you going to go out with the Mack?" I ask her, but I already know the answer.

"Yes! I invited him to the Kats and Kittys' Christmas party," Chanel tells me.

"Oh, right," I say, suddenly feeling strange that I don't have a crush on anyone.

"Who are you inviting to the party?" Chanel asks me.

"I don't know. I never meet any boys that I dig more than two hours," I say, embarrassed.

"Well, that's only because you're thirteen." Chanel giggles.

"Right." I chuckle and remember how happy I am that we finally got that out in the open. Now I feel closer to my crew than I felt before—especially Chanel.

"Wait till you're fourteen. You'll have a crush every other day," Chanel informs me.

"Word," I say, then check on Corky, Twinkie, and Pucci, who are running all around ogling all the different frogs in the vivariums. "You 'bout ready?" I ask Corky.

He nods his head, satisfied. "Now I wanna see the tiger!"

Shaking my head, we go to the museum store to buy some toy frogs. After about an hour, both Chanel and I are exasperated with Pucci, Twinkie, and Corky, who keep changing their minds about which frog they want. "Could you please pick one already!"

"This may be one of the most important decisions I make in my formative years," Pucci says, making a face. "You don't want to leave an emotional scar, do you?"

"No, Pucci, I don't," Chanel replies.

Pucci smiles like he got away with something.

"I want to leave a *physical* scar!" Chanel says, boxing him in his ears. "And one of the most important decisions I'll be making in my formative years is to go eat at Kickin' Chicken and leave you here to eat frogs for dinner, *esta bien*?"

"Awright—I guess I'll go for the boring green one," Pucci says, but he is smiling, so we know he is just joking.

After we buy little frogs for Pucci, Corky, and Twinkie, we head outside to go to dinner.

Chanel calls Galleria on her cell phone. Suddenly she starts screaming into the receiver and jumping up and down like a contestant on *The Price Is Right*. That's how I know something is definitely jumping off. I guess Bubbles has finally hooked the Red Snapper for a date.

"Let me talk to Bubbles," I say, motioning to Chanel.

"Quack, quack, quack!" Chuchie yells into the phone.

"Quack, quack, quack!" scream Corky and Twinkie.

"Put it on pause, *please*, Twinkie," I moan, taking the cell phone from Chanel. "Congratulations," I chuckle to Bubbles.

"Don't congratulate me. I don't mean to be bragging, but I told you that snagging Toto for our act was going to take us to the top, top, top!" screams Bubbles.

"What are you saying?" I ask, holding my breath.

"The Def Duck executives were so amped by our performance, and the fact that we put together the benefit like the Lone Ranger that they have put the fire under Mouse Almighty to finish that demo." Bubbles screams so loud, I have to take the phone away from my ear.

"That's what I'm talking about. You going with the flow now, Do'?" She screams once more—with feeling.

"So what does that mean?" I ask. Sometimes I don't understand Galleria, because she gets a little cryptic, like Dr. Seuss.

"It means that Mouse Almighty called Mom himself and says he'll get us back into the studio next week!" Galleria says, singing, "Go, Toto! Go, Toto! Go, Toto!"

Chanel and I both start jumping up and down and screaming.

Now Twinkie, Corky, and Pucci start jumping up and down and screaming with us, too. A few passerbys stop and smile at us.

"But what about Kahlua's record—isn't he working on that?" I ask, feeling hesitant about getting on this roller-coaster ride called the record business.

"Hold that thought, Do'," Galleria says, then screams, "Mom, come talk to Dorinda and Chuchie."

Now I feel stupid for sounding so insecure, but I just want to make sure this is all on the real tip. When you wish on a star long enough, you're bound to feel the world owes you a few twinkles for your troubles, you know what I'm saying?

"Chanel?" Ms. Dorothea says into the receiver.

"No, it's Dorinda," I reply.

"Dorinda, darling, trust me. Mouse Almighty called here eating humble cheese pie," Ms. Dorothea says sweetly. I can tell by the way she is talking that she is smiling. "He apologized profusely for not coming to the benefit. But the good news is, he has just handed in the master for Kahlua Alexander's next record and is ready to finish working on the Cheetah Girls' demo. He also very humbly hinted at the fact that he got a few urgent calls from Freddy Fudge and Tom Isaaks—meaning both coasts of A&R executives were blowing up his phone—as you would say. Well, suffice it to say, he is now firmly in agreement that the Cheetah Girls should 'Bring It On!'"

"What is she saying? What is she saying?" Chanel asks impatiently, grabbing my arm.

"Okay, I'm down for the twirl. Please tell Toto

thank you, because it if wasn't for him, we would be starting our own divette dogwalking service right about now," I say. Then I hang up the phone.

"They said the record executives agree—it's time for us to 'Bring It On!' and the Mouse is back to nibbling!" I explain cheerfully to Chanel.

"*Ay, Dios mío*, omigod, I can't believe it, *mija*!" coos Chanel.

Chuchie, Twinkie, Corky, Pucci, and me dance around in a circle for a few minutes. Looking at Chanel and my favorite brother and sister and Pucci, I realize that the "Bring It On!" benefit was the happiest day of my life—but this moment, right here, right now, is a *pretty* close second!

Bring It On!

Yeah, we saw those wannabes
Trying so hard to be prettily perched
But all they have are knobby knees
That shouldn't be seen in anybody's church

So by now you may be wondering
Why do we care about somebody else's
whacked reality?
For all we know there may be truth
That simply alludes us
Especially if we're thunderin'
So let us break it down like this

If you wanna dollar
You'd better stand up and holla
'Cuz the beat won't bite
And our street cred's tight
Laced with lyrics on the right

I said if you wanna dollar
You'd better stand up and holla
'Cuz the beat won't bite

And our street cred's tight
Laced with lyrics on the right

Alrighty for our groove
Alrighty for our moves
The Cheetah Girls are out.
No doubt. So bring it on till the break of dawn!

Now time goes on and still we see
Those wannabes are everywhere
Doing the same old thing
While we're out there standing our ground
And always coming up changing up
The style and sounds we bring

So maybe we should stop our caring
About all those who try to steal our flavor
Because we're gonna keep showing our spots
And that's all there is can be that we can savor
So let us break it down like this

If you wanna dollar
You'd better stand up and holla
'Cuz the beat won't bite
And our street cred's tight
Laced with lyrics on the right

Yes I said. If you wanna dollar
You'd better stand up and holla
'Cuz the beat won't bite
And our street cred's tight
Laced with lyrics on the right

Alrighty for our groove
Alrighty for our moves
The Cheetah Girls are out.
No doubt. So bring it on till the break of dawn!

The Cheetah Girls Glossary

The Beat Won't Bite: When the composition of a song is supa original. As in, "Don't hate on the Cheetah Girls' jammies, because the beat won't bite!"

Better Than Cheddar: When something is almost too good to be true. As in, "Guess who's coming to my birthday party? Kahlua Alexander! Now tell me that's not better than cheddar!"

Big Willies: VIPs (very important person) and other peeps rolling with the extra bling bling. As in, "Puff Daddy is such a Big Willy, he is coming to the party in his own private jet."

Breaking it Down on the Real Tip: Being totally and absolutely honest about something to the best of your ability. As in, "I'm not mad at you. Let me break it down on the real tip. I hope you!"

Bugaboo Chillies: When you get a creepy, scary feeling inside your tummy.

Chitlin' Circuit: Back in the day, especially in the segregated South, some black performers were forced to hop on rickety buses and tour the country to perform in broken-down clubs for very little money. This strip of clubs came to be known as the chitlin' circuit.

Crooky Snook: Someone who is a crook but is really shady about it and pretends to be an honest person.

Down for the Twirl: Ready and willing to represent for the cause. As in, "You can count on Danitra to perform in the showcase, because she is always down for the twirl."

Duckets in the Bucket: Money in the bank. Extra loot in your cheetah purse.

For a Change and Some Coins: To break away from the norm in double time. As in, "Can we go eat sushi tonight instead of Micky D's for a change and some coins?"

Foul: Wrong, ill, mean. As in, "You should have told me you didn't want to go to the mall instead of leaving me hanging. That was really foul."

"411": Information. As in, "Let's get the '411' on Kahlua and Krusher. I hear they're thick as thieves now!"

Freeze the Conversation: Stop talking about something. Move on. As in, "I wish she'd stop asking me about Eddie Lizard. She needs to just freeze the conversation."

Gagulating: When something catches you by surprise—both good and bad. As in, "I'm gagulating over Kahlua's new single. I didn't know she had skills like that."

Ghetto Getups: Tacky outfits or clothes that are supa baggy and boring.

Going to Town: Overdoing something, like eating or shopping. As in, "I wish we had duckets for Steve Madden—I'd be going to town on some shoes."

Goospitating: Licking your chops at a guy or girl like they're on the lunch menu. As in, "Did you see the way Derek was goospitating over Bubbles at the benefit?"

Horse-and-Phony Show: A smoke-and-mirror performance with a whole lot of faking. As in, "You'd better cut out that horse-and-phony show. I know you're not really sick, so you'd better get out of that bed and take your butt to school!"

Keep it Lite FM: When you're trying to stop static from jumping off. As in, "I know you had a beef jerky with Danesha, so I'm gonna keep it lite FM with both of you."

Majordomo: Bigger than huge. As in, "Every time the Lovebabiez song 'The Toyz Is Mine,' comes on the radio, she gets a majordomo attitude."

My Bad Bad: When something is really your fault and you have to cop to it. Doubly worse than "my bad." As in, "I was the one who stole your last stick of gum in gym class. My bad bad."

Off the Hinge-Y: Off the hook. Outta sight. Supa coolio. As in, "Check the new Jin single, "Senorita,"—it's off the hinge-y!"

Paradox With Lox and a Bagel: Something or someone that is *doubly* contradictory, but makes sense in its, or his or her, own way. As in, "Miss Thing only travels first class, but she won't eat the food they serve on the plane. Instead, she donates it to the homeless. What can I say, she is a paradox with a lox and a bagel."

Schmoozing: Trying to work a situation on the business tip. As in, "We have to schmooze with the Def Duck Records peeps so they don't forget that we're still here—ready and waiting for a record deal!"

Serious Sparklies: Diamonds, Austrian crystals— all the good stuff that puts a twinkle in your eye when you look at it.

Set it Off: Get things jumping. Make something happen. Get the party started. As in, "Let's meet at nine o'clock at Cheetahrama so we can set it off."

Showing Off Your Spots: Being yourself. Doing

the best you can in a situation. As in, "Don't be afraid to show your spots tonight, *mamacita*, because it's definitely on!"

Slipping on Your Own Banana Peel: When you get in your own way or mess things up for yourself without anybody else's help. As in, "I'm so nervous, I hope I don't get onstage and slip on my own banana peel!"

Sticky Fingers: Peeps who steal. As in, "Don't leave your bag open like that on the chair, because there are a lot of peeps here with sticky fingers."

Stinkhead: Someone who is a real pain the poot-butt. As in, "Please don't bring Tanasia to my party, because she is a real stinkhead and I'm not having it tonight."

Supa Shindig: Cool party. As in, "Now, that was a supa shindig."

Tasty Morsel: A cute guy. As in, "Who is that tasty morsel that showed up at the shindig?"

Throwdown at the Showdown: When it's time for you to do the best you can, like for a test, performance, sports event, or special event. As in, "Okay, Cheetahs, this is it. It's time for the throwdown at the showdown. We're definitely showing our spots tonight!"

Tripping: Off on the wrong tangent. As in, "No

way am I going out with Derek. You must really be tripping now."

What?: Don't try to step to this. As in, "Yeah, your shoes are whack. What?"

Twinkle, Twinkle, Cheetah Stars

To the ferocious onscreen Cheetah Girls, Kiely Williams (Aquanette), Adrienne Bailon (Chanel), and Sabrina Bryan (Dorinda), who are always flexing their growl power. *Ayiight*, you're tight, *mamacitas*!

Chapter 1

I'm probably the only person north of Houston, Texas, who knows what a good fake-tress my twin sister, Angie, is. (She truly deserves a ginger-bread-baked Academy Award.) Here we are trying to get ready, and Angie has just laid out an outfit on her twin bed that *she* wants me to think looks cute in this dag-on chilly weather—a white cotton peasant blouse, a denim skirt with a white dust ruffle underneath it, and white tights stuck inside black cowboy boots.

"Galleria told us that wearing white after Labor Day is a fashion crime that should *not* be committed," I say tersely, delivering a warning. "Why do you want to cause problems with the Cheetah Girls?" See, we are going to our annual Christmas meeting for the Kats and Kittys Klub—a national teen social organization that we originally joined in Houston and now belong to in the New York chapter. That's where we met Galleria and the rest of the Cheetah Girls—which is the best thing that could have ever happened to two singing thirteen-year-old twins who moved up from Houston to live with their dee-vorced father in the Big Apple and start a whole new life. (Daddy got the deal of a century on a duplex apartment through his boss.)

"We do not look like country hicks, Aqua—we look *tight*," Angie hisses back at me, standing defiantly in her white bloomers. Now my sister the fake-tress is imitating Chanel, the Latin spitfire member of our singing group who is the most obsessed with clothes, but unlike Galleria, would never say a mean word even if we showed up to the meeting in Big Bird costumes.

"Okay, Miss wannabe Hognate heffa," I humph at her, referring to the high school with the biggest cheerleading squad in Texas. "Don't forget your pom-poms."

Shaking my head, I change the paper lining in Porgy and Bess's cage (they're our treasured pet guinea pigs), then carefully lay out my blue denim skirt, brown turtleneck sweater, and black opaque tights on the bed, just to show Angie what I had in mind. Before I put on my tights, I run my fingers through them to check for holes (sometimes sneaky Angie runs my tights, then puts them back in the drawer!). Now I'm starting to feel uncomfortable about the meeting. See, some of the Kats and Kittys members didn't come to the Cheetah Girls "Bring It On!" fund-raising benefit. I guess that was their way of telling us that they really do think we're corny. See, Angie and I are on the volunteer services committee, but nobody seems all that interested in our plans for a food drive for the homeless at our church, either. Maybe we should have come up with a better idea. That reminds me about the flyers we made for the drive. "Don't forget to put the flyers in your backpack," I instruct Angie. Wiggling my tights up to my thick waist, I start thinking about the first time we met Galleria and the rest of the Cheetah Girls. She made a crack about my white frosted lipstick, so I stopped wearing it because I had to admit she was right—that shade did make my lips look like two flying saucers lost in space!

I guess you can tell by the now that Galleria is a handful. And do pardon my manners, please—the Cheetah Girls are Galleria "Bubbles" Garibaldi, who is the leader of our group as you will see by her extra-picky dress code; Chanel "Coco" Simmons (but she isn't the only Coco anymore, since we just named our new adorable puppy in her honor!); Dorinda "Do' Re Mi" Rogers (sweet as she wants to be); and us, of course, Aquanette Marie and Anginette Vivian Walker. Those are our full and proper names, even though we don't use our middle names since we moved in with Daddy.

"Why do you care a heap of beans what Galleria thinks?" Angie says, rolling her eyes around like pool balls, then answering her own question. "Because you liked that sneaky Eddie Lizard and he liked her!"

Now Angie is cutting deep. Eddie Lizard is this boy who slithered his way into Drinka Champagne's Conservatory, where we all take vocal classes on Saturdays. It's true that I liked Eddie and he liked Galleria, but it doesn't matter now, because, luckily, he has crawled back under whatever rock he came from in California. He even left without saying good-bye to anybody. I mean, it's obvious he doesn't have any "home training," as Big Momma would say, so I have gotten over him *real* quick.

"You know good and well that's water under the bridge," I say, shaking my head. It's true that I talked about Galleria behind her back to my sister, but now that the Cheetah Girls are finally going back into the studio with big-time record producer Mouse Almighty, to finish our demo tape (which

Twinkle, Twinkle, Cheetah Stars

Mouse is submitting to Def Duck Records in the hopes that we get signed to the label), I don't have time to think about that ole beef jerky.

"And don't change the subject. She is right about our outfits—that's all I'm saying," I moan, wasting my breath. See, Galleria talked us into wearing pink cheetah outfits for the "Bring It On!" benefit, and lo and behold, the Def Duck Records executives in attendance started quacking to Ms. Dorothea (our manager and Galleria's very fabulous mother) about getting us back into the studio with Mouse Almighty. Then faster than a Bisquick minute, Mouse called Ms. Dorothea and said he was ready to get back in the saddle with us.

I smooth down my hair one last time, then shuffled out of our bedroom and down the spiral staircase to wait for Angie to get it together before I bop her on the head. (Don't get nervous. Fighting with my other half is as natural to me as singing in a church choir—both of which we've been doing since we could get sound out of our vocal chords!) I figure if I leave her alone, maybe she'll come to her senses and change her outfit. That's all right, I'm gonna fix her broken wagon real good: this weekend, when Angie isn't looking, I'm packing all the summer clothes in the plastic garment bags, where they belong.

Landing in the living room, I notice a strong scent in the air. I sniff carefully, trying to place the aroma. One look at Daddy who is standing at the counter, filling his pipe with tobacco and I know what it is: Daddy is wearing some strange new cologne or aftershave. Something must be up, because he never wears anything that strong. And that's not all: Daddy is also wearing his black velvet sports jacket and dressy black slacks. In other words, Daddy is looking sharp and smelling like the gigantic fern plants they have at the botanical gardens.

"You look nice, Daddy," I say casually, to see if he will tell me where he's going—and most important—with whom.

"Thank you," Daddy says, staying tight-lipped. That's just like Daddy not to tip his hand (that's why he is real good at card games, even though he lost his card-playing buddies when he moved to New York).

Well, it takes more than that to keep my big nose out of somebody's business—even Daddy's. "Are you going somewhere, Daddy?" I ask cautiously.

"Yes, I am," he replies sharply, letting me know that this conversation is over.

"Well, we're going over to the Pizza Pit to meet the rest of the Cheetah Girls before the Kats and Kittys meeting," I say, defeated. That's also my signal for him to fork over some money for our dinner tonight.

"Oh, right," Daddy says, absentmindedly reaching into his back pant's pocket for his wallet.

I wish I could tell Daddy that his cologne is too strong, but I know better. Instead, I ask him if I can remove the lint from the back of his jacket. "Go ahead," Daddy responds gruffly, which I know means "hurry up." Now I realize Daddy is just waiting for us to leave, so he can go about his business, and I have a feeling that business has something to do with a woman. I freeze with fear for a second. *I hope Daddy hasn't picked up again with that kooky ex-girlfriend of his*. Let's just say that Angie and I were part of a plot (successful, I might add) to help rid Daddy of his last nut, High Priestess Abala Shaballa Mogo Hexagone, a whole lot of trouble in a head wrap.

While I'm brushing the lint off Daddy's jacket, Angie clumps down the staircase like a cow. Looking up, I see she is still wearing her cowboy boots and denim skirt and petticoat underneath, but at least she has put on a black turtleneck. From the way Angie scrunches up her nose, I can tell she is thinking the same thing I am. *Why is Daddy wearing some new stinky cologne?*

Daddy watches us carefully as we put on our

coats, and I know what he is thinking, so I grab my black-and-white checked muffler and matching wool hat from the closet so he can see we'll be dressing warm.

Angie stares at me hard. "That is *my* scarf!"

"No, it's not—you got the brown set," I hiss back. See, now when we buy stuff, we get different colors, even if we are getting the same thing. I mean, we're almost fourteen years old—we're getting a little too old to be dressing like twins. Angie stomps to the closet and grabs the brown-and-white checked knit muffler and cap. I guess we have borrowed each other's mufflers and hats so many times, Angie forgot which one was really hers.

Daddy yells, "Get to bed by eleven, you hear?"

"Yes, Daddy," I holler back, then stop myself from blurting out, "I'll see you later," since he is obviously trying to tell us that he won't be home by the time we get back from our Kats meeting.

"I know he has a hot date," Angie squeals as we run to the Pizza Pit. For once I think Angie is right about something.

When we walk into the Pizza Pit on Columbus Avenue—Galleria, Chanel, and Dorinda stare at us like hungry cheetah cubs.

"Starve a cheetah, why don't you?" barks

Galleria, then jumps up and gets on the food line. They obviously have been waiting for us before they ordered.

"Sorry, we had to change," I say, shooting Angie a look.

"What's this—your get-a-record-deal dress?" quips Galleria sarcastically.

"No," I say, paying her no mind. I have learned that Galleria doesn't mean anything by being a smart aleck, that's just the way she is. Besides, we only wear cheetah outfits when we're handling Cheetah Girls' business. Of course, for Galleria, *every* meeting and outing has to do with Cheetah Girls business, so it's normal that she is wearing her brown cheetah corduroy pants, turtleneck, and big cheetah fake-fur coat and hat.

As usual, Galleria's mind is moving like lightning, until she finds something else to flash on besides my outfit.

"Wait till all the Kats and Kittys hear we're in the house with Mouse again!" she boasts, her eyes darting with glee.

"I didn't hear you tell them extra cheese," Angie says, interrupting Galleria's gloating. Angie is a piglet when it comes to pizza. I think she'd eat it even if it was topped with a pile of hay.

Galleria twirls around quickly and says to

Angie, "Hold your horses," then twirls around to the waiter and says, "Hold the extra cheese, please."

"Galleria!" Angie protests.

"Before you dig in with your spurs, can we compromise?" insists Galleria, the boss of our sauce.

The look on Angie's face tells Galleria that compromise is not one of her strong points.

"Come on, let's pass on the lactose. I'm feeling gas-eous. That's even worse than feeling nauseous," admits Galleria, holding her ample stomach.

"That's not true, Bubbles. You don't want them to put on extra cheese because that guy called you juicy!" Chanel blurts out, giggling. Bubbles is Galleria's nickname, thanks to her infamous addiction to chewing wads of bubble gum nonstop since she was five years old.

"Well, I am tired of being the poster girl for big-butt comments," Galleria snaps back.

"Say it ain't so," Dorinda heckles.

"Uh-huh," Chanel says, nodding. "This wack-a-doodle guy walking behind us snuck up to Galleria's ear and hissed, 'Girl, you're *juicy*!'"

"That's truly foul," snaps Dorinda. "But don't let it shrink your ego, Bubbles—or your size.

Twinkle, Twinkle, Cheetah Stars

You're my role model on the real." Dorinda is extra tiny, but she obviously has big aspirations.

"Come on—how about two extra helpings of anchovies?" chides Galleria.

"Awright," Angie says, giving in to Galleria's insecurity attack.

Personally, I can't stand those fishy-looking things, but I don't mind taking them off.

"You can't get gas from anchovies?" Dorinda asks curiously.

"Nah, just puckered lips 'cause they're so salty," Angie says, licking her lips.

"Well, you'd better start puckering up, butter-cups," riffs Galleria, before asking the waiter for the disgusting addition to our pizza pie.

"Word, I can't wait till tomorrow night—I'm gonna suck on those oxtail bones so hard, some-body might call the police!" Dorinda laughs.

See, tomorrow night, the five of us are in for a real treat. We're going to Maroon's restaurant in Chelsea, with Ms. Dorothea—thanks to the gift certificates we won at the Harlem School of the Arts "Can We Get a Groove?" competition.

"I wonder why Mrs. Bugge didn't come to *our* benefit?" Galleria ponders thoughtfully.

"She couldn't fit it into her schedule?" Chanel queries gingerly.

"I bet she gets in a twizzle with all the preparations for the Christmas bash," adds Dorinda.

Galleria ignores both possibilities and continues chewing her gristle: "As a matter of fact, a lot of Kats and Kittys did a no-show."

"Well, it is a crazy-hectic time of year—for everybody," offers Dorinda, squirming in her chair.

"Yeah, well, I don't see why they're taking so long to ask us to perform at the Christmas bash," counters Galleria. "You know what I'm saying? Now that we're going into the studio—oops, maybe we won't fit them into *our* busy schedule."

"What happened?" Chanel asks, her eyes widening to the point that the pink sparklies on her eyelids look like they're about to burst into shooting stars. "They're probably going to ask us tonight, *mija*. Don't worry. *No te preocupe*."

Shoot, Galleria is right—going into the studio with a Grammy-winning producer is more important than performing at the Kats and Kittys Christmas bash. But I do hope Mrs. Bugge asks us anyway. "Do we know when we're going to work with Mouse again?" I ask, trying to shake off the left-out feeling like extra bread crumbs on a drumstick before it gets fried and tasty.

"Oh, my bad bad, as Dorinda would say."

Galleria pulls herself away from her pizza slice. "Cancel all extracurricular plans for the month of December. I mean all of them—Mouse has us on a very tight schedule. He wants to hand in the demo to Def Duck so we get first dibs on first quarter.

"What happened?" squeaks Chanel. She always asks "what happened?" when she doesn't understand something and feels embarrassed.

"Mom says that from January to March of every year—first quarter—is when record companies have the most money in their budget to throw around," Galleria says confidently, because she sure has got the music biz lingo down. "So that's when they decide on who they're going to bring into the fold."

Angie shoots me a look. I want to blurt out, "What's the matter—ain't half a pie of crawly creatures enough anchovies for you?" even though I know she is trying to tell me something with her eyes. As a matter of fact, I know exactly what she is thinking.

"Oh, Lord—what about Christmas?" I moan, letting my thoughts turn into spoken words.

"Oh, no doubt, we're not working on Christmas. But Mouse has to head to Holland the day after, and work on Sista Fudge's remixes, because her album is dropping in February," Galleria says without missing a beat.

Now me and Angie look at each other like the ghost of Christmas past has finally visited our table. "Galleria, we were planning to spend two weeks down South with our family," I say, my voice squeaking. Angie holds my hand underneath the table. We always do that when we're scared. It's funny how in one instant Angie and I go back to being two peas in a pod as soon as we feel like the outsiders.

Galleria stares a hole into me without saying a word. Instead, I'm the one who says what needs to be said. "Maybe we won't be going home."

"We have to talk to Daddy first," Angie blurts out. For the second time, she is right. Truth is, you'd have to be lying dead with pennies covering your eyes, in a coffin in Granddaddy Walker's Funeral Parlor, not to see that Daddy can't wait to get rid of us for two weeks. No way does he want us here in New York for the holidays!

"I don't know, Galleria—since we were born, we have spent Christmas with our family—*all* of our family," I mutter out loud.

"That's right—all two thousand of them," adds Angie. God bless her. For once, she is trying to defend the both of us.

Unlike her nature, Galleria bites into her pizza slice instead of chewing us out. Shoot, I'm sorry—if we don't talk to Daddy about this, we could get grounded—for life.

"You can come over my house for Christmas," Chanel coos sweetly. "Why don't the Cheetah Girls spend it together?"

The silence at the table tells Chanel that her idea isn't so swell. But for now, it's Dorinda who hits the nail on the head: "If we don't get to the Kats and Kittys meeting on time, Mrs. Bugge may pull our membership—for real."

Chapter 2

When the five of us walk into the Kats and Kittys Klub meeting at Riverside Church, Derek Hambone (aka the Red Snapper) and his rapping crony Mackerel Johnson light up like Christmas trees rigged with blinking lights gone haywire. Of course, they aren't looking at the fabulous Walker twins. No, ma'am. The dynamic duo are ogling Galleria and Chanel like they're cheetah-wrapped Christmas presents. See, Red Snapper and Mackerel go to Fashion Industries East High School with Galleria, Dorinda, and Chanel. Then they joined Kats and Kittys to be in the mix with "the objects of their affection." Since it's a free country (even if membership into Kats and Kittys isn't), Derek and Mackerel got their parents to plunk down $600 for the Kats membership, so Galleria couldn't do a thing about it.

Twinkle, Twinkle, Cheetah Stars

"Hey, Cheetah Girls," says Mrs. Bugge, the chapter president and treasurer. She's giving us a horse-and-phony-show smile, and even I can tell there's something lurking behind it. I cut my eyes over at Angie just to see if she's picked up on it, too. She has—I can tell by the way she shifts her eyes downward and doesn't look at anybody. Now I glance at Mrs. Rhodes, the head of the events committee: her weak smile isn't fooling us, either. Lord, there is definitely a fox stirring up things in this henhouse. Plunking down at the long wooden table, I tug at my denim skirt to pull it down—even though my legs are not visible under the table.

As if reading our minds, Mrs. Bugge starts in with a weak apology: "Girls, I'm ever so sorry I didn't attend your benefit, but my family obligations were out of order that weekend. Please don't let anyone else get married this month or I'm going to lose my mind."

"We understand!" Chanel says cheerfully.

"And getting everything organized for our holiday activities is about all I can handle," Mrs. Bugge adds, for good measure. Suddenly, I realize maybe that's why everybody is acting strange— they must feel bad for not supporting our benefit.

Devonta Weekes, who, like Galleria and Chanel,

is a teen adviser on the Party events committee, goes right for the bottom line: "How much did y'all rake in at that benefit, anyway?"

Dorinda stares at Devonta like a deer caught in the headlights. "Um, we raised the money for, um, my brother Corky—to get an injunction against a court order from Child Welfare." Dorinda stops, embarrassed about sharing her business. As it is, Dorinda already walks on eggshells because she got a free one-year membership to Kats and Kittys.

But it's Devonta who's embarrassed. Even though she is brown-skinned like Angie and me, we can tell she is blushing. I'm proud of Dorinda for squashing Devonta's overcooked curiosity. (Even though Dorinda didn't explain it correctly—the money we raised was given to her foster mother, Mrs. Bosco, so she could get an attorney and fight Corky's father from winning the custody battle.)

"So y'all didn't get to keep any of the money you raised?" Devonta pipes up again, like she can't take a hint.

"Look—the Def Duck Records peeps showed up and *supported*. That was reward enough," Galleria says firmly. "They got so hyped by our performance that they gave Mouse Almighty a jingle so he could tingle about the Cheetah Girls again. Now we're going back into the studio with Mouse to finish our demo. Why don't you nibble on that for a while?"

Galleria's explanation definitely dulls Devonta's curiosity about the duckets raised at the benefit. Everybody gets real quiet for a minute. Until finally, Indigo Luther, our teen chapter president, arrives so we can start our meeting. Miss Indigo is always late and I think she does it just so she can make an entrance. Already six feet tall (even though she is only in ninth grade, like us), and long-legged, she has enough attitude to fill a shopping mall. "Sorry I'm late, but I had an audition," Indigo coos, slipping out of her signature hot-pink rabbit-fur jacket, which makes her look like a Hollywood snow bunny. It also makes poor Chanel, our resident pink junkie, salivate every time she sees it.

"Really?" coos Brandy, who is not quite as tall as Indigo, and a whole lot sweeter. Brandy has the prettiest long wavy hair that is so thick it looks like bush-baby hair. And even though Brandy goes to the Bronx High School of Science, and is in the top-ten percentile of her school, she secretly wants to be a model, too, but she doesn't have Indigo's shameless confidence.

"Yes—it was nothing, though. Just for the swim-suit issue of *Elle Girl* magazine," Indigo sighs, pulling down her pink angora crop top to try and cover her belly button. "I got so cold standing around trying on all those bikinis. Who can think about what to wear at the beach when you're butt is freezing!"

"I thought they called those 'go sees,'" Galleria says, interrupting Indigo's lovefest with herself. We all look up at Indigo, waiting for her response. See, Galleria and Indigo don't exactly get along. You could say that their relationship is more like hot macaroni and cheese and cold potato salad— both can be served at the same meal, but they should stay on their side of the plate.

"Excuse me?" Indigo asks, flustered.

"Before, you said you went on an audition, but in modeling they're called go-sees," explains Galleria.

"Oh, right—sometimes I get confused because I'm acting now, too," Indigo says, tossing her long straightened hair out of her face.

"Oh, you're acting now?" Chanel asks. Indigo never said anything about acting before, but she's so dramatic, I shouldn't be surprised. Secretly I hope she stays right at Spence, where she belongs, and doesn't get any bright ideas about transferring to our school, the Performing Arts Annex. Lord, that's all we need.

"All right, Kats and Kittys, can I have your

attention, please?" Mrs. Bugge says, interrupting our Ping-Pong match. Everyone is quiet while she passes out the minutes from the last Kats and Kittys' meeting. "Aquanette and Anginette, would you please give us an update on our annual Christmas volunteer drive so that we may open up the discussion and finalize the details."

Angie takes out the flyer that we designed for the Christmas drive and passes it around for approval. "This year, we've asked the pastor of our church if we could host a holiday dinner on Christmas day for the homeless," I explain, trying not to be distracted by Indigo's short skirt and the fact that she is swinging her knee like she's testing her funny bone or something. "Plus, all the members of the church would pass out flyers in the neighborhood in advance, for clothing and toy donations, which will be given to the homeless people who stop in on Christmas day," I continue, wondering if I sound like a drone clone—boring and boring.

"And we would like to ask all Kats and Kittys members to distribute the flyers at your schools, supermarkets, and neighborhood bulletin boards, so that anyone can drop off clothing and toy donations to the church prior to Christmas day," adds Angie, because I left that part out.

"Thank you, Anginette and Aquanette. Let's vote on their suggestion for the Kats and Kittys Christmas Volunteer Drive so that we can get it into motion," Mrs. Bugge says. "First, we would like to now recognize all discussion from Kats and Kittys members."

Indigo raises her hand, then says, "Um, does your church have the space to hold enough people—in case a lot of, um, homeless people attend, because my church has a big recreation room—"

"Yes," blurts out Angie, cutting off Indigo and her lame suggestion.

Chanel tries not to show her little smirk, but she can't help it. Chanel is not going to be happy until Miss Indigo leaves her fur jacket "to her favorite señorita" in her last will and testament!

Mrs. Bugge waits a few moments to see if any one else has any bright ideas or suggestions to improve our Christmas Volunteer Drive. "Okay, I make a motion for the discussion of the Christmas Volunteer Drive be closed," she says. That means, whether they like it or not, our idea goes into effect for this year's Kats and Kittys' Volunteer Drive. Thank the Lord.

"Second that," says Galleria.

"Motion granted. Anginette and Aquanette will drop off flyers this week to our chapter headquarters, and they will be circulated to each Kats and Kittys member in the mail," Mrs. Bugge continues. "They have also agreed to drop off flyers at the Hallelujah Tabernacle Church for its members to circulate. Motion approved for this year's Kats and Kittys Volunteer Drive. I now open the floor to Devonta Weekes, our teen adviser for the party committee."

Galleria and Chanel look at each other in surprise. Usually they get to open the discussion for all our party and event activities. Since when does Devonta get to lead?

Devonta opens up a folder and pauses. "For this year's Christmas Eggnogger, we are going to throw it at the Weeping Willow instead of the Hound's Club, as was suggested by Galleria and Chanel. Also, each non-senior member is expected to invite five guests. Senior members are expected to invite ten guests each. Mrs. Bugge is going to dispense the tickets for everyone in attendance."

"If any of you would like to receive more than ten tickets—including non-senior members—now is the time to tell me," Mrs. Bugge says, smiling while handing out bright blue tickets. "Our Christmas bash has traditionally been the most well-attended event we throw annually. Last year, more than one thousand members attended—

The Cheetah Girls

from Washington, D.C., Connecticut, Philadelphia, and New Jersey chapters."

"Everybody knows we throw the best Christmas party," Indigo blurts out like a cheerleader. Well, it may be the best party, but I don't think Angie and I can get more than ten people between us to pay ten dollars a ticket. We are always hitting up everybody at school, Drinka Champagne's Conservatory, and church to come out and support us—and we just don't know a whole lot of folks in New York. "Are we going to have to sell raffle tickets, too?" I ask hesitantly.

"We'll get to that in a minute," Mrs. Bugge says. "Come on, someone here can take the initiative to sell more tickets—even if you contact Kats and Kittys outside of New York and get them to come—that counts as well."

"I'll take more than five tickets," flosses Indigo. I bet she is gonna twist everybody's arm at Clinton High to attend.

"All right, that's the Christmas spirit!" exclaims Mrs. Bugge, obviously pleased with Indigo, who cuts a sly smile over at Derek. It figures she'd like Derek! After all, he is tall as a willow tree, just like her. A dark cloud passes over Galleria's shiny face. I tap my foot nervously, because somebody is going to lay an egg before this meeting is over.

Twinkle, Twinkle, Cheetah Stars

"Okay, now I need five volunteers for the Eggnogger Cleanup Committee," moans Devonta, tapping her foot like she's imitating me. "Come on, y'all, the Weeping Willow is going to go boohoo if we leave their place a mess after our party."

A few reluctant members raise their hands to be on the cleanup committee.

"Okay, let's open discussion for the raffle prizes," announces Mrs. Bugge.

"My mom will donate a Chanel pocketbook," Indigo volunteers quickly. Her mother works in the publicity department of Chanel. *Hip, hip, hooray for her*.

"That's our lead prize, then," Mrs. Bugge says, handing Indigo a raffle ticket donation form for her mother to fill out.

Galleria winces. Ms. Dorothea didn't offer anything that fancy for the raffle. Knowing how persuasive Galleria can be, though, it's not because she didn't try. But nobody can blame Ms. Dorothea. She worked her butt off to help us put together the benefit. And thanks to her, it went off without a single hitch, thank you, ma'am. Galleria tries to disguise her pout: "My mom will donate a Toto in New York silk leopard scarf," she mumbles almost to herself.

"That's great," says Mrs. Donnell, one of the volunteer parents, trying to keep up the morale. "Listen up, Kats and Kittys, this is *not* a competition."

Angie pokes me under the table as if to say, *This is so a competition!*

Secretly, I wish there was something we could donate—but Daddy works for a bug spray company. That's probably why I feel a twinge of jealousy when Chanel announces proudly: "My stepmother will donate a gift certificate to her Princess Pamela Pampering Palace."

Talitha follows with a pair of tickets to the Broadway play *Beauty and the Beast* because her father is a Broadway producer. Devonta's mother, who is a personal trainer at Crunch gym, has gotten the fancy health club to donate a one-year membership. Devonta takes the floor to discuss the entertainment plans for the Christmas party. This, of course, is the part that we're all waiting to hear about. "We have secured Deejay Millie Shakes for the party," Devonta announces, like it's finally official.

"What happened to Deejay Bisquick?" protests Galleria. She had her hopes up that we would be using the same deejay that she secured for last year's Eggnogger.

"We thought having a female deejay would be a nice change-up," Devonta goes on to explain. "Some of the parents complained that the deejay last year played too much hip-hop music."

"Well, what else is there?" squeaks Dorinda, before turning red.

"Well, she deejayed a birthday party for the Bakers, in Atlantic City, and we thought she did a great job," chimes in Mrs. Donnell, letting us know how Deejay Millie Shakes got in the mix.

"All right—but I hope she doesn't get her needle stuck in the old-school groove," Galleria whines, "That's all I'm concerned about."

"No, Galleria, she got the party rolling. I know we're old, but you have to trust us on this one." Mrs. Donnell laughs and shakes her head.

"She also met our price, too," Devonta adds, letting us know the commitment stands. Galleria's pout becomes more prominent. I know she is fuming that no one discussed this with her and Chanel.

"Okay, now on to the entertainment portion," Devonta leads in, ignoring Galleria's dissatisfaction. "This year, um, we thought it would be the warmest welcome if our newest members to the metropolitan chapter of the Kats and Kittys Klub— Derek Ulysses Hambone and Mackerel Johnson, aka Mackerel and the Red Snapper—um, if they would perform at the Christmas Eggnogger."

At last, the fox has finally come out of the hen-house!

"Um, what do you mean?" blurts out Galleria, leveling her intense glare at Mrs. Bugge. "I thought you said we could perform."

"No, I didn't say you could perform. I said I would think about it, Galleria," Mrs. Bugge says, like she's in a courtroom giving testimony. "Our organization is called *Kats* and Kittys—so sometimes we have to allow our male members to participate more fully. The Cheetah Girls performed at the Halloween Bash."

"Yeah, and we raised a lot of duckets, too," Galleria mumbles, folding her arms tightly across her ample chest.

"Yes, our Halloween bash has traditionally been one of the two fund-raising events we throw every year," Mrs. Bugge explains, like she's letting us know that the Cheetah Girls were not responsible for the funds raised. "And the entire accounting of those funds are in the minutes I've handed to you this evening—donations were sent to the Riverside Youth Fund, the Pediatric Illness Fund, as well as ACS, the Division of Foster Care, for aid allocation to Gaye, who is in the temporary custody of Mrs. Bosco."

"I know that," Galleria says, like she's winding up for round three.

Ignoring Galleria's defensive stance, Mrs. Bugge says with authority, "I move that we close the meeting. All Kats and Kittys are to hand in their ticket sales to me up to the day of the event."

"I second," says Indigo with such force, I thought she was going to pull a gavel out of her Chanel purse and pound it on the table!

Although Angie and I are usually slow to rise after the meeting, we jump up like jackrabbits, because we know Galleria wants to hightail it out of there.

But we're not the only ones chasing her tail. "Wait up, Galleria," Derek calls out, chasing after her like he's hooked to her heels. Galleria stomps in her tracks and Derek pulls her aside to try to calm her down, but he might as well have spouted saltwater in her face instead.

"I'm not fretting, so don't sweat it," Galleria protests, trying to free her arm from the Red Snapper.

"We really had nothing to do with—"

"Whatever makes you clever," Galleria cuts in, interrupting Red Snapper's plea.

The Red Snapper, though, isn't trying to give up. "What do I have to give you for one tiny kiss?"

"Cyanide?" Galleria snaps back, referring to a deadly poison.

Meanwhile, Chanel does what she always does best when there is drama in her midst—turns chirpy and sweet. "I'm so sorry to hear about the hurricane," Chanel coos to Mackerel, referring to the mischievous "Mabel" who blasted through the Pensacola region of Florida, where his family lives. "I saw it on the news!"

"Guess we know who'll be kissing under the mistletoe," remarks Dorinda, trying to lighten up the situation. It's obvious Mackerel and Chanel are smitten with each.

Galleria, however, isn't in the mood for jokes. "Let's bounce," she announces loudly.

"You think they'll have mistletoe at the Eggnogger?" Chanel giggles to Dorinda, ignoring Galleria's orders.

"I can't believe they pulled that okie-doke behind our back," huffs Galleria, intent on staying angry.

"I think it's *tan* coolio that Mackerel and Red Snapper get to perform together again, *mija*," Chanel says sweetly. When she sees the dejected look on Galleria's face she quickly adds, "I mean, we don't have time for that now anyway, since we're going into the studio."

"Right about now—all I have time for is stewing and brewing," moans Galleria, getting the final say.

Angie and I walk home, glum as plums. Along the way, my mind keeps going back to the same dreadful thought: How are we going to get to stay in New York this month so we can finish the demo for Mouse Almighty?

"We were waiting forever to hear from him—now we gotta jump?" I complain to Angie.

"Daddy is going to have a conniption fit when we ask him," Angie groans back.

"I know he wants us outta here," I mumble, dangling my cowboy-boot-shaped leather key ring by its toe.

"What do you mean?" Angie asks, like a dunce.

"Dag-on, Angie—you know Daddy is seeing *somebody*."

"Oh, right," she says in her forgetful manner. "You think he's going out with Aballa again?"

"I don't know what I think," I say, realizing that I'm starting to perspire even though we just came in from the cold. I guess I'd rather face Count Dracula instead of Daddy any day of the week!

Chapter

3

Daddy must have come home in the wee hours of the morning, because I didn't hear him. "Even if Hurricane Mabel took the roof off our room, you'll still be sleeping with your mouth open, and drool dripping by the faucet-full," Angie humphs while we make up our twin beds before going downstairs for breakfast.

"And you heard him?" I ask, testing Angie's veracity.

"Yup, I heard him come in, but I didn't see any reason to wake you," the fake-tress continues. "Just as well we ask him after he's had his two cups of coffee."

"What time did he come home?" I ask. She can tell lies as greasy as burnt bacon.

When Angie doesn't respond, I realize I'm right. She was out like a log, too. Patting down the corners of my ugly bedspread, I fantasize about a shopping trip at the Galleria Mall when we go back home. I'm getting awfully tired of this powder-blue bedspread with the annoying nubby pom-poms that shred after each machine wash.

"Did the Ooophelia catalog come yet?" I ask Angie. I know she snatches the catalogs out of Daddy's mail pile and hogs them all for herself.

Sure enough, Angie pulls the catalog out of her cheetah backpack. "I don't think you should bother Daddy, because he is going to say no anyway," Angie warns me, dropping the catalog on my bed.

"About staying in New York for Christmas? Or getting the cheetah shelf organizers and matching comforter?" I ask, even though I already know the answer.

"Both," Angie retorts, then puts on more tape to secure the upper left corner on the Mariah Carey poster hanging on our wall. Pointing her finger at Mariah's pouty image, Angie quips, "Don't give me no drama, because you're not my mama!"

By now, you've probably figured out that we're both scared of Daddy. Our puppy, for example, Coco, that Galleria and her mother, Ms. Dorothea, gave us? Well, Daddy wouldn't let us keep him here until he is housebroken. God forbid, the adorable creature should pee in his kitchen. But don't get us wrong, Daddy isn't always mean: sometimes he surprises us. Like the poster of Mariah with her navel hanging out—he bought it for us after her concert at Madison Square Garden and even let us put it up on the pristine white walls in our room. I guess we should be grateful— but I'm sorry—our bedroom is still too plain. I wish we could redecorate it in cheetah, like Galleria's and Chanel's bedrooms.

Taking a deep sigh, we climb down the stairs to face the music. Angie whispers, "It could be worse, we could have Dorinda's bedroom."

"Hush," I shoot back. Poor Dorinda has to share her bedroom with two other foster sisters, and it's a mess. Actually, her whole apartment is shabby. It's a dag-on shame that Mrs. Bosco doesn't use some of the money we raised from the benefit to fix up that awful apartment.

Meanwhile, Daddy looks all bright-eyed and bushy-tailed in his white shirt and tie, even though I know he probably didn't get much sleep. He obviously had a good time with whomever he was tipping out with. "Where did you go last night?" I ask him, even though I know our tight-lipped father probably won't take the bait.

"None of your concern. How was the meeting?" asks Daddy, proving me right.

Twinkle, Twinkle, Cheetah Stars

"It was real good. Um, Daddy, we need to talk to you about something," I blurt out, because I can't take the anxiety anymore. "They're throwing a Christmas Eggnogger, which we want to go to, and we are in charge of the Christmas Volunteer Drive at our church—"

"But you told them you're going home for two weeks, so you can't go," Daddy says, glancing at me for a second, then looking back down at his newspaper. I stand silent, peering at the article Daddy is reading: about a six-foot baby giraffe making his debut at the Bronx Zoo. I know Daddy doesn't care about giraffes—he's just trying to ignore me.

"Well, that's not all," I start in, feeling winded already before the battle begins. Angie stops scraping the mayonnaise jar with the butter knife, and the kitchen alcove gets real quiet. We already know what Daddy is going to say: because the only place he wants us to be is out of his hair until after the ball drops in Times Square on New Year's Eve!

"Um, Daddy—you know how well that benefit went for us—I mean not just us raising the money for Mrs. Bosco's attorney and all for the court case," I say, babbling on. Angie just stands there holding the butter knife in midair, like a mime taking a break! I can't believe she isn't helping me. "Well, we didn't know that the producer, Mouse Almighty, was going to work with us again—you know—back in the studio."

"What does a Mouse have to do with the benefit—he wasn't there, was he?" Daddy asks sternly, like he is a prosecutor trying to trap a witness in a shaky alibi.

"No, but the Def Duck Records people were there and they—well, that's not the point," I stutter, pulling the yarn on the sleeve of my turtleneck sweater.

"Well, I wish you would get to the point, because I have to go to work, and I've got meetings all day for the spring campaign," Daddy announces gruffly. Suddenly I feel guilty for making Daddy go from cheerful to stressed out in the span of two minutes.

He does have so many responsibilities with his new job as marketing manager of SWAT, the biggest bug repellant company in the country, but killing cockroaches can't be more important than his own daughters getting a record deal!

"Daddy, we have to stay in New York to finish our demo tape so Mouse can take it to the record company because he has to go to Amsterdam and work on Sista Fudge's remixes," I spit out quickly.

"You mean, not go to Houston for two weeks?" Daddy asks.

"Yes, sir," Angie says, *finally* piping up in our defense.

"Have you both lost your minds?" Daddy responds sternly, shaking his head in disbelief.

"No, sir," I say quietly.

Angie chimes in a "No, sir," right behind mine.

"Um, we just want to finish working on the demo tape," I add, after another beat has passed.

"There are a few things I would risk in life," Daddy starts in, then pauses, putting the newspaper down on the kitchen alcove counter, "but crossing your grandmother and raising her blood pressure is not one of them. Y'all are going to Houston."

"Big Momma would understand. She loves us being in the Cheetah Girls!" I say, getting hysterical. I can't believe that Daddy is going to stand in the way of us making our dreams come true. He knows how hard we have worked to make this happen. We love our family more than anything. He knows we would never do anything to hurt Big Momma, or Ma, or *anybody* in our family.

"Oh, yeah, you think Big Momma will understand?" Daddy asks, challenging us. Then he points to the telephone on the wall. "Get her on the phone right now and find out."

We stand there awkwardly for a second.

"Go on," repeats Daddy.

I wipe the sweat that has piled up on my forehead with the sleeve of my sweater.

"Don't do that. Get yourself a tissue," Daddy barks at me.

Angie runs and hands me a tissue. I pick up the phone, my hand shaking, and dial Big Momma's house. The phone rings. Inside I'm praying she doesn't pick up the phone, but I know it's too early in the morning for her to be tending her garden. She is probably sitting right there, sipping her sweet iced tea and eating her biscuit with peach or strawberry jam.

"Hello." Big Momma answers the phone in her deep morning voice. By midafternoon, her voice always gets a little softer.

"Um, hi, Big Momma—it's Aqua," I say softly, trying to hide the anxiety in my voice. I should have known I couldn't fool my smart grandmother, though.

Sure enough, she asks quickly, "What's wrong, Aqua?"

"Oh, nothing," I say before I can stop myself from telling a lie.

"Hush your mouth," responds Big Momma. "You wouldn't be calling me at this hour if nothing was wrong." Who do I think I'm fooling? Angie and I always speak to Big Momma on Sundays—usually after church. She can see through my lie clearer than she can see an army of red ants climbing into her cabbage patch in the backyard.

"Remember we told you about that record producer who put us in a studio to make a demo?" I say, stalling while I try to figure out how I can explain this to Big Momma so she won't get upset.

"Yes—y'all been waiting to work with him again," Big Momma says, proud of herself for remembering something that is important to us.

"That's right!" I exclaim breathlessly. I can just see her sitting in that house all by herself. My heart starts sinking again. "Well, we can't come home for the holidays, because we have to work with him right now."

"What you mean, you can't come home?" Big Momma says in such a startled voice that my heart sinks even lower. "Pauletta and her kids are coming in from Galveston. Jelsetta got the week off so she can take y'all around. Uncle Skeeter done arranged a party for y'all. And Indigo and Egyptian will be beside themselves if they don't see their favorite aunts."

"I know that, Big Momma," I say, close to tears, "but this is the break we've been waiting for."

"Your father got something to do with you not coming?" Big Momma asks curtly. I can hear the wheels turning in her mind.

"No!" I say quickly.

"'Cuz your mother would come up there and slap him till next Tuesday, you hear me?" commands Big Momma.

"Yes, ma'am," I say quickly, praying she doesn't ask to speak to Daddy.

"So I don't care what you do, you just get your butt over my house like you do every year, you hear?" Big Momma says in the same tone of voice Reverend Butter uses when he's finished talking at the podium—it means, the sermon is over.

"Yes, Big Momma," I say, caving in. I feel like my chest is going to collapse.

When I get off the phone, Daddy stares at me with a steady gaze. "I see that went very well."

"Yes, it did," I say defiantly. Then I start crying like a baby who didn't get her pacifier in time.

"Stop that," Daddy says gruffly. He rises from the alcove, leaving behind a full cup of coffee and half-eaten English muffin.

"Well, now you really did it!" Angie says desperately, letting the knife free-fall on the counter.

"I didn't do anything," I protest. "Nobody will listen. What am I supposed to do?"

Twinkle, Twinkle, Cheetah Stars

"Well, Big Momma sure crunched you like corn chips," Angie says sarcastically. "You're the one who's going to tell Galleria and Ms. Dorothea tonight at dinner that we can't stay and finish the demo because we have to go home and eat peach cobbler instead!"

I resist the temptation to scratch out Angie's eyes. I can't believe her nerve, standing there with her twitching eyebrows, giving me orders like she's been anointed the Wicked Witch of the Upper West Side.

By the time we walk to the subway, I have calmed down, but I'm racking my brains trying to think if there was anything I could have said differently to Big Momma. All of a sudden, this lady with a double-carriage baby stroller knocks me from behind and doesn't even say excuse me, or nothing! The rude woman has snapped me out of my daze and got my heart pounding.

"These women with the baby strollers ought to have a license," I moan to Angie, but she doesn't say a word. I know what she is thinking: how could this be happening to us? Of all the people, we thought Big Momma would be on our side.

"You remember that time Big Momma was watching us—when Ma and Daddy had to go to an Avon convention?" I ask Angie, ignoring the fact that she isn't talking to me—a habit I developed a long time ago when I realized I was stuck being a twin.

"Yeah, I remember," Angie pipes up. "When Big Momma nodded off after lunch, we thought we were cute strutting around in Ma clothes, until I fell down the stairs and broke the heel off her red shoes."

"I couldn't believe she fixed the heel for us and didn't say a word about it to Ma," I say, my eyes tearing up again. "We were real lucky Ma didn't get hurt when she wore those shoes out and the heel got wedged in the sidewalk grate."

"Yeah, Big Momma was never real good at fixing stuff—not like Uncle Skeeter." Angie chuckles. Big Momma used to give Uncle Skeeter five dollars to walk around the house in her new shoes so he could break them in for her. Big Momma can't stand her feet hurting for five minutes.

"What are we gonna do?" I ask Angie as soon as we get to the Performing Arts Annex at Lincoln Center.

Angie doesn't have time to answer, because we run right into Malcolm Extra and JuJu "Beans" Quinnonez.

"Are you all right?" JuJu asks, like she cares, but I know she doesn't. This is just her way of letting me know that I look a mess. I guess there is nothing like coming to school with puffy eyes to draw attention.

"Yes, ma'am, I'm fine and dandy," I say, pretending I have no idea what she is talking about. I shoot Angie a look like, Do my eyes look *that* bad? By the way she shrugs her shoulders, I realize they do.

"Oh, Miss Aqua—my bill is in the mail," Malcolm Extra coos in his singsongy voice.

"For what?" I ask, startled.

"For that fabulous performance I gave at your benefit," Malcolm Extra shouts. "I may be free, but I'll cost you!"

"Yes, m'—I mean, sir. I know those kind of thrills never come cheaply," I say, chuckling. Malcolm Extra performed at our "Bring It On!" benefit. He is quite a character and we were lucky to have him. He sings in a falsetto voice that even rivals disco artists like Sylvester from the 1970s. (Once a month, we meet at Galleria's house for Seventies Appreciation Night and watch videos of artists from back in the day so we can be on top of our game.)

"Oh, well, one day, let's hope there is a payday in this picture for one, for all!" Malcolm Extra shouts louder, sailing down the hallway to his class.

The Cheetah Girls

Plopping down in science class, I stare glumly at the blackboard, waiting for our teacher to start the class. Out of habit my eyes move to the big sign in red letters tacked to the side of the blackboard. SCIENCE SAFETY RULES: 1) NEVER MIX UNKNOWN CHEMICALS JUST TO SEE WHAT HAPPENS. . . .

Maybe that's what I'm trying to do—mix things together, but instead I'm making a terrible mess. I mean, here we are in New York City, with the Cheetah Girls and all our big dreams. Then there is our whole other life back in Houston, where we always have to try to make everybody happy and get them to understand our new program. Yeah, well, I guess it sure has backfired. I get the feeling the whole thing is going to go *kaboom*!

Chapter 4

I thought the time to go meet the Cheetah Girls and Ms. Dorothea at Maroon's restaurant was *never* gonna come, but then the drop-the-boom hour has finally arrived, and now I just dread it. Well, I hope you understand what I'm babbling about, because I sure don't. Neither did Daddy. He made it real clear to us when we left the house to go meet our gang that we'd better just blurt out the truth, "or, so help you God, I'm going to ground you two for a long, long time." Daddy did not want to hear any more nonsense about the recording schedule Mouse Almighty has mapped out for us. Daddy ended his "sermon" by saying that we have to go to Houston for two weeks, just like he planned, even if that means we don't finish the demo. And that, "if we tell the truth, then God works in mysterious ways to make it all work out."

Well, Angie and I may have to listen to Daddy, but we know better than to believe everything he says.

What we do have to do right now is show up at Maroon's restaurant, even if we feel like the Lion in the *Wizard of Oz*, who is in desperate need of some spare courage. Angie and I drag ourselves into the restaurant, shaking in our boots. A real pretty lady wearing a blue polka-dot dress and happy red lipstick greets us at the entrance.

"Welcome to Maroon's. I'm Sarongeh, your hostess for the evening. I'll take your coats to the coat-check room while you join your party."

Sarongeh's warm greeting thaws my inside, so Angie and I take off our matching blue quilted down coats and hand them to her willingly.

"Howdy, pardner!" interjects Galleria from the bar area, waving like a hula girl. She is clutching a Caribbean cocktail with a pink umbrella thinga-majig like she's ready for a beach party.

"We're with them," I tell Sarongeh, but I gather she already knows that by Galleria's racket.

"Omigod, you have to try this—it's the bomb-ditty *boom*!" Galleria says gleefully as we approach. She shoves a punch glass filled with an exotic blue concoction toward me.

"What is it?" I ask curiously.

"It's called Jamaican Mama Brew!" heckles

Twinkle, Twinkle, Cheetah Stars

Galleria. "Sounds right up your rodeo, doesn't it?"

"Hi, ladies," Ms. Dorothea says, interrupting Galleria's giddy behavior. (If I didn't know any better, I'd think someone had slipped Galleria some tutti-frutti punch.) It's obvious that Galleria is as happy as fried clams to be "in the mix," as she puts it—and out at such a nice restaurant on a weeknight. Angie and I would be enjoying this special treat a whole lot more if it weren't for the fact that we have to spill the barbecue beans. My other half shoots me a look, and I know what she's thinking: "Galleria may be grinning now, but she'll be stinking mad later."

Ms. Dorothea swivels around quickly on her bar stool, her pretty, colored, fox muffler swiping Chanel on her right temple in the crossfire. "Oh— I'd better check this, too," she says absentmindedly, handing the muffler to Chanel like she's on coat-check duty. "Aqua, you and Angie look perplexed." Suddenly, I shriek inside. Leave it to Ms. Dorothea to know something is up with the Huggy Bear Twins. After all, she can read people faster than the *New York Post*.

"Let me make it real simple for you," Ms. Dorothea continues, depositing a drink menu in my hand. "All you have to do this evening is order the most exotic cocktails right now, then once we sit down, the most succulent appetizers, entrees, and desserts this establishment has to offer, because, my darlings, the price is definitely *right*."

I take a deep guppy breath, then let out a chuckle. Ms. Dorothea is right. We don't have to pay for this special treat, and we earned that gift certificate, so we might as well enjoy it. I break out into a grin of relief. Thank goodness Ms. Dorothea isn't on to us—just yet. After all, we don't want to ruin the fun for everybody the *whole* time we're here—just part of the time—and preferably after dessert! (I don't care what Angie thinks, I'm waiting till everyone has a full stomach before I tell them our sad, sorry story!)

"I was almost tempted by the Caribbean Calamity—coconut, mango juice, and cherry syrup. Sounds like a tasty solution to me. What do you think?" probes Ms. Dorothea.

Dag-on this is hard. Ms. Dorothea is so nice. Usually, we are so glad to see her, but tonight, seeing the Grim Reaper would have been a more welcome sight. I tug at my skirt riding up my thick thighs.

"Where's Mr. Garibaldi?" I ask, wondering if he is still at their factory store filling orders for Christmas.

"Working," Galleria hoots back, confirming

what I thought. Then she mumbles mischievously, "Better him than me."

We're glad Mr. Garibaldi isn't here. Not because we don't like him—we like him a whole heap. But he gets upset when Galleria is upset. Obviously, he's the opposite of Daddy, who doesn't give a hoot when Angie and I are miserable.

"Yoo-hoo, Aqua!" Ms. Dorothea repeats, trying to get my attention.

"Oh, I'm sorry. Yes, ma'am, I'll have a Caribbean Calamity," I say, clearing my throat. *Just what we need—another calamity!* Angie shoves me in my side. Galleria levels her trademark furtive glance in my direction, like she wants to ask, "What's up, buttercups?"

"You look nice," Angie interjects politely to Ms. Dorothea, deflecting my plea for help.

I nod in approval. Ms. Dorothea has the most unique way of dressing than anybody we've ever seen—even in New York. "I think this is the first time I've seen you wearing an outfit that isn't leopard print." Tonight Ms. Dorothea is wearing a sort of glittery knit poncho with a big crochet flower at the neckline, and a matching flared wool skirt in some sort of juicy peach color that makes her skin glow.

"Predictable is boring—always leave them guessing," Ms. Dorothea quips.

"I can't believe even your shoes match!" Angie says in awe, staring down at Ms. Dorothea's peachy-looking tweed pumps. This is so much fun—Lord, why do we have to face the music tonight? I want to grab Angie so we can scuttle to the bathroom, get right down on our knees, and pray about this. *Please, God, just give us a sign telling us what to do. Any sign. Is that too much to ask?*

"Ladies, your table is ready," Salongeh announces, interrupting my plea for help from the Almighty.

"Let's get lovely," chirps Galleria, springing off her bar stool and following Salongeh's sashay into the dining room. Following right behind them, Angie and I glance at the huge, old-timey black-and-white photos in vintage frames scattered on the walls. They remind me of the old pictures Big Momma has stacked in her photo albums. One photo in particular catches my eye: a pretty brown lady wearing a fox stole, strands of pearls, and a tight skirt cropped at the knee. She has her dainty purse clutched in her hand, and she looks like she is strolling about her business.

"I like that one," Angie says, pointing to the picture right next to it—a young boy in his Sunday best, standing next to a tall vase stuffed with roses on an antique marble end table.

Twinkle, Twinkle, Cheetah Stars

As we turn the corner into the main dining area of the restaurant, the din of chatter and noise in the crowded room makes me feel self-conscious all of a sudden. Sarongeh parks us at an empty table wedged in between two occupied tables. Of course Galleria motions for *us* to pile into the chairs against the mirrored wall. I examine the narrow space between the tables like a tightrope artist speculating the odds of pulling off the latest fantastic feat. Tiny Dorinda has already slithered into the space and is sitting down. At Angie's prodding, I turn sideways so I can squeeze in between the two tables while trying not to look down at the man's head that is directly parallel to my sucked-in stomach! A smirking Galleria sits facing us, flanked on both sides by Ms. Dorothea and Chanel. Dag-on, this is the one thing we don't like about New York—everything is so crowded and cramped.

When I do squeeze into my seat, I make sure my eyes don't meet the man at the adjoining table. I'm so embarrassed! My shame vanishes when a bus-boy plops a piping-hot basket of corn bread and biscuits in the center of our table. Just as quickly, a tall and dark bald man with flashy white teeth arrives at our table and announces himself grandly. "Good evening, ladies. I'm Mechel Thompson, the owner, and I want to welcome you to Maroon's!" he says, revealing a foreign accent.

"Hi, darling. I'm Dorothea Garibaldi and these are the Cheetah Girls," responds Ms. Dorothea. "What a lovely place you have here."

"Thank you. We want to make sure that you are served to your satisfaction—I understand you girls won the Harlem School competition," Mechel continues enthusiastically. "I'm sorry I couldn't attend, but we had to get things properly sorted out here that evening for a private party."

"*Sorted out*." I repeat the phrase to myself while I try not to stare at him.

"Where are you from?" asks Galleria, while holding a piece of corn bread hostage in her left hand.

"London," Mechel informs us proudly, "but I moved to Jamaica when I was just a tiny pup."

Quickly I have a flashback of the vintage photos on the wall. "Is that a picture of you on the wall?" I ask sheepishly, hoping that I'm not wrong. When I was little, I used to hate when people would confuse me with Angie. Even though we are twins, we are distinct and different in our own way.

"Yes, back in Mandeville. My grandmother used to like to dress me up and take me to a photo studio." Mechel giggles. "The other photos are of my partner,

Arlene, her mother, and some of our other relatives."

"I hope we get to go to London—and Jamaica," Galleria pipes up wistfully, then adds in her usual confident style, "we're going to be in the studio for the rest of the month with Mouse Almighty."

"Oh, *brilliant*. Kahlua eats here all the time when she's in town," confides Mechel, letting us know that he is quite familiar with the recording artists in Mouse Almighty's roster. "Well, I wish you girls much success. I'm sure you'll be trotting around the globe, holding court in Buckingham Palace, and drinking Earl Grey tea with the Queen!"

Galleria looks at him in amazement. "I can't believe you said that! I—I mean—we—I mean, me and Chanel, because we started the group together before we hooked up with—anyway, we would sit around and fantasize about all the places we were going to perform. . . ."

"Well, people with big dreams do think alike, darling, don't they?" Ms. Dorothea riffs at Mechel, like grown-ups sharing a trade secret.

Mechel giggles again and swipes his bald head gracefully like a gazelle. "This is true. Arlene and I opened this place five years ago, with pennies in our pocket and big dreams in our heads and buckets full of charm for the landlord when we didn't have our rent money!"

"Trust me, I know. The Texas chain gang didn't work half as hard as I did to get my boutique off the ground," Ms. Dorothea says, assured that the accuracy of equating prison labor to opening her boutique Toto in New York . . . Fun in Diva Sizes cannot be disputed even in a court of law!

"I should have known you were a fashion diva, because you are *working* that pink outfit for points." Mechel rests his wrist gently on Ms. Dorothea's shoulder. "That color looks genius on you."

"Well, actually it's not pink," Ms. Dorothea says hesitantly, "it's a shade of salmon."

"Yes, I know, but I didn't want to say that, darling," Mechel whispers, leaning over Ms. Dorothea, "in case it sounded fishy!"

Ms. Dorothea howls at Mechel's wit and I can tell these two will be breaking a lot of corn bread together in the future.

"Well, nice to meet all of you—and I'll send a waiter over *straight away*!" Mechel gushes, then marches off.

"*Straight away!*" howls Galleria. "I dig his vocab!"

"Word." Dorinda is obviously tickled pink by the exchange between Mechel and Ms. Dorothea, because her cute dimples have deepened. "He's

550

right, though—you are *working* that outfit. I don't mean to be 'knit-picking,' but it's silk, right?"

"Fresh out of the cocoon," Ms. Dorothea chuckles.

"Cocoon?" I blurt out without thinking. I'm sorry, but Angie and I are as green as spring tomatoes when it comes to textile science—one of the courses Dorinda takes at Fashion Industries East.

"The silkworm's cocoon," explains Dorinda, who can tell that the Walker twins are still not on the same fashion page as the rest of them.

"Lemme explain the silky situation. Legend has it that an Asian princess discovered silk back in the day—I mean *waaay* back in the B.C. day—Before Christ—"

"We know what B.C. means, Dorinda. We do go to church *every* Sunday," says Angie. "Just tell us what happened with Princess Cocoon already!"

"Sorry—so she was sipping her Oriental tea, right? And one of the cocoons fell in her cup—" continues Dorinda.

"Just fell from the sky like SpiderBabe?" Galleria asks in a skeptical tone.

"Let her finish," moans Ms. Dorothea.

"I don't know—maybe the cocoon fell from a closet or something that was near the table where she was drinking the tea—so, anyway, she fished

551

the cocoon out of her cup and the silky threads were exposed because the liquid had dissolved the cocoon."

"I see, said the blind man—so Cinderella isn't the only fairy tale to come out of Asia?" quips Galleria.

Even though I didn't know about the origin of the Cinderella story, either, I clamp my mouth shut.

"Thank you, Dorinda for that 'fabrication.' What says you about the attorney 'situation'?" Ms. Dorothea asks, fishing for an update on Mrs. Bosco's battle.

"Well, Mrs. Dropkin, the attorney, says Mrs. Bosco should hire a private investigator, just in case they can dig up any extra dirt about Mr. Dorgle—Corky's father," Dorinda explains carefully. "She said it could only help the case."

"Well, that makes sense—everybody is hiding *something*," remarks Ms. Dorothea.

Angie has a knee-jerk reaction to that comment and kicks me under the table. Luckily, the waiter comes over and hands us each a pretty, colored menu. Ms. Dorothea eyes the menu like a prisoner just released from lockdown. She pants, "Decide quickly, girls, so we can order, *pronto!*"

"Which appetizer should I get—jerk chicken

wings or codfish critters," I mumble to Angie. Meanwhile, I can't help overhearing tasty tidbits from the couple at the table to our right.

"I can't believe you expect me to pay dog alimony!" hisses the man. He plops his glass down firmly on the red-and-white checkered tablecloth. "What will you think of next. Getting a dog nanny?"

We all pretend that we aren't paying attention to the dueling duo, even though we are. Now I even feel sorry for the poor dog that is getting dragged into the middle of their mess. It reminds me of Angie and me when our parents separated. I can almost feel the same sensation in my stomach. We were walking around with so many cherry pits in our stomach we could hardly concentrate in school. Our seventh-grade science teacher, Mrs. Chummins, even called our parents to find out what was going on at home that had us so distracted in class.

"Aqua!" Galleria barks, rescuing me from eavesdropping. She has her left hand wrapped around the bottle of Walkerswood Jankanoo Hot-Pepper Sauce like it's Aladdin's lamp. "This is off-limits for the fabulous Texas Walker twins, okay?"

"Yes, ma'am," I respond automatically.

According to Galleria, "stars don't carry Hot

Papa sauces in their purses." Well, we learned our lesson all right: We still carry it, but we just don't whip it out in front of the Cheetah Girls anymore!

"Ending the Civil War was easier than weaning these two off their spice of choice," Galleria says, making another jab in her "needle point."

Before I can open my mouth to make a smart retort, other words start falling out of my mouth: "Daddy says we have to be on that plane going to Houston next Friday. He doesn't care if we don't finish the demo."

Galleria gives Angie and me that shocked-bunny look she can do on cue. Then she looks at her mother, Chanel, and Dorinda, then down at her plate—which is pitifully empty except for a few scattered corn bread crumbs.

"So I guess it's true, huh? There's no place like home?" says Galleria, dripping with more sarcasm than fat on a bacon strip. Angie and I know what Galleria thought of us when she first met us: that we were two Houston hickory sticks that had to be cured to her liking to be part of the Cheetah Girls.

"Galleria, we wish we could click our heels three times and be in the studio with y'all, and back home with our family so we could make everybody happy!" I stutter, fighting back my anxiety.

"Well, then I guess we're going to have to finish

the demo without the Fabulous Walker Twins. Because the demo is getting *done*," huffs Galleria like she's a courtroom judge delivering a hefty jail sentence. "But I take it you can show up every afternoon at Mouse's studio up until next Friday? Or will you be *toooo* busy with pedicure appointments and other primping perks in preparation for your holiday travel plans?"

Ouch. Galleria knows how to deliver a sting better than any yellow jacket bumblebee in operation.

"No, Galleria. We will be at the studio every afternoon, like we're supposed to," I retort, still smarting from her mighty sting.

Angie pokes me on the side—this time, hard. I can't even get mad at my cowardly other half for her sneaky jab. For once, she was right: peach cobbler topped with melted vanilla ice cream sure would have made this whole thing go down a lot easier. I should have waited until after dessert to spill these burnt barbecued beans!

Chapter 5

The announcement of our Houston-bound holiday trip dampened the rest of our evening. I don't mean to sound like a Southern debutante in distress, but I'm *not* exaggerating. Usually Galleria eats macaroni and cheese with the enthusiasm of a mongoose swallowing a mouse, but instead she poked her fork around her plate like she secretly wished it was our faces instead!

And if enduring such a *dreadful* "last supper" isn't bad enough, as soon as we get home, Daddy serves up more unappetizing news. "Big Momma had a flare-up. Your mother is expecting a call from you—right now."

I sigh and take my coat off, then turn to go to the bathroom, but Daddy jumps down my throat like a bumblebee determined to get his buzz on, "Do it right now!"

"How bad is it, Daddy?" Angie asks, panicking. See, Big Momma has had rheumatoid arthritis since we can remember—it's a terrible disease that never goes away, and nobody on God's green earth knows what causes it. When we were little, there were times Big Momma would just lay in bed, moaning and calling for the healing powers of the Lord. Once, we cried to Daddy because we thought somebody put a spell on Big Momma. How else could you explain the fact that she would be fine one minute, then in agony? I'll never forget when Daddy sat us down and told us everything about "RA." That sometimes it makes Big Momma's joints so stiff and inflamed, it causes excruciating pain.

I pick up the phone and dial Big Momma's house. I feel like my throat is on fire. Ever since Daddy told us about RA, I conjure up these horrible images of Big Momma's joints being "on fire." I just don't like those words "inflamed" or "inflammation." They sound like the work of the Devil, if you ask me.

"What do you think you girls are up to?" Ma barks into the receiver, but doesn't wait for my response. "How could you call Big Momma and tell her something like that without talking to me first? Have you lost your minds up there?"

I recoil from Ma's sting. I've been stung so many times this evening, I'm tempted to reach for the calamine lotion before another word comes out of my mouth!

"No, ma'am, we have not," I reply calmly. There is no point in telling Ma that we only called Big Momma first because Daddy forced us, on a dare. We learned a long time ago, when Ma's midnight train of terror rolls out of the station, the best thing for us to do is stay out of her way.

"Do you know that the neighbors had to go over and help Big Momma out of bed this morning because she couldn't move? Doctor says the inflammation is finally spreading to her internal organs. Now what do you have to say about that?" Ma barks at me mercilessly.

"We're coming, Ma," I say, surrendering to the guilt eating away at the lining of my stomach. Even though it's irrational, Angie and I have always felt responsible for Big Momma's flare-ups. But this particular time, it's obvious we *are*.

"Oh, I know you're coming home, but you'd better call your grandmother in the morning and talk to her. Do you hear me?" Ma threatens, but doesn't stop for refueling: "If it wasn't so late I'd make you two call her right now. But she is worn out and we finally got her into a peaceful sleep.

Now, I don't want to hear anymore nonsense like you're some big-time singing group."

Obviously we're not! I want to scream at Ma, but I know better than to sass. "Yes, ma'am," I squeak instead, and hand the phone to Angie so Ma can chew her out, too.

Afterward, we hightail it to our bedroom, just in case Daddy gets riled up again. Lying in my bed, I think about Big Momma sleeping peacefully. I'm glad that at least one of us will be sleeping well, because I'm not going to. Meanwhile, it doesn't help that Angie is fumbling with leftover wrappings in her bed. I try to decipher the smells wafting from her side of the room—hints of cinnamon and white frosting. "Why are you eating in the dark?" I whisper. I turn on the lamp on my nightstand. Angie is lying there, bug-eyed, swallowing dawn a slice of red velvet cake, which we found out tonight is a Jamaican dessert.

I am so anxious about Big Momma that I don't even ask Angie for a bite. That's why she knows that I'm so upset my stomach is hurting.

"What is it, butterflies?" Angies asks, concerned.

"No, elephants," I moan. I lie down again and try to sleep while the light is on and Angie is munching away. Suddenly, I have a vision of Angie and me sitting on a back porch in Houston with a ten-pound bag of green beans and a big metal strainer like we used to have when we were little. But in the vision, we're old and wrinkled, and have such bad arthritis that we don't have even the strength in our fingers to snap the ends off the beans! I'm so frightened, I jump up out of bed and go to my desk and turn on my computer.

"You're gonna do homework now?" Angie asks me in disbelief.

"No," I mumble, ignoring her. I sign onto the Internet and search Google for "Rheumatoid Arthritis." "There has to be something we can do to help Big Momma." Scanning information on the different sites, I try to decipher all the fancy medical language and understand what this thing is that Big Momma has. Angie gets up from her bed and looks over my shoulder. Talking out loud, I try to explain. "When you have RA, something in the body's immune system starts attacking healthy joint tissue and eating them up. That sounds horrible."

"That's why we always thought something was attacking Big Momma—it is," Angie says with a sigh.

Poor Big Momma. Tears well up in my eyes. I decide when we get to Houston, I'm going to spend more time with her. I keep searching, trying to find more information. (Secretly, I know I'm searching for something else, too—I want to know if the flare-ups are caused by being upset, but I can't find anything.) After visiting a lot of sites, I realize that nobody seems to know what causes this type of arthritis. "The cause of rheumatoid arthritis is not yet known."

"It seems like there is nothing we can do," I say, defeated. I turn off the computer, feeling more confused than before.

"Do you think they are going to make the rest of the demo without us?" Angie asks, crumpling the tinfoil and stuffing it back into the brown paper doggie bag she got at Maroon's.

All of a sudden, I feel like a card-carrying member of the I-don't-know club. "I don't know," I mumble emphatically to Angie, clutching the ugly blue bedspread around my neck like it's going to protect me from all the fears and worries that are sweeping me into a nasty avalanche. I close my eyes and decide to pray again, but not in the spiritual way that we were taught to pray, but in the "I can't help it, because I'm desperate" way. *Please, God, don't take Big Momma from us.*

The next day, I can tell that Angie is just as scared as I am. Not because she's acting afraid, but because she asks me what we should wear to go to the studio instead of just putting on anything she pleases, which usually doesn't please Galleria.

"Something cheetah," I reply, knowing that's exactly what would make the Cheetah Girls' committee happy. Thank goodness Daddy has called to tell us he is working late. Otherwise, he would drive us to the studio, and I'd prefer if he didn't. I'm sorry, but it's true. I don't want him coming up and being stern with us in front of the Cheetah Girls. It's going to be embarrassing enough to face them without him there causing more friction.

"Let's wear the pink cheetah stuff," I say emphatically.

"We just wore that to the benefit," Angie protests. Before she gets her itchy fingers on that white petticoat again (which I still haven't had time to pack away, with all this drama going on), I pull out both of our pink cheetah tops and skirts, and shove hers into her chest, ordering her to "just put it on."

"We should call Big Momma *again* before we leave," Angie warns me. "I just feel so bad about everything." My nerves are still numb from speaking to her this morning. I mean, Big Momma didn't mean to sound like she was in a lot of pain, but it wasn't hard to tell. The biggest tip-off was she didn't ask us anything about the Cheetah Girls. Usually she wants to know every detail. Things like, "What is Miss Galleria up to? That girl is something else."

"She knows we have to get to the studio," I moan, but I know she's right. We should call Big Momma anyway. I don't care what I read about rheumatoid arthritis on the Internet, I know she had a flare-up because of my big mouth. Angie levels one of her you-know-we're-in-hot-water looks at me, and I cave. We hurry up and finish dressing, then hightail it downstairs to hit the phone, dialing Big Momma's house as we put on our coats.

"Praise the Lord." Big Momma answers the phone in her usual manner, which makes my heart skip a beat. *She must be feeling better!* See, that's what I mean about this rheumatoid arthritis business—it's strange to me how Big Momma can swing from one end of the pendulum to the other.

"Angie and I just wanted to tell you that we love you," I coo.

"All right, now, Nettie One," Big Momma says using the nickname she gave me. "Well, I'm especially glad to hear from y'all. I got a surprise for ya'll."

"Really?" I respond, turning into a little girl

again, excited by Big Momma's Christmas presents. When Angie and I were six, Big Momma gave us the biggest dollhouse this side of Toy World. It was so big, we had to put it in the basement instead of our bedroom. We practically lived in that basement, telling our mother, "Bye, we're going downstairs to *our* house now!" "Go 'head," Ma would say. "Just don't forget to pay your mortgage." We sure did take care of that dollhouse like it was a real house. One thing you have to know about our family, there is nothing more important than owning your own home. Guess that dollhouse was our start.

"Yes, really," Big Momma retorts. My heart starts to swell. I can't believe how selfish we were for even thinking about canceling our trip home. As Big Momma would say, "God don't like ugly." Well, I bet God sure doesn't like the Walker twins at this moment.

"You're not going to tell us the surprise?" I ask Big Momma.

"No, ma'am, I won't," Big Momma says, her breathing heavy.

"I'll let you off the hook this time," I say, kidding her. "You want to speak to Angie?"

"Yes, put on Nettie Two," she says.

Handing Aqua the receiver, I start feeling guilty

about all the preparations everybody back home is doing for our visit. I bet Big Momma has Uncle Skeeter running around like a rooster looking for a cheetah surprise for our Christmas present. I just can't stand how much we have upset Big Momma with all our drama.

"She is just so tickled by how we dress now that we're part of the Cheetah Girls," Angie says, putting her arms through mine as we leave our house.

"Yeah, well, she sure ain't tickled by our selfish behavior," I snarl back. I take another deep sigh as we head off to the recording studio—to nibble on some tunes.

Chapter 6

As soon as we get out of the elevator onto the sixth floor, which opens directly into Mouse Almighty's reception area, our eyes meet Ms. Dorothea's. She is standing near the glass reception door, with her leopard hankie clenched in her left hand and held against her chest. Before I can extend my arm fully to grab the knob, Ms. Dorothea nudges the door ajar, sticking her head out. She is perspiring so heavily, and if I didn't know any better, I'd swear she was sweating oxtail juice from last night's dinner at Maroon's. Now I start sweating and wringing my hands, anticipating that she'll tell us something dreadful: *She probably told Mouse Almighty we aren't staying to finish the demo and he has thrown us to the wolves. We're probably banned from his studio!*

Patting her forehead with the hankie in a

staccato manner like a mechanical Chucky Doll, Ms. Dorothea yelps, "Dorinda is not here yet. Did she call you?" While waiting for my response, Ms. Dorothea quickly scans us from head to toe.

"No, she didn't," I answer, secretly hoping that we register satisfactorily on the cheetah meter. Ms. Dorothea scans us up and down again while releasing a faint smile. Relieved, I let the air out of my stomach like a hot-air balloon. Now I feel bad that we didn't talk to Dorinda today. I know she has a lot to deal with right now. Even without the custody battle over Corky, the Bosco residence always seems like it's one boiling-hot kettle away from blowing its lid. If Dorinda called anybody, it would have been Chanel, since they are the closest, but I'm sure Ms. Dorothea has already checked that angle.

"If I have to get that girl a cell phone myself, I will," Ms. Dorothea says, finally ushering us into the recording studio's reception area and flashing her "I'm so fabulous and so are you" smile at Cindy the receptionist, who looks up from her desk. In return, Cindy gives us a glad-to-see-you're-back smile, which makes me feel just like that: glad that we are back "in the mix with Mouse Almighty."

Galleria and Chanel are plopped comfortably on the black leather beanbag couch.

"Hola!" Chanel coos. She looks so cute—she has on a red hoodie sweater with a big pink heart on the front, over a black-and-white cheetah-print skirt; Galleria has on a brown cheetah jumper with matching cheetah boots. Now I'm relieved that Angie and I are looking equally as cheetahfied as they are.

"Howdy," Galleria says tersely. Joining Galleria and Chanel on the couch, my eyes dart around the office at all the framed photos and RIAA certified plaques for platinum- and gold-selling records. (RIAA stands for the Recording Industry Association of America—the national organization that monitors record sales.) Eventually my eyes settle on the signed photograph of the LoveBabiez, the Pampers-wearing, thumb-sucking singers who just got dropped from Def Duck Records.

"Guess their group is a testament to at least one thing," says Galleria, joining my gaze.

I don't respond to Galleria's probing, but leave it to Angie to take the bait and nosily inquire, "What?"

"That diapers should only be worn by *real* babies," Galleria retorts.

A shudder tingles across my shoulder blades as

another wicked thought pops into my mind: what if the Cheetah Girls get booted back to the jiggy jungle?

"At least they have one gold record—that's something to tell their grandchildren," Chanel says hopefully. She's right. All we have under our cheetah belts are a few talent shows and gift certificates. Getting people to buy your albums is a different slice of blackberry cobbler. I can't take the silence, so now my eyes wander over yonder—at the shelves behind Cindy's desk, filled with exotic bottles of hot sauce. I try not to stare too long—lest Galleria comes up with some new clever comments. But I find myself hypnotized by all the different-shaped bottles filled with red, green, yellow, and orange hot sauces—lined up like a spicy rainbow that leads to hot-sauce heaven. The last time we were here, Cindy told us that the audio engineer, Son Seven, collects hot sauce from all over the world. One day, I'm going to have my own collection—hundreds of bottles, displayed right in my kitchen.

Ms. Dorothea shoots us a look like she has to say something on the down low: "Mouse is in there with Heidi Klum and Seal," she whispers carefully.

I feel embarrassed, because I don't know who on earth she is talking about. Obviously, they're

"Big Willies," as Galleria would describe them, but who are they? I shoot a glance at Angie and I can see she is in the dark, too. Galleria stares at us evenly, like she's thinking, "Hmmm. The Houston hickory sticks still need more curing!"

I roll the names over in my mind. *Heidi Glum and Seal?* They sound like a circus act. I know there is Siegfried and Roy, Barnum and Bailey . . . *Heidi Glum and Seal?*

"Seal is a very important recording artist on the London soul scene," Galleria says, picking up on my blank stare. You know, from back in the day."

"Back in the day?" Ms. Dorothea interjects, puzzled. "His first album came out in the early nineties—that's ancient history to you?"

"Yup, it is. A long time ago in a galaxy far, far away, " Galleria says, flashing a mischievous smirk at her mother. Daddy would slap us straight into Sunday if we talked to him the way Galleria talks to her mom. Her tone and facial expressions are too sassy for Daddy's stringent tastes.

"Perhaps a Nineties Appreciation Night should be in order," counters Ms. Dorothea.

"Well, anyway, Seal has had about four albums," Galleria says, making her point, and turning to me to readdress our ignorance. "He's from somewhere in Africa."

"No. He was raised in England, but his parents are Nigerian and Brazilian," retorts Ms. Dorothea, proving once again that she always knows the "411," because she reads *Billboard* magazine like Big Momma reads the Holy Bible.

"I probably heard his music," I add quickly, so I don't seem so ignorant.

"And who is the other person he's with?" Angie asks.

"Heidi? I know that one up and down like a see-saw," Galleria pipes up. "They interviewed her on MTV like, last week."

Well that explains it. We have don't have the time to be watching MTV—not with all the chores Daddy gives us.

"You don't know who she is, *mija*?" interjects Chanel.

"No, we don't," I answer for both of us.

"She is a *big* supermodel. I mean *major*," Galleria says emphatically, to get her point across. "Let's just say she *is* Victoria's Secret—"

"Besides Tyra Banks," Chanel adds quickly.

"No doubt," Galleria chimes in. "They're *both* major."

"Oh, I see," I say, nodding. We used to always peek at Ma's catalog when we were back in Houston. Now that I think about it, we haven't seen a catalog since we started living with Daddy.

"Anyhoo, Heidi and Seal are quite 'the toasty' these days. You've got to start reading something else besides the astrology page in *The Post*," Galleria chides us. By "toasty," I gather Galleria means that they are boyfriend and girlfriend.

"When you brush up on your geography, Aqua and Angie will expand their newpaper reading to more than astrology," Ms. Dorothea says, referring to Galleria's mistake about Seal's origins. "And Ms. Heidi, by the way, is from Cologne, Germany, in case you were wondering."

Cologne, Germany. Now I wonder if Heidi's hometown is where the word "cologne" comes from, but I don't ask, because the door flies open and in walks a very harried Dorinda. "I'm sorry I'm late."

As she cuts across the reception area and plops down next to Galleria, I get a whiff of the strangest odor. It's a chemical scent that reminds me of one of Daddy's SWAT bug sprays.

"Speaking of 'cologne,' why aren't you wearing any?" asks Galleria, embarrassing poor Dorinda.

"I did put some on, Galleria," Dorinda responds, flustered, "but the apartment was *bombed*—"

"What happened?" Chanel asks, interrupting Dorinda's tale of woe.

Because of Daddy and his job, I realize what Dorinda is probably trying to say. "You mean the apartment was bombed for, um, roach infestation, right?" I probe gently.

Dorinda nods her head, because she is almost too upset to talk. "Mrs. Bosco forgot to take all the clothes out of the drawers—before the exterminator came. If she had just told me before I left this morning for school, I would have helped. But she is so absentminded because of this Corky thing, and—" Dorinda stops in midsentence to catch her breath, then recharges like a Chucky Doll, "now all our clothes smell like a chemical factory, and I had to sweep up all the dead roaches lying around before I came here!"

"Don't worry, *mija*," Chanel coos, shuffling through her purse until she finds her bottle of Yves Saint Bernard cologne. She spritzes it heavily into the air, like an airplane glider releasing insecticide spray on an innocent peach orchard. Chanel is so enthusiastic about camouflaging the "Roach Motel" scent, that poor Dorinda starts sneezing and ducking for cover.

"Oh, that's nice, what is that?" asks Cindy, the receptionist, oblivious to the drama because she was too busy fielding calls on the switchboard.

"Yves Saint Bernard," Chanel retorts quickly.

"Oh." Cindy nods her head in approval. "That's the *bomb*."

Lord, why did she have to use that word? We all stare at her dumbfounded, like we're the newest dummies installed in Madame Tussaud's Wax Museum. Cindy senses the drama in our midst, so she quickly picks up the newspaper on her desk like she forgot to check something important.

"Can we check our horoscope?" Angie mutters to me.

My mind starts racing, wondering what my horoscope says today: *Mercury is in retrograde, stirring up mess, which means all Virgos should have stayed in bed today!*

"Backstabba is going solo," announces Cindy. She is obviously reading something in the newspaper about the lead singer of our least favorite girl group—Karma's Children—who hail from Houston like we do.

"Say it ain't so," moans Galleria, slapping her hand against her face in a mock gesture. "Another star in the galaxy seduced by the dark side of the force—fame, fortune, and standing solo in the hot spotlight in a sequin gown!"

Next, Galleria levels one of her you-should-have-told-me looks at her mom, then asks, "Did you know about this?"

"Of course. I don't miss an issue of *Billboard* even if the seams are splitting on my customer's orders!" Ms. Dorothea huffs back.

"Her solo album is dropping soon," Cindy reports further.

Suddenly, the soundproof door to the recording studios swings open, and out walks Mouse Almighty with two interesting people. Galleria fans the air hysterically with her hands, like she is trying to vanish all the comingling scents—the roach bomb and Yves St. Bernard. I try not to stare at the couple, but they are both really tall and interesting looking. I gather Heidi is the tall blond lady with the chiseled features—anybody can tell she is a model, even if they lived in another galaxy. Seal's features are chiseled, too, but he's real dark, with these unusual marks on his cheeks. Mouse waves at us and sniffs the air curiously before continuing his conversation with the famous couple.

"Yes, that would be *brilliant*," echoes Seal. I notice that he has the same accent as Mechel, the owner of Maroon's. I can't wait till we visit London one day.

"Oh, let me introduce you to this new singing group I'm working with," Mouse says to Seal and Heidi, beaming in our direction.

The Cheetah Girls

We all stand up quickly, but I spurt out, "It's so nice to meet you Ms. Glum and Mr. Seal!" I extend my hand to Heidi first. Out of the corner of my eye, I can see Galleria wince, but that's too bad. She doesn't always have to be the first one speaking for us.

Heidi smiles politely and says, "It's Klum."

My face turns more purplish than any Texas beet in the goosefoot family snatched from its roots at birth! "I'm so sorry, Ms. Plum, but I just love—um—your stuff."

Just when I thought it wasn't possible to turn a deeper shade of purple, Heidi replies sweetly, "It's *Klum*."

"We've been watching your show," Galleria interrupts quickly, trying to help me save face. I wonder what show Galleria is talking about, but I dare not ask now.

Heidi catches my "I'm a dunce" expression and tries to console me. "Oh, don't worry—it's just one of those funny German names," she says graciously, revealing a hint of a foreign accent. "Who are you girls?"

"They are the Cheetah Girls," Mouse responds on our behalf.

"Nice to meet you," Heidi says, while feeling in her purse for something. She pulls out a Palm

Pilot, one of those gadgets that Daddy has for organizing everything.

"Oh, you got a raspberry, too—just got mine. Aren't they divine?" Ms. Dorothea says to Heidi, and they launch into a discussion about the pros and cons of blackberrys and raspberrys until I can't keep all the fruit groups separate.

"Call us straight away when you get to Amsterdam," Seal says, cupping Mouse's hand into his.

"Will do," Mouse assures him. "And don't worry, Heidi, Son will even the score out. She's always a half beat off most of the time, a little wobbly but her vocal styling is tight. I'll have first edits ready by January for the finale show."

I wonder what they are talking about, but it's obvious it has something to do with music that Mouse Almighty is producing for, I guess, Heidi. After Heidi and Seal leave, we stand there, breathless from all the excitement, until Mouse whispers to the receptionist to "turn up the central air-conditioning."

Dorinda winces, because we all know that Mouse's request has to do with us turning his reception area into an "odorama factory."

Galleria fans the air again with her hand, when Mouse turns his back to talk to Cindy. "Tell Seth to hang tight, *ayiight*?"

The Cheetah Girls

When Mouse turns his attention back to us, Galleria blurts out, "Oh, I remember you were working on the tracks for 'So You Wanna Be a Star.' How'd that go?" Mouse seems impressed by Galleria's good memory. The last time we were here, we met the show's producer, Seth Seidelman. All of a sudden, I hear a little voice inside shriek: *Maybe we should try to get on that show, 'cause we can't even finish a demo!*

"Okay, Bubbly one, let's focus on the work we're doing for you." Mouse Almighty has invented his own version of Galleria's nickname, which is Bubbles.

"You mean that we're already stars and we don't need to be here?" Galleria queries jokingly.

"Not exactly. First, we have to get Def Duck Records quacking about your product," Mouse starts in, getting serious. "You girls are gonna have to 'bring it,' so we can make that happen."

"Right, I know," Galleria says, shrugging her shoulders like an ingénue ready for her close-up, even though there isn't any film in the camera!

Chapter 7

We follow Mouse Almighty, a short, wiry producer with unusually large white teeth, behind the soundproof door, like he is the Pied Piper. As we pass more walls filled with *more* framed RIAA certified gold and platinum sales plaques, I start feeling ashamed about leaving the Cheetah Girls in a lurch. I can already picture Ms. Dorothea trying to explain to Mouse how the Goody Two-shoes twins have to go back home to Houston, like sacrificial piglets on a rotisserie for Christmas dinner!

Mouse motions for us to sit down on the metal chairs scattered outside the sound studio. I scurry toward a chair, but stub my toe because I am so lost in my shameful thoughts.

"So what have you girls been up to?" the Grammy-winning guru asks while stroking his goatee. I can detect his whiskers trying to sniff out what is going on with the five divettes-in-training to whom he is about to lend his Midas touch.

"They've been so-o-o-o busy," interjects Ms. Dorothea, playing her manager role to the hilt. "First, there was the Harlem School of the Arts competition. Then they had to get ready for the 'Bring It On!' benefit. And with Christmas around the corner—tinsel bits have taken over my house."

"If we hit the ground running, we should be finished with you girls right before Santa makes his chimney drop," Mouse Almighty says, chuckling, then sits down and crosses his legs like a master Jedi about to school his pupils. "By the by, I'm sorry I couldn't make the benefit—what was it for again?" Mouse asks respectfully. He is so busy, we're surprised he even remembered our "Bring It On!" benefit.

"Dorinda, why don't you tell him?" Ms. Dorothea says proudly. But Dorinda starts fidgeting like she's afraid she's going to sneeze again.

"Um, we raised money," Dorinda says, stopping in midsentence. The rest of us sit silent, like a bunch of hungry kids waiting for her to whack the piñata so we can eat the candy that falls out.

Mouse Almighty scans our faces quickly, like the MetroCard machine at the subway turnstiles, computing instantly that there aren't any more fares left in this conversation. "Well, let's get going. We've got a full rehearsal ahead of us," he says sharply. "The work you girls did on 'Not a Chance' is a good start, so let's break off a little something, something else."

"*Ayiight*," Galleria breaks out, imitating Mouse.

Meanwhile, I wrack my brains trying to remember the name of the songwriter who wrote the first song we recorded for the demo, but the only thing I can remember is that Galleria didn't like the song. As a matter of fact, I'm surprised she hasn't already asked Mouse if we can record one of her songs yet.

Jumping out of his Jedi pose, Mouse motions to Son Seven, and orders him to "cue up the Midget Man track."

"Now, this tasty morsel comes from a songwriter I've been working with—he's got real tight lyrical skills—sweet with a lot of bite. Personally, I think that's what the Cheetah Girls are all about—so you should be able to really sink your teeth into this jammy," Mouse coaches us. "We're gonna try it two ways. I've had it arranged with more snares and tighter piano riffs, and raised the tempo up a notch to keep the energy bouncing. Really sweet. Then we'll hit it mid tempo with a keyboard and bass arrangement that might make it a little more, well, sour."

I quickly look over at Galleria to see if she is feeling what Mouse has said. Mouse Almighty hands us the sheet music to the Midget Man song, "It's a Jungle Out There," and tells Son to "hit the Midget Man track A." The bass-heavy track fills the room. I snap back to the present, my clammy hands stuck on the sheet music as I stare at the lyrics for the first verse:

"Don't take your toys and go home and leave me alone in a world that doesn't care about my rhythm. Just keep watching my back and I'll watch yours—because that's what friends are for in this crazy world of a mixed-up jungle of a jumbo size prize inside of a Cracker Jack box."

"Are you feeling it?" interjects Mouse after the first stanza.

I nod my head, still frozen in my foolish thoughts but trying to force myself to concentrate.

"I'm not sure I can hit a High C like that," Dorinda says, squirming in her chair. The chorus on this number has a slightly falsetto feel, which Angie and I can handle just fine, but it is definitely a strain for Dorinda and probably even Chanel.

"Come in here for a minute, Dorinda and Chanel," Mouse Almighty says, motioning for the two of them to step out so they can work in the other studio. "Listen, the rest of you girls marinate—we're gonna work in here."

Marinate. That's the first time I've ever heard anyone else besides Uncle Skeeter use that expression. I start thinking about how glad I'll be to see him next week.

Galleria jumps up and announces, "I have to go winky tink." If I didn't know better, I'd swear Galleria doesn't want to be alone with us. I look up, trying to get her attention, but she doesn't look at me, confirming my paranoid suspicions: she has something up her sneaky sleeve. That's it! *They are probably searching for alternate Cheetah Girls. Or maybe they're already lined up, just waiting for us to get on that plane—and good riddance to the Walker twins!*

I shoot Angie a look like I used to when we were little and sitting in church and I had to go to the bathroom in the middle of the preacher's Sunday sermon. Angie signals me back. She *knows* too!

Mrs. Dorothea whispers to Angie, "Are you okay with the chorus?" A startled Angie ponders the question for what seems like a whole Minute-Rice minute, then nods her head in the affirmative. Then Ms. Dorothea puts her arms around my shoulder, "Don't worry about Galleria. Leave that to me. You girls just show up here every day after school, and we'll work out the rest. I'm taking care of it."

What does Ms. Dorothea mean by she's "taking care of it"? My heart sinks to my feet like it's dropping to the depths of the Armand Bayou back home. Now I'm positive: our Christmas geese are cooked and practically ready to serve on a silver platter surrounded by freshly glazed cranberries!

"How long do you think it's gonna take us to finish this demo?" I ask Ms. Dorothea, hoping she'll tell us the truth. We might as well find out if they're going to lower the boom on us.

"Well, it takes what it takes," Ms. Dorothea says, shrugging her shoulders like, "Sorry, I can't let you off the hook."

When Galleria comes back, she moans to her mom about the lyrics to the song we're rehearsing, "I don't like the whole idea about toys—we don't play with toys anymore—you know what I'm saying?"

Since Galleria isn't asking *our* opinion, Angie and I don't say bo-peep. We like the song—it seems to go more with our whole "global groove."

"What should you be singing about—*boys*?" Ms. Dorothea queries, concerned. "Trust me, darling, it is a jungle out there—and that's a very good message to be getting across. So, please, Galleria, for once, pretend you don't have a mouth—and just follow the bouncing ball."

The door to the adjacent studio opens up, and Dorinda and Chanel come through, smiling like they've regained their singing stride. Mouse has obviously worked his magic. I wonder if he has had to coach other singers—even powerhouses like Sista Fudge.

"Okay, Aqua, Angie, you'll be soprano, Galleria—alto as usual, and Dorinda and Chanel—mezzo is your move," orders Mouse Almighty, then puts his hands up like he wants to slow down the choo-choo train. "Now hold up, I need to talk to you girls for a minute." Mouse Almighty pauses, rubs his goatee, then starts in, "You girls have an advantage that artists twice your age don't have."

I like when Mouse Almighty refers to us as "artists." It makes me feel like we're not the same girls who came in second at the Apollo Amateur Hour contest. Or the same girls who were afraid of the Sandman pulling them off the stage with his hook.

"What's that?" Galleria asks, like it's the prize behind door number three she's been panting for.

"You know who you are—you're the Cheetah Girls—so relax, even though I'm gonna work you till you believe in Santa—hang in there, 'cause this is supposed to be fun," Mouse Almighty says, trying to get us into the recording spirit.

"How are we supposed to relax—this is so-o-o-o important," Galleria moans.

"We have one very simple goal here—to get the A&R peeps at Def Duck excited enough to get behind this demo, take it to acquisitions—in front of a whole boardroom of corporate Big Willies who make the decision about which new acts get signed—it's no biggie!" Mouse chuckles. "In order to do that, you've got to be yourselves—then trust me, growl power is gonna *rule*."

"Were you a cheerleading squad leader in high school?" asks Ms. Dorothea, chiding Mouse on his motivational speech.

"I could have been." Mouse kicks up his leg like he's doing a cheer. "Okay, get your hides into rehearsal mode!"

After two hours of rehearsal and trying out different melodies, Mouse decides it's time to lay down the track. "Are y'all up for it? We can wait till tomorrow if not," he asks, egging us on.

"We're down for the twirl, so let's swirl," Galleria riffs.

"Those are tasty lyrics, young lady—I may have to take you up on your songwriting skills," Mouse says.

Twinkle, Twinkle, Cheetah Stars

Galleria's eyes light up like the fifty-foot Christmas tree on display at the Galleria Mall in Houston at Christmastime. Mouse motions for us to go into the sound room and put on headphones.

We sing the first verse of the song at least five times—and each time Mouse has Son Seven stop the takes. Through the headphones we can hear Mouse tell Son to "cut the playback." Then he says to us, "The five-part harmony is off."

I cringe inside, wondering what he needs for us to do. Maybe Angie and I are singing too high— but we are singing in this key to accommodate Dorinda and Chanel's range.

"Okay, let's take five. Son, cut the second verse, pop back into the chorus, and we'll go again," Mouse says, like he's calculating a new strategy. We look at each other, puzzled. Mouse orders us to come out of the sound room while Son fixes the tracks.

"I think it's time we rely on the nourishing powers of Chunky Cheese," Mouse says, rubbing his stomach. "I'ma tell Cindy to hook us up."

I'm relieved. We're so hungry, we could slap our Daddy, but we didn't want to say anything until the rest of the Cheetah Girls said something. When Mouse walks out of the room, Chanel asks in a jittery voice: "Did I hit the high C, okay?"

"Chanel—it's okay. Let's just eat, and we'll work out the harmonies after. They obviously still need tweaking," Ms. Dorothea says, consoling us all. For once, Galleria doesn't look at me and Angie like it's our fault. There is nothing she can *ever* say about our singing—that's for sure. But we can't help but wonder if we are the real reason the harmony is off.

"Well, whatever it is, Mouse will tell us how to fix it," Galleria moans.

Dorinda seems to second that motion. "Judging from all his plaque attacks," she starts in, referring to the framed record plaques on the walls, "nobody needs to tell this man how to make a hit record."

After we down our hamburgers and sodas, we are back in the studio, ready to try something different with the song. Mouse has given us new harmony lineups, and we're going to try yet another version—this one more uptempo so we can lower our range. After seven takes, Mouse comes into the studio grinning, "You hit it hard, girls. Now hit the sack. See you tomorrow. I have to take this conference call."

Galleria is so groggy, she starts riffing off her own Dr. Seuss rhymes: "Look at me! Look at the bee! Look at the sow! It is fun to have sun. But you have to be a cow!" she yelps.

"Okay, Miss Cat in a Hat, enough of that," Ms.

Dorothea counters, unwrapping a pack of Tums antacid, popping two in her mouth and chewing them like she's crunching bones. "That was O.T.T. even for you."

I scrunch up my nose, trying to figure out what "O.T.T." means as we shuffle into the reception area. Miss Dorinda comes to my rescue by tugging my sleeve and mouthing to me, "Over The Top."

"Oh, right," I say out loud.

Galleria turns her head like she just got whiplash. "Thank gooseness it's time to break out," she groans.

"You sure you don't want us to wait with you?" Ms. Dorothea asks as the rest of the Cheetah Girls pile out the studio.

"No, ma'am," I reply quickly. We have to wait for Daddy to pick us up. I'm sort of disappointed that he wasn't eagerly waiting for us in the reception area.

Turning back around, Ms. Dorothea asks, "What do you think? That Mouse really knows how to nibble on a song, huh?"

"Yes, ma'am," squeals Angie. "He could sell sour milk to cows!"

Cindy waves good-bye. I wonder what time she gets to go home. She obviously works really long hours.

"Hurry up and wait, isn't it always the case," Angie whines, plopping down on the comfortable beanbag couch. "I wish we had one of these bad boys at home."

I wish so, too—like the hot-pink one they have in the Ooophelia catalog, which I pull out of the my backpack and devour the pages. The only comfortable chair in the living room is the leather recliner chair, and that's Daddy's domain. We don't even sit it in when he isn't home.

The phone rings and Cindy answers, then yells out to Mouse, "London on line one!"

I guess that is the call he has been waiting for. I wonder which Big Willie is on the phone. I know it can't be Seal, since he was just here a few hours ago. Even on the fastest flight—from New York to London it takes hours."

"I liked the second version of the song," Angie says, rubbing her eyes.

"I liked the last one," I retort.

"Well, we'll see which one he picks," Angie counters. "That is, if he picks any at all."

Right now, the only thing I wanted to pick is a new bedspread out of the Ooophelia catalog. I rest my head on Angie's shoulders. "Do you think Ms. Dorothea told Mouse yet?" she asks, mumbling.

"Don't know, don't care," I answer back and for

once I really mean it. I close my eyes and, before I almost drift off, I mumble to Angie, "Don't you wonder who Daddy is seeing?"

"All's I know is, she'd better not be bringing over any recipes for brews," Angie mumbles back, then jabs me sharply in the side like she's wielding a red-hot cattle prod. I whip my head up so I can "cuss her out," and there's Daddy coming into the reception area. I sure didn't hear him open the door! Mouse should put musical chimes on his studio entrance, like the ones they have at Pepto B's hair salon, Churl, It's You!

"Good evening," Daddy says, tipping his cowboy hat to Cindy. She smiles warmly at him, even though she is on the phone. Daddy has been "tippin' out" with someone special—*again*. He only wears his cowboy hat and leather coat when he wants to look sharp. I can tell that Daddy had a good time, too. "How did your jam session go?" Daddy asks, pleased.

"I think it went real good," I say, looking to Angie for collaboration. I like that term Daddy uses—"jam session." I know it's an old-school term folks use when talking about jazz and blues musicians who used to play in smoky basement clubs and used real instruments like the saxophone, upright bass, and clarinet. Daddy loves jazz.

"Yes, sir. It went just fine. If the record company doesn't like the harmony we laid down on the Midget Man track, then they must have wax in their ears," Angie says, getting awfully chatty.

"Midget Man?" Daddy asks, raising his eyebrow in a suspicious manner. "The things people name their children."

I decide it's best not to point out to Daddy that Midget Man's mother probably had nothing to do with his music industry moniker, but I decide to clamp my mouth shut instead. Little does Daddy know how kids used to tease us in school because of our nursery rhyme names—Aquanette and Anginette.

After we get in the car, Angie asks Daddy, "You talk to Big Momma tonight?"

"Yes, I did," Daddy says, keeping his eyes on the steering wheel. "Her legs done swelled up like watermelons."

We both get real quiet. Big Momma is having all these problems because of her selfish granddaughters. I can just hear her voice scolding us, *"Nettie One, Nettie Two, you should be ashamed of yourselves!"*

Chapter 8

By Saturday, Angie and I are so tired from our wannabe-stars schedule—going to school, then the recording studio, then back home to do homework and finish household chores—we're dragging our behinds like Deputy Droop-A-Long and her dim-witted sidekick. But that's not the only reasons we're stressed out: on top of all that, we still have to get ready for our trip to Houston while we walk on eggshells with the rest of the Cheetah Girls, who are *furious* at us for leaving in a lurch!

"Well, I guess we should thank the Lord our voices are holding up," I grunt at Angie, secretly wishing we didn't have to go to our vocal classes this morning at Drinka Champagne's Conservatory.

"Yeah, but my butt isn't," Angie moans, knocking me in the side with her stupid backpack. "And I'm sick of the way Galleria is treating us. Do you really think they're going to replace us behind our backs?"

"Well, there has to be some reason why Ms. Dorothea hasn't told Mouse Almighty yet that we're leaving, right?" I whisper to Angie. "I wish they would say something already."

Daddy, who is whispering into the phone, snaps his fingers at us to get our attention. We shoot each other knowing looks. *Yup, he is definitely talking to a woman in that quiet voice!*

Acknowledging Daddy's command with dutiful nods, we stand like statues by the front door, waiting patiently for Daddy to finish cooing like a canary into the phone. After a few more minutes, we both start fidgeting with the zippers on our down coats like we're doing a musical duet. *Zip, zip, zippety zip!*

When Daddy hangs up the receiver, we both stand at attention like army recruits waiting for our orders. Knowing Daddy, he probably wants to give us our travel itinerary and go over everything a *thousand* times. Daddy is particular when it comes to us flying the friendly skies.

"I need for you girls to come straight home today after your lessons," he barks, motioning for us to come closer.

"We always come straight home," I shoot back.

Twinkle, Twinkle, Cheetah Stars

"Don't you go out with your friends afterward?" Daddy challenges me.

"Yes, sir, we do—to eat lunch," I say, backing down.

"So, like I said, I need for you to come straight home. I'll fix y'all lunch here. We have to get this house cleaned today," Daddy orders.

We stand there dumbfounded, because Daddy can't be serious. He knows we always go out for lunch with the Cheetah Girls after school, and how important that is to us. *Why don't you clean the house yourself?* I want to scream at him, but my good sense kicks in and I respond, "Yes, sir."

"I can't believe he expects us to clean the house so he can impress some *heffa* while we still have to pack and get ready for Houston!" I fume at Angie when we are out of Daddy's earshot.

Angie shakes her head in agreement. "I can't believe he won't let us go to lunch after class with the Cheetah Girls."

"Yeah, that too!" I add as I chew on the *real* dilemma: now Galleria is going to be doubly upset with us. 1) We can't stay in New York to finish our demo. 2) We can't have lunch with the Cheetah Girls after vocal classes today because we have to go home and clean the house like Cinderella-wannabes instead of wannabe stars.

"Well, I'll guess now they'll really be glad they're replacing us," croaks Angie, her big brown eyes widening with fear as we enter the reception area of Drinka Champagne's Conservatory.

Suddenly, a disco tornado almost knocks us off our feet. "There they are—the fabulous Walker twins!" Drinka Champagne announces gleefully, startling us because she has never greeted us like this before. Clad in a tight red jumpsuit decorated with dangling Christmas ornament balls, Drinka's high-voltage smile is frozen on her face like she's getting ready to perform her 1974 hit dance single, "Bubbles of Love," at a concert or something!

The corners of my mouth curl up on reflex, wondering why she is being so nice to us. Oh, I get it: *She probably already knows that we're getting kicked out of the group!*

"Aqua, are you feeling all right?" Drinka asks, concerned.

Embarrassed that I'm not as good a fake-tress as my other half, I quickly stammer: "Oh, I'm fine, Drinka—just tired because we've been in the studio all week with Mouse Almighty."

"So I've heard!" Drinka says proudly, putting her hands on her hips. "Go join your crew before they talk everybody's ear off about the Cheetah Girls latest *beau-coup*."

Twinkle, Twinkle, Cheetah Stars

I wonder what a *beau-coup* is—probably a fancy French word. Drinka has traveled all over the world performing—unlike us, who probably won't get farther than Texas, because we can't even finish one stupid demo tape! I moan to myself, my heart sinking to my toes by the minute.

Drinka isn't the only one who "peeps" my gloomy disposition.

"Feeling *twizzled*?" Galleria asks glumly when we walk into Studio One. She is huddled with the class "regulars." Besides the rest of the Cheetah Girls, that would be Danitra, Malcolm Extra, Harmony Jones, and Melanie Melody.

"Mouse is definitely pushing you to the *Borderline*," hums Harmony.

"Can it, Madonna," Danitra heckles, whacking Harmony on the shoulder.

Drinka was right. Galleria has probably told everybody all the details about our recording sessions fifty times over. Flashy Malcolm Extra suddenly interrupts with a standing ovation.

"Can we all give the weary-teary Cheetah Girls a big *braaavo, divas!*" he sings in his falsetto voice, jumping up from his chair and clapping his hands. Now we're really blushing like beets.

Galleria and Chanel take a bow. Dorinda grins sheepishly, and I get a sinking feeling in my chest again. Malcolm won't be applauding us when he finds out the truth: *that the fabulous Walker Twins couldn't even stay in New York to finish the Cheetah Girls' demo!*

"Hey, Aqua and Angie, I found something for you," squeals Melanie Melody, pushing a book toward us. Melanie goes to The Julliard School in Lincoln Center, which is right next door to Performing Arts High East, but way more prestigious—and expensive.

"When you gonna tell us your name is *made up*?" Malcolm Extra challenges her.

"It's my real name—"

"Yeah, that's what Jessica *Rabbit* said before she got sued by Roger!" Malcolm throws another one of his infamous darts at Melanie, who he constantly uses for verbal target practice. (We all know Malcolm is crushed that he can't afford to go to Julliard and has to attend the lowly Performing Arts High East instead.)

"Yeah, well I have a birth certificate to prove it—unlike you, orphan Extra!" quips Melanie, then continues shoving the book at me. "Check out your Style horoscope."

"Don't try it, Miss M&M, because I'll truly see if you melt in my mouth for real!" Malcolm snaps. "I'm not an orphan—I live with my aunt—

not a pack of hyenas, like *some* creature critters."

Dorinda freezes. She really is an orphan and doesn't have a birth certificate. At least Malcolm got to live with his aunt when his mother went to prison for credit card fraud, instead of being put in a foster home like Dorinda. I mean, Dorinda doesn't even know what really happened to her birth mother.

Everyone gets silent for a second before Chanel changes the subject. "What happened?" she asks, grabbing the book out of Melanie's hand. Chanel flips through the pages, then squeals, "Style-strology? That's so *coolio*."

"What is it?" Galleria asks curiously.

"Style-strology—get it, *mija*?" coos Chanel. "Here's your sign, Bubbles: 'Gemini is fickle when it comes to fashion, changing her look at the drop of a floppy hat. Being up on the latest trends is more important than seeing the latest movies. Accessories are another *must* since this girl likes to play. Cosmic twin: Naomi Campbell. Must-own item: *Juicy* couture pink cashmere sweater, $250.'"

"Very funny—ha-ha, I get it, Chuchie," Galleria says, acknowledging Chanel's emphasis on the word "juicy." "But I'm not fickle. Whoever wrote this guide doesn't have a Blue's Clue about a

Cheetah Girl's dedication to showing her spots."

Now Galleria swipes the guide from Chanel. "Give me that, Chuchie, before you read yours. That's all you need is another excuse to shop. What about you, Dorinda, do you want to hear your Style-*strology*?"

"Um, no, that's all right—at those prices, I might have to drop out of the zodiac," Dorinda responds, chuckling. We're glad she's not upset about Melanie and Malcolm's foolishness. That's what we love about Dorinda—she lets things roll right off. Unlike Miss Galleria.

"Okay, that leaves the Walker Twins," Galleria says, tearing through the pages until she finds the page for our style-strology: 'Image is *everything* for a Virgo. This girl is always pulled together, favoring clothes that are tastefully understated—rarely trendy or attention-grabbing. Cosmic twin: Sista Fudge. Must-own item: Burberry trench coat, $400.'"

"Well, we like Sista Fudge," Angie says, shrugging her shoulders.

"Oh, I'm sure you can find a Burb trench coat at the *Galleria* when you're back down in Howdyland," Galleria says, handing the guide back to Melanie. Then she pulls a cheetah tissue out of her bag and loudly blows her nose.

"Howdyland—that's funny," says Danitra, giggling.

Yeah, real funny, I think, blushing with embarrassment. Just because we're going home doesn't mean we have money to shop at the Galleria Mall (which Galleria is named after because her mother shopped there when she was a model). Our mother has a humble job as district manager at Avon Cosmetics. She has better things to do with her hard-earned money than buy us $400 Burberry raincoats!

"Is there anything Cheetah you don't have?" Malcolm Extra asks Galleria as she throws her soggy tissue into the wastebasket in the corner of the studio.

"Yeah, tampons—so if you run across any, let me know!" Galleria says sarcastically.

"Sorry! That's not my department," hisses Malcolm Extra, making a circle with his forefinger. "But it's a good thing you have cheetah tissues for your *issues*."

Galleria throws Malcolm a look like, *Whatever*.

"How's Derek?" Danitra bursts out. She obviously has been dying to ask about Derek since she met him at our "Bring It On!" benefit, where they both performed. It looked like she was trying to get her hooks into him all evening.

"Why don't you ask him yourself, since you're obviously *goospitating* over him?" counters Galleria. "Or didn't you get the digits?"

Galleria and Danitra stare at each other like they're at a Mexican standoff.

"Can you believe Christmas is next Saturday?" asks Melanie, trying to break up the tension. "Are you gonna celebrate finishing up the demo?"

"Yeah, we would celebrate, except Aqua and Angie are going to Houston on Friday," Galleria says, exasperated.

"But we could have a mani-pedi party at my house on Tuesday night, couldn't we, *mija*?" Chanel says sweetly. "This way your toes will look nice for the trip, *está bien*?"

"That would be real nice," I say, nodding at Chanel. Bless her heart.

Angie looks at me, then turns back to Chanel, "Yeah, that *would* be nice. Daddy would be happy, too, if we saved money."

"Can I come and get my toes done too—even though I'm not going anywhere?" begs Danitra, staring down at her raggedy *Boomerang* toenails speckled with traces of hot-pink glitter polish that looks like it was applied last year.

"Attention, everyone!" Wolfgang, the pianist, announces when he walks into the studio—our signal to take our seats. Miss Bettina, one of the vocal instructors, comes in right behind him and begins class.

"Since I won't be seeing you until next year," Miss Bettina starts in, acknowledging our upcoming holiday break, "I thought we should concentrate on upper register work today. And you will continue your exercises at home, right?"

"Right," we groan back. Upper register work is the hardest for most of the students—especially Dorinda, Chanel, and Melanie.

"Okay, warm-up time." Bettina instructs us, guiding us through our breathing exercises. I try to relax into it, but all I can think about is how much I dread telling the rest of the Cheetah Girls we have to run home today like little kids.

By the end of the class, I have gotten myself so worked up that I can't wait to grab Angie and nuzzle next to her, whispering in her ear, "Maybe we should go live with our mother?" Maybe all this aggravation we go through in New York isn't worth having to put up with Daddy and his mean behavior. Coaxing Angie to come to a decision, I try to sweeten the pie: "We could just take Porgy and Bess—and Coco—back home with us. Ma would gladly welcome them. And we can just go to regular high school instead of a performing arts school."

"What are you two whispering about?" Chanel asks, quickly siding up to us as we all exit the studio.

"Nothing," we reply in unison.

Chanel absorbs our fib like a sponge: "Did I sound okay?" she squeaks, looking for reassurance.

"You were medi-okra," Malcolm Extra says, cutting in.

"You're so-o-o-o *mala*, Malcolm," Chanel hisses.

"Don't listen to him," Dorinda offers. "You hit all the notes—on point, *mamacita*. I'm the one who should be worrying."

"Where we going—Mo'Burger or Mo'Betta?" Galleria asks.

"What's Mo'Betta?"

"Anywhere besides Mo'Burger, that's what," Galleria says, holding her lip gloss wand to her mouth and pursing her lips in midair.

Angie looks around like she doesn't have anything to say, which annoys me, because that means I'm going to have to do the talking as usual. "Um, we have to straight home today," I mumble so low that nobody hears me over all the cackling. I don't have the nerve to say it again, so I just walk, embarrassed, into the reception area. Ms. Winnie smiles at us, then chortles, "All right now, Cheetah

Girls, y'all keep giving that Mouse something to nibble on in that studio!"

As we're waiting for the elevator, Drinka Champagne yells out from Studio Two, obviously trying to catch our attention. "Don't you girls leave without saying good-bye!" she quips, startling me again.

"No, ma'am," I reply automatically. I'd swear Drinka was looking directly at me when she said that, but she probably was talking to all of us.

When she comes out and places her hands on the hips of her red jumpsuit, causing her Christmas ornaments to really "jingle," I realize that I'm right. "So, you girls are all set for the holidays?" she asks, staring directly at Angie and me.

"Um, yeah," I stammer.

"Well, I'll be seeing you girls *real* soon," Drinka says, her long false eyelashes fluttering along to their own private Morse code.

"Yes, ma'am," Angie replies.

"Why is Drinka up in your barbecue grill?" Malcolm Extra queries as we pile into the elevator. I guess even he noticed that Drinka showered the fabulous Walker twins with some "Bubbles of Love."

"I'm surprised she didn't ask about that 'handsome father of yours,'" Galleria says, mimicking

Drinka. "You should have seen Mr. Walker's face when Drinka was showing off her concert photos. He blanched like an almond!"

"Who wouldn't? She dressed up in metal chains and was carried onstage by bare-chested body-builders, hello?" heckles Harmony.

"That cowboy hat your father was wearing was, well, *extra*!" Malcolm Extra chimes in, practically cracking himself up.

Now I'm blushing from ear to ear.

"You are so-o-o *malo*, Malcolm," Chanel says, shaking her head. "Bad boy."

"As long as he digs it—since he's wearing it," Dorinda says, sticking up for us.

"Okay, for real—let's get some Atomic Wings," Galleria says, gazing down the block.

"Um, we have to go straight home," I say in a louder voice. This time I know Galleria can hear me.

"What happened?" Chanel asks. "You're not coming with us?"

"What's up, whack attack?" Galleria asks, annoyed.

"We have to go home—that's all," I say, stammering.

"Whatever makes you clever," Galleria says, staring at me with that piercing pout she puts on when she's really annoyed. "Come on, let's bounce."

The rest of the Cheetah Girls follow Galleria, as Angie and I put our cheetah tails between our legs and walk in the other direction toward the subway.

"Maybe you're right," Angie moans. "We should stay in Houston. They don't want us in the Cheetah Girls anymore."

Chapter 9

By the time we get home, Angie and I look as sullen as two convicted jailbirds reporting to work in a chain gang. Only thing we need now are those ugly striped gray jumpsuits so we can look like real prisoners! Daddy has obviously been busy all morning. He has put up the Christmas tree in the living room, and points to the boxes of ornaments on the floor. "Y'all can start putting those up after lunch."

Trim it yourself! I want to scream. It's not like we're gonna be here on Christmas Day to enjoy looking at it—all lit up. Angie and I march to the kitchen and stare at the plate of tuna sandwiches on the counter. I'm so upset that I poke out my mouth like Galleria does when she's mad.

"Tuna's okay?" Daddy says, wondering why we are sitting at the counter like statues. He goes to the kitchen and starts unpacking bags of groceries from the Piggly Wiggly. He obviously went to Home Depot, too, because there are a ton more bags lining the dining-room wall. Angie and I eat our sandwiches in silence.

After Daddy finishes putting the groceries in the refrigerator, he lays out a clear plastic throw by the windowsill. I notice the can of paint and brushes and rolling pans. Daddy notices me staring at the paint utensils and says, "Don't worry—I'll do all that. I'm gonna touch up the windowsills."

Now I know a woman is coming over, because Daddy has clearly lost his mind! I can't believe we have to go through all this trouble to clean the house, when we're the ones going away. We're not entertaining anybody—he is!

"I'll need for the both of you to clean the guest room and put new sheets on the bed in there," Daddy says. "Did you hear me?"

"Yes, sir," Angie mumbles.

"Aqua?"

"Yes, sir," I say, fighting back the tears. If he knew how dumb we looked today in front of the rest of the Cheetah Girls, he wouldn't ask us to do another dag-on thing till we leave!

I roll my eyes around like pool balls. Then I notice the big plastic bags next to the painting supplies. I hope Daddy didn't get our Christmas presents at Home Depot, or I'm putting *myself* up for adoption!

"Can I look inside, Daddy?" I ask, pointing to the bags stacked like potato sacks in the corner. Daddy has gone on quite a shopping spree, and I'd like to know *why*.

"What is all that stuff?" Angie asks, curious by all the packages as well.

"Go find out," orders Daddy.

"Oooh, look at these," Angie says, pulling out two black frosted glass vases. I wonder what she is "oohing and aahing" about. They just look like plain flower vases to me. Angie catches my expression and quickly adds, "We can make our own designs on them—see, here's the chalk," she says, pulling out a package of chalk from inside the vase.

"I'm not in the mood for arts-and-crafts class at the moment. I have to go clean the guest room," I mumble, feeling glum as a goat.

Angie starts making heart shapes on the vase. "Don't overdo it," Daddy says.

"Yes, sir," Angie says, happily drawing away like she's discovered her inner artist. I want to bonk her over the head so she can start discovering the Lysol spray and sponge! I jab her in the side and motion for her to follow me upstairs. At least we'll be alone up there—slaving away.

"Cinderella has got nothing on us!" I gripe, grabbing the clean linens out of the closet and shoving a pile toward Angie.

"I bet Ma put him up to this, just so we could learn our lesson," Angie grumbles back.

"Yeah, so we'll be real grateful to see her Wednesday. So grateful, we won't mind cleaning her dirty house, too!" I wince.

Angie nods in agreement. We couldn't believe how messy Ma's house was when we visited her for Thanksgiving. I bet she has reverted back to her old ways in our absence. She confided in us how lonely she is being divorced from Daddy and not having us to look after.

"We better not say one word about Daddy dating anybody," I advise my nosy twin sister. It still makes me so sad thinking about Ma sitting all by her lonesome in our old house.

"Maybe she's dating Fred Fish," chuckles Angie, referring to the homeless man in the band, Fish 'N Chips, who performed with us at the "Houston Helps Its Own" benefit. Fred and Ma got along like, well, fish-and-chips. Ma even invited Fred over for dinner right before we left Houston.

"Big Bird would stand a better chance," I snarl

back. We both know the truth about our parents: Ma is *real* snobby and Daddy is *real* mean. "At the rate Daddy's going, I'm gonna have to borrow a magnifying glass from science class to find the rest of Daddy's good points," I moan in despair.

By the time we finish cleaning the guest room, our bedroom, and the bathrooms, we drag ourselves to our room without brushing our teeth. I am so tired that I fall on my knees to say my prayers. All I can think of to say to God tonight is: *Please tell Daddy to hire a maid while we're away!*

When I open my eyes on Sunday morning, I just want to praise God and shout "Hallelujah!" because it is a brand-new day, indeed. Yesterday was just like watching a bad remake of *Nightmare on Elm Street* over *and* over again. Don't get me wrong, everybody knows that I could watch horror movies twenty-four hours straight—as long as the bad guy gets demolished in the end—but we all know that's not what happened yesterday, 'cause Daddy sure didn't get his!

"What is that smell?" Angie says, sniffing the air.

"If I didn't know any better, I'd swear Daddy was cooking Texas barbecue," I humph, wondering if my big flared nostrils are deceiving me. "Lord, I must be hallucinating from all that housework!"

Twinkle, Twinkle, Cheetah Stars

"I bet *she* is coming over for dinner tonight!" Angie gripes, referring to Daddy's mystery date. For once I think Angie is right. Crawling out of her bed in a huff, Angie puts on her white terry-cloth bathrobe—no, I take that back—*my* terry-cloth bathrobe, and peers at her face into the etched heart-shaped mirror hanging over our dresser. "Just what I need, a stupid pimple," Angie says, trying to poke away the whitehead with her index finger.

"Well, it's in good company," I mumble. "You'd better stop sneaking those sodas at school—and could you please put on your own bathrobe, ma'am?"

Angie switches bathrobes while taking a swipe at my soda-drinking habits: "Take it, you guzzle queen." She's right. I drink Coca-Colas every chance I get, even though Daddy says soda is not good for our vocal chords. Well, our vocal chords are working just fine—but if Daddy keeps giving us all these Cinderella cleaning assignments, our complexions are going to break out from all the chimney soot!

As I bend down to get Porgy and Bess's water bowl, I feel a terrible crick in my neck. "Oh, lord, my neck is gonna fall off. Can you massage it for me?" I ask Angie, who is standing by our bureau, carefully placing her silver cross in its designated compartment in the white jewelry box Big Momma gave us last Christmas.

"Only if you massage my feet!" Angie says, grabbing her tube of Pineapple Slush-Fuss Body Scrub and limping into the bathroom.

"What's the matter, your dogs are barking?" I ask her sarcastically.

I follow Angie, wedging my body in between the bathroom door. "I can't believe Daddy hasn't even given us our Christmas shopping money so we can buy our presents before we leave on Friday."

"Well, call the SWAT roach spray team and tell them!" Angie says, pushing me out of the bathroom and shoving the door shut so she can shower. I can't believe my own sister still feels uncomfortable about getting undressed in front of me. After all, we are twins with the same identical body—big hips, big butts, and big feet with corns and bunions!

Flopping down on my bed, I stare at the pile of sneakers squashed in the bottom of the closet like a bunch of grungy rug rats. I try to ignore them, but I can't. I must be turning into an inspector from Mr. Clean, just like Daddy! I fold my hands across my chest defiantly and force myself to look anywhere else but in the bottom of the closet. It doesn't do much good, because now I notice the dust on the bureau! Getting up in a huff, I wipe the dust off the bureau, then rearrange the shoes and sneakers in the closet.

I can't help it: all we want to do is please Daddy. I try to stay angry at him, but I realize that our room does look more organized. Too bad I can't invite somebody over, to show it off!

When we get downstairs half an hour later, it turns out that staying mad at Daddy isn't going to be hard at all: he is down our throats again like a drill sergeant in the Marines.

"Did you clean your room?"

"Yes, sir, we did."

"You made your beds, too?" he asks, challenging our definition of clean.

"Yes, we did," Angie and I say in unison.

We sit there speechless, looking at all the food preparation. Now Daddy is sticking pineapple slices on a roasted glazed ham. Daddy must have gotten up with the crows at the crack of dawn to do all this cooking!

"I need for you two to peel the potatoes and cube them for the potato salad," Daddy says, pointing to the metal strainer in the sink filled with whole cooked potatoes.

"I wish you had told us you were cooking for—um—someone. We would have helped you," I stammer. What, is he ashamed of our cooking, all of sudden?

"Well, you're helping me now," Daddy retorts.

"But don't we have to go to church?" I ask, because Daddy knows we leave at nine-thirty on Sunday mornings for the early service.

"No, you're not going to church today—we have too much to do before—" Daddy stops himself in midsentence. "Just help me finish, all right, instead of sitting there doing nothing."

Doing nothing? My cheeks are stinging from bee bites again! But before I say something that will get me into trouble, I march over to the sink and start peeling the potatoes. Angie gets an onion out of the refrigerator and sets it on the cutting board, then thwacks the knife in a loud, staccato rhythm to cube the onion slices.

"Don't forget to put some bacon bits and relish in the potato salad," Daddy barks to Angie. We shoot each other looks to communicate our surprise: *He's using Big Momma's secret potato salad recipe to impress some heffa!*

At last one thing is clear: the mystery date can't possibly be Daddy's kooky ex-girlfriend, High Priestess Aballa Shaballa, because she *hates*

Southern food. All she ever indulged in were disgusting Mogo Hexagone shakes and brews—that's how we knew she was up to no good. No normal person would pass up corn bread dripping with butter for dee-gusting concoctions from a galaxy we never even heard of.

After we spend all morning helping Daddy cook his Sunday feast, Daddy tells us he has to go upstairs and change. Then he comes back down in a clean white shirt and slacks, while we're still cooking and preparing the rest of the food. "Y'all set the table. I'll be back around three o'clock."

"Where you going, Daddy?" I ask. I can't take his mysterious behavior anymore.

"Never mind all that—just do what I tell you," Daddy says, plugging in the Christmas tree lights, then grabbing his white Stetson hat off the coatrack. Angie and I run to the window and peek through the blinds while Daddy tears down the street in his white Bronco like he's in a big hurry.

"I bet you he's going to pick *her* up," Angie says, pursing her lips.

"You're on," I counter, even though I'm unsure what to think. "Shoot, Daddy could be going to the Twilight Zone, for all we know. 'Cause he sure is acting spooky." Looking at Angie, I know exactly what she is thinking: too bad we can't call

Galleria to ask her what she thinks about all this. She always knows the answers to everything, but she is too mad with us right now for us to call and indulge in "cheetah chatter."

"I'm gonna call Dorinda and see how she's doing," I say. Angie nods in agreement. Truth is, I'm hoping Dorinda will spill the barbecued beans about what's going on behind our backs. If Angie and I are being replaced, then we might as well find out sooner rather than later. "Wouldn't you hate to come back from Houston and find out we are cheetah-less?" I ask Angie absentmindedly.

"So, what are we betting?" Angie asks, ignoring me. "You can do my math homework for a week when we go back to school?"

I want to wipe that "smugly" expression off Angie's face, but she's probably right about both things. 1) Daddy is going to bring home some strange woman. 2) What's the point in fretting about being replaced.

Clearing my head, I counter Angie's bet: "Or, you do my Spanish homework if you're wrong. How do you like those apples?"

Angie moans. She hates Spanish homework more than I do. "Well, I won't have to worry about that, *mamacita*, because I'm gonna win. So you'd better giddyap and sharpen your pencils for all that math homework," Angie says, sashaying over to the kitchen counter and twirling the head of lettuce.

"Yes, ma'am—you're always right," I nod, dialing Dorinda's home.

One of Dorinda's sisters answer the phone. I can't tell which one, so I just say "hi."

"Hi," she responds, then gets silent.

"Hi," I repeat again, waiting for her to say something.

"Who is it?" I hear someone yelling in the background.

"It's for me!" the unknown sister snaps back.

I hear her sister break out into a wail of giggles as Dorinda takes the receiver from her and speaks into it. "That was my sister Twinkie—she wishes she had her own phone."

"Don't we all," I say, chuckling. "I just wanted to see how my favorite Cheetah Girl is holding up."

"This schedule is no joke." Dorinda laughs. "Mrs. Bosco is real cool about the situation, though. I mean, she's happy I'm doing my Cheetah Girls' thing. It's just that she's going bonkers now that I can't help her after school."

"Lord, I can imagine," I respond sympathetically. Since Dorinda brought up the word "schedule," I decide to dive right into my cheetah-fishing expedition. "Look, I know Galleria and everybody is upset that Angie and I are going—"

"Handle your Houston business—don't worry about that situation," Dorinda says, interrupting me. My stomach sinks like a crab pushed to the bottom of a barrel. She *does* know something. Using her cheerful Southern drawl, Dorinda adds, "Y'all must be getting ready today for your trip, huh?"

"Well, not now—we're cooking," I blurt out, feeling sorry for the poor Walker twins who might be kicked to a Houston curb in a minute.

"Give me the phone," Angie says, swiping the receiver from me.

"We got Texas barbecue—yes ma'am," Angie says, nodding enthusiastically.

I wonder why she is showing off. Daddy is the one who cooked the meat, not us.

"Texas barbecue is all about the meat—you don't smother it in sauce or nothing. You just cook it enough so it falls off the bone when you eat it," Angie explains like she's on a cooking show talking to the studio audience!

Angie ignores my glare and goes on and on about all the food we're preparing, till I can almost hear Dorinda salivating at the gills. I grab the phone back and talk to Dorinda some more.

"Please mind her manners. We would invite you over if we could, but Daddy obviously has some other plans for all this food."

Dorinda can tell I'm upset because she finally tells me for reassurance: "Aqua—stop sweating it. Nothing's going to stop our cheetah train. That's all I'm saying."

"Well, I hope you're right," I sigh deeply, then tell her about all the drama that is going on in our house, and she tells me about all the drama that is going on in hers.

"Now Corky's father is trying to make it sound like he's suing for custody because Mrs. Bosco is an unfit mother," she whispers.

But the screaming gets so loud in Dorinda's house that she can hardly hear herself talk. Apparently her sister Twinkie is yelling about getting back down to the laundry room before someone steals their clothes. Now I feel bad for keeping her on the phone, so I tell her good-bye and to "hang in there."

"I will—like a chimpanzee," Dorinda chuckles.

"Okay now, but watch out for Tony the Tiger!" I yell before hanging up. We still can't believe that one of the tenants in Dorinda's building was keeping a four-hundred-pound tiger in his bedroom until the police discovered it. Now I realize how lucky we are that we don't have to live in the proj-ects, with pets that are ready to pounce—*literally*.

I plop down on the couch and yawn. All I want to do now is take a nap, but I know Daddy would skin me alive if he came home and found us sprawled out on *his* couch. Shoot, maybe living in the projects wouldn't be so bad after all! I sit for a few minutes staring at the blinking Christmas lights on the tree. It sure does look pretty. Angie and I did a real good job of decorating the tree. We trimmed it with all the white ornaments, garlands, and lights, just the way Daddy likes it.

Yawning again and drifting into a daze, my mind starts wandering from "I wonder if Dorinda has a Christmas tree" to "Shoot, Daddy didn't even thank us for making the house look good."

Leave it to my sister to snap me back to the drudgery at hand. "Get your butt in here and help me!" Angie snarls from the kitchen.

Dragging myself back to the dining room, we start fixing the dining table and side table and get-ting everything ready for the feast we're going to share with somebody who could turn out to be a mean ole witch. "The hearts look real nice," I say to Angie, admiring the designs she painted on the smoked-glass vases Daddy bought. They're filled with big bouquets of pretty yellow roses, which makes me think about Ma, because she loves yellow roses. "Too bad she's not here to see them," I mutter under my breath.

Angie and I polish the crystal glasses in silence until she blurts out exactly what I have been thinking: "If somebody came in here and saw how pretty everything looks, they wouldn't know we are now living with a crazy man!"

Chapter 10

True to his word, Daddy pulls up in the driveway at half past three. Angie rushes over to the window, but I call her back. "Don't do that!"

We sit our butts down at the counter, waiting for Daddy to open the door.

"Please don't let her be a witch!" I grumble. Angie and I sit with bated breath like those anxious contestants on *The Price Is Right*, waiting to see what is behind Doors Number One, Two, and Three.

When the door pops open, we can't believe our eyes.

"HONEY, I'M HOME!" screams our Uncle Skeeter, bursting into the living room. He plops down his suitcase and stands there with outstretched arms. Angie lets out a big squeal. Tears well up in my eyes as I sit frozen for a second before I run over and wrap my arms around my favorite uncle in the whole world.

Angie runs outside and I can hear her squealing, "Omigod!"

"Go help your Daddy with the rest of the bags," Uncle Skeeter says proudly.

I am crying so hard, the lapel on the left side of his jacket is soaked. "I'm so sorry, Uncle Skeeter—this is a real nice suit!" I say, admiring the burgundy pinstriped suit he is wearing.

Uncle Skeeter gives me his handkerchief, and I blow my nose before Daddy sees me carrying on like a big fool. He takes the used hankie from me and gently pushes me outside the door. I stand frozen in the driveway, watching Angie hugging Ma real tight.

"You got us *real* good! We didn't know you were coming!" Angie squeals with delight, like Babe the pig. Then she starts jumping up and down and squealing even louder.

Ma breaks out in the biggest grin. "Shoot, you ain't the only drama queen around here. You got it from me!"

Suddenly our upstairs neighbor pulls back the curtains in her front window and glances at us to see what the commotion is all about. Ma looks up and waves at the window. Our neighbor, Mrs.

Solomon doesn't wave back. She just smiles tersely, then lets the curtain drop. Meanwhile, Daddy is helping Big Momma out of the Bronco. She stands in place holding onto her cane, and I start bawling like a baby all over again.

Big Momma looks right in my direction. "Come here, Nettie One!" she says with a sly smile on her face. I try to stop crying, but I just can't. Through my slobbering tears, I try talking: "I can't believe you came."

She pats me on the back. "Now, we couldn't be getting in the way of y'all making some record. Come on now." Big Momma says, smiling.

"Well, we ain't exactly making a record. It's a demo so we can see if the record company will give us a deal," I explain, embarrassed. I don't want Big Momma to get her hopes up too high.

"Never you mind—the Lord will find a way to make it happen," Big Momma says, making me realize that I'm the one who's worried about getting too hopeful.

But right now, looking at Big Momma's grin, I feel like we can soar higher than Wonder Woman. "Yes, ma'am," I say, putting my arm under Big Momma's as we walk inside.

"When you leaving?" Angie asks excitedly, trying to peek inside of the Uncle Funky's shopping bag Ma is clutching tightly in her hand. It's obvious the bag is stuffed with Christmas presents. Ma knows that Uncle Funky's Boutique is one of our favorite stores in Houston.

"We just got here—you trying to get rid of us already?" Ma asks, slapping Angie's hand and pulling it out of her shopping bag. "We're going back on Monday."

When we get inside, everybody oohs and aahs over the Christmas tree. I beam at Daddy with pride. I'm so embarrassed for thinking all those terrible things about him earlier that I can hardly look him in the eye.

"Lord, look at his snow globe collection—it done grown twice in size!" Big Momma exclaims as Daddy proudly shows her his latest purchase—the Times Square snow globe. Angie and I carry their luggage upstairs and put it in the guest room. "Put mine in your father's room," Ma instructs us.

"So you're sleeping in Daddy's room?" I ask, hoping it means what I think it means—that maybe they're getting back together. But Ma sticks a pin in my balloon.

"Yeah, but Mr. Walker will be sleeping on the couch," Ma announces.

As we set Ma's luggage down on the floor in

Daddy's room, Angie chides, "By the time they leave, I bet you they'll be sleeping in the *same* room."

"You still owe me from the last bet!" I exclaim to Angie in disbelief. She's not wiggling her way out of this one. "You lost—Daddy didn't bring back no new girlfriend!"

"Well," Angie says, twisting her neck, poking out her mouth, and putting her hands on her hips. "Technically, I didn't lose the bet, because I said he was probably going to get *her*, and that is exactly who he brought back to this house! I didn't say which *her*!"

Clapping my hands, I retort, "And the Academy Award for Best Fake-tress—oops, I mean, Actress—goes to the trifling Anginette Vivian Walker!"

"Thank you, ma'am—I'll take any award I can get," Angie says slyly. All of a sudden, Angie's eyes light up, and I realize that she is thinking the same thing I am: "Daddy did go out on a date last week with *somebody*, didn't he?"

"He sure did," I say, staring over at his dresser and catching a glimpse of his new cologne. Picking up the bottle, I try to pronounce the name on the label—*Homme Sensual*, but I can't, because I don't understand French. "I'm sure it means 'stinky scent'!" I say, giggling.

Angie and I head back downstairs. Ma takes the

presents out of the shopping bag and puts them under the tree. Daddy goes into the closet and pulls out a shopping bag from the back. Angie and I shoot each other a look. We didn't even see that one! He puts some more presents under the tree, till it looks like Christmas for real! Before dinner, Uncle Skeeter entertains us all by playing his harmonica. "I'm so glad you're still playing that!" I exclaim, remembering how much fun we had at the "Houston Helps Its Own" benefit. When we performed there with the Cheetah Girls, we even hooked up Uncle Skeeter up with the homeless band Fish 'n' Chips.

"We were so proud of you performing with them!" Angie exclaims, hugging Uncle Skeeter so hard, he loses his concentration.

"Fred Fish has been over a few times for dinner," Ma says, a wicked smile creeping into the corners of her mouth.

"You're in love!" I say, embarrassing Ma. "Mr. And Mrs. Fish 'n' Chips!"

"Don't push it, sister." Ma gives me a firm look. "Only thing I'm in love with is paying my bills, young lady. That's true love, okay?"

"I know that's right," Big Momma says, chuckling at our nonsense.

"All right, everybody ready for dinner?" Daddy

asks, jumping up from the couch. Somehow we get the feeling that talking about love has made Daddy uncomfortable.

Angie and I help Daddy put all the food on serving platters to set on the sideboard.

"Thank you, Daddy," I say quietly, when the three of us are alone in the kitchen.

"You're welcome," he says. And without missing a beat, he takes the glass Pyrex dish filled with his famous macaroni and cheese out of the oven. I'm so proud of him for being such a good cook. I guess that's another thing we have in common with Galleria: we both have fathers who can cook up a storm. All of a sudden, I can't wait to talk to Galleria and tell her everything!

"Oooh, the crust is perfect," I exclaim with delight.

"Always is," Daddy says confidently. I look over at Daddy and stare at him when he's not looking. All this time, we thought he was a mean person (you have to admit, not letting us bring Coco home was a real misde-mean-or in our book!). But no *real* mean person would do all the things that Daddy does for us. Or make the kind of sacrifices he has made for us since we came to live with him in New York. No, sireee, it turns out Daddy isn't crazy at all. But he sure can keep a secret.

Twinkle, Twinkle, Cheetah Stars

When we sit at the table, Big Momma says grace, and it brings tears to my eyes.

"Lord, thank you for allowing me to make the journey up here to spend time with the only people in the world who matter to me—my precious family. I know you move in mysterious ways, and we're grateful to have the good sense to follow you wherever that may be. Thank you for watching over my precious granddaughters as they make their way—wearing all those wild clothes and doing what you put them here to do—singing. And thank you for this wonderful feast we are about to eat. Amen."

"Now I know why Daddy made Texas barbecue!" Angie says, squealing at Uncle Skeeter like she finally figured out a prize-winning riddle.

"Yes, sirree, because everybody knows I'm a *carnivore*!" Uncle Skeeter shouts, then lets out a laugh that could scare coyotes back into the hills. "And everybody knows that my favorite animal is a *rack of lamb*!" We chuckle at our crazy Uncle Skeeter and watch with amazement as he chomps on the ribs like a prisoner on parole. "Mmm-hmm—Johnnie Walker—you sure put your foot in this food!"

"The girls helped, too," Daddy says proudly.

"Indeed—don't think I don't know my own potato salad recipe when I taste it!" Big Momma says, nodding in approval.

After dinner, Angie and I can't wait to pull Ma aside. "Can we call Galleria now and have you just say hi to her and her mom, Ms. Dorothea?" I ask excitedly.

Ma smiles and dials Galleria's house. "Yeah, let's see what Miss Galleria is up to."

"Good evening—who am I speaking to?" Ma says, putting on her professional, sweet voice. After the person responds, Ma says proudly, "This is Mrs. Walker—the twins' mother." Ma shakes her head at us, grinning. "How are you doing, Miss Galleria. People are still talking about the stir you caused in Houston!"

We can't wait to grab the phone from Ma. We stand there and let them talk for a few more minutes until we can't stand it anymore.

"We're in the house with Mouse until you need us!" I yell into the receiver before Galleria can say anything.

"Well, I do declare, you sure gave us a mighty scare," Galleria says, giggling and using her ridiculous Southern accent. Angie and I are holding hands and jumping up and down. Daddy shoots us a stern look but doesn't say anything.

"My mom wants to talk to your ma," Galleria says, tickled by the exchange.

I hand the phone to Ma again. After Ma finishes

talking to Ms. Dorothea, Angie grabs the phone like she always does before someone can finish a conversation in peace. "Were you going to replace us?" she boldly asks Ms. Dorothea.

I follow my sister's rude manners and grab the phone from her. "What an imagination you two have," Ms. Dorothea says to me, surprised. "We will see you tomorrow evening?"

"Yes, ma'am," I reassure Ms. Dorothea. "We will be there with Christmas bells on!"

Ms. Dorothea chuckles. "Darling, leave the bells and whistles at home—just bring your cheetah-licious selves, okay?"

I feel my cheeks glowing in the dark. This was the first time Ms. Dorothea ever called us *cheetah-licious*. It really is a brand-new day, indeed! I want to scream praise from the rooftop, but go over and give Big Momma a big hug instead, and plant a big kiss right on her forehead: "Guess we know where we got our cheetah-licious-ness from in the first place!"

Chapter 11

I think Ma is more excited about going to Mouse Almighty's studio today than we are. And believe me, we're excited—now that we have *finally* squashed our barbecued beef jerky with the Cheetah Girls at last. As a matter of fact, Angie and I plan on raising the roof off Mouse's studio this afternoon, like Southern church-choir girls should.

"Yes, ma'am. If we don't get a record deal with Def Duck after this, it's not going to be the Huggy Bear Twins' fault," I say confidently to Angie, using the nasty nickname Galleria gave us behind our backs when we first met her and Chanel at the Kats and Kittys' Fourth of July barbecue. We found out later that they were aghast at how many hot dogs we were shoveling in our mouths while swatting flies.

Ma is standing by the security guard in the

building lobby, looking like an eager fawn about to dart into the woods. "Do I look cheetah-licious enough for Ms. Dorothea?" Ma asks nervously, fussing with the yellow carnation in the lapel of her powder-blue suit. "I hope so, 'cause I musta changed three times!"

Even though Ma looks more like an Avon representative about to unleash the latest spring bouquet fragrances on the world instead of "growl power," I smartly decide to heap on a big helping of encouragement. "You fit right in the jiggy jungle!"

"What about my shoes?" Ma says in an agitated tone. "See that scuff mark there?"

We both examine Ma's ivory pumps like forensic psychologists looking for clues. "There, I see a little dirt mark right there on the side," Angie says, pulling an antibacterial wipe out of her purse and bending down quickly. (We have learned the hard way to always be prepared for anything in the Big Apple.)

"I was over on Fifth Avenue, and this woman was walking so fast, she stepped right on my foot," Ma exclaims in surprise. "I yelled after her, 'Excuse me, you forgot to step on my *other* foot!' I mean, where are these folks's manners?"

"Fifth Avenue is always crowded with buffalo

about to stampede. They don't have any manners," Angie chuckles, then jumps up. "There, it's off."

"Well, alrighty, then. Thank you, Nettie Two," Ma says, flashing her pretty smile as we climb into the tiny, cramped elevator that looks like it would collapse if Fat Albert stepped into it.

I notice Ma eyeing the dirty ceiling, so I blurt out, "There's a lot of old buildings in New York like this." I just don't want Ma to think that Mouse Almighty is nibbling on his last piece of cheese or something.

"And I bet he is paying an arm and a turkey leg for the privilege of risking his life every morning in this rickety contraption!" Ma smiles and, folds her beige overcoat over her arm. "How they get away with these rents should be against the law."

Now I can't help wondering if Ma is freezing to death wearing such a lightweight coat in this icy weather, but I know the only other winter coat she brought with her is a red wool wrap coat. Even though it's probably warmer—it doesn't match her outfit. Trust me, Ma would rather freeze to death than not match. I guess that is what makes her a "diva," just like Ms. Dorothea, even though the two of them couldn't be less alike. Speaking of divas, Angie and I have our fingers (and toes) crossed in hopes that the two "divas" will get along. We're also wondering if she and Daddy are getting along. They certainly haven't argued since Ma has been here—at least not in front of us.

"Are you and Daddy getting back together?" Angie asks, nuzzling up to Ma.

"Have you lost your mind, Nettie Two?" Ma responds sharply. "Only reason I'm here is because I know how important this whole thing is for y'all."

"Yes, ma'am," Angie replies quietly.

My eyes start to tear up.

"Don't ruin your makeup," warns Ma.

"If we get a record deal, first thing I'm getting you is a fox-fur coat with gray silver tips," I say proudly.

"Never mind all that, Nettie One. If I were you, my first agenda would be replacing those ugly bedspreads in your room!" Ma says, chuckling. Angie and I howl. We knew Ma wouldn't like the way Daddy fixed up the apartment. "Lord, what was he thinking? It looks like a field of blue mushrooms growing on your beds."

Angie and I try hard to suppress our desire to burst out laughing at Daddy, but we just can't.

"What y'all fretting me about anyway? He's got some new girlfriend," Ma says, nodding her head like a psychic making a prediction.

"He told you?" I ask, being nosy. I can't wait to hear all about this mystery woman who may wreck havoc in our lives.

"He doesn't have to. Why else would he be wearing that awful cologne?" Ma shoots straight from the hip, like she always does when she knows something is true.

Now Angie and I are trying so hard to squelch out giggles that it looks like a pair of twin canaries are hiding in our cheeks. Finally, Angie lets out a loud cackle, and I join her.

"Hush now," Ma warns us gently as the elevator door opens into Mouse Almighty's reception area.

Ms. Dorothea's diva radar goes into full rotation when her eyes set on Ma. "Welcome to the Big Apple!" she says, stretching out her arms like a big cheetah ready to pounce. "Just what we need—another 'Mamacheetah' in the jiggy jungle!"

Ma chuckles, then steps daintily into Ms. Dorothea's "fold" for a fierce embrace.

We can't help but notice how teeny-tiny Ma looks next to Ms. Dorothea, who is six feet tall. She looks more like a baby bear hugging a mama bear instead of a "Mamacheetah."

Dorinda notices, too, because her dimples have deepened. She turns to smile at me, because she is so tickled at the sight before us. I smile back faintly.

Twinkle, Twinkle, Cheetah Stars

I feel like a pecking hen for insinuating that something was going on, like there was a Cheetah Girls conspiracy, or something.

"The girls said you were larger than life," Ma says, beaming up at Ms. Dorothea. "But they were wrong—you're even *larger* than that!" Suddenly, Ma blanches from embarrassment. "I didn't mean—"

"I know," Ms. Dorothea says. "I can't tell you how much it means to all of us that you came up here so the girls could finish the demo."

"Thank you," Ma says humbly.

"Let's just say you've earned a lifetime supply of cheetah points for this passage," Ms. Dorothea gushes earnestly.

"I'll consider that an investment for my stock portfolio," Ma says, sounding very businesslike.

"I see we've made an investment in Cartier as well," Ms. Dorothea says approvingly, mesmerized by the diamond-covered face on Ma's wristwatch.

"Well, let's just say my boss made an investment—in my future, Ma says proudly. "Honey, I told him in advance he'd better come up with something better than a Timex for my Christmas bonus this year, or it was time for me to take my record-sales history somewhere else!"

"Speaking of records, I want you to know your daughters are pushing this demo over the cheetah meter!" Ms. Dorothea says, pursing her lips with approval.

"Do you think it's good enough for the record company?" Ma asks hopefully.

"*Time* will tell," Ms. Dorothea says wistfully.

"Speaking of time," Chanel says, imitating Ms. Dorothea, "can I look at your watch, too, Mrs. Walker?" Gazing at Ma's prized possession, Chanel gets starry-eyed from all the diamonds. "Wow, you've got more karats than Bugs Bunny!"

"Don't you worry, Chuchie—one day we're going to get a few twinkles for our troubles," Galleria says confidently, then reaches into her cheetah backpack and pulls out a cheetah-wrapped present. "Here's a Christmas present for the fabulous Walker twins—just our way of saying thank you for not leaving us to the wolves."

Galleria hands the present to me, and tears form in my eyes. "Why, thank you, Miss Galleria, Miss Chanel, and Miss Dorinda!"

Angie pokes me in the side.

"Oh, and thank you, Ms. Dorothea," I add quickly, handing the present to Angie, since I know how much she likes to hold presents.

"Well, open it!" commands Chanel.

640

Twinkle, Twinkle, Cheetah Stars

I carefully pull at the corners of the cheetah wrapping paper so that we can recycle it later. "Oh, it's Seal!" I exclaim at the four CDs by the recording artist we met a few weeks ago right here in Mouse's studio.

"Wow—he really is famous," Angie says, ogling the CD collection.

"We can't wait to listen to them," I say, extending my hand for a Cheetah Girls' handshake.

The intercom at the reception desk chimes, and Cindy answers it. It's Mouse Almighty's voice telling her to send us back.

"Okay, girls, it's showtime. Today let's try and remember that you've got to give a few twinkles to get a few," Ms. Dorothea instructs, ushering us all back to the sound studios. "I expect you to shine like shooting stars today."

"Yes, ma'am," Dorinda says, imitating us.

"Oooh, this is exciting," Ma says enthusiastically.

Galleria nudges us, "You're coming over on Christmas, right? Daddy will lay a cannoli if you don't!"

"Yes, ma'am," Angie and I say in unison.

"Wait till you meet Mouse Almighty—the genius at work," Ms. Dorothea declares to Ma.

I cringe inside, however, when I see what the

"genius" is wearing today—a white oversized T-shirt that has the face of an old-time black man with big red lips and the words "Buy Black!" in big bold letters right below it.

"Oh, no!" I want to moan. Ma hates this kind of black Southern memorabilia. She thinks it's real offensive. Angie pokes me in the side while we stand there uncomfortably. Ms. Dorothea picks up on the situation quickly, like she always does, and goes into diva mode playing the hostess with the mostest. "Um, Mouse, this is the twins' mother, Mrs. Walker—who is visiting for the holidays from Houston!"

Mouse Almighty carefully places his long dreadlocks behind his ears like he knows they aren't "Ma-approved" either. Then he gently extends his hand to shake hers. We hold our breath as Ma quickly studies Mouse before shaking his hand, then says, "Nice to meet you. That's a very interesting T-shirt."

"Oh, yeah—I had this artist's image silk-screened onto my shirt because I dig the painting so much but I can't afford it," Mouse Almighty says softly. It's obvious that Ma doesn't like it. "As a matter of fact, he's from Texas, too—Michael Ray Charles—you know, his paintings be clockin' about sixty-five thousand these days."

Twinkle, Twinkle, Cheetah Stars

Ma nods her head. Knowing her, she probably can't stand the way Mouse Almighty talks, either. Now I realize Ma probably doesn't understand how, well, different people in the music business are from other folks.

"Oh, word, I never heard of that artist before," Dorinda says curiously.

I never heard of the artist before either, but I don't say a word.

"His stuff looks like the stuff we've seen at the Black Collectibles Fair back home," Angie says, because the silence is unbearable.

Ma still doesn't say anything, but I know what she's thinking: *Nettie Two, have you lost your mind. You know I hate that "Mammy-looking" mess they have at the Collectibles Fair!*

"Well—would you like to hear what the girls have been working on?" Mouse asks Ma hesitantly. We're not used to hearing him sound like that. Usually he is so gung ho.

"Yes, sir," Ma replies.

Angie holds my hand as we head into the sound room to listen to the playback. That means she wants us to bow our heads and say a silent prayer, because she feels scared, too, about Ma liking our music. My prayer is, *Lord, please let Ma like our music!* (Later, I'll ask Angie what she said in her prayer, but I bet you it's the same thing.)

"I've been working with this songwriter—Midget Man—who's been wrecking shop with his floetry style," Mouse says.

I cringe again. Lord, help us. From the look on Ma's face, I can tell she doesn't have any idea what on earth Mouse Almighty is talking about!

Mouse Almighty picks up Ma's judgmental look, too, because he motions to Son Seven, the engineer, through the glass window. "Cue up—'It's a Jungle out There.'"

I guess he realized explaining music production to Flipper would be easier than trying to explain it to Ma.

Galleria cuts in. "Mrs. Walker—he's trying to say that the Midget Man cut is the jointski!"

A sly look creeps across Ma's face as the song plays—kinda like a fox let loose in a henhouse, wondering what the poor little critters are up to. I try not to watch her face as the song continues:

> Don't take your toys and go home
> and leave me alone in a world
> that doesn't care about my rhythm.
> Just keep watching my back
> and I'll watch yours—because

Twinkle, Twinkle, Cheetah Stars

that's what friends are for in this
crazy world of a mixed-up jungle
of a jumbo size inside of a Cracker Jack box.

At last Ma starts tapping her foot. I shoot Angie a gleeful look: *Thank God, she likes it!*

But when Ma opens her mouth, I realize that I leaped for joy too soon.

"Don't you think that song is too mature for the girls?" Ma asks defensively.

How can she think that? What does she want us to sing about—bobbing for apples?

Ms. Dorothea comes to our rescue: "Junifred, let's go over here for a second and have a little cheetah chat." While the two of them have a hushed conversation for a few minutes, I smile at Mouse Almighty. He whispers at us, "She doesn't like my vibe." Then he pulls out a handkerchief and pats the perspiration on his forehead.

"It's not easy being greasy," Galleria says, smirking.

Mouse Almighty flashes his big grin, baring his oversized white teeth. I chuckle quietly. I know what Galleria is saying—and she's right. It's not easy being different. Sometimes people won't like you. I guess our prayer didn't work.

When Ms. Dorothea and Ma come back from

their little "cheetah chat," they sit down while we are instructed to take our places at the micro-phones.

"We're going to mix the song one more time," Mouse instructs us.

"For each of the songs on the demo, we do two different versions—one that has a radio-friendly format, and the other one is a little more creative," Mouse explains to Ma, who nods her head like she finally gets it. I guess Mouse Almighty has finally figured out how to talk to her—just keep it plain and simple.

After we try five takes on the song, Son Seven instructs us through the headphones: "Let's take five. Could you girls come out of the studio, please?"

"We must be doing *something* wrong," moans Chanel, taking off her headphones like she's bid-ding them good-bye.

An even worse thought than Chanel's pops into my head: *maybe Ma has put her foot down and is yank-ing us out of Mouse's studio!*

"Say hello to the Ghost of Christmas Past," whines Galleria, putting on her famous pout. As usual, I'm not sure exactly what Galleria means, and I don't feel like asking her.

"Hold up about the ghosts or ghouls—or even

the Sandman. We've come too far for tricks—now it's all about the treats," Dorinda says nervously, before asking for approval. "Right, everybody?"

Instead of answering, I march behind Galleria and Chanel, wringing my clammy hands together.

Now Chanel starts humming the melody from *The Wizard of Oz*, which makes us snicker down the hallway.

"Cheetahs and Prada and glitter, oh, my!" Dorinda throws in for good measure.

When Son Seven comes out of his booth and follows us into the reception area, we *know* something is up. He never leaves the production booth.

Ms. Dorothea and Ma are already waiting for us in the reception area. Mouse Almighty is standing with a man we've never seen before. He is wearing a chartreuse sharkskin suit that almost matches his eyes. I also notice that he has hair growing out of his ears like a Dr. Seuss creature from *The Cat in the Hat*.

Judging from the blank look on Ms. Dorothea's face, I can tell she doesn't know what's going on, either. It seems we're all waiting with bated breath for the reason Mouse interrupted our recording session.

"I was feeling so good about the work you girls have been doing that I sent some of the songs to Def Duck already," Mouse Almighty starts in.

"Oh, really?" Ms. Dorothea says, obviously impressed.

"Yeah—just give them a taste, since I've got to jet to Amsterdam next week," Mouse goes on, rubbing his goatee.

I glance over at Ma and she seems more relaxed than before, thank goodness.

"So let me introduce you to Frankie Fly, the new A&R executive at Def Duck Records. Well, I'll let him do the talking." Mouse moves over and motions for Frankie Fly to take the floor. My stomach sinks again. I guess he's here to tell us that we may be cute, but there isn't any room at the label right now for our cheetah-ness, "blah, blah, blah. Good-bye. See ya!"

As soon as Frankie Fly starts in, I realize that I may be right.

"Before I begin, I just want to apologize in advance," Frankie Fly says, then stops for a minute while he suppresses a cough. "Excuse me, but I haven't gotten used to this weather yet."

While we're waiting with bated breath for Frankie Fly to finish his speech, Ma asks him, "Um, where are you from?"

"Miami," Frankie replies, putting his hand over his mouth to suppress yet another coughing spurt.

"We love Miami!" Galleria says nervously, like a windup doll. We've never even been to Miami. I guess she is trying to soften the blow.

At last Frankie Fly continues, "I would have liked to have had the opportunity to meet with you girls before, but there is no time like the present, and we'll have plenty of time to get to know one another."

Mouse Almighty jabs Frankie Fly in the side and blurts out, "Would you go ahead and tell them before they fall off the couch!"

"Ladies—um," Frankie Fly starts in again, then takes a deep breath. "I'd like to welcome you to Def Duck Records."

The five of us stare blankly at Frankie Fly, wondering what he means.

"He's signing the Cheetah Girls!" blasts Mouse Almighty, snapping us out of our daze. "A little jumping up and down is in order, please!"

"OMIGOD," screams Galleria, jumping up and grabbing Chanel.

"We did it, *mija*," Chanel says, staring deeply into Galleria's eyes, then grabbing my hand while Dorinda grabs Angie's.

"Together forever!" we scream loudly in unison, then throw up our hands over our heads.

"Okay, now that you've gotten that out of your

system, here's the real deal," Mouse Almighty says, putting his arms around us. "It's gonna be a lot of work, and there are no guarantees, but we'll hang in there like pros until we go platinum, or bust."

"Oh, this is so blazin'—it's amazin'," Galleria chants.

Frankie Fly breaks out in a big grin. "You girls have a way with words."

"Praise the Lord for that,' Ma says, tears welling in her eyes, and putting her hand to her chest.

"We'd better call Daddy and tell him," I blurt out.

"And Big Momma, too!" Angie adds.

"And my dad, too!" Galleria chimes in.

"And Mrs. Bosco, too!" adds Dorinda.

"Okay, put away the cell phones—hit the switchboard," Mouse Almighty commands us, pointing to Cindy. "The only reception you're gonna get on cell phones in here is to Mars."

"Well, let's get back to earth, shall we?" Ms. Dorothea says, motioning for Ma to use the phone. "Guests go first."

Ma dials our home and speaks to Daddy. "I think Def Duck Records' newest recording artists deserve cuter bedspreads," Ma says, starting in. "Hmm. Hmm. Hmm. Really? Is that right?"

Twinkle, Twinkle, Cheetah Stars

Now we wonder what Daddy said on the phone to make Ma go, "Really?"

"Well, you tell them yourself," Ma says, handing us the phone.

"Hi, Daddy!" I scream into the receiver.

"I'm proud of you girls. I knew you could do it," he says, then pauses. "Um, there is someone here who wants to talk to you."

Angie looks at me like, *What is going on?*

I shrug my shoulder, waiting for Daddy to put, I guess, Big Momma on the phone.

"All hail the fabulous Walker Twins!" Drinka Champagne shouts into the receiver.

"Drinka?" I exclaim, shocked beyond belief.

Galleria's ears perk up. "What's up, buttercup?"

"Well, there is no reason to keep it a secret any longer, but your father and I have been dating," Drinka informs me while my mouth hangs open. "Your grandmother is a mess—and so is your Uncle. We are all going to be waiting for you, to celebrate when you get home!"

"Yes, ma'am," I say, still dumbfounded. I hand the phone to Angie and shake my head.

"I knew it. I told you so!" Galleria says, jumping up and down.

Mouse Almighty and Mr. Frankie Fly stand around smiling like Cheshire cats, until we clue them in on the latest goings-on in Cheetahville.

Angie screams when she gets off the phone: "I won the bet!"

Now I cave in. She did win the bet. Fair and square.

"Seems like we've all won the bet." Mouse Almighty chuckles. "I gambled on you girls because I knew you'd come through. So I want you to know, we're in this together."

"I don't mean to get giddy like P. Diddy, but can we give ourselves a shout out?" Galleria asks.

The five of us put our hands on top of one another's and join her in a group scream, "TOGETHER FOREVER!"

Twinkle, Twinkle, Cheetah Stars

Being fierce is no child's play
We work hard at it every day
That's why Sunday is not our fun day
Because we can't always get our way
So if you think we're at our wit's end
And that drama and kaflamma will make us bend
You're wrong about the message we send
As a matter of fact we're here to mend
What some say are our puffed-up ways
We're here to tell you that we got a payday
Through Def Duck Records
And something better
So here we are with our sneak preview
That's just for you
Our mighty-tight fans
Through and through
Both far and near
We're simply here
To give you a message
That's totally clear
We're talking about the time to twinkle
and bring on the Christmas cheer!

From all of us—we number five
The Cheetah Girls got something that's totally live
Our way of saying
You're the reason why we climb
And drop the lyrics

We wish you a CHEETAH CHRISTMAS
We wish you a Cheetah Christmas
We wish you a Cheetah Christmas
And a Happy New Year!
(Chuchie, why you asking what I got you for
Christmas? It's not about you, mamacita. *Peace*
and hair grease. The Cheetah Girls are out!!)

The Cheetah Girls Glossary

Big Willies: VIPs. Very Important Persons. Celebrities. Famous peeps who usually travel with an entourage or posse because they are so important in the real world (or in their own minds).

Bomb-Ditty Doodle: Fantastic. Out of this world. As in, "Where'd you get that bubble fake-fur jacket? It's the bomb-ditty doodle!"

Break out: Move on. Leave. Bounce. Let's roll. As in, "Okay, girlies, if we want to get to the movies in time, we'd better break out."

Brilliant: An English expression. Used when something is fabbie poo. As in, "I heard the Mango Room is jumping off tonight. Brilliant. Let's go there!"

Busy-Body Attitude: Someone who thinks they know everything, and thinks it's their business to tell you so you will know, too, and can keep up with them.

Cheesin': Trying to manipulate or suck up to someone for a purpose. As in, "Don't trust Miss

Shanequa, because she is always cheesin' for something on the down low."

Cheetahfied: Someone who is wearing "hot spots." As in, "Oooh, Miss Chanel, you are looking extra cheetahfied today!"

Cheetah Meter: The only true gauge for how fabulous something or someone is. As in, "The new Karma's Children album is off the cheetah meter!"

Clankety: Someone who clanks about, making a lot of noise, just to get the point across. A distant cousin of "yakkity yak," except the person who is talking in a "clankety" manner is usually a grown-up or person of authority. As in, "I don't know why my grandmother didn't tell my Mom in advance that she wanted blackberry cobbler for dessert instead of being so clankety about everything at the dinner table."

Collaborate: To get support from someone about going along with your "story," point of view, opinion, factual evidence, or even your lame excuse. As in, "Mom, if you don't believe I was at the library after school, you can ask my math teacher, Mr. Dizz Wizz, because he'll collaborate my story."'

Crispy Mad: When someone is super hot under the collar. Madder than angry.

Drone Clone: Someone who is boring and talks like everybody else. As in, "I wish Talitha would shut up already about her plans for Christmas. She sounds like such a drone clone."

Exiled to Siberia: Banished to the far reaches of Russia and stuck in a frozen ice pond for good measure.

Fabbie Poo: Fabulous. Wonderful. Great. As in, "Miss Dorinda, I think you are so-o-o fabbie poo!"

Feeling or Acting Daffy: Feeling light in the head, or acting a little cuckoo. As in, "Derek must be feeling daffy today, because he asked me to be his date for the Kats and Kittys' Christmas bash, when he knows I'm going with my crew."

The "411": Information of the real-deal kind. Not the kind of listings information you get when you call the telephone operator. As in, "I heard Brittany got grounded, but ask Denasia for 'the 411,' because she was at Brittany's house when it happened."

Gosspitating: Looking at someone like he or she is a juicy lamb chop with mint jelly on top. As in, "I know you're goospitating over Derek. Why don't you just admit it?"

Jumbalaya: Slang for a scenario that is part fiction,

part desire, and part cheesin'." As in, "I want to go to the skating rink instead of the Hokie Podown, but I have to figure out some 'jumbalaya' to tell my mom so she'll let me go."

Lite FM: Keeping a conversation superficial and not getting too deep. As in, "Derek, I'm trying to keep things Lite FM with you, because I'm saving my precious energy for the talent-show audition."

Marinate: Chill. Hang loose. Hang tight. As in, "I'm gonna head to the little girls' room for a winky tink. Why don't y'all marinate here for a second, okay?"

Mija: Spanish term of endearment. Means "honey," "sweetie," "precious one." As in, "*Mija*, lets go get some Mango Smoothies after school today."

On the Low, Low: When something is a secret, but still not as confidential as "on the down low." As in, "On the low, low, I heard that Performing Arts High may be cutting back on the amount of applicants they accept for the vocal and dance departments."

Putting on the Peach Glow: Acting like everything is mellow yellow on the Lite FM tip. Acting like there isn't any static going on. As in, "I heard Chantelle got cut from the volleyball team, but she was at the Christmas party just putting on the peach glow."

Sharp as a Tack: Smart. A brainiac. Someone who doesn't miss a trick. As in, "Don't be fooled by the banners and the balloons, that girl is as sharp as a tack."

Smugly: A combination of smug and ugly. As in, "Did you see how smugly Sade was acting at cheerleading practice yesterday?"

Spill the Barbecued Beans: Reveal a well-kept secret, sham, or scandal. As in, "Why did you tell Jessica you'll see her at the party on Saturday? It was supposed to be a surprise. Now you just went and spilled the barbecued beans!"

Straight Away: An English expression. Means "right away." As in, "Once we land in London, we must head to Harrod's straight away and buy some knickers for the masquerade ball!"

Stringent: Strict, sharp, tight, rigid. Someone like a teacher or parent who has a tendency to rain on your parade a tad too much. As in, "Aquanette's father is nice and all, but he can be a little too stringent for my taste!"

The Toasty: Hot item. Fabbie poo. As in, "Did you see that dress Karlana was wearing. It's quite the toasty."

Tippin' Out: Going out to have fun—usually when you're "looking sharp as a tack and all that." An expression used "back in the day." As in, "Why are you lying around here in your raggedy bathrobe and hair rollers? I know as soon as I leave for bingo, you're gonna be getting sharp as a tack and tippin' out on me. Yes, indeedy, Miss Eartha, you don't fool me a bit!"

Twizzled: Tired. Burned out. Deflated. As in, "I can't go to Mo' Burger with you after school today, because I'm feeling too twizzled."

Up and Down Like a Seesaw: Down pat. When you know something by heart. As in, "I'm not worried about the trig test. I know the equations up and down like a seesaw."

Whirly: Strong, harsh gust of hot air. As in, "Why was Dezaedra getting all whirly with you after tap class today? She was staring so hard, I thought your head was going to open up like a chimney and let out a big gust of soot!"

You're So-o-o-o Mala: You're so wicked, bad, terrible. As in, "I saw the way you were goospitating over Quincy at lunch. You're so-o-o-o mala, *mamacita*!"